The Descendants of the Pirate Pegleg Josiah Johnson

a remembrance by Rudy Briggs

a work of fiction by
Alec Clayton

Cover art and design by Gabi Clayton, back cover photo by David Ammons, cropped from the original.

Fonts on this book's cover and title page: Bitter and Bellefair. Inside book text: Times New Roman.

 Mud Flat Press

DISCLAIMER

This is a work of fiction. The characters are the product of the author's imagination. Resemblance to any person living or dead is coincidental.

Note: There are many descendants of the pirate Pegleg Josiah Johnson. For readers who find it difficult to keep track of who is who, there is a family tree at the end of the book that might be helpful.

ACKNOWLEDGEMENTS

I am indebted to so many people for their invaluable help, starting with first readers Ned Hayes and Courtney Shrieve.

I am grateful to Don Martin and Jack Butler for their brilliant and insightful editorial suggestions, and as always, my final editor, my wife Gabi Clayton.

Thank you to Paul Zmolek, a dance instructor who helped with the section where Lizzy teaches Sitara to dance the Martha Graham way.

Gery Gerst and Kristy Gledhill were helpful in describing their experiences on Orcas Island. Although our family had camped on the island, we had never been inside any of the resort hotels, and I needed their help to give the "Peter Puget Resort" a feeling of verisimilitude.

Thanks to Madeline Morgan for teaching me about some of the finer points of golf and for editing the chapter about Billy's golf game with Betty Kent and the other Billy.

Everything I know about Sunil and Mira's life in India and their move to Seattle and Olympia came from Shree Nath. My friend Pug Bujeaud talked to me about how long Covid might have affected Kaylee.

ALSO BY ALEC CLAYTON

Fiction
> Until the Dawn, 2000
> Imprudent Zeal, 2004
> The Wives of Marty Winters, 2007
> Reunion at the Wetside, 2010
> The Backside of Nowhere (Freedom Trilogy Book 1), 2009
> Return to Freedom (Freedom Trilogy Book 2), 2012
> Visual Liberties (Freedom Trilogy Book 3), 2015
> Tupelo, 2016
> This is me, Debbi, David (bonus nine stories), 2018
> Teacher, 2021
> Locked In, 2023

Non-fiction
> As If Art Matters, 2003
> What the Heck is a Frame-Pedestal Aesthetic?, 2020

Short stories included in:
> Mud Flat Shorts (mostly fiction), 2022

JOSEPHINE AND THE TIGER

It was the Sumatran tiger that killed Hairless Harlan Johnson's young bride.

Stunned silence from the audience filled the stadium-style seating surrounding the dusty ring. It was as if the townspeople in the bleachers and the clowns in their tattered costumes and the ringmaster in his black top hat and all the animals were characters in a television show and somebody punched pause on the remote. The stunned pause lasted a full minute, and then everybody at the two-bit circus fled while the ringmaster and cat handlers and big-tent workers rushed to get the tiger out of the tent and into its cage and to lift Josephine's mangled body and carry it out.

From the front row, a giant seated with an infant on his lap rose to his feet. That was Harlan, all six feet, six and one-half inches and almost three hundred pounds of him, cradling his infant son Billy, Josephine's baby. He watched them carry his dead wife out of the tent.

Swarming spectators rushed out through the open tent flap through which Josephine's limp and mangled body had just been carried. They knocked a small boy and an old lady to the ground in their rush to escape the horror. A circus worker pushed through the panicked crowd to reach the woman and child, and he lifted them to their feet and helped them out of the big tent.

Big Hairless Harlan watched in silence as they hauled Josephine's body out, and then he walked in the direction they had taken her. When he got to where they had lain her body out, he scolded his deceased wife with, "I told you this job was dangerous."

Times Picayune Columnist John Brighton wrote the story for the issue of the paper dated September 28, 1935.

BIG CAT TRAINER MAULED BY TIGER

Buckingham International Circus assistant lion tamer Josephine Warnock Johnson was attacked and killed by a tiger in front of two hundred horrified spectators during a performance Monday afternoon.

The blonde beauty was only fifteen years old and the mother of a six-month-old son, Billy Johnson. She had married into the Johnson family so recently that she had never even met her brother-in-law Bryce or any of her husband's family members. She was one of very few female big cat trainers in America. "I reckon she might be the onliest one. Onliest one I ever knowed of," said ringmaster and part owner of the circus Parker Little.

The feisty young trainer had stepped into a cage with three lions and the Sumatran tiger. Wielding a whip and wearing a red and gold halter top and skin-tight black leggings, Mrs. Johnson pranced around the circular cage and herded the big cats onto three-foot-high pedestals where they sat on their haunches in obedience to her commands until the Sumatran, suddenly and without noticeable provocation, leaped on her and mauled her to death.

Lion tamer Josh Grant and a handful of assistants rushed into the cage and forced the big cats out of the arena while other assistants removed Mrs. Johnson's body.

Mrs. Johnson was married to Houma resident Harlan Johnson, a fisherman and sometimes oil rig laborer. She had been with the circus less than a year. During that time, she often worked with the Sumatran tiger named Sumo. The lion tamer said Sumo had never been aggressive. He reported that on the day the big cat attacked Mrs. Johnson she wore a new perfume and speculated there might have been something in the new scent that caused the tiger's aggression.

Mrs. Johnson was the granddaughter-in-law of the once-famous but now mostly forgotten pirate Pegleg Josiah Johnson.

The other front-page headline for that issue, in even larger type, was TULANE TRAMPLES TEMPLE IN SEASON OPENER.

...

Off the record, Ringmaster Parker Little said to a reporter, "That knockabout Hairless Harlan was a no-good self-important SOB. Tell you the truth, I'd feel sorry for the girl's family if we could find them, not for Harlan Johnson. But that S.O.B. seems to be the only family she's got. He was known as a lady-killer, although I'll be goddamned if I can figure out what it was about him that any woman could find attractive. Maybe it was his hairlessness, or maybe his size. He was huge. And strong like a fucking King Kong. Excuse the bad word. He was just a kid hisself, and so was she. But don't you go writing none of that in your newspaper. Nothing but their ages. That's all right to say."

Within minutes after his young bride's mutilated body was carried out of the cage, Harlan telephoned his girlfriend, Viola Parker. "Hi, hun," he said. "There was a terrible accident. That motherloving tiger went and attacked Josephine without provocation. I mean she hadn't done a blessed thing to make him mad. He had her for lunch."

"Had her ... is she ..."

"Dead? You bet she is."

1899 to 1920
BEAUREGARD CALLED BOBO

Hairless Harlan Johnson's grandfather was the notorious pirate Pegleg Josiah Johnson who roamed the waters of the Caribbean and the Gulf of Mexico from Florida to Texas back around the time of the war between the states. Hairless Harlan's wife, Viola, the one he married hardly any time after his first wife Josephine was killed by that mad Sumatran tiger, talked about her father, Beauregard called Bobo, as if he were a god. Hercules or Zeus or one of them. It's hard to point a finger to what kind of man Beauregard called Bobo was. He wasn't a particularly big man, but at about two inches shy of six feet tall he was, I guess, slightly larger than average, and as strong and ferocious and as gentle as a papa gorilla.

Bobo started out with nothing and built himself a fair fortune in practically no time. But he never thought of himself as a worthy person. Oh, he was full of bluster and back-slapping good cheer, but that was all an act. What he truly wanted more than anything in this world was to be respected, and he never felt he truly was. He wanted to be king of his domain, the patriarch and benevolent dictator of his own ever-growing family.

Born and reared in the bootheel of Missouri, Beauregard called Bobo escaped home and landed in Seattle on his way to the Klondike in 1899—going to strike it rich in the gold mines. He ran away from Clarkton with thirty-five dollars in his pocket, hitched a ride with a family of four going to New Madrid, where he hired on as a deckhand on a riverboat going up the Mississippi to St. Louis.

He was sixteen years old, had dropped out of school in the tenth grade after being suspended multiple times for fighting, and finally said to hell with school and Missouri and with his worthless family and decided to seek his fortune in the wild Northwest where he had heard that gold nuggets could be picked up in creek beds as easily

4

as catching tadpoles. He didn't know where the Klondike was, but he had heard that St. Louis was the starting-off place and figured he could find his way from there.

Bobo was a vicious fighter and was known for beating up much larger boys. (In Seattle he would learn to control that temper.) It was his third day on the boat. He was stowing ropes on deck along about suppertime when a tipsy young man approached and said, "I hear you think you're tough."

Bobo didn't reply.

The man said, "Well I think you ain't tough for shit."

Bobo, ignored the drunk, went about his business.

"Hey, you too good to talk to me?" the guy challenged.

When Bobo still didn't say anything, the drunk hauled off and hit him in the face. Bobo shook his head and went about his business, gritting his teeth and holding back tears, afraid that if he fought back he might get fired. He wished some of the other deckhands could see what was going on. Maybe they would know how to deal with the situation. He wanted to see a whole gaggle of deckhands rush in and grab the drunken bully and toss him overboard. *I'm just a kid. These here other guys are grown men.*

The guy danced around to face him and said, "What are you, chicken? Cluck, cluck, cluck. Come on, put your dukes up." And then he hit him again, once in the gut and then his jaw. The one to the jaw felt like it broke something in there. Bobo couldn't take it anymore. He reached around the drunk with both hands, picked him up and slung him away like a rotten hunk of fruit. The man slammed into the boat's guardrail and bounced over it and into the water. Bobo rushed to the rail and looked over and saw his drunken attacker flailing in the muddy Mississippi then sinking out of sight, leaving nothing but a spreading circle of brown water as the boat continued northward. Should he call for help? Get the captain to go back and fish him out? His hesitance cost the life of the drowning man. Or so Bobo supposed. Speaking to the muddy water, Bobo said, "That there's gonna haunt me as long as I live." He swore then and there he would do whatever it took to avoid fighting ever again.

For a little while there was murmuring onboard the boat about a deckhand that must have quit and taken off during the night. But such murmuring lasted only a few days.

…

From St. Louis, half a dozen hitched rides took him by water and road to Seattle. By the time he landed there, he was flat broke, having spent and gambled away all of what little money he had.

It was cold for a summer day and rainy. The streets were muddy, and so were most of the people, who sloshed through the streets and sat where they could and when they could. Bobo could not afford to go any farther. He saw a man seated on a packing crate of some sort in front of a bar. The hand-lettered name of the bar was BAR-BAR. *Now ain't that something, Bobo and Bar-Bar*, Beauregard called Bobo thought. *All them Bs and all that repetition. It's downright poetic.*

A woman in a long black dress sat on the lap of the man seated on the packing crate in front of the bar. The top of her dress was cut so low Bobo could see all of her titties except her nipples. He had never seen such a sight except for pictures on a deck of playing cards he bought for a dollar at a traveling carnival. He stared and stared, and she saw that he stared, and she smiled at him. She had a missing tooth, and her eyelashes and eye shadow were heavily slathered on. "Hey kid," she said, beckoning him with her hand, "C'mere. Do us a favor. Go in there and buy us a bottle of booze. Any kind. Don't matter."

Bobo didn't say anything else for a moment while ogling her bulbous breasts. Neither did the man upon whose lap the woman sat. "Here," she said, holding out a fistful of dollar bills, "This oughta cover it and a little something extra for your trouble."

He took the money and stepping gingerly from almost dry spot to almost dry spot, he walked into the bar where a player piano was tinkling out a waltz. "Whiskey," he said to the barkeep. Don't matter what kind."

The barkeep gave him a bottle and took his money and handed back his change. Bobo asked, "You wouldn't happen to be hiring, would you?"

"Hiring for what?"

"Anything. Whatever you need."

"How old are you, son?"

"Eighteen years old," he lied. He'd never had any trouble convincing people he was older than he was. Not that anybody cared.

The barkeep said, "I reckon I could use somebody to do some cleanup and carrying cases and whatnot. You sure as shootin' look strong enough for that. What's your name?"

"Beauregard. But everybody calls me Bobo."

"I'm Ned. I don't know how old I am, but it's probably more'n eighty."

...

So, on his first day in Seattle, Bobo got a job at Bar-Bar. That was where he met his wife-to-be, Nellie. She was a bar girl and—to put it bluntly—a whore. She worked the streets and the bars from the time she was fifteen years old in March of that year and up until she married Bobo late in August and after that up until she became Hairless Harlan Johnson's mother-in-law. The one he never saw and never spoke to but heard plenty about.

But I'm getting ahead of myself.

...

"You gotta quit going upstairs with them guys," Bobo said. "We's married now. I'm supposed to be your one and only."

She said, "How else are we supposed to earn enough money to live offa?"

"I'll ask Ned to give me more work for more money."

"You jest ask him and you expect he'll do it?"

"Yep."

Soon thereafter she quit taking men upstairs and Ned gave Bobo a bit of a raise, and Bobo quickly took on more and more responsibility until he was managing the bar. They move into a little apartment behind the blacksmith on South King.

It was clear to Bobo and to Nellie that old Ned was rolling in money even though he lived like a pauper. He lived in a little room above the bar next to the whoring room and never went anywhere. He never visited the whores either. Not since ... hmm ... musta been twenty years ago. He hardly ever bought a thing for himself, had only two pairs of dungarees and two shirts and one winter coat. Never ate out. So the money kept growing.

Ned took a liking to the industrious and likeable young man right away. Bobo was quick to do whatever Ned asked of him and was friendly with the customers. Except for the ones who got nasty when drunk.

When one of them got belligerent, and especially if he got nasty with one of the girls, Bobo would insert himself between the drunk and whoever he was hassling and back him out the door. No fisticuffs ever ensued; they always backed down, because there was an intensity to Bobo in his silence more frightening than any amount of threat or bluster.

In addition to carrying cases of booze and putting the bottles on the shelves behind the bar and sweeping and mopping, Bobo was Bar-Bar's unofficial bouncer.

Ned said to Bobo and Nellie, "Maybe y'all can care for me when I get old. The day's a coming quicker than you think. I ain't likely ta last much longer."

"Good lord, don't I know it," Bobo said with a grin. "I thought you was dead long ago." He had learned that Ned liked that kind of kidding around.

Ned put Nellie to work behind the bar and gave her what she thought was pretty good pay. He said, "I kindly think of you as my children since I ain't got no real children of my own."

They knew the old man wasn't likely to last much longer. Bobo said, "I betcha my bottom dollar if we treat him right, he'll leave it all to us. He ain't got nobody else."

As predicted, he didn't live much longer, and he did leave it all to Bobo and Nellie. Ned's will was one paragraph signed by his lawyer who might or might not have been licensed and notarized: *To Beauregard Parker and Nellie I leave everthin. The bar called Bar-Bar and ever red cent in my bank account lessen a hundred dollars to lawyer Sam Snoek for signing this my will and making it official and legal and whatever extra it costs him to get it notarized.*

8

Lawyer Sam handed Nellie the letter and a key to Ned's lockbox saying, "I'm giving this to you, young lady, because I learned long ago that women are more to be trusted than men when it comes to money matters."

...

Nellie and Bobo moved into the room above Bar-Bar, and seven months later Nellie gave birth to a baby girl. They named her Viola.

Bobo announced he had a plan for cleaning up Bar-Bar and making it respectable before Viola got old enough to hear all the cussing and what all else went on in the bar, which meant no more gambling and no more whores taking clients upstairs. He told his male customers to bring their wives and children. "This here's gonna be a respectable family drinking establishment."

He put up a sign that said NO CUSSING. He got checkers and dominoes and such for the kids and whatever grownups might be inclined to play and added lemonade and soda to the selection of drinks. He banished the whores, who simply migrated to a bar down the street. Soon he and Nellie had more money than either had ever dreamed of and over the next few years they added to their wealth by buying a hardware store and a funeral parlor, all in or near Pioneer Square. Bobo told their customers, "You're all family here." He was well loved by their customers, and he and Nellie loved them in return.

Nellie was not as easy-going and trusting as Bobo. She became suspicious, for no reason Bobo could detect, and thought that pretty much everyone was out to bilk them out of their money. There were times when she remained upstairs alone for days, and times when she couldn't sleep at night. "You done gone clean off your rocker," Bobo told her.

"So" was her only rejoinder. He didn't know what to do with her. She thought he was seeing other women. She was afraid someone would break in and steal everything. She accused Bobo of wanting to kill her, and behind his back, she hired a locksmith to put a lock on their bedroom door and would sometimes lock herself in for hours and not let him enter. Some days their sweet child Viola would have to scrounge the refrigerator and cabinets to feed herself because Bobo was working and Nellie would forget to do it. Bobo begged her to see a doctor, but she insisted there was nothing wrong with her. "Seems to me you might be a bit sick in the head," Bobo said.

On Viola's fifth birthday, Nellie left their home and took Viola with her. She didn't tell Bobo she was leaving him; she didn't leave a note. The only things she took were clothes and the two hundred dollars Bobo kept hidden in a plastic bag in the freezer.

"Look, honey, look," Nellie said as the train drove through the splendor of the Cascade mountains.

Viola's only response was to look down at the floor and kick the back of the seat in front of her.

"Don't do that," the man in front turned to say.

Nellie said, "Mind your own business."

Viola had been alternately crying and pouting since leaving Seattle. It was not until they were through Idaho and rode into Utah that she finally broke her silence. She asked her mother where they were going.

"Phoenix," Nellie said. You'll love it there."

"Why?"

"Why what?"

"Why did we leave Daddy?"

"I just had to get out of Seattle. I couldn't take another cold and wet winter there."

"But Daddy? Don't you love him?"

"Sure I do. Acourse I do. But I just ... You'll understand when you're older."

Months later, broke and afraid, Nellie called Bobo and said she was sorry she had left and begged him to forgive her and take her back.

There was an uncomfortable pause followed by, "Are you there, Bobo? Say something."

"Uh huh. Yeah, I'm here."

"Well can I come back or not? Please. Viola misses you."

"If you promise to see a head doctor," he said.

"Yes, yes I will. I promise."

"I love you, and I love Viola. Can you put her on the phone?"

"Hi Daddy."

"Hi Sweetie."

"It's hot here all the time. I saw Santa Claus, and he was wearing short britches. Can you come?"

"I wish I could, sweet thing."

"Please, please, pretty please."

He said, "Your mama's going to bring you back to Seattle so y'all all can be with me again," hoping he was right. They talked for only a minute.

Back in Seattle, Nellie visited a psychiatrist once but refused to go back. "I just don't like him," she said, "I don't like the way he looks at me. I think he's going to … going to, gonna, gonna want me to do stuff with him, and he's gonna get in my head and make me want to do stuff 'cause head doctors can control your thinking like that."

She figured he recognized her as a former whore and figured once a whore …

Nellie stayed in their home above Bar-Bar for no more than three weeks before taking off with Viola again. This time for good. She carted Viola around the country picking up the only kinds of jobs she knew how to do—tending bar and walking the streets in Denver and in Kansas City, Phoenix, and finally settling in New Orleans where she would eventually meet big Harlan Johnson.

Whenever she needed money, she would call Bobo. To his pleas for her to come home, she would say, "I promise I will, honey. Just give me a little time."

Knowing full good and well she was never going to come home, Bobo sent her money anyway. He dove into his business. He expanded his empire beyond Seattle. He bought another hardware store, this one to the south in Olympia, a good half-day drive. Later, he took over ownership of a Ford dealership even farther south in the little town of Centralia.

1935 to 1944
The Big Easy

As she had in Phoenix, in Denver, in Tucson, in Memphis, and finally now in New Orleans, where she would soon meet Harlan, Nellie continued to get by as best she could, working the streets, picking up odd jobs here and there, cleaning house and cooking and taking care of spoiled-rotten kids in a rich woman's house in the Garden District; and dancing (not very well) in strip clubs in the French Quarter where the posters out front promised GIRLS! GIRLS! BEAUTIFUL GIRLS FULLY NAKED but the dancers stripped down only so far as thongs (G-strings I think they called them) and pasties. Nellie dragged sweet little Viola with her from rooming house to rooming house and club to club and boyfriend to boyfriend. Often Viola was left to fend for herself. She was lonely much of the time and often afraid. She loved her mother and terribly missed Bobo.

In New Orleans, Viola attended Benjamin Franklin High School. Hairless Harlan Johnson was also a student at Ben Franklin and lived a few blocks away from Nellie and Viola. They did not know each other, but Viola often saw him at school and on the streets. She found him fascinating to look at. How could she not considering his size, his handsome face, and his absolute starkly shocking baldness?

...

Harlan of the hairless head was the oldest living child of Auvergne Johnson, and his wife, Wanda (called Bluebird). Auvergne was the oldest living child of the pirate Pegleg Josiah Johnson. So there's the piratical connection that runs through this widespread family that I married into. Hairless Harlan grew up an only child since his brother Wilson died in infancy. Auvergne and Wanda and Harlan lived in a second-floor apartment on Bourbon Street where they could sit on their balcony and watch the revelers during Mardi Gras. The

12

only way to reach their apartment was to climb metal steps that were essentially a fire escape. The ancient building housed Broussard's Oyster House and next door to Broussard's a striptease joint called Hot Desire. Nellie and her daughter Viola lived in a room above Hot Desire.

Did you ever watch one of those crazy comedies wherein the stars keep buzzing around one another like bees, in and out of doors, never meeting but frequently coming within feet of bumping into each other? That's what Harlan and Viola were like when they were growing up. Before settling in New Orleans, each of them knocked around various little waterlogged towns south and west of New Orleans, including Cut Off and Bayou and Dulac and Houma, where Harlan eventually lived with his teenage bride—not Viola, but the one that came before her, the lion tamer.

...

Harlan's baldness was from birth. Not a single hair on his head, not on his arms or legs or anywhere. "It'll grow," his mama said when he was an infant and then a toddler. "Lots of babies don't have hair at first, but it always sprouts sooner or later."

But it didn't. His hairlessness was a condition called hypotrichosis. When his daddy told people about it, he said hypotrichosis (he pronounced it hyperchosis) was Latin for no hair nowhere. Harlan always thought his daddy was kidding about it. For years he held out hope that it would start growing, but when he was sixteen years old and had not yet begun to sprout a beard or hair on his arms and legs or pubic hair, boys in the locker room at school began teasing him about it. He asked a doctor what was wrong, and the doctor told him his condition had a name. *By God, Papa was right.* Once he knew it had a name—a big, impressive name at that—he bragged about his hairlessness. "Hypertrichosis. Bet you can't even say it, but I got it."

...

Harlan loved the female sex. And I don't mean by that that he was simply horny like any ole teenage boy; I mean he really loved,

13

not just lusted after women and girls, all of them. It was not the challenge of the conquest that excited him; it was much more than lust. He adored women, he adored their spirit, their quiet strength, their intelligence. He thought the world should be ruled by women. He wished that he could marry them all and raise their children. And they loved him back because he loved them, because he listened to them as other boys did not.

He was sure this predilection was inherited from his grandfather the pirate (whom he had heard of but never known) and probably from other Johnson ancestors going back generations.

When Viola Parker relieved Harlan of his virginity, they were still kids. He was smitten with her from the moment he laid eyes on her. She was a diminutive, svelte beauty with hair as sleek and black as a panther's fur. She was seated at a table in the school library, her face in a book, glasses down near the bulbous little tip of her nose. She was holding her book with one hand while running the other hand through her hair. From time to time, she glanced up at Harlan and gifted him with what he thought of as a winsome smile. After about her third smile, Harlan unfolded his body from his seat at a nearby table and took a few steps to stand next to her. Looking down at her, he said, "You must be new."

"Uh huh."

"Where you from?"

"Everywhere, but mostly Seattle," Viola said.

"Where's that at?"

"Seriously? You don't know where Seattle is? Nevermind. It's way up in the northwest corner of the country, almost in Canada. It's a great big city, even bigger than New Orleans."

"Well hot damn," he said. "Ain't you something."

He grinned down at her, melting from the heat of her beauty. She said, "You don't have to be such a snot about it."

He said, "You are the most beautiful girl I've ever seen."

"You get right down to the meat o' the matter, don't you?" She took in a deep breath and let it out with a gush of wind and then closed her book using a matchstick for a marker. He sat beside her, noticing that the librarian was looking at them as if she were their jailer, as if they were going to rip off their clothes and go at it right then and there, which was precisely what he dreamed of doing. He picked up the book, looked at the title, *The Sound and the Fury*, and pronounced that he had tried to read it once but didn't like it. "It was hard to make heads or tails out of it, and after the first chapter, I couldn't keep track of who the hell was telling the story. It kept changing."

"I know, but it's kind of exciting. Weird but exciting." She was impressed that he had even tried to read it, pretty sure that nobody she knew, except maybe the English teacher, had even read the first sentence.

"I kindly liked Benji, but after I got to the part where Quinlin was telling the story it set my head to spinning."

They talked about what classes they were taking and about the upcoming dance in the gym. He said he never went to dances. She said, "I guess I'd go if I had a date, but there ain't no boys I'd want to date in this school. They're all so juvenile."

He said, "I played football at my last school, and I'm going to go out for the team here."

"Well la dee da," she said.

He gathered she didn't care for football.

She told him she lived over a club called Hot Desire and explained that it was a striptease joint.

"I know what Hot Desire is," he said. "It don't bother me none. You living there and all. I been by there plenty of times."

She asked if he'd ever been inside.

" Acourse not," he said. "They don't let kids in there."

"Well I've been in there," she said. "I even been in the dressing room and watched the dancers change their costumes and watched from behind the stage when they did their shows."

He repeated what she'd said earlier. "Well la dee da,"

She chuckled at that and said, "When I was really, really little, I lived over a bar my old man owned. It was called Bar-Bar, silly name, and it was none too savory."

"How little were you?"

"I don't know. Hardly more'n a baby. But I remember it. I got a picture of my mama and papa standing in front of it."

...

15

Harlan and Viola soon became almost inseparable. They wandered the streets of the French Quarter together, past all the eating places and jazz joints and strip clubs. They wandered through St. Louis cemetery; and down by the Mississippi River; shop-lifted; smoked cigarettes pilfered from their parents; and drank beer and wine out of bottles hidden in paper bags in the alleyways off Bourbon and Royal and Iberville Streets.

They both dropped out of school, but they were not stupid. Both were voracious readers who spent hours two and three days a week in the library.

Alone and somewhat hidden by trash bins behind a bar on Bourbon Street one afternoon, Harlan said to her, "I'll give you a dollar if you let me see your tits."

Puffing out her chest like a boy pigeon trying to seduce a girl pigeon, she said, "Make it two bucks and you can not only see 'em, you can feel 'em too."

He practically ripped the seams out of his pockets grabbing two one-dollar bills. She pulled her shirt up but not all the way off. She was wearing a bra that gleamed whitely against her deeply tanned skin.

"That's just fifty cents worth," He said, "Gimme the full two bucks worth."

"I'll do it if you let me see your thing."

"You already said you'd do it."

They peeked out from behind the trash bins to see if anyone was passing by. She pulled her shirt all the way off. And her bra.

Suddenly panicked, he said, "Put your shirt back on."

She shrugged her naked shoulders and laughed but made no move toward dressing. "Your turn. Chicken if you don't."

He unbuckled his belt and dropped his britches and underpants down around his knees. They looked at each other while furtively glancing around to make sure nobody could see them. "Get dressed," she said. And they did. But before saying that she said, "Where in tarnation is your hair down there?"

He enjoyed telling her about his hypotrichosis.

16

In days to follow there were a few more times she allowed him to look but look only. And then one day he reached out with both hands—trembling hands—and cupped her breasts. They were just big enough to fill his hands and were soft yet firm like a balloon blown up almost to the bursting point. He was surprised to know that nipples felt hard like leather and that the part in the middle (he didn't know there was a word for it) got longer like his penis which was, not surprisingly, hard. She saw and she smiled, and she reached to touch it. Two more times touching like that, and then they went all the way on the back seat of Viola's mama's boyfriend's car when it was parked in front of their house one night in early September. He told her he loved her and couldn't live without her. She said, "I will follow you anywhere,"

And she did.

His daddy picked up jobs all over South Louisiana and dragged Wanda and Harlan from job to job to job. They might drive to some little bayou town for a day job and back to New Orleans at night, or they might go for a few days, a week or a month, and rent a room in some motel or some little cabin on a bayou. Wherever Harlan's daddy took him, Viola found a way to follow, always on her own, since her mother insisted on staying in New Orleans and didn't worry about her daughter venturing out on her own.

One day Viola came home to the little apartment above Hot Desire and found her mother dead on the floor. She never knew what killed her and never much cared. Bobo was still sending her money and telling her by mail that she was welcome to come back home anytime she wanted. Viola thought that was sweet, but she didn't want to go back to Seattle. She'd had enough of family. *Daddy Bobo thinks I'm still a baby*, she told herself. *Now that mama's dead I can be my own woman. 'Sides, Harlan's here.*

In 1925 Harlan's daddy got a job clerking in a general merchandise store in Houma, a thriving little community set smack dab in the midst of bayous and sugar cane plantations, and he moved his little family into a one-bedroom rental. Viola, now easily passing as a grown woman of twenty-five or thirty, got a job in a café two doors down from the store where Auvergne worked, and she rented a room in the home of a widow three-and-a-half miles away in Bayou

Cane. She walked to and from work every day, sashaying on the dusty road in her flapper skirt. Men passing her on the road offered her rides, but she turned down the offers unless she recognized them from the café. Harlan often drove to Bayou Cane to pick her up after work.

...

Viola and Harlan considered themselves married but just without the rings and the license and the ceremony. Even though they didn't live together. She was true to him and assumed he was true to her. And then she found out otherwise.

She was enjoying a smoke break in the kitchen with her coworker and current best friend, who announced, "Oh honey, I had the best sex I ever had. It was a guy I just met. Lord, lord, lord, I never do that, but he came on to me so strong and was so sweet that before I knew what was happening, we were doing it, and oh my god, you'd never believe how ... I mean like it was explosive. We practically devoured each other."

In the midst of her gushing, she said, "You oughta see him. He's the biggest man I've ever seen and God if he ain't beautiful. And get this, "I'll be damned if he ain't completely bald. I mean not a single hair anywhere on his body. And he's just a kid. I mean like maybe seventeen or eighteen."

How the tears and recriminations did flow. But Viola forgave her friend, knowing it wasn't her fault; she didn't know the guy was Viola's practical husband, couldn't have known.

Viola confronted Harlan. He did not deny it. Not in the least. He said, "That's what men do, honey. We can't help it. We're just made that way. But I'll always love you and you're the one I'll always come home to."

For three days she wouldn't speak to him, wouldn't let him touch her, then she quickly made up her mind that if she wanted to keep him, and oh my did she ever, she needed to look the other way and let him have his little flings. That's just what men did. He said it, and so did her mama. "If you don't want to end up an old maid," Mama said.

And then Harlan met Josephine. She was small and fierce and self-possessed, and she had a laugh so infectious that everybody who heard it started laughing too, even if they had no notion whatsoever what was so dang funny.

Harlan was fascinated that she was in training to be a big cat handler with the fly-by-night Buckingham International Circus, which was in no way international but traveled throughout Texas, Arkansas, and Louisiana. He hung around the periphery of the circus and watched the work of rigging and the feeding and grooming of animals and performers practicing their acts, including Josephine in skin-tight leotards working with three lions and a sleek Sumatran tiger. None of the circus workers and performers bothered him or even seemed to notice him. But Josephine noticed and flashed him meaningful looks. Just like Viola had in the library, just like so many girls and even grown women did. He took it as his due.

He followed Josephine behind the big tent and told her, "I'm Harlan Johnson, and I'm madly in love with you."

They made love the first night they were together and were married two months later. Viola went berserk when he told her. "If you had any goddamn hair I'd pull ever last out by the roots," she screamed at him. She already knew he was sleeping with another woman (besides her coworker who dropped him when she found out he was Viola's guy). She was willing, reluctantly, to look the other way. But marrying a hot little teenager? And expecting her to stay true to her while he was married to another girl? That was a step too far, far, far too far.

"How could you?" she demanded to know. They were out on the bayou fishing in a little flat-bottom rowboat. She picked up a paddle and slapped the water with it, splashing him, and she drew it back with the intention of hitting him, but she backed off before swinging it at him.

"I didn't want to marry her," he told her, throwing his hands up to protect his head. "It's still you that I love."

He meant it, and she sensed he meant it.

"But the thing is, you see, I knocked her up. I should have known better than to do it without protection, but we drank too much bourbon and didn't know what we were doing. Now I have to take care of her and the baby. She said I had to make an honest woman of her."

They argued; he begged; she finally said she understood. "Making an honest woman of her is a noble gesture. 'Sides, you can divorce her after the baby comes. You and me and my daddy Bo, we can pay for taking care of the baby. Daddy Bo will understand."

...

Harlan was a busy boy. He worked odd jobs and went to the circus to watch his young wife perform with the wild lions and the lone tiger and cheer her on whenever he could, and he continued seeing Viola once or twice a week. He didn't hide it from Viola that he was still sleeping with his wife. Of course, he was. Viola had the occasional romp with other men as well. They told each other they were a thoroughly modern couple who were advanced in their morality beyond the conventional.

Viola never went to the circus. If she did, she told Harlan, she would cheer for the lions. "Just joking," she said. That was only days before the Sumatran tiger killed Josephine.

1935-1944
FIVE LITTLE JOHNSONSES

Harlan and his lion tamer in training had been married barely long enough to get to know each other before her tragic end, but they were married long enough to bring a baby boy into the world. Billy Byron Johnson. Redfaced, with hair to match, Billy was born mad at the world. Three years later, Viola, still "living in sin" with Harlan but with the blessing of the lord, or so she said, gave birth to a beautiful baby girl they named Renae, the strong one, the industrious one, the daughter that took over all the cooking and house cleaning—quickly to be followed by big Bryce the clown, who would grow to be a giant of a man and a beloved history professor at Washington State University. And then there were Lizzy the dreamer and dancer who gave up dance for love of a biker dude, and finally Marilou, the soul of patience and the love of my life. We've been married now long enough to have middle-aged kids.

...

One of the first words Billy ever said was *Mama*. Viola said, "I'm not your mama," and little Billy broke into tears, not so much because of what she said—it's unlikely he could understand the words—but because of her dismissive tone of voice. He didn't call her Mama again until after his little sister Renae was born. That time. Viola said, "I'm *her* mama, not yours. And don't you forget it."

And again, he cried.

"Now don't you go crying like a baby," she said. "I ain't saying that because I don't love you as much as I love your baby sister. Because I do. Be that as it may, howsomever, it's a matter of importance that you know your proper place in this family." Pointing back and forth to Renae and herself and then Billy, she said, "Mama, daughter, STEP son, STEP mother. You got it? No real kin."

He did not get it.

Harlan had not been there to hear the first time she denied her maternity, but the next time he was. He stood aghast for a long moment, and then he hit the roof. Literally. "Don't you dare let me hear you say anything like that again," a deep panting breath then, "I don't give a hoot whose womb he popped out of, you're his mama now, and if you don't make sure he knows it without any doubt I'm going to leave you and take both kids with me."

"A'right, a'ready," she said. "But if I'm gonna be a mama to your kid, then you have to marry me. That's all I've ever wanted."

"Well how come you never told me? I'd a married you long time ago."

"Really?"

"Yeah. Sure."

...

The Johnsons spent some time in Dulac and Port Fourchon, where Harlan scraped out a meager living working at a variety of temporary jobs: shrimp boats and offshore oil rigs and fetch-and-carry gigs on construction crews. He also engaged in a bit of bootlegging and the selling of pilfered goods such as watches, rings, and bracelets—not a thief but a fence, he explained to his little boy Billy. "Like my grandpappy the notorious pirate," he bragged.

Billy, of course, had not the slightest idea what his daddy was talking about, but he looked up at him worshipfully.

...

Viola, meantime, could not quite let go of the mama conflict. After all, Billy came out of another woman's belly. She tried once again to explain to Billy why she wasn't his mother but that she loved him anyway. He cried and cried and cried.

"Aw, quit your crying," Viola said. "It ain't like I don't love you like I love my real children."

A few years later, Billy's youngest sister, Lizzy, also reminded him that *her* mother—and Renae's and Marilou's and Bryce's—was not *his* mother. "You're not my real brother. You're not none of us's real brother," she said. Viola had taught her that.

22

After they were all grown, the issue of Billy's parentage was raised again, and he said, "It's a wonder I didn't grow up hating every damn one of y'all."

Bryce said, "We thought you did," and they all laughed. Even Billy.

1944-1958
THE GANGLY BOY

"That boy is all arms and legs," Harlan said.

Viola agreed. "He's like a young colt or a baby giraffe."

"So gangly. It's a wonder he can get from here to the kitchen without tripping over his own two feet."

"You're right. He can be so clumsy at times." A pause, a small laugh, both shaking their heads in wonderment, and then Viola said, "I reckon he'll grow out of it."

"He'll grow up to be another Jim Thorpe or, what's his name, the British miler that ran it in under four minutes. Look at them legs, them calf muscles. He's gonna be a runner for sure."

Fourteen years old and already taller than his mother, Billy was playing soccer with his half-sister Renae in the dead grass without a net but with stakes driven into the ground to mark the goals. Billy's still reddish hair now grown thick and long on top waved in the sun like wheat. Their little sister, Lizzy, was running circles by herself, shirtless and wearing shorts. Viola said, "Look at Lizzy. I swear she'll be able to outrun both of them before long. Lizzy was fidgety, constantly on the move. Couldn't sit still to save her life. More often than not she ate her meals standing up at the table.

It was a sweltering summer afternoon. Breathing the outdoor air was like sucking in bayou water. The interior of their rented cottage on the shores of Charley Pond was bearable only after midnight and before about nine in the morning. They did have a large box fan, but the belt had snapped during the night a week earlier. Harlan kept saying he would replace it. In order to tolerate the heat, Harlan and Viola had carried iced tea out to the back porch, three heaping spoons of sugar in hers. From there, they could look across a broad expanse of grass where the kids were playing, seemingly oblivious to the heat. At the edge of the field where land met water stood three ancient oaks draped with curtains of moss. Cypress trees stood in the knee-high water like an army of ghostly guards ten to twenty yards out from shore. Harlan and Viola loved to fish that lake from a leaky old skiff that required constant bailing. They caught bass and bream and crappie and the occasional big catfish. Harlan once reeled in a fifty-pound cat. They dined on that cat for days. Harlan always carried a .22 caliber pistol and a big stick when he went out on Charley Pond as protection from Alligators and water moccasins. The kids were not allowed out in the boat alone, and swimming was strictly forbidden. None of them knew how anyway. They had never seen a gator, but they were all sure there must be some in Charley Pond.

The field where the kids were playing stretched from the old no-longer-used outhouse to the lakeshore. Like their littlest sister, Billy and Renae both wore shorts and were shirtless. "That's fine for Lizzy," Viola said, "But I reckon Renae's getting big enough we ought to teach her to cover her tits. She's getting to be a young lady."

All of the Johnson kids matured early. Physically anyway. Tall, slim and muscular.

Harlan said, "I wouldn't bother. It's just us. Family. Let her be free of such for at least another year."

"I don't know. I've seen her checking them out in the mirror. She's well aware of them."

It was the sight of their legs, not Renae's budding breasts, that brought about the discussion of Billy's calf muscles. "Look at those muscles," Harlan said. "He's gonna be a pass catcher and a track star."

Billy overheard and was pleased with himself, overjoyed with his papa's pride. *Yes, by god, I'm going to grow up to be an athlete, a winner, the fastest runner in South Louisiana*, Billy thought. And then: *no I ain't. I ain't never going to be as good as I want to be.*

Self-doubt was never far from Billy. *I've gotta live up to Daddy's expectations. If I don't, he's going to be terribly let down.* Pleasing his father and being accepted into the family where he could never be his mama's boy were Billy's primary goals in life. *Of course he's smart as he is, big and strong. He's a Johnson after all* was a sentence Billy dreamed of hearing from Harlan or Viola or any of his siblings.

Harlan sent contradictory messages to his eldest son, the son he could not forget had been carried in Josephine's womb. He could brag on his son and belittle him at the same time. Sometimes his teasing seemed loving and sometimes just downright mean to the young boy who feared and idolized his father. Harlan had told his children he had been an outstanding athlete in his youth. He told them he ran the hundred-yard dash in ten seconds, an outright lie, but none of them doubted it. Athletic prowess—strength, agility, and the guts to constantly try your best—that, in Harlan's mind, was the mark of a manly man, that and pride of family. Harlan drilled those precepts into his children, and when Viola birthed the other kids, both parents told Billy he had to set the example because he was the oldest.

At recess in the third grade at Pioneer Elementary, Billy stepped on the low end of the playground seesaw and held out his arms like an eagle spreading its wings and walked like a tightrope artist up the angled board. When he reached the fulcrum, the board tipped toward the other side, and Billy fell off. Nearby kids laughed at him. Billy got up, knocked off the dust, and tried again. More kids gathered to watch, and again they laughed when he fell. On the fourth try, he managed to hold his balance and walked like a conquering hero to where the board touched ground on the other end, turned around and walked back to where he had started. His schoolmates shouted, "Betcha I can do that!" "Me too!" "Watch me do it!" They tried and failed. Even sixth graders. Billy was dubbed King of the Playground.

Billy ran all the way home after school to tell his father who, as it turned out, was not at home. He told his mother, and he told Renae and Bryce, neither of whom could quite grasp the concept from Billy's description. Nevertheless, Bryce told him he thought that was great. Renae shrugged and walked away. Billy was not able to tell his father until the next day. Harlan said, "That's good, son."

A hero for less than a day, Billy nevertheless gloated in his father's weak praise. He wanted so much to earn his father's love, and he figured the way to do that was by excelling in sports. After all, the old man still bragged about his athletic accomplishments in his own schooldays, and he spent every weekend seated in his old easy chair with a can of Falstaff in hand listening to football or basketball or baseball on his RCA Victor radio—laughing at Dizzy Dean's uproarious butchering of the English language—and years later he sat in the same easy chair with eyes and ears glued to the TV screen. Often

Billy sat cross-legged on the floor by his chair and listened to and watched the games with Papa Harlan, but even more often he was outside practicing his pitchi and running.

He gave it his all. He had the grit of a champion but came up short on speed and strength, which was a disappointment to his papa. He was perpetually second-best in baseball, football, track and field, and basketball. He competed with gusto but was never a winner. On the other hand, he was never a loser either.

...

Seated on the porch overlooking the makeshift soccer field by the shores of Charley Pond, Harlan shouted, "You go, girl!" when Renae made a sliding tackle and a neat steal from Billy. Viola stood up and clapped. Renae didn't have the muscular calves Billy had, but her legs were sleek like the body of a snake. Three years younger than Billy and with the presumed disadvantage of being female, Renae competed valiantly against Billy in most sports and was confident that by the time she was in high school she'd be big enough and strong enough to beat him.

Billy had no choice, realistically, but to accept that he would never be first across the finish line, would never score the winning touchdown or hit a grand slam homer. He took his frustration out on his younger siblings—studious and excitable Renae; little Bryce, eight years younger and easily cowed; Lizzy, on her way to becoming a beatnik and later a hippie farm wife; and Marilou the baby, a year younger than Lizzy and so precious to them all that even Billy would never bully her.

Billy never complained about perpetually being a little less than a winner but he never gave up. No matter the sport and no matter how badly he was beaten, he kept on coming. Harlan admired the hell out of that, but never told Billy.

In Billy's sophomore year of high school, he was a bench warmer on the school football team. He had played no more than three cumulative quarters in actual games (as opposed to scrimmages on the practice field).

"Hey, Johnson. Over here!" the coach shouted.

27

Billy jumped up off the bench and hustled to the sideline where the coach stood.

"Yeah, Coach."

"You think you can catch a pass?"

"Yessir."

"All right. Let's see what you can do. Get in there at right end."

Billy hurried onto the field. The next play in scrimmage against what they called the A team, Billy ran a slant pattern across the middle twenty yards deep. The QB sent a pass sailing his way. It drifted too high. Billy leaped for it, and a defensive back knocked his arm down. The ball fell to the ground. "What the hell was that, Smitty?" the coach shouted from the sideline. "In a game that would cost us fifteen yards. Hit the bench, Smitty. Packard, get your butt in there. Show Smitty how to defend without interfering."

Not on the next play but soon enough thereafter, they ran the same pass pattern, and this time the QB hit Billy in stride, and he ran it in for an easy touchdown. That play didn't win him a starting position on the team, but it did get him playing time in the next game and the next one after that. In those two games, he caught three passes for a total of twelve yards. Nothing spectacular, but by God he had made the team.

Next came the game against Metairie, their bitter rival. Into the third quarter and trailing by a field goal, Houma had the ball on Metarie's thirty. The play sent Billy flying, and the QB let loose with a too-high pass. Billy leaped for it, and a defender cut his legs out from under him. The ball hit the turf inside the goal line, and Billy hit the ground hard. He felt and heard his ankle snap. Down with intense pain in his left ankle, Billy was done for the season. An ambulance was called, and he was rushed to the nearest hospital, where his ankle was taped. He spent the night in the hospital and afterwards he walked with crutches for more than a month. Some of the girls made over him like he was a genuine hero, and he relished in the attention.

The football season was almost over, and Billy knew he would not get to play again that year, and maybe not ever. Homecoming was coming up. Beverly Smith, the prettiest and most popular girl in school, approached him after school. "Are you coming to the homecoming dance?" she asked him.

Astounded and confused but ecstatic that she had asked him, he stammered, "I can't dance. Look at me." He was standing on the outer edge of the basketball court, leaning on his crutches.

"Oh, don't worry about the crutches," Beverly Smith said. "I just want you to be my escort. We can watch the other kids dance, and we can all get together for sodas after. It'll be fun."

She asked me. Beverly Smith wants to go to the dance with me. Naturally he accepted her invitation.

At the dance in the gymnasium, they sat with another couple. Beverly Smith helped Billy into his chair. Before sitting next to him, she leaned forward and kissed him. What a night! What a night! The next day he asked her out on a date, but she said she couldn't. And not much longer after that she started going steady with another boy.

…

The younger Johnson kids hated and idolized Billy, and Billy both idolized and bullied each of them except for Marilou. Poor Bryce got the worst of it.

"Mama!" Bryce cried out for help when Billy had him pinned to the floor and was administering a hard noogie. Bryce—normally happy-go-lucky except when Billy's bullying got out of hand—was eight years old and no match for his big brother.

Their mother in the kitchen shouted back, "What?"

Billy clamped his hand over Bryce's mouth to keep him quiet and answered back, "What time is it?"

"It's almost six o'clock. Supper'll be ready soon," she shouted back, and Bryce gave up, knowing Billy would hold his hand over his mouth until doomsday if need be. He always got away with the what-time-is-it bit, no matter how many times he did it. Plus, Bryce granted it was funny, even as it pissed him off. *One of these days. I won't always be the littlest, and I won't be so fat and weak. One of these days I'm going to bloody his smartass mouth.*

That was the way all of Billy's younger siblings felt about him. They admired and wanted to emulate him while fearing and hating him, not recognizing that they were making their big brother into another Papa Harlan. Like his papa, Billy was a brilliant jokester when

29

he was being playful, and when he was picking on his siblings it was more maddening than hurtful. Little did any of them suspect that young Bryce would grow up to be much like their father, only bigger, stronger, and jollier.

Lizzy was the only one who never picked on Bryce. They competed in games of physical and mental skill, and she often let him win. Once she challenged him to a quarter-mile race, one complete circle around the high school track. "I'll spot you twenty yards," she said.

Bryce, thirteen years old at the time and a good twenty-to-thirty pounds over what a kid his age and height should have weighed, knew that Lizzy was faster than him but gladly accepted the generous gift of a head start. Twenty yards was twenty yards.

"Bang!" Billy shouted from where he watched by the start/finish line holding a cap-pistol starting gun. Lizzy and Bryce took off, Bryce dashing ahead as fast as his legs could go, Lizzy easing along with a relaxed loping stride. A hundred yards and more to where the track curved to the straightway heading to the finish, Bryce began to gasp for breath and lose speed, with Lizzy closing the gap step by step. Ten yards and then five to the finish line, Bryce a couple of strides ahead of her, it looked like Bryce was going to hold his lead by the tiniest when Billy stuck out his foot and tripped him. He went down, reaching out with his hands to break his fall. He landed on all fours, cinders digging into his palms and bloodying his knees. Lizzy stopped running and bent over to help Bryce to his feet. She turned and shouted at Billy. "You just wait, you ... you bully. One of these days I'm going to beat the shit out of you."

"Me too," red-faced Bryce shouted.

"Aw, I never meant to hurt you, buddy." Billy stifled his laugh.

Helping Bryce walk to the house and washing and bandaging his skinned-up knees, Lizzy blurted out something she had never before said out loud. She said, "I hope he rots in hell."

Bryce was stunned into silence for a second, and then burst into laughter.

It was around this time that Bryce was made to walk around and around and around the flagpole—the most dreaded but actually meaningless and easiest punishment ever doled out by the principal at

Bayou Junior High. The flagpole stood outside the front entrance to the school. Three flags hung from the pole: the Confederate battle flag, the state flag of Louisiana, and what Bryce called the misnamed American flag. He was made to walk round and round and round the flagpole because he helped another kid with his homework. "I was just trying to help her," he complained, but the teacher said he did the problems for her, and that was cheating.

Since he was extremely likable, a number of his friends stood around the flagpole and chatted with him while he was walking off his punishment, and he explained to them why he claimed the American flag was misnamed. He told them there were three parts of America, North America, Central America and South America; and the United States was only a small part of North America and clearly not the entirety of the continent. "Yeah, that makes sense," one of his friends said, and another one marveled, "How do you know stuff like that?"

That was the moment Bryce decided he wanted to be a teacher when he grew up. He could hardly wait to tell the family about his momentous decision. "I'm going to be a teacher," he blurted, to which Harlan and Viola both said, "That's great," assuming he'd change his mind multiple times before he was grown.

Later, when their parents weren't around, Billy told Bryce, "Teaching is what people do when they can't do anything else."

…

Running, jumping, you name it—Lizzy could beat all of her siblings except Billy, and it was clear that she would be able to best him also before too awfully long. She also showed signs that she'd grow up to be the smartest and the most lovable. But the dear little girl was constantly in trouble at school because she could not sit still. She would get out of her desk and run around or dance in place, and her teachers would have to punish her. They didn't want to because she was so precious, but they felt they had no choice. They made her stand in the corner and made her write on the blackboard a hundred times I WILL NOT GET OUT OF MY DESK UNTIL DISMISSED. And she was often sent to the principal's office where she would sit and watch the hypnotic movement of the hands on the grandfather clock.

At home, she was punished by being made to go to bed without supper for getting out of her seat at the dinner table without being excused, and sometimes being made to go out in the yard and get a switch off the willow tree. All because she could not make herself sit still.

...

A quarter mile down the two-lane road from where the Johnsons were living at the time there lived a young girl named Belle. She stood barely over five feet tall and had a lovely figure, the kind that was called hourglass, curly hair and big lips that were juicy and red even without the aid of lipstick. She habitually licked and chewed on her lips. Her arms and legs were as muscular as any of the boys in school. She and Billy met in a most unexpected way.

It was the summer before Billy was going to start high school in Houma. Their houses, his and Belle's, were a good distance out of town near old Bobby Jenks's farm. The Hairless Harlan Johnson family had rented and crammed themselves into the little shack on the south edge of Mister Jenks's pasture only a week earlier. Mister Jenks had a little pond on his farm where he let kids in the neighborhood swim. On a blazing summer afternoon, Belle was the only kid swimming in the pond's murky water. "It's a nasty pond. You couldn't pay me to stick a foot in it," her mama had warned her, but to Belle it was deliciously cool and soothing.

Belle said, "It's the only place we can go swimming."

"Well all right. But I warn you, never go in that pond alone. Anything can happen. You could get a cramp and go under and drown with nobody there to pull you out."

Mom's a worrywart, Belle thought. But getting a killer cramp while swimming alone was exactly what happened.

It started in her left calf and quickly shot down to her ankle and foot. Panicking, she began to flail in the murky water, and her head went under, and she swallowed a mouthful of the foul-tasting water and fought to the surface and spit it out. Billy Johnson, who was heading to the swimming hole, saw her floundering and came running like a fullback crashing through the line, and dove into the pond and grabbed her and swam to shore with one hand reaching across her shoulder and into her armpit the way he'd been taught by illustrations in *Boy's Life*.

On her back in the grass with Billy on top of her pumping her chest, Belle gasped and spit out pond water, looked into his face and thought he was the most handsome boy she had ever seen. She sputtered a wet, "Hi. I'm Belle, Who are you?"

"I'm Billy Johnson."

"Hi, Billy Johnson," still sputtering with choking breath. "I think I need mouth-to-mouth."

She giggled a wet giggle at her clever remark.

...

Lizzy never did beat the shit out of her big brother like she said she would, but after they were grown, she told Renae, "If Billy ever tried to beat me up the way he did Bryce, I'd a torn him a new asshole." That was shortly after she came home from her summer in New York—came home full of piss and vinegar and disdain for her family, all but Bryce who had emerged as the smartest and funniest and most loveable of the Johnson kids, and Renae who had confessed to Lizzy and only two of her best friends that she thought she might be a lesbian. Lizzy thought that was cool. Daring. "There were a couple of lesbians at the dance studio in New York, and they didn't care who knew it. Can you imagine that down here?"

...

Something unexpected happened to chubby little Bryce between the ages of thirteen and fifteen. He grew up. And all that chub turned into muscle. His siblings had not noticed how much time he spent shut up in old man Jenks's toolshed lifting weights and doing calisthenics. He was also a bookworm. That much they knew. They thought he was spending all that time in the shed with his nose in a book, not molding his body into six feet and two hundred pounds of rock-solid muscle and still growing. Billy, by then, was a fully grown man, but in many ways, still the kid who, in his own mind, was never good enough, who took his frustrations out on his younger siblings.

33

He no longer lived full-time with the family but had pretty much moved in with Belle. Harlan and Viola and Belle's parents had reluctantly agreed to the arrangement after Billy and Belle laid down an ultimatum. "Yes, we are sleeping together," they informed both sets of parents. "It's the twentieth century for Christ's sake. At least we're using birth control. We are aware and responsible adults." It was Belle who said all of that while Billy stood by with a puffed-out chest and smiled at her.

One day while visiting the family, Billy called Bryce a fat slob. Easygoing Bryce ordinarily would have shrugged it off or come back with a comical jab, but it had been a rough day at school, and he had suppressed his resentment of Billy for years, and all those years of frustration with his big brother coalesced in his reaction to that remark. He hauled off and socked Billy smack dab in his big mouth. Billy fell to the floor, and Bryce pounced on top of him and held him down and took him by his hair and banged his head against the floor and shouted, "What time is it, Mama? Huh? What time is it? Huh? Huh?" Their mama was not even at home at the time.

Well into old age, Billy would carry the mark of that encounter in the form of a crooked tooth.

1958
THE JOHNSONS MOVE TO WASHINGTON

Harlan and Viola and their passel of children lived hand-to-mouth during their time in Louisiana, but that was soon to change when the kids met up with their grandpa on their mother's side of the family. Beauregard called Bobo, the king of the wheeler-dealers up in Seattle. As Harlan put it, "That son of a gun's richer'n God."

First, they had to escape Louisiana. Summers from hell, air you could drink, mosquitoes large enough to pick up a baby and carry it off into the swamps. Beauregard called Bobo sent them the magic ticket out of Louisiana.

. . .

Viola opened the mailbox, looked in, and pulled out an envelope with a Seattle P.O Box for a return address written in her father's familiar handwriting. She laughed out loud and ripped it open, expecting the usual hundred-dollar check and a short but sweet note from her dad. She treasured his sweet notes and saved them all in a scrapbook. She laughed some more when she read it. She said, "I don't fucking believe it."

The kids were shocked. None of them had ever heard her use that word. Coming from Papa Harlan it was as common as molasses on pancakes, but coming from Mama Viola it was shocking. Despite having grown up around whores and drunks, Viola seldom cursed.

Marilou asked, "What is it?"

"Oh, nothing much. Just a letter from y'all's grandpa Bobo." (None of the Johnson kids knew Bobo. To them he was a heroic myth.) Viola said, "I'll share it with you after Papa and Billy get home,"

Billy at the time was working with his papa building a boat dock on Bayou Cane for the owner of the bowling alley in Houma. Viola stuffed the letter in the big pocket of her pants and refused to talk about it until Harlan and Billy got home. The kids, mostly grown or practically grown by then, were like seven-year-olds on Christmas morning waiting to see what Santa brought.

Four hours later when Harlan and Billy got home, Viola met them at the door screaming with joy, "Looka here, looka here, looka here!" She waved the letter like a victory flag. "It's a letter from my old man in Seattle. Out of the blue. Look what he has to say."

Harlan thought she was being ridiculously over-excited considering that the letter from her father was in no way out of the blue. Her old man had been writing to her regularly since she left home, starting when she could barely read. "Ain't nothing worth that much hollering," Harlan said.

"You think not? Well listen to this."

The family gathered around to listen to Viola read her father's letter.

My dearest daughter,

I know times is tough, but I'm doing pretty doggone well up here, and I could use some help running the business. Make that businesses. If you and Harlan and the kids could see fit to come up here, y'all could be a big help, and I promise you, you could make a fine living at it. I'm talking about—get ready for it—millions of dollars. Y'all'll never have to worry about where your next meal's coming from. You, my precious Viola, will never have to do the things your mama had to do.

Your loving father, Beauregard "Bobo" Parker.

She folded the letter with trembling hands and put it back in her pocket and said, "Don't that beat all? What we gonna do about that, huh? What we gonna do about it? I think we oughta do it."

"Do what?" Harlan asked.

"Whaddaya think? Go to Seattle, silly. Go to work for my daddy."

"And what if ..." He couldn't think of a worthwhile what if. Viola had told him that her father was a man of his word, and he knew the old man, huckster that he was, loved his daughter and was rolling in dough. What else did they need to know?

"What about your mother, Nellie? Ain't that her name?" Harlan asked.

"What about her? Have you ever even met her? Do you really care about her?

Presumably, Nellie was still whoring in the French Quarter. Viola hadn't seen her or heard from her in years.

...

On the day before they left Louisiana, Harlan walked to his favorite spot near the banks of the Atchafalaya River, sweltering on a depressingly hot August afternoon. He carried the old fishing pole and casting reel he had bought off of Buster Williams for two dollars, and he set himself down on the old bench that had sat there since forever and plopped his little box of hooks and corks and a can of nightcrawlers in the grass. He didn't cast out his line right away but reached into his pocket for the worn-ragged paperback of *The Illusive Pirate Pegleg Johnson* by Robert Creel. He opened it and thumbed through it looking for phrases he had highlighted, phrases of Creel's ridiculous hyperbole like "Old Pegleg practically invented guff, but he didn't take none of it off nobody" and "all he had to do was look sideways at a woman and she'd drop her drawers" and "never was there a woman so big, so strong and so beauteous as Hurricane Gertie Duchamp." There were so many sayings like that. Harlan had memorized pages worth. He had owned that copy of the book about his notorious grandfather since he, Harlan, was twelve years old, and had read it cover-to-cover more than a few times. His eldest son, Billy, had also read it repeatedly, and they sometimes enjoyed swapping Pegleg and Gertie quotes. He came to the place where the book described Gertie as the most illustrious madame in New Orleans, and he smiled his satisfaction at that and then closed the book and slipped it back into his pocket, patting it as if to satisfy himself that it was really there. On a whim, he picked up his fishing pole again and tossed it in the river and threw the other stuff in after it and watched it slowly go southward with the ebbing tide, wondering if the worms could swim. *I'm done living in the past,* he told himself. *We're going to Seattle, and we're going to build a different life. No more shrimping and no more bootlegging and buying and selling useless junk and no more sneaking around on Viola, and by God I'm gonna love our children and raise 'em up right like the good lord intended.*

...

Creel's book was but one of two published books about Pegleg Josiah Johnson. There was no definitive evidence that any of the legendary stories about him were anything more than unsubstantiated fairytales. Documented evidence suggested he was not an actual pirate but a privateer or possibly a rumrunner who sold alcohol to bootleggers in coastal towns from Cape Coral to Corpus Christi and that he lived with and fathered children with the famous New Orleans madame Matilda Gertrude Hildegarde Duchamp, a.k.a. Gertie or Hurricane Gertie—legendarily one of three or more women with whom he cohabited and fathered children, none of whom knew about the others.

The bulk of Pegleg Johnson's descendants had scattered around the country like locusts—primarily in cities and towns bordering the Gulf of Mexico—and had long since been lost to history. The only descendants about which much was known were Hairless Harlan and his children.

They had lived a hardscrabble life in Louisiana, and they were sick of it—going from town to town, shanty to trailer court, sometimes ahead of pursuing lawmen. It had been a freezing February evening when Harlan said, "Let's do it." It was August and the heat and humidity were skyrocketing when they finally packed the family possessions in Harlan's doddering Ford station wagon and hitched a trailer behind the old Chevrolet, and the two-vehicle caravan moved north to Seattle.

"Oh my goodness, this is a big move we're making. I hope the old man is sincere about wanting us to move up there." Harlan was scared and skeptical, which was why he had put off the move so long.

Viola said. "He asked us to come, didn't he? He'll give us both good jobs. He did say he wanted us to help with his businesses. That's gotta be like managers. Right? I mean he wouldn't stick his daughter and her husband in some entry-level job, would he?"

"Nah, I guess not. Or maybe that's exactly what he's got in mind, and he figures he won't have to pay us good 'cause of we're family."

"No, no, no. He's not like that. Not at all. He's got oodles of money, and he's generous with it. He'll probably give Billy a job too. And maybe even Renae. She's old enough to work, and right smart too. We're gonna be managers. Probably wear nametags. *Harlan Johnson, manager. Billy Johnson, sales Manager, like that.*"

Harlan remembered tales Viola had told about her mother, Nellie, how she had run off with her and dragged her from town to town and how she had sponged off Bobo and how loyal and supportive Bobo had been to her despite it all. Harlan knew in his heart that Bobo would treat him and his wife and children well. Shyster though he might have been, Harlan was confident that Bobo was their ticket out of the swamps of destitution—but still scared he might … nah, couldn't be.

…

Viola and the Johnsons' young son Bryce squeezed in the front seat of the station wagon with Harlan; the back seat was fully loaded with their possessions. First son Billy and his sisters Renae and Marilou and Lizzy, along with Belle, followed in Billy's old Chevvy with a small trailer pulled behind.

"We're modern day Joads," Lizzy said.

Belle and Billy by then were virtually married but without the ring and a preacher to make it official. She had found a discarded crib left on the sidewalk and got Billy to repair and paint it. "We don't know when, but one of these days we're going to need this." It now topped the household junk on the trailer, painted a festive red with white flowers.

On the road to Washington, Belle was fascinated with everything she saw. She asked questions like "What's that?" (a silo) and wondered "Why would people choose to live in a place like that?" (miles from the nearest town, or so it seemed from her vantage point)" and "What are we gonna do about eating and sleeping?" (we eat and sleep in the car) and "How long till we get there?" (until we get there) and "Are we gonna cross the Mississippi?"

"No silly," Billy said in response to that last one. "The Mississippi is over thataway, east of here, and we're going north and west." He answered many of her questions with made-up stories. Such as when she asked how Bobo got so rich he said, "He got started playing poker, probably cheating. Then he made smart investments. He was smart thataway."

Marilou kept her nose buried in Jane Austin's *Pride and Prejudice* and kept her mouth closed pretty much all the way to Seattle. It took the family seven days to get there, stopping along the way to camp and eat picnic style alongside the road and to replace Billy's transmission when it bit the dust near Salt Lake City. It was a decrepit garage that installed the rebuilt transmission that they would later find out was stuffed with sawdust. The transmission lasted long enough to get to Seattle but not a month longer before it bit the dust again.

Their two-car-seven-person caravan arrived midday on day eight at Bobo's home in the Laurelhurst section of Seattle. It was a two-story, four-bedroom house with a deck over the front porch. The deck, which Bobo had furnished with a table and chairs and a big red umbrella to shade from sun and rain, overlooked Lake Washington. Bobo stepped gingerly out on the porch with the help of a cane and with a lovely young woman in a nurse's uniform holding the crook of his arm. He shouted with a booming voice, "Bout damn time y'all got here. Come on in the house."

Viola was shocked at how wraithlike Bobo had become, at his wisps of white hair and at how the hand on his cane shook. The years since she last saw him had not been easy on his body. When she reached the porch, carrying a large suitcase, Bobo said, "Drop that damn suitcase and com'ere and give your daddy a hug."

She complied, feeling for a moment like an anxious little girl eager to please her father. He gave her a big hug and then kissed her on both cheeks.

"Damn, Daddy!"

"Damn your ownself, gal. It's so good to see you."

He gave Harlan a big slap on the back and said, "This must be that notorious Harlan Johnson that married my little gal. Welcome to Seattle, son. Welcome home."

Viola said, "I can't hardly remember seeing you, Daddy. I didn't even remember what you looked like."

"Well I looked a good deal younger," Bobo said.

Harlan said, "He looks like you, Honey."

...

Settled down in the large living room, their suitcases put away in two separate bedrooms, they talked about plans for the immediate and distant future. "So here's the deal, I'll put you all to work in my establishments—those of you that are old enough I mean—so you can learn the ins and outs of running a business in the Bobo Parker way. And then I'm gonna send y'all down Olympia way to run my establishments down there. Don't want you too close to home. Family oughta be close enough to visit time to time but not so close to be a constant irritant. Y'all will be happy 'bout that 'cause I can be a bear of a bother to be around all the time."

"Not Lizzy and Marilou," Viola spoke up. "They're too young to be put to work."

"No we're not," they protested.

"Hellfire, that's the spirit. I like gals with gumption," Bobo said. "Now tell me who all is who."

As they talked, the nurse carried Bobo's empty glass into the kitchen and brought back a glass filled with amber beer.

"I'm Lizzy, Lizzy said, and Marilou said, "I'm Marilou."

"And I'm Renae," piped in Renae.

Billy introduced himself and said, "This beauty here is my girlfriend, Belle."

"Girlfriend, huh? You come all the way from Louisiana with him and you ain't married yet? Y'all oughta get hitched," Bobo pronounced.

"Don't you go talking like that, Papa," Viola said, and Bobo said, "I gotta hand it to you, honey. You sure hatched a passel of handsome children, and I can't hardly believe you're fully grown up your own self."

Viola reverted to little-girl shyness in her father's presence. Not so Harlan. Harlan admired and reveled in Bobo's boisterous good humor and from the start was anxious to leap at his every request. He went to work for him, first at Bar-Bar and then in his hardware store in Pioneer Square. Bobo pulled Viola into his web and trained her to take over as bookkeeper for the businesses and set up an office for her off the display floor in Bobo's Ford. "Bookkeeping's what your mama did for me, and she only stole a little bit."

He put Billy to work as a used car salesman. All three of them thrived in their new jobs. Harlan's cheery personality made him a popular bartender and salesclerk.

Despite having little formal education, Viola was a wizard with figures and a fast learner. *How did Bobo know she would be a good accountant? Because her mother had been a wiz at math.* She found errors the former bookkeeper had made that saved the businesses thousands. "Errors my hind quarters," Bobo said, "That motherlover was stealing from me. He can thank the gods that I don't know where to find him, squeaky little faggot that he was." Bobo used words like faggot and queer freely, and Renae cringed whenever she heard, but said nothing in protest. The others of the Johnson clan seemingly thought nothing of Bobo's casual use of homophobic and racist words. After all, hadn't they heard them a thousand times down in Louisiana?

Billy sold cars like nobody's business. He was the first of the Johnsons to be made manager of his own shop, Bobo Ford of Centralia, a hop, skip and a jump south of Olympia. It was not a thriving business when Billy first arrived, but he was determined to change that, and he did. He started by crafting himself as a personality. First with a big sign out front announcing UNDER NEW MANAGEMENT followed by HONEST BILLY JOHNSON, GREAT GRANDSON OF THE NOTORIOUS PIRATE PEGLEG JOSIAH JOHNSON WELCOMES YOU TO BOBO FORD with a cut-out picture of himself in a pirate costume.

"That's an advertisement declaring you're going to rip folks off," Harlan said.

"No it ain't. Watch and see."

He filmed a series of commercials starring none other than himself. The commercials ran on area stations and always featured Billy wearing his pirate hat and standing on the used car lot next to a late model car. Standing by his side was a pretty girl in a bikini. "This is Honest Billy Johnson coming to you from Bobo Ford of Centralia, and this little beauty (pointing to the car and to the bikini babe who was also pointing at the car) can be yours for a fraction of the asking price." People laughed like hyenas at the Bobo Ford commercials. School kids parodied them. Their smartass parents said Billy was the dumbest pirate ever. But when it came time to shop for a new car, Bobo Ford was the first place they shopped.

…

Billy and Belle moved into an apartment in Olympia and soon produced three children, and not long after that Harlan and Viola also moved to Olympia to run Bobo's other hardware store. Soon all of the Louisiana Johnsons were living together in two units of a downtown duplex. A short walk away was the area near the Fourth Avenue Bridge where the Deschutes River flowed into Puget Sound, linking the east and west sides of town. It was an area of small businesses on the east and small homes on the west, an area once popularly known as Little Hollywood (I don't know why) and described by one historical document from the 1920s as an area that housed the less acceptable elements of Olympia society, including immigrants, prostitutes, and alcoholics; men, women and children in clothes so worn a strong wind might strip them naked, men and boys standing on curbs and pissing in gutters, women and girls doing their business in alleyways; illegal sales of drugs, whiskey and stolen goods taking place in plain view. The perceived history of Little Hollywood as Harlan and Viola saw it appealed to them; they thrived in that atmosphere.

…

Belle got a job cashiering in a department store in a strip mall in Lacey. Or maybe it was in Olympia; you couldn't tell when you left one town and entered the other. With Billy and Belle both working, they were well off enough to plan on getting married. The wedding was in June, two years after the Johnson clan moved to Washington.

That same summer Billy talked the owner of a drugstore in Olympia into hiring his sister Renae. She was the oldest girl at twenty-two and anxious to get away from home and live on her own and was happy to settle in Lacey, which she called Northeast Olympia.

Belle kept her job in the mall for a little more than a year after she and Billy were married and until she was six months pregnant with the first of three children. After the baby came, they bought a nice little house on Bethel Street.

"I don't want to inherit this dealership," Billy told Bobo. "I want to own it outright, and I want it to be right now. What's more, I don't want you to give it to me; I want to buy it with my own dang money earned by my own wiles and ingenuity."

"Well, all right. That's some goddamn gumption. Good for you, son. You and that gal of yours, y'all are all right," Bobo said.

That was about the time Billy began to lose all his hair. He said, "I think I might have hypotrichosis like my daddy."

"No you ain't got that," Belle said. "If you did, you'd a had it all along and you'd not have a lick of hair anywhere on your body, and believe me, I know where you got hair and where you ain't." With that, she kissed the top of his balding head.

...

It wasn't long before Belle found out that Billy had been cheating on her. Those damned Johnson men and their philandering ways. It was one of her friends at work who told her. The friend had seen Billy with a blonde seated together in a diner and holding hands across the table. When Belle confronted him with it, he readily confessed. "It was a one-time thing," he said. "I don't know what came over me. It just happened. But I swear it'll never happen again."

"Did you sleep with her or just hold her damn hand like some lovesick teenager?"

"I slept with her." His demeanor was casual. *So what, no big deal.*

"Damn you, Billy Johnson."

Billy's confession of infidelity took place over lunch in the same diner where he had been seen with the other woman. It was convenient to work and convenient for a tryst between Billy and the parts department receptionist, a fiery tall and skinny blonde named Brenda who lived in a small apartment next door to the diner.

Belle's eyes were red-rimmed. She grinded her teeth. She had not touched the coffee she had ordered. She took a few deep breaths, loud on the outtake, and put her hands flat on the table to keep them from shaking. Her already pink face was glowing. Between clinched teeth she said, "I don't hate you, Billy. I should, but ..." A painful pause and then, "Yes I do. I want to ... I, I, I ..." And without uttering another word she stood up and ran out of the diner and down the street in the direction opposite the way to the dealership with no idea where she was going, just desperate to get away.

She needed space. And time. To recover from the shock. To clear her head. She didn't want to leave Billy. Yes she did. She wanted to never see him again, never hear his name. She wanted to smash his face. She didn't know what she wanted to do. Get drunk, maybe. Cry for a day. Cut his thing off. *Let's see how you're gonna fuck around now.*

She called Renae. "We need to talk. Please. Can we meet somewhere?"

They got together for drinks. She said, "Billy is having an affair. With the bimbo parts department gal."

"Oh my sweet lord," Renae said. "I'm so sorry."

Belle asked if she could sleep on their couch for a little while. "Just until I get my head straight, figure out what I want to do."

Renae said, "Sure."

"And Sally? She'll be all right with me crashing?"

"Of course. The more the merrier. Sally loves having company, and she loves you."

Renae and Sally were lovers. Had been for almost a year. Sally worked part-time at Smithfield Café where the bulk of Olympia's gays and lesbians hung out. They lived together in a cabin a little way out of town. Renae had already come out to the family, and none of them were surprised or upset. "We've known all along," Viola said. "It makes no difference to any of us. We love you just the way you are."

"Oh my god, that's such a relief. But why in the world didn't you tell me? It would have saved me a ton of grief."

By this time in the Johnson saga, the three younger children, Lizzy, Marilou and Bryce, were the only ones still living at home with Harlan and Viola. None of them were shocked to learn that Renae was a lesbian; they also had sensed it all along.

...

Billy and the receptionist sleeping together was not a one-time thing. They had been doing it for more than two months, and it did not stop just because he got caught. Billy was a rake just like his father and apparently Johnson men going back forever. He was absolutely confident he'd never get caught again, or if he did, Belle would overlook it. He had once justified his philandering by saying, "A hard dick ain't got no conscious," which was evidenced by the behavior of all the Johnson men except for Bryce.

A hard dick ain't got no conscious was practically a Johnson battle cry. Billy's buddies (underlings) at the dealership acted like it was the funniest thing ever said. And it spread around Bobo Ford. Belle relayed that little bit of Billy Johnson wisdom to Renae. "Screw that," Renae said.

Days later Belle said, "I've been thinking on it and ... you know, as much as I hate to admit it, a man's going to be a man, and if you love a man—and God knows I do love that man, I can't help it—you just got to live with it."

Sally shook her head in dismay and didn't say anything. Renae said, "I know, honey, I know. Bless your heart." In the privacy of their home, Sally and Renae agreed the whole Johnson family was crazy with their lackadaisical attitude toward fidelity.

LIZZY IN HIGH SCHOOL

At fourteen years of age, five-foot-eight and fencepost skinny, Lizzy, sometimes called Lizzy, was teased in school because she stood so much taller than the other girls, even most of the boys, and because of her bayou country accent. Some of the other students joked that she was "just one of the boys." That didn't hold water because there was no denying her girlish face and figure, skinny be damned (skinny in her own estimation, sleek and sexy as a mermaid in the eyes of at least a good chunk of the high school boys). She had no friends back then, but some of the boys at school thought she was ripe for being fondled if not for friendship. Like Bobby Emerson, who stood all of five-foot-three and was called Squirt by his classmates. He tried to reach his hand inside her skirt once. They were in the cafeteria, in line to be served. Smack dab in front of the other students from Miss Marion's fourth-period algebra, with no warning and not a hint of subtlety, that disgusting little Bobby Emerson reached his hand down around her knees and upward under her skirt. Lizzy slapped his face so hard that his eyeballs rattled around like marbles. He tearfully tried to apologize, and with an icy voice, she said, "You ever do that again, I'll break every one of your goddamn fingers. Starting with the one you got up your nose all the time, you disgusting little turd."

That elicited an eruption of laughter from classmates. Both Lizzy and Bobby turned red in the face. Word spread around campus. Kids who had never spoken to her approached her over the next few days to tell her how much they admired her for standing up to Bobby. "The squirt ain't nothing but a worthless piece of excrement," one of the older girls said. Lizzy loved that. She loved that the girl used the word *excrement* rather than the more common curse word she had used.

After putting the squirt in his place, she was slightly more popular in school. Only slightly. She was still the beanpole with the funny accent. But the message got around that Lizzy Johnson was not to be messed with. The girls were nicer to her, and the boys were respectful and leery. Still, she never completely felt like she belonged among the popular kids at Olympia High.

A few junior and senior boys worked up the nerve to ask her out, but she was hesitant, even downright fearful of accepting their invitations. The same older girl who had called Bobby Emerson excrement said, "They just wanna fuck you," and Lizzy had a strong sense that she was right. She didn't date. At least not for another year or two. She developed a reputation for being standoffish.

What passed for a social life for her was bowling and skating and going to movies with her sister Renae and Renae's girlfriend, and with Marilou. They went together to see Marlon Brando in *The Wild One*. As soon as Brando appeared on screen, Marilou said, "Oh my dear lord. I want him, I want him, I want him."

"Not me," Renae said. "He's ugly and sleazy looking. I'd be afraid to let him touch me."

"Meaning he's a man," Marilou said.

Lizzy didn't say anything. Two girls in seats behind them said, "Hush your mouths."

...

During the remainder of Lizzy's school days, only three boys asked her for a date. She gave in and let one kid named Oliver take her to one of the Friday night dances in the gym. He was a decent dancer, and she enjoyed the date until he took her home and walked her to her door and shook hands with her. She had expected at least a goodnight kiss. She was all puckered up for it. She said, "Didn't you have a good time?"

"Sure. I reckon," he said, and never asked her out again.

Another boy, called Gerald and nicknamed Speedo, took her to the drive-in movie and they smooched and petted in his car and hardly watched the movie, but he never asked her out again either. *I must be toxic to boys. God knows why.*

She decided to give up on boys, at least for a while. Until Brando or Paul Newman or Elvis came calling. She took up dancing and studied for a while with a local dance instructor, and she performed to scattered applause in a school talent show. She decided at the moment of bowing to applause at the end of her performance that she was destined to be a professional dancer.

Betty Hanson, a cheerleader and president of the Home Economics Club, and Betty's brother Randy, who was just about the most popular boy in school, were both impressed with Lizzy's dancing. They became close friends for a while, and Randy said he liked her a lot and eventually, after a couple of enjoyable dates, said, "I think I'm in love with you."

It was her senior year. No one had ever said that to her. She was flabbergasted, overjoyed. *Did he really say love? Could that be possible? Didn't he look a little bit like Brando?* She hugged him and kissed him and said, "I think I might be in love with you, too." They started sitting together in the cafeteria and hanging out after school. Everybody knew she was Randy's girl. Suddenly she was popular.

They were the same height, and other kids said they looked good together. They went to the drive-in movies in his Ford sedan, which coincidentally he had bought from Lizzy's big brother Billy. She had never done such things as smooching at the drive-in. They sometimes double-dated with Betty and her boyfriend. There was a time when Betty and her boyfriend went all the way on the back seat. Lizzy didn't dare look over the seat, but she could hear them and knew exactly what they were doing. For weeks she struggled inwardly with should we or shouldn't we, and soon handholding and kissing and fondling led to more serious petting in his Ford, and she finally let him do what he wanted to do, and the morning after when she entered the school building one of the boys shouted out, "Guess who's not a viiir-gin anymore!" A crowd of juniors and seniors stood nearby, and as Lizzy walked by one of them shouted, "Cherry, cherry, who got Lizzy's cherry!"

Randy stood with the crowd with an uncomfortable grin on his face and looked down at the ground when Lizzy caught his eye. Had she been older and wiser, she would have been able to interpret his expression more clearly. It was a mix of pride, humor and shame. His friends badly needed standing up to, but Randy was not the boy to do the standing up. His popularity with the other boys was more precious to him than was his romance with a girl he truly cared for but for whom he couldn't bring himself to sacrifice his schoolyard status. Randy's sister Betty was in the crowd too. She shot her brother wilting looks and spun around and pushed her way past some of her classmates. Lizzy could tell that Betty was furious at her brother for telling the other kids he had gone all the way with her and mad at the others for being so mean. But she was no more willing to stand up to the other kids or to apologize to Lizzy than was her brother.

Lizzy never again spoke to Randy or Betty, and they never again spoke to her. She refused to cry or to let anyone know how absolutely devastated she was by the way Randy used her and threw her on the trash heap and how her first-ever sexual experience made her the butt of a schoolyard joke.

She finished her high school years friendless and practically in silence. At home, things were not a heck of a lot better. Her home life was like Cinderella before the ball. When floors needed sweeping and mopping, dishes needed washing, laundry needed to be put away. Her brothers and sisters seemed to have a magical ability to be scarce, and none of the family, including her mother, showed any appreciation for all the work she did—not in Lizzy's opinion, anyway.

If she was sad or hurt or enraged, she didn't let it show. She whistled and sang and danced while doing chores. Among the various household jobs she was expected to do was the laundry. Their old washing machine made chugging noises that in Lizzy's ears became musical. She would dance to the beat while washing clothes.

Home from work in the middle of the day one day, which was unusual, Harlan stood in the doorway to the laundry room smoking a Chesterfield and watching Lizzy dance in front of the washing machine.

"My darling daughter," he said, "you're just about the best dancer I've ever seen."

"Aw, Daddy, you're teasing me." She curtsied.

"No I'm not teasing. I mean it. You're really good."

"Thanks. Gosh, do you ... uh, this is crazy, but do you think I'm good enough to become a professional? That's what I think I'd really like to be more than anything."

"I think you could, baby. I really do."

For a time after that, she swam in a stream of pure joy, feeling like she could conquer the world, fantasizing about being on Broadway or in the movies.

Before school let out for the summer, Harlan told Lizzy he was going to pay her tuition and expenses to attend a summer session at the famous Martha Graham School in New York. To Lizzy, Martha Graham was a goddess and New York was Camelot.

1961
WHEN MARILOU MET RUDY

Rudy Briggs. That's me. 'Bout time I introduced myself.

I'll never forget when I first met Marilou Johnson and through her the rest of Harlan Johnson's brood. Lizzy and Marilou were as different as sisters could be. Long-legged Lizzy lived inside her head much of the time. She was a quiet and dreamy girl who lived for books and music and dancing. She liked having friends well enough but could live with or without them. Marilou, shorter with a lighter shade of hair (Marilou's rosy taupe to Lizzy's cocoa), could be mischievous and playful and had many more friends at school than Lizzy did. Her manner of speech was animated and usually joyful, accented with a constant flailing about of hands and head, and a deep laugh. Whether being humorous or serious, once she got on a roll—watch out. She never met a dare she couldn't answer. The one thing Lizzy and Marilou had in common was that they were both, as Bryce put it, boy crazy. Marilou made a point of sharing her male friends' every interest and loved to talk about them, be it cars or sports or the intricacy of words and numbers. She cuddled and smooched and danced with her boyfriends and went to the proverbial next step at a much younger age than most girls, while Lizzy wistfully admired boys from a distance and longed to do all of those things but for the talking about cars and baseball and hunting, all of which bored her.

I was in Marilou's English class. I hadn't quite grown up all the way. I was an inch shorter than Marilou and somewhat pudgy with perpetually rosy cheeks. At that age, an inch to me was like a foot, meaning that when I stood next to someone like Lizzy, or even Marilou, I felt like a midget.

I spent much of my time in English staring at Marilou and quickly looking away when she caught my eye. I could imagine what she was thinking. *He wants me the way a dog wants a bone.* She was right too.

Walking to school one day I found a pamphlet, or I guess what you'd call a small magazine, from the Arcadia Nudist Community. It was called *Living Naturally,* and it was in the middle of a stack of magazines piled by a trashcan. In front of God and everybody, as they say, I stood on the sidewalk thumbing through the magazine studying the pictures of naked people of all ages. When I saw a couple of kids walking my way, I quickly stuffed the magazine in the big inner pocket of my long black coat. I wore that coat every day no matter the weather—thought it made me look cool and dangerous.

The thing about the *Living Naturally* magazine was that none of the naked people—men, women, children; even grandpas and grandmas—were like traditionally gorgeous creatures. Lord knows I had seen enough of those in *Playboy* and *Penthouse.* These were just ordinary people. Somehow that excited me more. I kept it stuffed in my jacket for months. Until Marilou found it.

OK, I might as well confess it, and here it is. I'm sort of a wannabe exhibitionist. I love getting naked, and I'm titillated with the idea of doing it in public. For a while the previous summer I went skinny dipping with some other boys in a semi-hidden pond beyond a stand of trees that marked the edge of a new subdivision on the edge of Lacey where there was a good chance, in my imagination, that a group of luscious young women might happen by and see us, and I got all gigglyheaded with desire thinking about it. I imagined all of us chest deep in the water, teasing the girls, telling them we were naked and daring them to strip off and join us. Of course, no such cadre of luscious girls ever showed up, but imagining it was thrilling. Or streaking. A few years later some friends in college did it on campus. I wanted to run with them but did not have the guts.

...

I almost forgot about Marilou after graduating Oly High and never once saw her during my college years at TESC. It was my first year after college. I was holding down an entry-level job with the state Department of Transportation, I was shamefully still a virgin and feared I always would be. I had never even seen a naked lady, and no lady had ever seen me naked. In my life so far, I had dated only two girls, both in college. The first was a math major named Barbara Ann who wore clear-rimmed, round glasses and wore her straight hair down below her shoulder blades. I took her to dinner at a little diner called The Ribeye—my favorite. I ordered a cheeseburger; she had a salad only. "You should have told me you were a vegetarian, I would have picked a different restaurant," I said. Talk about getting off to a lousy start.

"No, that's OK, really," she said. She did most of the talking, deadeningly dull talk about her classes, while picking at her salad. It was my first and only date with her. The second girl I dated turned out to be much more exciting. She was short and curvy, and even before she accepted my invitation to go to the drive-in movie, she talked unabashedly about sex—implying if not coming right out and saying she was ready and willing. The film was *La Dolce Vita*, which I thought would turn her on. At the drive-in we petted on the backseat of my car. She let me reach inside her blouse. She wasn't wearing a bra. Oh boy. The same thing—not the drive-in but the reaching inside her blouse and nothing more—happened almost every afternoon for two months on her couch when her housemates were not at home and in my apartment and on the two-person slider swing slightly secluded near the rose garden in Priest Point Park. But there was a limit to how far she was willing to go. So much for her being ready and willing. My relationship with Rita drizzled to a stop shortly after that.

My lack of a sex life was probably typical of boys my age, but I thought I was the only twenty-two year old virgin in America.

And then Marilou Johnson walked past me from behind when I was looking through *Living Naturally,* and I could tell that she could see the open pages with the photos of people cavorting naked. My reflex response was to slam shut the magazine.

In the cafeteria at work later that day, Marilou approached me and said, "Hi. Can I sit here?"

"I, uh ... OK." And she sat and said, "I know we kind of know each other, but we've never really met. High school English class. Remember? I'm Marilou Johnson."

"Sure. I remember you."

We sat quietly for what seemed a full minute. Then she said, "What was that magazine you had? Some nudie mag?"

"Sorta. I mean, oh, nothing. Just something I found."

She didn't persue that, but she sat by me in the cafeteria again the next day and the day after. We talked about books—discovered we both loved reading and liked some of the same authors—and talked about our families and where we came from and what we wanted to do with the rest of our lives, and then one day she asked again about the magazine.

I confessed it was from a nudist camp. "There's pictures. Families. Kids. Old people. All naked as the day they were born."

"Really? A nudist camp?"

"Yeah. Uh huh."

"Do you still have it? I'd like to see it."

"Nah, I mean yeah I have it, but nah I ..."

"Chicken."

"Aw-right. I got it right here." I pulled it from inside my jacket and we thumbed through it together.

"This is kinda sweet," she said. "I mean it's so natural. Just families having fun in their altogether."

I told her I had often thought I would like to go to a place like that.

"Are you some kind of exhibitionist?"

"Kinda, maybe. I mean just in my mind." I was blushing but determined to be honest with her. I said, "The, uh, the idea of like, you know, being naked with other people, it's like something that, you know, kinda excites me. But I'd never have the nerve to really do it."

"I would," she boasted.

If ever in my life I dropped my jaw, that was the moment. "Really?" I said.

"Sure."

"I don't believe it."

"Why not? Naked bodies are nothing to be ashamed of. It's the way God made us."

"I don't think I believe in God," I said.

She surprised me again by saying, "Me neither. I just said the way God made us because ... you know. It's an expression."

After what was to both of us a surprisingly long silence, Marilou said, "That place, Arcadia, it says it's near Hoodsport. That's a beautiful wild place. I've been there."

"The nudist camp?"

"Not the nudist camp but a regular campground near there. It's not all that far from here. We could go. I'd go with you if you wanted me to."

I couldn't believe she was saying that. I said, "I'd love to go but I could never. Not in a million years."

"All right. You don't know what you might be missing."

Marilou and I were cafeteria buddies only. Never saw each other after work and didn't date. We never went to that nudist camp either. I guess we could have had our own private nudist camp, I mean just me and Marilou stripping down with nobody else around. That was another thing that never happened. . . back then.

Summer 1962
DANCING WITH MARTHA GRAHAM

Lizzy packed clothes that were ridiculously out of style and her transistor radio and a half dozen paperback novels, and caught the train to New York, discovering when she checked into the YWCA on Lexington that other students at the Martha Graham School were staying there too, and they were just as much out of style and out of place as she was. In other words, she felt less out of place than ever. One of the girls said, "We're misfits together."

"That's it! Misfits together," one of the others said, "Like the Three Musketeers."

"A code word."

"Our mantra."

And such they became. Someone should have written a song.

When not taking classes, Lizzy entertained herself by wandering the streets of Manhattan, walking fast down 42nd Street dodging other pedestrians the way she used to dodge Billy when playing football on the grassy field next to Charley Pond, then slowing down, watching, watching, watching the myriad variety of people in the city who taken altogether were like all the characters in all the movies she had ever seen. There was a James Dean lookalike, Elizabeth Taylor. Could that woman on 42nd Street who smiled at her really be Carol Burnett? *I want to see her tug her ear*, she thought.

Making up stories about many of the people she encountered, stopping to give a few coins to a barefoot man sitting on a curb on Sixth Avenue, she wandered the streets in a kind of daze, feeling that she had found her true home at last. But not always wandering the streets alone, because she made friends more easily among the other dance students than she had made friends back home. Her new friends, whom she feared she would never again see once the summer class was over, enjoyed meandering Times Square and quirky Chelsea and the Village as much as Lizzy did. Most of them were from small towns in Kansas or Florida or Mississippi and had never before been to the big city. Alone or with other dance students, Lizzy marveled at how watching the denizens of Times Square and down around the Village was like watching circus performers or characters in a Fellini movie, colorful hippies with their patched jeans and long hair, street vendors, buskers, hustlers and pimps and half-dressed strippers and prostitutes, and the families and runners and skaters in Central Park, and the old men who played bocce ball and chess in Washington Square Park and the flamboyant queers in Sheridan Square—one wearing a wedding dress with roller skates—and the remnants of the beats scattered throughout the West Village. She was neither attracted to nor repulsed by the sleazier aspects of the city but viewed it all as a spectacle that in an unexplainable way didn't touch her and in another way left her feeling as if she were in a movie that had become real.

She attended an impromptu all-night dance party with the cast and crew of a strange play she did not understand but loved nevertheless, in a theater on the Bowery. She had been invited to the play and the after-party by one of her fellow students who had a small part in the show. There was a moment in the play when an actor wearing a tutu began walking in circles singing "Someday my prince will come," and her top kept slipping down and she kept stuffing her boobies back inside while the audience laughed uproariously. Bare breasts on stage. Lizzy had never seen anything like that. She wondered how the woman in the play got her top to slip down on cue without touching it. Was there some kind of wire underneath her top that she could pull without it being noticed? Maybe it was psychokinesis.

She was drunk with joy, swept away by the music and the thrill of dancing with strangers of both sexes. They didn't dance together as couples but danced in mass movement, each doing their own interpretive moves.

One of many highlights of that summer's adventure was visiting the Metropolitan Museum and the Museum of Modern Art, and along with much of America, discovering pop art, seeing paintings and silk screens by Warhol and Lichtenstein "in the flesh." She would never again enjoy the banal art shown in the mall or the armory show back home.

She wandered through Chelsea where she visited a little store called the Boggle Shop where giant fantasy-creature stuffed dolls were on display. The proprietor called them soft sculptures. He was a tall man, a monk's tonsure on top and a long twisty mustache. He spoke softly with a Southern accent. "Hey there, what part of Mississippi are you from? He asked.

"Louisiana, not Mississippi. But jeez, how could you tell?"

"How could I not tell? The sound of your voice. It's *almost* unmistakable."

He said, "I'm from down there too, a little town in Mississippi that nobody's ever heard of. Eupora. Not far from Columbus." Lizzy had never heard of Columbus either.

"What's your name?" she asked. "I'm Lizzy. Or Lizzy."

He said, "People call me Geezer."

She enjoyed visiting with Geezer that afternoon, but she never saw him again.

...

One night she went to a little folk music club in Greenwich Village with three fellow dance students, Mel and Cathy and Bobby. The name of the club was Gerde's Folk City. Cathy, who seemed to know everything, said it was a famous club where 'all the best' played. They were going to see John Lee Hooker. At least Lizzy was familiar with him. He was from her part of the world.

The joint didn't look like anything special to her. It was smoky and crowded. They found a small table near the bandstand, and they ordered drinks. Soon the host stepped on stage to announce the next performer. It wasn't John Lee Hooker. Cathy explained that they always had lesser-known performers do warm-up acts before the main star. A short, skinny guy with curly hair in jeans and a plaid shirt hovered on the back edge of the stage while the host said, "From way out west in his first ever New York appearance, welcome to our stage Mister Bobby Dee."

The guy played a bunch of standard folk songs. Lizzy thought he was all right but nothing special. And then John Lee Hooker walked out on the stage without an introduction and to stormy applause, and he put his arm around the warmup guy and said something to him that the audience couldn't hear. Lizzy had heard of John Lee but had never heard him sing.

...

The dance classes were demanding and exhausting. The students complained that Martha Graham was a tyrant. She pushed them relentlessly. They grumbled, but they admired her; even worshipped her. Often, after her classes, Lizzy went home to the Y and took long hot soaks in a tub to soothe her aching muscles. She took pain pills and took up smoking, regular cigarettes and sometimes marijuana, which relaxed her. After smoking a joint music sounded fuller, colors were brighter. Glancing at her own reflection in a mirror made her laugh. She wished that when her time studying dance ended she could find some way to stay in New York, but she knew that was impossible.

...

Back home in Olympia at the end of the too-short summer, everything she could think of doing seemed empty. Olympia was so provincial. She had never had many friends there anyway. Now there was no one she wanted to be friends with. Big brother Billy and her dad said she should go to college. She thought, although she hated to admit it, they might be right. It was what she should do, but she didn't want to. And where would she go? What would she study? She could major in dance, but after Martha Graham, studying dance in some state college would be like going back to ... what? Tenth grade? She thought it might make sense to put off college for a year or two and get a job, sock away some money until she could make the move back to New York. Just as Billy had bought the dealership with money he earned himself rather than accept it as a gift from Bobo, Lizzy wanted to make her move, whatever her move might be, with her own money. At least then she would not be beholden to her dad. But how? Surely she could go to work for one of the family-owned businesses, but that seemed like a cop-out to her. She never appreciated, or rather it never meant much to her, that after a childhood in rural poverty she now enjoyed the privilege of being part of a wealthy family. Besides, she didn't want to constantly be under the eye of Billy or Renae or her parents. Once she had a stake in the quicksand that was the family business, she might get sucked further and further in. Goodbye dreams of Hollywood. Goodbye dreams of Broadway.

She could get a secretarial job or clerking in a bookstore or department store. Maybe that wouldn't be so bad after all. A bookstore especially could be cool. Would she get free books? Or waitressing in some fancy restaurant where the tips would be good. Get a little place of her own and save some money. If she worked hard and saved enough, she could go back to New York and take more classes with the Martha Graham School and maybe even get accepted into the company, become a professional dancer. Not yet. But soon. She didn't want to wait too long either or her chance would slip away. She imagined herself sixty years old and working as a volunteer usher at one of the local theater companies, married to some old man who was just some OK guy. She imagined her beauty and strength and energy evaporating, and she could see herself sitting on the porch of a rundown track house somewhere in Lacey looking out at other track houses and regretting her life choices.

She wandered somewhat aimlessly around Southwestern Washington in the rusty VW bug she had bought from Billy for $50, visions in her head of Anna Pavlova, Isadora Duncan, and of course Martha Graham herself.

Now we're getting to the meat of the story. It's a continuation of the story of Lizzy as a young woman, my favorite of Harlan's daughters—God knows I would have married her if I'd had the chance. Instead, I married her sister, and I'm glad I did.

. . .

Shortly after noon on a gloriously bright Saturday afternoon in the waning days of summer, she took off in her VW wearing a short-sleeved cotton shirt, tie-dyed with a scoop neck and no bra. Patched bellbottom jeans. Viola raised hell about the way she dressed, especially the no-bra look, but Harlan said, "Let the girl dress the way she wants to."

She parked near the lake where the Deschutes River flows under the twin bridges at Fourth and Fifth Avenues and watched the swimmers for a while, wishing she had brought her bathing suit but decided that watching was better than doing, especially when she saw Randy Hanson roughhousing with two other swimmers and took that as a cue to hightail it out of there.

Randy Hanson. There's a good reason to go back to New York. Imagine him forty years from now reliving his glory days as a so-so high school football player, bragging about deflowering Lizzy Johnson.

Back in her car and heading east on Fourth Avenue, up the hill to Puget and then a cut over to State, she circled back west to the lake again and parked and got out and danced alone and barefoot in the grass to a song in her head—catching a sideways glance of Randy Hanson watching her, damn his soul—and then back in the VW and back up Fourth to Pacific and to Lacey Boulevard, windows rolled down, enjoying the breeze. She pulled to a stop at a red light by a small café on Lacey Boulevard. The cafe looked homey and comfortable, white siding, a red roof, flower pots in the windows. There were two cars parked on the side of the building and a motorcycle out front. She could see through the window that the place was empty but for one man sitting at the bar nursing a beer. He was wearing a black leather jacket. *Leather in the heat of summer. Must be a motorcycle dude; bikers are crazy like that.* She took all of that in in the few seconds before the light changed, and then, making a last-second decision, she whipped into the lot, got out of her car and opened the restaurant's front door. A little bell tinkled, and the beer drinker looked up at her with the slightest hint of a crooked smile—or was it a sneer? It was a sneer, an upturned Elvis lip—and he immediately looked away. Lizzy turned to look back at the front window, halfway expecting to see the name LEEKERS on the glass like the scene in *The Wild Ones* when Kathie met Johnny, because that was what the scene at the little café with the biker at the bar was like. He and she were Kathie and Johnny—Marlon Brando and whoever the actress was that played Kathie—oh god, visualizing him in that scene made her hyperventilate. That brooding look, and later the scene in the woods when Johnny kisses Kathie. (Years later she watched a rerun on television with Buddy and thought Brando's forced kiss bordered on sex abuse, and it creeped her out; but in the summer of '63 when she watched it with Renae and Marilou at the Skyline Drive-in that kind of scene was commonplace. The strong silent man forces himself on the woman, and she gives in reluctantly at first and then with fierce passion; and the girls watching it on the big screen project themselves into the scene, having been conditioned to admire just that kind of take-charge man.)

"Hi," she said to the beer drinker who on second thought didn't really look like Brando at all but did have a Brando-like brooding expression on his big lips and in his deep black eyes. And he wore the leather well.

She asked, "Is that your motorcycle parked out there?"

"I'm riding it. It belongs to a friend. I can't afford my own bike, but someday I will."

"I can dig it," she said. She was still standing, not knowing whether to sit or not or if to sit, where. Next to him? He swiveled in her direction with his booted feet on the bar at the bottom of the stool. He looked her in the eye, and neither could hold the gaze. He swung back toward the bar and glanced over his shoulder at her. *He's shy*, she thought, this big, bad motorcycle man.

But perhaps he's not shy after all, she thought as he let his gaze undress her. Unabashedly. He could see that she had a willowy body, small breasts underneath the tie-dyed thin cotton shirt. He liked that she was long-waisted with muscular hips and legs. *She could crush a man between those thighs*. After looking at her for quite some time, he said, "Have a seat. My name is Wendell Bundrock. Everybody calls me Buddy."

"Hi. I'm Lizzy."

"No it ain't. Sounds too prissy for you. I'm a gonna call you Lizzy. Lizzy's got some spark to it. It's saucy and playful."

"Whatever." A bubbly little laugh trickled from her mouth.

From the time she entered first grade until the day she met Wendell "Buddy" Bundrock, Lizzy hated it when people were presumptuous enough to apply nicknames to her without her permission. If anyone called her Lisa or Lizzy or any other variation, she would politely say, "Please don't. My name is Lizzy," which landed on them like a request from a respected adult, and maybe made them feel ashamed of themselves.

But when Buddy called her Lizzy, Lizzy it was, from that moment forward.

She ordered a sweet roll and coffee; Buddy ordered another beer. He poured his beer into a glass. He poured too fast. The beer foamed up and out. "Uh oh," he said, laughing, but didn't drink his beer for quite some time, idly blotting the foam with napkins. Lizzy remained quiet too. And then the Brando-looking guy said, "Backwards talk can't betcha."

"What? Is that even English?" And then, "Wait a minute. I get it. You said you bet I can't talk ... I mean Backwards talk can't betcha said you."

"Ah ha. It do can you."

"Can I yes," she smugly replied, proud of herself for catching on so quickly. They looked at one another with laughing eyes and sparkling teeth. Flirting with backwards talk. She had come a long way since her tentative and disastrous flirtation with Randy Hanson in high school.

Her sweet roll was toasted, the sugary coating dripping. She sliced off a bit with the side of her fork and ate it, then took a sip of her coffee. He drew a heart with his finger in the condensation on his glass and lifted it for a big swallow and said, "My second and my limit. I'm not a big drinker."

Already thinking of a long-term relationship, Lizzy was relieved to hear that he was not much of a drinking man. *What other vices could he have? Is he the kind of man who beats on women? Is he a two-timer?* She knew that Billy and her father were both two-timers. *Are all men? Is that just the way they are? Oh God, is he married?* During the time it took her to finish her sweet roll and ask for a refill on the coffee, he sat with his hand on his glass looking directly in her eyes. He mopped up the spilled beer, and then finally he tipped up his glass and took a final big slug. They both laughed, and she swiveled her stool in his direction, and their legs touched. They rubbed their legs together as they swiveled their barstools back and forth and practiced talking backwards until she could spit out long backwards sentences without having to stop and puzzle it out, and then he said, "Yamaha my of back the on ride a like you would?"

"Yeah, I'd love to, but I don't have a helmet," she said (switching to forward speak).

"I can take care of that," and turning to the waiter he said, "Hey Mel, ask Johnny in the kitchen if I can borrow his helmet. I'll have it back soon."

Mel stepped into the kitchen and came back out carrying a helmet.

...

"Hold tight," Buddy said as Lizzy straddled the bike behind him and reached her arms around his stomach. She hooked her thumbs under his belt. He kickstarted the bike, and soon they were headed out Carpenter Road. "I love it!" she shouted against the wind and the roar of the Yamaha. For a second or two, the bike lurched, and Lizzy tightened her grip on his belt and shouted, "Whoa boy!"

At Long Lake, he pulled to a stop near the swimming area, a cozier, more familial watering hole than the one by the bridges in Olympia. Couples and families and teen groups lounged on beach towels with umbrellas and coolers; kids of all ages ran into the water shrieking and splashing and ran out onto the wooden pier and dove in and rushed back out shivering and wiped themselves with towels and fished sodas out of Styrofoam coolers. Lizzy and Buddy sat in the grass and smoked cigarettes. "What do you do with yourself?" Buddy asked.

Lizzy said, "Oh, I just cruise around Lacey picking up motorcycle dudes. No, really, I kill time doing mostly nothing. I was just down at Capital Lake watching the swimmers. Now I'm here watching the swimmers. That's the kind of boring life I lead."

They ground their cigarettes out in the grass. "No, really," he said. "What do you do?"

"Really. Nothing. I just came back home from a summer studying dance in New York, and I haven't figured out what to do next. What about you?"

"I'm a cop."

She said, "No, seriously."

"I am serious. Well, almost a cop. I'm in the police academy."

"No shit. Wow! I'm dating a cop."

"Oh, we're dating are we?"

She dug another cigarette out of her pack and said, "It's a good thing you were not drafted and sent to Vietnam."

It was his turn to say no shit. He said it was pure luck that he hadn't been drafted. "It's a horrible fucking war. We shouldn't be over there at all."

She asked, "Are your fellow police trainees cool with that?" His response was, "Are you kidding? Most of them want to go over there and join in the fight. They think they can beat the entire Viet Cong army in hand-to-hand combat."

That perked her up. With bubbles like champagne in her voice, she said, "Now right do to want I what know wanna?"

"Yeah, I want to know what you want to do right now. I'd love to know."

She said, "I want to do this," and she pushed herself up to her knees and flung her arms around his neck and kissed him.

He said, "Well you're a bit of a tiger, aren't you?"

And she growled at him and laughed and said, "Maybe. I never did anything like that," and they kissed again, and she said, "That's kiss number two. How long do you think it will take to get to a million?"

"Oh, I'd give it about two days."

They lingered in the grass and continued kissing and talking and kissing some more. "That was twelve. Long way to get to a million."

Buddy said, "I've got some weed in my bag. You up for that?"

"You bet." And they surreptitiously smoked it by cupping the joints in their palms and blowing the smoke out with confidence that they were far enough away from the nearest people that they couldn't smell it.

"It's funny that you called me a tiger. Not funny funny but ... you know. My big daddy's first wife was killed by a tiger.

"Whaaat! Aw come on, tell the truth. That can't be true."

"But it is."

She told him the story Harlan had told all the kids about Josephine and the tiger.

From there, the conversation turned to dance. They had settled into more relaxed positions with her head in his lap. Buddy was idly rubbing her belly. "I studied with Martha Graham. She's about the most famous dance teacher in the world."

Buddy had no idea who Martha Graham was. He said, "I get it, I think, that when you talk about dance you ain't talking about the twist or jitterbug or whatever but like ... like whatever."

"Uh huh. Trying to explain what dance is to me is overwhelming. It's bigger than the sky, bigger than love. It *is* love. Dance—my kind of dance—is not like doing the twist or the frug or the monkey, or even something classical like the waltz. Dance is more. I'm talking about CAPITAL D DANCE, not dancing. You know? It's expressive movement. It doesn't even have to be to music. It's expressing love or hate or anger or heartbreak through bodily movement. It's like making love." All of that came out in a gush. All he heard was "making love."

Teasingly, he said, "You mean to say you know what making love is like, little girl?"

"Ha! Are you asking if I'm a virgin? Is this your sneaky way of seeing if you've got a chance of getting me into bed?"

"You're damn right it is," he shot back with laughter, and she kissed him again and said, "We'll get to that when the time is right."

"So we're going to get to it?"

"You better believe it," she said with as much hutzpah as she could muster up. And then she flushed scarlet.

"You're a virgin," he suddenly realized. "You're pretending to be brave and acting all worldly and experienced. But you're just about scared out of your drawers."

She said, "Not quite true, but pretty close."

"Explain wanna you?"

"No."

"OK."

67

1966THE FAMILIAR GIRL

At work, I was a paper shuffler glued to a desk in a large room where many more drone-like workers were glued to similar desks with typewriters and Rolodexes and file cabinets and telephones with lots of buttons that lighted up. I usually lunched in the company cafeteria, but sometimes went to a nearby burger place.

I noticed a young woman in the cafeteria who looked familiar. She usually sat with others and often—so it appeared from where I was sitting—dominated the table talk. She was stunning in her flowered miniskirts, the oddly colored lipstick she often wore, and long blonde hair with bangs cut straight above her eyebrows. It was summertime, warm outside but cool in the air-conditioned office building. She wore sleeveless tops and a light jacketI couldn't get over the feeling that I knew her.

There came a day when she was eating alone, and when she saw me take a seat, also alone, she stood up and carried her lunch over to my table and said, "Hi, Rudy. Mind if I join you?" *She knew my name*!

And then I recognized her. Of course. She was Marilou Johnson from school looking even sexier than I recalled. It was the blonde hair that threw me off. Back in high school it had been kind of a reddish sand color. "Did you ever go to that nudie camp?" she asked.

"Oh my god no. I can't believe you remember that. That was just a juvenile fantasy. I could never." But I still thought about it, and now that I had met her again, I knew I would still dream about seeing Marilou Johnson without any clothes.

"Lordy, lordy, you haven't changed a bit. Betcha still have that pamphlet."

"No I don't. But I guess you're probably right that I haven't changed much."

I was fascinated with the way she ate her lunch, moving food around her plate with her knife and fork, using them like a pair of chopsticks and often holding a bite of fish or the delicious cubed and broiled potatoes aloft between the tips of her implements while talking. I was amazed she never dropped anything. And why had I never noticed that quirk before?

I said, "I remember you had a grandfather or uncle or something who was notorious. Who was he again?"

"My great grandfather, the notorious pirate Pegleg Josiah Johnson."

"Right. Did he really have a peg leg?"

"That's what they say. My grandfather Auvergne said it was like a fancy carved table leg, and he said he could cut a rug on the dancefloor and run as fast as most men with two good legs. That sounded far-fetched to me. The way he lost his leg also seemed far-fetched. Grandfather Auvergne said it was in a sword fight with another pirate, and said he killed the other guy."

"People knew he did it and he got away with it?"

"I guess there's no jurisdiction out at sea. Additionally, I heard the story secondhand. I never even knew my grandfather Auvergne."

I finished eating before she did and waited for her to finish, watching her move her food around as if it were some form of Zen meditation, trying to think of what to say. I never was good at chit-chat.

She finished chewing one last bite and laid down her knife and fork and said, "Let's hit the dessert line."

We got ice cream in cut-glass bowls the size of demitasse cups. When she finished hers, she lifted her bowl to her lips and licked every last bit of ice cream with her long, fat tongue. I was embarrassed and fascinated and sexually aroused.

"I never saw anyone do that," I said.

"Me either," she replied. "Let's get some more."

And we did, and this time I followed her lead and licked my bowl clean. People at the next table stared at us, and Marilou smiled at them and shrugged her shoulders. I never felt so liberated. Or so daring.

...

Eating lunch together became a regular thing. And then one day I worked up the courage—not an easy thing for me—to invite her to have dinner at my house. "Do you like fish?"

"Wha' kind?"

"Salmon. Blackened. My own special recipe." I had never baked any kind of fish, but I had blackened salmon in a restaurant and loved it.

She said, "I love it to death."

I stopped at the library on the way home and scoured cookbooks for a recipe.

...

I opened the door for her and tried to rush her through the front room and the kitchen before she noticed the mess, and quickly out to the patio where we could sit at a table and enjoy before-dinner drinks. "Wait," she said, holding out her hand to stop me. "I want to see the art. I noticed it when we passed through."

I said, "It's all copies. I can't afford originals."

"That's cool. I want to see what you have."

There was one of Modigliani's portraits of a longnecked woman and one of his nudes, a couple of van Gogh's and Edward Hopper's "Morning Sun."

"I like your taste in art," Marilou said. Indicating the Hopper, she said, "Would you believe I have a copy of that same one on my wall?"

"That's quite the coincidence. I guess we do have similar tastes. Speaking of taste…" I escorted her back out to the patio where the table was already set with wine and water and paper napkins.

She was wearing a lightweight long-sleeve shirt with the top two buttons open. *Women don't show that much cleavage unconsciously*, I told myself. *She's sending a message. I hope, I hope, I hope.*

"The fish smells great," she said. "What kind is it?"

"Salmon," I said. "Just like I said. Baked and blackened. It'll be ready in ... " glancing at my watch, "ten minutes."

The oven timer went off, and I dished up dinner and brought it out to the patio. It was not yet sunset. The fish was flaky, and she ate it with a fork and a spoon. Like spaghetti. After dinner we shared a bottle of wine and then went inside when the evening cooled down. She went straight for my bookshelf. "This is some pretty heavy-duty literature, she said, "Milan Kundera. Whew! Cormac McCarthy. You must be really into reading."

"Uh huh. I guess I am." She shouldn't have been surprised; we had talked about literature a lot back in school. I wanted to tell her I was a writer but didn't.

...

Not long after that, she invited me to a party. It was at the apartment she shared with her sister Lizzy who was there with her boyfriend Buddy, whom Lizzy referred to as the motorcycle dude. There were other couples there as well. They all quite obviously knew each other well, and I had little to say other than answering specific questions like "Where are you from?" and "What do you do for a living?"

"Oh, uh, I work for the state. With Marilou. Not actually with her, but same department anyway." Why was it so hard to answer such a simple question? I wanted to discuss my writing, but writing was not the kind of thing you bring up unless someone asks about it. Otherwise, it's just bragging. And at the time I hadn't told anybody I wanted to be a writer. There are too damn many no-talent dreamers who think they are writers, and I don't want to be lumped in with them in anybody's opinion. I had only recently accepted that I wanted to be a writer and had bought books on the art and craft of writing and had tried my hand at writing a few short stories. I wished I knew someone who could read and critique them. And most importantly, my whole frigging life since sometime in high school, if you must know, I'd been working on what I thought of as my opus, a monster novel based on my own life. I knew people would think of that as audacious and stupid. I'd gladly let Marilou read and critique my stuff. Even the

71

opus. Yeah, Marilou could read them. She'd say, *"These are marvelous. I've never read stories so captivating. I mean you could be right up there with Steinbeck and Hemingway." Or maybe Jane Austen. Yeah, she was probably big into Austen. And she'd say of the opus, "Is this based on you? You must have had a fascinating life so far."*

No. I'd had a nothing life so far, and if she read my stories, she'd probably hate them. She'd advise me to give up writing. Quit wasting my time.

I was drifting into fantasy when someone at the party put Miles Davis on the turntable, and Marilou's sister Lizzy got up and danced to his seductive tones. "You're really good," I said when the music stopped. She thanked me, and Marilou said. "She studied with Martha Graham."

I'd heard of Martha Graham—recognized the name but didn't know who she was. I was beginning to think Marilou and her sister and their friends were out of my class.

I finally, reluctantly, told Marilou I should probably go. It was after midnight, and everyone had left except Lizzy and Buddy who had retired to their bedroom. I felt, suddenly, that I had overstayed my welcome. But Marilou didn't think so. She said, "No, don't go yet. Let's have one more drink." I looked around and was frightfully aware that we were alone. She sashayed to the kitchen counter and mixed us each another Manhattan, and we settled together on a loveseat. The drink was slightly sweet and had a nice punch to it.

She said, "You hardly said a word all evening. Are you just shy or what?"

"Not shy," I said. "I just never know what to say, or I think nobody will be interested in whatever I have to say, and when I do think of something I kind of write it and rewrite it in my head to get it right, you know, before I open my big trap. And by the time I've done that the conversation has moved on to something else."

"Wow and gee wiz," she said. "That's not like me at all. I just blurt out whatever comes to mind." In saying that, her arms moved in gestures that reminded me of the dance Lizzy had done.

"Maybe I am hesitant like that because I'm a writer. That's the way writers talk, I think." There, I said it. It wasn't so hard. It was the first time I had ever told anyone I was a writer.

"You *think* that's the way writers talk? You don't know? I mean if you're a writer and that's the way you talk, then that's the way writers talk. Right?"

"I'm not really one yet. I'm trying to become one." I said I didn't know any real writers to talk to. She told me she had majored in English Lit in college but had never done anything with her degree. "I mean what the heck can you do with an MA in Lit in Lacey, Washington?"

We finished our drinks, and I asked her if maybe she would be willing to read some of my stories and critique them sometime.

"Sure," she said, I'd love to," and then, "If we got married, we would together constitute one bipolar person. I would be the manic pole and you'd be the depressed pole. Except you're not depressed, you're just quiet."

"Sometimes I'm depressed," I said. That was the only response I could think of. What my brain was filled with was *if we got married.*

. . .

When we went to bed together for the first time, it was Marilou, not me who was the aggressor. She pushed me down onto her bed and pulled my pants down, and she stripped buck-damn-naked while standing at the foot of the bed, and then we did it. She was on top.

NOT LIKE OTHER BOYS

I married into the Johnson family and thus became a descendant-by-marriage of the notorious pirate Pegleg Josiah Johnson. It didn't take me and Marilou long to crank out two little pirate sons. First Larry, and then Parker, eighteen months apart. And that was enough for us. From the get-go, Larry was independent, an imp who, starting in kindergarten, was constantly in trouble with his teachers and, of course, with me and Marilou, not for anything serious, but for little things that were funny after the fact. He invented things that never quite worked, and he made up outrageous stories; he took up art at a young age and is now a working artist in New York City. Parker ... well, he tended to blend in wherever he was. He was a nice-looking kid of maybe above average intelligence, and a sometimes sparkling personality. He grew up to marry his childhood sweetheart who happened to live right next door to us (her parents still do). Delia Rappaport. She was a nice enough girl who grew into a nice enough woman. I gotta admit it, hate to but gotta. Parker and Delia were sort of invisible. Like me, I'm afraid. They gave birth to a daughter named Marianne in the same year they were married and did not have another child until fifteen years later, a son they named Randolph who, until he was five or six, thought his big sister was his mother. The sister, Marianne, doesn't live at home with us now, but Parker does. He and his wife and child. Jesus Christ, he's middle-aged now. Parker, not their child.

Marianne is a lesbian. She lives across town with her girlfriend.

Back to Larry. He was never like other boys. For one thing, he was gorgeous from birth and still is. Not fairytale princess gorgeous and not like a beautiful movie star, not in an effeminate way, but manly gorgeous. As an infant and more so, as he grew into a precocious toddler and a fun-loving child, and then a teenager other teenagers wanted to be. He believed—and everyone else believed as well—that he was put on earth to be worshipped. Yet ... how to explain it? ... he was not arrogant, but supremely and naturally self-confident. He was so smart and happy and amazingly good-looking that it simply made everyone happy to be in his presence. One of Marilou's co-workers said to her, "I wish I could adopt your precious little boy," adding, "Kidding of course." That was when Larry was two or three years old. When Marilou retired thirty some years later, that same co-worker said with a wink, "I'd still like to adopt your kid."

"More'n likely you'd like to marry him."

"Whoever does is going to be one damn lucky lady," Marilou's friend said.

When Larry was in high school, he spotted a book on the library shelves called *From Bohemia to the Beats* which was all about the artists and poets in Paris in the early 1900s who lived what was called the Bohemian life, and about how many years later in New York's Greenwich Village the beatniks took up similar lifestyles. He was fascinated but knew of such things only through books. Nobody in his lived experience was anything like a Bohemian. With the possible exception of his Aunt Lizzy. She had spent that summer in New York, studying dance with the great Martha Graham. (Larry had never seen Martha Graham perform, not even in films, but he knew she was a legendary dancer and teacher.)

In his imagination, there was a connection between his Aunt Lizzy and legends of the art world that could be traced all the way back to Gertrude Stein's salons in Paris that were attended by no lesser figures than Picasso and Matisse and Hemingway and Scott Fitzgerald. He had read all about them with great longing. In college, he developed the same worshipful longings for the legendary gatherings of literary and entertainment giants that clustered around Dorothy Parker in the Chelsea Hotel and for the abstract expressionists who drank together in the Cedars Tavern. He read Ginsberg and Kerouac. He read *On the Road* three times. He drew constantly, filling sketchbooks with fantasy figures of beautiful men and women—nudes and superheroes, and he complained that he was born into the wrong generation.

It was the year O.J. Simpson was arrested and charged with the murder of his ex-wife and her boyfriend, the year Paula Jones accused President Clinton of sexual harassment. It was the year fifty-year-old Lizzy regaled her seventeen-year-old nephew Larry with tales about hanging out in coffee shops with artists and writers and musicians and seeing art by artists who are now famous but then known only by fellow artists.

Lizzy was still as attractive at fifty as she had been at eighteen. Her hair, dark and silky, flowed down to her lower back. Her figure was not as voluptuous as the women in Larry's sketchbook but was slim and sleek. He thought of her body and the way it moved as a gazelle or a deer or a panther or, for a more human reference, an Olympic figure skater.

Larry wanted to know who some of the artists were she had seen in New York. "Whose paintings and sculptures did you see?"

"Let's see. I'll have to think about that. I did see Willem de Kooning and, I think it was Robert Motherwell, once in a café, but I couldn't muster up the courage to speak to them. OK, there was this one show at the Museum of Modern Art called *Americans*. It had works by some of the early pop artists and others before they became really famous."

"Like who? Who? Who?"

"Gimme a sec. Let's see. There was Lee Bontecou. Do you know her work? Great stuff."

"I'll look her up."

"And early stuff by Robert Indiana, and the sculptor Marisol. She was really famous back then and later kind of drifted into obscurity. I don't know if she's still alive or not. Oh, and Claes Oldenburg. I know you know who he is. You know, I think that by the time you're my age you'll see that the sixties proved to have been a harbinger of the political and social climate of times to come, a time of awakenings. You'll see it's all connected somehow. Vietnam and drugs and protests and the art and music. Be aware of all of that but beware of the drug culture."

Larry said, "Nobody says things like harbinger of the political and social climate. Backwards talking as crazy be would that." She had told him about talking backwards with Buddy, and Larry was bright enough to get it.

He told her he was going to be an artist when he grew up. "I told my mom, and what do you think she said about that?"

"What?"

"She said, 'If you've made up your mind you're going to be an artist, then you're going to be an artist, and that's that.' And then she said—Get this, I love this—she said, 'I know you, honey. You're determined to do whatever you set out to do, always have been.'"

"That's just like your mom. And I can certainly relate to that," Lizzy said. "I was like you when I was your age, determined and starry-eyed. But then I fell in love, and oh boy, that changes everything. I was going to be the next Josephine Baker and ended up wading in chicken shit."

...

Larry showed his aunt Lizzy some of his drawings. They were derivative, of course—to be expected of an artist so young—superheroes and monsters and cheesecake nudes drawn with a natural facility in his handling of lines and in his shading. *This kid has the goods.*

She loaned him books about artists, and she created a drawing instruction book for him with her own drawings as examples, a creation of which she was vastly proud. Her book included an explanation of linear perspective with drawings of a railroad track and a street lined with buildings receding to a vanishing point with ruled lines in red to illustrate the principle. She demonstrated the proportions of an ideal human figure as measured by head width and height: an ideal man's shoulders were three heads wide, a woman's two and a half, a man stands seven heads tall, a woman six; and faces are measured by the eyes. Eyes are positioned halfway between the chin and the top of the head, "Beginners always put the eyes too high." There should be one eye width between the eyes, the bottom of the nose falls halfway between the eyes and chin, and the mouth halfway between the bottom of the nose and the chin. She included explanations of how to create illusions of three-dimensionality, modulating, light and dark, and how to draw cast shadows, and of the use of balance, and examples of such design principles as repetition, harmony, and contrast. She included basic color theory with a cut-and-paste color wheel and value chart. She encouraged him to draw large and freely with big sweeps of the pencil or charcoal or paint brush, and she told him to never be afraid of making mistakes.

"Once your drawing or painting becomes precious to you, you've ruined it. Remember that. Don't ever let it become precious."

"What does that mean?" he asked.

"It means if you're afraid to change a certain part of a painting for fear you're going to screw it up. That is exactly the part you need to work on. Wipe it out if you must."

Larry had faith in his ability. He was willing to test himself against the New York art market, which he instinctively knew could be fickle and unfair. But he was not one to dive in the deep end without first learning how to swim. He got a bachelor's degree and an MFA in drawing and painting from the University of Washington, and then with a thousand dollars saved up over three years and a bus ticket bought by me, he crossed the country to New York, awake the whole way, marveling at the changing scenery through Wyoming, South Dakota, Nebraska and Illinois and on across the rust belt and finally to New York. The sun burned blindingly on snow-covered streets in Manhattan the day he arrived. Brown slush in the gutters. The year was 2001, and he was twenty-four years old. He rented a room in a fifth-floor walkup in Chelsea and started looking for a job and a gallery. He picked up day labor jobs from an outfit in the basement of an old hotel near Washington Square. The jobs ran the gamut from pouring concrete to painting apartments to dog walking. He worked for a few weeks as a Shabbos goy in a temple in midtown Manhattan, and for a month flocking silly lamps in a four-person factory. One day he and a dozen other laborers worked at a rolling paper company, sitting around a conference table stuffing thinly folded papers into little packages. The brand was one all of his friends back home used for rolling joints. The workers were given a fifteen-minute smoke break, and they passed around a joint, rolled, naturally, in the company's paper. Later came a half-hour lunch break with another shared joint after lunch, and then another smoke break in the afternoon. The weed was provided by the company of course.

He got a job pushing an obese guy in a wheelchair around Brooklyn, and another day a crew of six piled in two cars and drove to a neighborhood on Long Island where every house had six steps up to the front porch and a swimming pool in the backyard. Their job was to hang ads on every doorknob.

Nights, usually until two or three in the morning, and all day on Sundays, he painted. There was no room for an easel if he had one in his one-room apartment, so he propped canvas boards on his knees while seated on his bed. He had slides of his earlier paintings that he had left in his parents' house back in Lacey, and he sent the slides to galleries, and hoofed it from gallery to gallery with a portfolio of small paintings—actually crayon drawings of crayons spilling out of their boxes.

"Maybe we can give these a try if you can do them large in acrylic," one gallerist said. She looked to be in her forties, straight black pageboy hair, big, round glasses. She was the tenth gallerist he had shown his work to.

"But you don't get it," Larry tried unsuccessfully to explain, "These are drawings of crayons drawn *with* crayons. The ultimate irony, the ultimate pop art. Conceptually, they're like Warhol's Brillo boxes."

"Yeah, I get it." He didn't think she did. "But nobody's going to pay good money for crayon drawings. Do them big in shocking colors and you've got something."

He talked the guy who owned the flocking factory into letting him paint in a corner of his warehouse. Two months later he went back to the same pageboy hair-glasses-wearing gallerist carting half a dozen four-by-five-foot paintings in a pickup truck borrowed from the same factory owner. The paintings were not little drawings of crayons with crayons or scissors cut out with scissors and pasted to paper; they were geometric abstractions four and five feet square in mostly primary colors. She said, "These are kind of derivative of Mondrian and Burgoyne Diller. I don't think I can sell them. If you can apply the same color and design sense to something more popish, I might could do something with that. Something like the little ones you showed me but big and splashy. Isn't that what I asked for?"

"I tried that, but they just didn't work at that scale." *I'll be damned if I'll let you or any other dealer dictate what I'm going to paint.*

"I know but I just don't know," she said.

The other galleries he approached gave him even less hope. He did eventually—after more than a year trying—get two paintings accepted into a group show in Chelsea and one more in another group show on West Thirteenth Street. In his first four years in the city, he managed to get into eight group shows, and one gallery, the Greg Sullivan Gallery, sold one of his paintings.

Even though his paintings were usually non-objective, he still liked drawing figures. He carried a sketchbook everywhere and sketched people seen in coffee shops and city parks. He attended figure drawing sessions at the Art Students League and hired on as a parttime model. He was almost too nervous to strip for the first modeling session but soon became comfortable with it. *What would he think if he knew that his father (that's me) was strangely obsessed with thoughts of exhibitionism but would never in a gazillion years act on it? I'm sure he thinks of me as staid and probably boring.*

He became friends with another artist named Arnie and Arnie's girlfriend Jodi, who was also a model. Arnie asked him if he'd like to share his loft in Brooklyn. "The studio space is huge, and there's ample living space. We can pick up a bed for you for practically nothing, and the rent is cheap. Hey, I can really use some help paying the rent, and you need a place where you can paint. It should be perfect for both of us."

The rent, as it turned out, was less than he had been paying for his tiny room in the Chelsea brownstone. Instead of picking up a bed for practically nothing, they scrounged a mattress from the street and he slept on it the floor.

1998
BILLY PLAYS GOLF

While waiting for the golfers in front of them to get on to the next fairway, Billy talked to his latest paramour and golfing buddy, Betty Clyde Remington. *Paramour* is what he called her in his mind; he loved words like that—archaic and romantic to his way of thinking. Like his father before him and mostly, if the legends could be believed, his father's father's father, the illustrious pirate Pegleg Josiah Johnson. He flaunted the same penchant for flowery language. Also like the pirate, Billy had been a Casanova all his life. He loved his wife like no other, but that didn't stop him from crawling in bed with other women when he got the chance. Even at a youthful and vigorous sixty-three years of age.

"I saw your old lady at the co-op the other day," Betty Clyde said. "She ain't looking in none too good a shape. She was moving like an old lady."

"Well hells bells, honey," Billy said, "she's just old. We're all old, for love's sake. We all got aches and pains and false teeth and hearing aids that barely do the job they're supposed to do. I hate to bust your bubble, honey, but I wear dentures and hearing aids too. And even with 'em, I can't hear diddly squat unless it's like one-on-one. And if I get a little bit of food or the tiniest seed under my dentures, it feels like a goldarn rock digging in up under there, and it's painful to chew. Growing old. You can have it."

"Pshaw," she said dismissively. "I'll take it when it comes my way. Meantime, I feel like I ain't a day past thirty, and I can count my blessings that I've got hot youngish lover like you. Old man or not."

Billy's mind jumped to how old folks constantly talk about being old, about illness and pain and medication and why they can't sleep at night for peeing every hour on the hour, admitting he was as guilty as any.

Betty Clyde was pushing sixty herself, but she was, Billy had to admit, as strong and supple as a woman ten or fifteen years younger.

"Goddamn, you're lovely hide! Why can't I be as youngish as you? He said,

She said, "Hey, don't put yourself down. You still got what it takes."

"It's all relative, I guess. My sister Marilou, she's the youngest of us all, ten years younger than me, I swear she looks not a day over thirty; and Lizzy, the next youngest, she acts like she's the oldest. She looks like she got so old she forgot to die. But you, you're like a young filly, like Marilou. I reckon I can count my blessings too. By the way, did Belle recognize you in the co-op?"

"No. She's never met me."

"Good. Let's keep it that way."

Betty Clyde was a tall woman with muscular arms and legs, looking like Lizzy would look if she had taken care of her body all those years. She (Betty Clyde, not Lizzy) had been a champion golfer in college and had gone professional but never made it to the top ranks, and retired after three years. Now she played against men mostly, always teeing off from the men's tees and more often than not beating them. She said other women were no match for her. Besides which, she loved humiliating men who thought they were god's gift to the game of golf, who thought no woman could possibly compete with a manly man. She and Billy were a good match, and unlike many of the other male golfers, he was not humiliated when she beat him.

He had grabbed his favorite clubs that morning. PXG clubs from top to bottom—driver, fairway clubs, irons, wedges, putter, even the bag itself was PXG. "Not because they're the best," Betty Clyde teased, "but because they're the most expensive. Show off." She understood that Billy didn't have to have the best of anything; he simply had to be seen as having the best of everything. Betty Clyde teased that he had more money than talent. More mouth too. But she had to admit he was pretty good in certain areas. For starters, he was the strongest man of his age she had ever known, a bull on the golf course and in bed. (Both her previous lovers were in their forties and couldn't measure up to Billy Johnson.)

So Billy carried his favorite clubs in his favorite black and white leather bag and put them in the back of his black BMW and headed for the club early in order to hit the greens before it got too hot. Their club was the Indian Head Golf Club thirty miles from Billy's house but only two miles away from her house, where they usually went after playing nine holes and downing a couple of beers in the clubhouse.

They teamed up with another guy named Billy—Billy Franklin, forty-eight years old, small and wiry, and a fair to middling golfer who could never beat Billy Johnson or Betty Clyde but enjoyed their company and was content to chalk up the money he lost on their matches as the cost of playing the game. Billy Franklin was the kind of guy who never asked what something cost; he just handed over his credit card.

Billy Johnson's one concession to age was playing nine holes instead of eighteen.

Betty Clyde suggested a simple $10 Nassau bet. Billy said, "Let's make it a hundred bucks."

"All right, sport. It's your funeral."

The other Billy reluctantly agreed. He might as well just fork over a hundred before they started, and he knew it, but he was loaded and figured it was worth it for the good company and for watching Billy and Betty Clyde play—playing golf and playing with one another; they were nothing if not obvious.

The first hole was a straight-ahead hundred and sixty yards, par three. No sand traps, no water hazards. "Piece a cake," Billy Franklin said.

Billy Johnson hit it straight down the fairway and watched it roll to the edge of the green. Billy number two followed with an impressive drive of about a hundred and twenty yards. With luck, he figured he'd score par or maybe a bogy on that hole. He figured the other two would get par or better.

Betty Clyde was up next, and she drove it within a foot of the hole for an easy tap-in for a birdie. "Not half bad," Billy said.

The toughest hole on the course was number five. Not the longest hole, but the trickiest. It was a mean dogleg left, about 450 yards with trouble lurking everywhere in the form of out-of-bounds, water hazards and sand traps. By the time the trio got there, Betty Clyde was clearly winning, and Billy Johnson was within two strokes. Billy number two wasn't out of it yet, but he had two more strokes than Billy number one.

Billy number one placed his tee and pointed at the bend of the dogleg and said, "Right over that tree, straight as an arrow. Who's willing to place a side bet that I can't do it? Another ten dollars just for fun?"

"I'll take that bet," Betty Clyde said.

He made it easily. It was a beautiful shot that landed past the bend and dead center on the fairway. "All right, hot shot. You win ten dollars. For another ten, I'll bet I can beat that."

"You're on, babe."

She teed up and drove her ball over the same tree where it landed in the same spot Billy's ball had stopped, and hers rolled ten yards closer to the green.

"Lucky roll," Billy said.

"It's all in the way you hold your mouth."

On the ninth and final hole, Billy Johnson and Betty Clyde were all square. The other Billy was out of the competition but played on.

The ninth presented them with a three-forty-yard drive over trees that cut the corner of a dogleg, caught the downhill speed slot on the other side that made the ball roll forever, and ended up—assuming gargantuan luck or skill or a combination of both—in the fairway with the perfect angle for a 110-yard wedge to the pin. That was where Billy and Betty's balls stopped on their drives. Billy Franklin landed near where the dogleg bent and rolled into tall grasses where he had to take a penalty stroke.

The green was guarded by bunkers and steep run-offs around the edges. Betty Clyde offered another side bet. She wagered she could birdie number nine. Billy was confident she couldn't because he knew it was a fast green and she tended to put too much juice on her putts. So he took the bet and lost again. She got a wedge shot onto the green and a killer twenty-yard putt into the hole. Billy did exactly what she thought he was going to do. He missed the hole by inches, and the ball rolled right off the green and into a sand trap. It took him three more shots to get out of the trap and into the hole. He owed Betty Ken $120. He said, "The clubhouse is calling. You're buying 'cause you've got all my money."

The overhead sun was brutally hot, but the deck at the clubhouse was shaded and cool, a good twelve-degree difference. They bought beer and grabbed a table overlooking the first tee. "Good game," Billy said, and raised his glass.

She laughed and said, "Sure was, and I won't scoff about winning all your money."

He questioned her about being a woman amongst men. He was fascinated with the way she played with and flirted with men. Big, brassy and ballsy, is how he thought of her, and a woman who exuded sex appeal. Billy had grown up at a time when sex was all about conquering and being conquered and women didn't talk about it so freely. He said, "I'll bet you get hit on all the time."

"Yeah, I do."

"Is that flattering or ..."

"Depends. If they're gentlemanly about it ... well yeah. Sure. But if they're crude about it and make me feel like a slab of beef they plan on eating raw, well then I make sure they never hit on me again."

"How do you do that?"

"If a man ever lays a hand on me without permission, which happens more frequently than you might imagine, I slap the bejesus out of him. I punched a guy in the mouth once, right on the seventh green. He grabbed my ass and I hit him. I think I broke one of his teeth. They banned me from the club and didn't do a damn thing to him."

Billy liked that. Belle could be like that sometimes too. Feisty. Take no crap from nobody. But she never broke anybody's tooth.

...

Belle was bound to find out about Betty Clyde. And she did, and when she did, she didn't let Billy know she knew, not right off the bat anyway. Growing up next door to Harlan and Viola, being around Johnsons all the time, even knowing about Harlan's affair with Viola when he was married to Josephine, she learned from them and even from her own mama and papa that men can't keep it in their pants and women had damn well better put up with it if they want the nice house and all the nice things in it. She was long since reconciled to Billy chasing after other women. That was just the way life was. Men cheated. Women too, sometimes, and she decided, "Fuck it. If he can do it, I can too." That's what she said when she told Billy's sister Lizzy that he was having an affair.

"He's schtupping his golf partner?" was Lizzy's response, delivered with a mixture of astonishment and laughter, followed by "If he can do it you can too? Do you really mean that?"

"You're damn right I mean it. Why not? It's only sex. So long as he still loves me and brings home the bucks, we ... well, you know. What do I care what he does when he's off in Yelm or Chehalis or wherever? Just keep bringing home the bacon, baby."

"Yeah but what if ..."

"But what? They never told us what life was like for Cinderella after she married the prince, did they? I suspect it was like being in a fancy prison for dear old Cinderella while dear Prince Charming was getting it on with the scullery maids. I didn't marry Billy with my eyes closed. I married him for security, for a fine home. And if the sex was good, and it was honey, believe you me—then enjoy it while you can. And if you want a little side meat. Well, there's love and there's sex. Sometimes they go together and that's cool, and I guess that's ideal. But sometimes they don't go together, and that can be OK too. What's the old line? Something like if you can't have the one you love, love the one you're with?"

"Do you really believe that?"

"I do," she said. But she didn't.

Lizzy said, "Sometimes I wish I could be that blasé about things like that."

Belle asked, "What about Buddy? Has he ever cheated on you?"

"No."

"How do you know?"

"I don't. But I know Buddy. He would never do that."

In all the thirty-three years Buddy and Lizzy had been married, neither of them had cheated. Of that, they each were sure. See? A least some of us in the Johnson clan had a sense of right and wrong.

...

For Buddy, Lizzy had given up her dream of being a dancer. They had bought the little farm south of Olympia and he resigned from the police department, and together they fought to eke out a living from farming. In all those years, they had never made more money than it took to barely subsist. Buddy was ashamed of his inability to provide for Lizzy the kind of comfort—downright luxury—his Johnson in-laws enjoyed.

...

In their first years together, Buddy told Lizzy that his time in the Navy had been the defining moment in his life. "Everything important that I learned about myself and about life I learned in the Navy. I learned to navigate by the stars, to be comfortable with aloneness. To tie a secure knot; and after all, don't people talk about getting married as tying the knot? I learned to look into my heart and see myself for what I truly was."

A gunner on a patrol boat on the Mekong River in Vietnam, Buddy learned to trust his mates with his life and to know their lives depended on him. "We loved and protected and were willing to sacrifice for each other," he told Lizzy.

Long before going to 'Nam, he developed a keen sense of knowing who to trust and who not to. Nobody who owned a Ferrari or a Porsche or lived in splendor was to be trusted. Bosses and authorities were not to be trusted. But if a man—any man, black, white, dirt poor, queer, you name it—treated you like a brother, you treated him the same. Before joining the Navy, he had never known anything about race or racism. He had not known more than two or three Black people and had not thought about how they were discriminated against. Sure, he had heard what was now politely called the n-word being casually tossed around by white people—

poorly educated hayseed bigots, but also by people who were educated and in most other areas liberal, and he wasn't deaf and blind to incidents of racial hatred that showed up on the news. But he thought that was the exception, not the way of the world. In the Navy, he got to know many more Black men than he had ever before known, and he learned from them that things he had never given any thought to were hurtful to them. He realized that he had done and said such hurtful things himself and had never truthfully looked into his own words and actions deeply enough to see it. He said to his Black mates, "I am deeply sorry for any racist remarks I have ever made, and if you ever hear me say anything racist, please call me on it. Even if it's clear I don't mean anything bad by it."

The other thing he learned about in the Navy was homophobia. Looking back all these years later, he knew damn good and well he had uttered homophobic remarks and told queer jokes and laughed at other people's queer jokes without once thinking it was hurtful. "Back then, everybody laughed at queer jokes, even queers. They saw themselves as pathetic and laughable, and if comments from others hurt them, they stuffed it in and pretended to enjoy the humor. Same thing with Blacks. Play along to get along."

Lizzy nodded agreement and continued to listen. He said, "I'll tell you what I thought about and what drove me fucking crazy. I was scared I might be queer myself. I don't mind admitting it now. It was a feeling that came over me at certain times around certain people that ... well, I never acted on it, and it's been years since I felt that way, but the thought that I might be one of them scared the living shit out of me. The thought of it made me sick."

Lizzy said, "You know my sister is gay, don't you?"

"Yeah, I know. And if I ever get the chance, I want to apologize to her for every homophobic thought I've ever had."

Lizzy said, "I don't think that's necessary. It would probably make her uncomfortable."

"Yeah, maybe."

"Another thing you should know. If it turned out you really were gay, I would still love you. We'd work it out somehow. I don't know how, but we would."

They were quiet for an uncomfortably long time until Lizzy said, "You're not done with this, are you? There's something else."

"Uh huh ... I was remembering a guy called Sol. Never knew his front name. A seaman apprentice. Little guy, no bigger'n Truman Capote or what's his name, Leslie something, that funny little actor we both like. Anyway, Sol's last name was Solomon. In the military, you know, it's always last names or nicknames. Nobody's ever called Bill or Joe. Anyway, somebody—I don't know who—but somebody got the notion that Sol was gay. He didn't act gay or talk gay in any of the supposedly traditional ways so far as I could see, but word got around, and everybody believed it, and they called him queer and fag and cocksucker right to his face, and Sol never denied it or fought back in any way but just stuffed it and tried to keep to himself as much as he could. This was later in the war. I got assigned to a ship in the Mediterranean as far from 'Nam as could be. Our sleeping quarters were two levels below deck and crowded. Triple-decker bunk beds that were no more than swinging hammocks. Sol slept on the one above me. To my everloving shame, I kidded about him too, but never to his face. At least I don't remember ever doing it to his face.

"One night when the ship was docked in Barcelona or Naples or one of those Italian ports, some guys ganged up and raped Sol in the showers and beat the crap out of him. He came out of the shower room all bruised and bloody.

"Oh my god," Lizzy said.

"Everybody knew who did it, but nobody saw it happen or had any evidence. They just knew. And I'm pretty sure nobody would have said anything if they had the evidence. I could'a asked Sol if he was all right or at least I could'a told him I was sorry about what they did to him, but I never said a thing. He never said anything either. Never reported it. Kept his mouth shut and kept to himself.

"After we got back to the States and pulled into port at Norfolk, two civilians in suits and the executive officer escorted Sol off the ship, and we never saw him again."

"Jesus. They arrested the victim?"

"I don't think it was that, not exactly," Buddy said. "Being gay in the armed forces was illegal then. That's why they hauled him off I think. What they usually did was tell them they'd quietly give them an honorable discharge if they confessed to being homosexual. But if they refused to confess, they'd throw them in the brig and there'd be a trial and they'd be dishonorably discharged and publicly shamed. We never knew what happened to Sol."

POST MILLENNIAL LARRY

People who knew the art scene in New York started referring to Larry as a mid-level painter or a mid-career painter. B-list. "I don't know what that means," he said. "Like I'm good but not good good? Like an old character actor everybody recognizes but nobody knows their name?"

"Yeah, something like that," Arnie told him. "It ain't good and it ain't bad, but it's better than the rest of us suckers who can't even get our stuff through the gallery door. Go with it. Be happy."

"Like my uncle Billy," Larry said.

"What's that mean?"

"Uncle Billy was an athlete, good but never the best. He was like the guy that always comes in second."

If Larry had been comparably successful in any other city, he would have been considered one of the best artists in the region. Like if he had stayed home, he would have been celebrated in Olympia and Tacoma, and maybe even a little bit in Seattle. But nobody in New York or LA or even Topeka would have ever heard of him. It was big fish, little fish, depending on where he was. Actually he was a hell of a lot more successful than Arnie or any of his other painter friends, and he knew it. It just so happened that at the moment he was feeling down on himself.

One of his paintings had been included in a group show at MOMA. That's huge. And not one, not two, but three were in a traveling show that made it all the way to the Tacoma Art Museum where his parents and Lizzy and Eva and Helen and me and Marilou got to see it. There we were, all of us Johnsons standing in a tight group in the Tacoma Art Museum gaping at paintings by our own Larry Briggs, my son, in a show including famous artists from the Museum of Modern Art. Talk about proud! Oh my god. Even two of Larry's high school classmates emailed him congratulations. By the summer of 2017 when Billy paid for Larry to fly out to Washington for the annual family weekend on Orcas Island, his paintings were in collections all over the country, and he was represented by the respected Greg Sullivan Gallery in Chelsea. He even got a positive mention once in the *Times*. That was big-time success by any measure, as we liked to brag, but it was not financial success. A parallel: Even after *Life* posited in print that Jackson Pollock was the greatest living painter in the United States, Pollock was practically broke. That's the way it goes. Funny business, art business.

The average dude in any town would not recognize Larry Briggs's name. He was barely scraping by, sharing the loft in Brooklyn with Arnie and picking up the occasional day job—house painting, some rough carpentry, even dog walking. He also continued modeling occasionally for figure drawing sessions at the Art Students League. He didn't do that for money. He probably couldn't tell you why he did it, but I suspect it was because it made him feel more a part of the arts community. Maybe it was the exhibitionist gene from me.

Larry's paintings remained what they had been almost since he first moved to the city, square and rectangular blocks of bright colors that alternated between contrasting and harmonizing with adjacent color blocks. Reminiscent, you might say, of Piet Mondrian, his hard-earned teenage skills in drawing superheroes and naked ladies and his clever gestural drawings of crayons having long since been abandoned in favor of geometric abstraction.

He was proud of the work but bothered by the nagging feeling it had all been done before.

Some of his paintings were small, ranging from twelve-to-thirty inches on the longest side, and others were big suckers, six, eight, ten, even as large as twenty feet square. He mixed his own paint with powdered pigment and acrylic medium and was able in that way to come up with colors that were rich and luminous, velvety reds and deep blues and electric yellows.

...

Once—it was the summer of 2012, I remember because it was the last summer Lizzy and Buddy went to the island and, well, because it was a momentous summer—Marilou and I went to New York for a weekend visit. We stayed in a once-elegant hotel not far from Larry's studio. We saw a delightful off-Broadway play called—if I remember this correctly—5 Lesbians Eating a Quiche, and did the obligatory touristy things: the ferry ride to Staten Island and back past the Statue of Liberty, a visit to the site of the Twin Towers, and an elevator ride up to the top of the Empire State Building. What a splendid view from there! Larry went along with us and said he'd never done any of those things. Picture that. All those years living in the city, and he'd never visited any of those places that every tourist absolutely has to see.

Larry took us to art galleries in Soho and Chelsea. In each gallery, he introduced himself to the gallery owner with some variation of the opening: "You might remember me. We met at the Kyle Jones show (or so-and-so's opening or ...) You might have seen my work at MOMA or at Greg Sullivan's. Larry Briggs."

"Oh yeah, yeah. I remember. How're you doing?"

While walking to the next gallery on our tour after the second time I heard him use that intro, I said, "You sound like you're trying to sell yourself,"

"Uh-huh. It might sound crass," I stopped, my hand on the door handle of the next gallery, "But you gotta understand, in this business, you have to keep reminding people who you are, that you've been recognized by people in the know, because it's a crazy damn business and most of the people who make the decisions about what is real art and what art to show and what to buy don't know diddly squat about what's good and what's not. They go by what others say, by who's buying what. My dealer, Greg, is no exception. You never know but what you might need to find a new gallery someday."

"Why?"

"Well, because Greg might die or sell his gallery to somebody who might want a different kind of art."

"That's not good business," I said. "Good business would be to keep showing the kind of work that's, you know, already selling. And then expand into other work that will bring in new customers. But what do I know? All I've ever been is a paper pusher for the state."

"Yeah. Uh-huh. Or he might just close down altogether. You never know. What I'm saying is if I have to start the grueling slog of presenting myself to dealers all over again, I want them to already know who I am and that I've had some success. In this racket, people are quickly forgotten."

…

Among other things, Larry augmented his painting income by doing a bit of acting and voice work. I kind of knew that, but not much. He joined Actor's Equity and picked up the occasional gig. Sometimes commercials for local businesses. And some odd jobs. And he had a podcast. He said he did that for his own enjoyment, not for the money, 'cause there wasn't any. The hook of his podcast was that he strolled through such public gathering places as Prospect Park and Washington Square, struck up conversations with people he met, and asked if he could interview them for his show. The interviews were presented as spontaneous and impromptu, like he never knew who he might bump into in his wanderings; yet his guests were always artists, writers, or actors, meaning they were planted as surely as the trees in the park. Nothing spontaneous or happenstance about it. He planned the recording sessions ahead of time with his guests and met them in Washington Square or on the Hudson River Walk or in his favorite coffee shop in Brooklyn—the ambient chatter in these settings sometimes made it hard to hear his guests but gave the program an authentic feel and sense of immediacy.

"Hello, friends. This is Larry Briggs again coming to you from Prospect Park in Brooklyn, U.S.A. where I bumped into the painter Randy Smith whose show just opened at Granger's in Chelsea. Tell us a little something about your paintings, Randy."

He also liked to hang out in the Harvest Moon Tavern, a bar around the corner from his studio where he had come to know the bartender. He would usually go early in the afternoon before the place got busy and an hour or so before his live podcast was to start. He would set up his microphone and laptop at a table near the back and sketch the bar and the bartender and the few early customers while sipping beer. Usually a Samuel Adams, his favorite, but sometimes a porter.

"Hello, friends. This is Larry Briggs again coming to you from Harvest Moon Tavern enjoying a Samuel Adams lager. Hey, I just ran into Helena Humbolt, an actor who is playing Nora in *A Doll's House* at The Backdoor Theatre in Soho. Tell us a little about yourself, Helena, and about playing Nora."

Although most of his guests were friends or friends of friends or artists or entertainers who listened to his podcast and emailed him asking to be interviewed ("We've got this great little band that's playing down on Bleeker Street, and we'd sure like the attention your podcast could give us") he sometimes legitimately and accidentally bumped into interesting artists in the tavern or in the park.

GEARING UP FOR ORCAS

Well into the first quarter of the twenty-first century there was a heaping load of Pegleg Josiah Johnson's great-grandchildren in the state of Washington. Most were long since grown with children and grandchildren of their own, all but Lizzy, who still lived childless with Buddy the biker dude in their small farmhouse on the outskirts of Olympia. They weren't childless by choice. Twice Lizzy had found herself ecstatically pregnant, and both times she had a miscarriage. After the second miscarriage, her doctor said he was afraid she could not carry a pregnancy to term and that another miscarriage could be dangerous. "We can't chance me getting pregnant again," Lizzy said.

Buddy offered to have a vasectomy.

"No, it's not on you; it's on me," Lizzy said. "I can have my tubes tied."

After much discussion and many tearful days, they agreed that Buddy should have a vasectomy.

…

Most of the Johnson descendants lived in or near Olympia. But Harlan and Viola's youngest daughter, Renae, still called the baby, in her thirties, by most of the family and her life partner, Sally, lived in Portland, where they ran a little vegetarian café that was popular with students at Portland State. Before moving to Portland, Sally and Renae had campaigned vigorously for equal marriage rights, but after domestic partnerships were legalized in Washington, and then marriage equality became law throughout the country, Sally said she didn't want to get married.

"For heaven's sake, why not?" Renae asked. I know you're all for gay and lesbian marriage."

"Yes, damn right. For other people. Not for us."

"I don't get it."

"Marriage is an institution that's fine for those who need it, but I don't want to live in an institution."

"Oh, you crazy freaking rebel you."

It was almost time for Pegleg's grandchildren and great-grands—or maybe it was great and great-great grands, I never can keep the generations straight in my mind—to muster the troops and leave for the annual family retreat at the Peter Puget Resort on Orcas Island. Sally and Renae drove up from Portland past Olympia to Shoreline to spend the night with Renae's niece, Helen and her wife, with the intention of then driving back down to Olympia the next day. "That's a hairbrained idea," Sally said. "You mean to say we're gonna drive seventy miles past Olympia to see Asher and Diane ..."

"And Bryce and Emma driving all the way from Pullman. Don't forget, they got us tickets to that play."

"Right. Oh my god, I did forget."

...

Before coming out as lesbian—first and hardest of all to herself, and then to her best friend in middle school, a girl whose name she could barely remember thirty years later, and then to her father, and before meeting Sally and falling in love with her—before all of that there had been a string of horny high school boys in Sally's life. She was fifteen years old when she gritted her teeth and clenched her fists and let the first of that string of boys have his way with her; and those boys in turn told their friends, "Sally Crawford's a nympho." That was similar to but even more humiliating than Lizzy's classmates teasing her about having sex with Randy Harmon. Sally didn't want to do it with those boys. She didn't enjoy it, and she felt dirty afterward. But it was her desperate attempt to convince herself she was not queer.

Her ill-thought-out period of hetero promiscuity got her pregnant. She had to confess to her daddy. It was always her daddy she opened up to first.

"Daddy, I'm so sorry, so, so sorry. I'm afraid I went and got myself pregnant. Please don't be mad at me, Daddy."

Not shouting but with a sad whisper, he said, "How could you? Have you not heard of birth control?"

She looked down at the floor, tears in her eyes. He said, "You're too damn young to be having sex anyway. Your mother should have taught you better."

"She did, Daddy. Don't blame Mama for my stupidity. 'Sides, you had sex at my age. I'll bet you anything."

"It's different for boys," he said.

Sally came back with, "I don't want to hear about different standards for boys and girls. Don't you dare ..."

"And don't you go talking back to your father."

For a day and a half, he was beside himself with anger, but then he calmed down. "It's OK, honey. Everybody makes stupid mistakes at your age. God knows I did. So did your mama. I just hope the boy that did this to you is willing to take responsibility."

They argued. Always had. And they always settled. He was stubborn but eventually gave in; Sally typically threw a hissy fit and then agreed. She had always been able to confide in him, even when she could not confide in her mother. Choking between words, she spit out, "I don't know who he is, Daddy."

"Who who is?"

"The father."

"Oh my god."

She put her hands on her head with elbows bent, almost as if getting ready to fend off blows.

Calmly he said, "It's all right, honey. Whoever he is, if he's not a big enough man to accept responsibility, he's not good enough for you. You just need to find yourself a good boy who will love you and take care of your child as his own."

"But I don't want to be with a boy, Daddy."

Red-faced now after reaching the point where he was almost ready to graciously accept the situation, her daddy said, "Well, you kind of have to unless you expect me and Mama to raise the child for you, and that ain't gonna happen."

"That's not what I mean."

Tearfully, she told him that she was attracted to girls, not boys. "Yeah, yeah, I did it with all those boys. I was… I don't know why."

That was when the flood of tears came.

"Oh you poor darling." He surprised her, saying, "Don't you dare let nobody say you ain't normal. There's nothing about a girl loving a girl that ain't just as normal as spit. Me and you and your mama, we'll raise your child together, and we'll love him or her, and someday you'll find the right woman to love you and your baby. Rest assured of that. I know it'll happen, and sooner than you think."

. . .

Sally gave birth to a healthy baby boy with red hair and large blue eyes. She named him Asher. Over the following months, Sally lived with various friends and worked at temporary and part-time jobs as the baby in her belly grew. until she landed the job cooking at the Smithfield Café downtown. It was there that she met and fell in love with Big Hairless Johnson's youngest daughter, Renae.

She gave birth to a baby she named Asher, and Sally accepted him as her own. But when he was six months old, Sally said, "I want a baby with you."

"We already have a baby," Renae said.

"Yeah, but he's not yours."

After weeks of discussing the possibilities, Renae agreed to a sperm donor. They named the baby Heather. She was born red-faced with wispy blonde hair. A little sister to Asher. Both children grew up to be beautiful and brilliant. When classmates teased them about having two mothers, they stood up to them. Their strength and no-nonsense attitudes won over some of the bullies and intimidated the hell out of the rest.

. . .

Time, time, time. It speeds by so fast. From an unmarried couple (one large with child) to parents of children with children of their own, seemed to have happened overnight. It was the summer of 2017, and it was their son Asher and his family that Renae and Sally were going to visit in Shoreline.

...

Helen and Eva called their property Sappho Farm. Their house was a white shingled cottage with a little blue Kia parked on the grass in front and the pair of overly laden apple trees that passed as a grove in their lexicon. In the shade of the trees, Helen and Eva gathered fallen apples while Lil' Bit the yorkie and Max the mutt played around their feet, barking and digging at the ground and batting fallen apples. Helen, the taller of the two, picked the low-hanging fruit and shook the limbs, and Eva picked them off the ground. Bees swarmed all around but did not sting the women or dogs. The goats and Fatima the cat watched from a distance.

Lil' Bit and Max ran down the slope to the pond and jumped in. Eva said, "Renae and Sally should show up in a couple of hours."

"Maybe, but I expect they'll be much later. They're going to that play, remember. I hope they'll text us to give us a heads-up."

They finished filling baskets and carried them into the house where they washed them, spread them on towels to dry and culled the rotten ones. Tired but excited at the prospect of seeing Renae and Sally, they set to washing dishes and sweeping and mopping and putting fresh linen on the guest bed.

Renae and Sally were on the road. They had left home hours earlier when Portland was socked in with early morning fog. Renae texted Eva: "We should get to your place before midnight. Don't wait up for us."

Eva texted back, "The spare key will be in the usual place."

...

"Pray for light traffic on the way back down," Sally said. "I'd like to get to Helen and Eva's farm early enough to get a good night's sleep. The trip from there to Orcas is not going to be a picnic."

he lights on the bridge crossing the Willamette were haloed like a scene in a mystery set in foggy boggy England. But that was short-lived. By the time they had driven past Olympia and reached the rest stop north of Tacoma the fog had begun to lift and a warm sun was beginning to light up the day. They rushed into the rest stop's restroom, washed their hands after peeing, dried them with the blow-drier that shut off automatically too fast, and finished wiping them dry on their pants. They lunched at a picnic table before heading north again.

Just south of Seattle, Sally's GPS warned of a traffic slowdown and suggested getting off the freeway and taking Highway 99. "When the phone says do something, we have to do it," Sally said.

"The phone is god."

"Goddess."

"Right. Her majesty."

Their GPS's voice was female with a British accent. They called her Diana and talked back to her even though she never responded. "Diana, you're an idiot." "Diana, why do you want us to turn here? "Diana, can you find a fecking bathroom?" (Renae had sworn off swearing years ago when she worked in a daycare center; *fecking*, in her mind, was not a swear word. Sally said it wasn't even a word.)

They drove past some sleezy motels, which they had heard were notorious for drug dealing and prostitution, and past several shops and restaurants—a mile of sleaze on the northern edge of Seattle as they came into somewhat more bucolic Shoreline.

Asher and Diane's home was a small two-story with clapboard siding and a low picket fence around the front yard. A gate kept the youngest child from wandering into the street. The boys rushed out to greet Sally and Renae as soon as they saw them park and get out of the car. The oldest boy stopped a few feet away and said, "Hi," and the more exuberant middle child leaped at Renae and hugged her. Little Luke, wearing a diaper only, waved exuberantly. Asher opened the front door and from the stoop he shouted, "Boys! Give 'em a chance to get their stuff and come on in before you crawl all over them."

Kids' toys and clothing were strewn about the floor. A pedal car, a map-of-Washington jigsaw puzzle, books, blocks, things that flashed and lighted up and beeped and whistled, shorts, underwear, a stack of folded diapers. "Just step over stuff," Diane said as she waved across the cluttered floor. She shuttled a pile of freshly folded laundry from the couch to the coffee table and said, "There you go, have a seat."

The boys were pushing and practically climbing over one another to show Renae and Sally their latest games and toys and drawings and finger-paintings. Asher said, "Bryce and Emma oughta be here soon."

"They're coming here?" Renae asked, bright surprise in her voice. Bryce had always been her favorite sibling.

Asher said, "Well yeah. Wasn't that the plan?"

"Not exactly. We were expecting to meet them at the theater tonight. But good. I'm glad they're coming here first."

They had tickets for *My Name is Rachel Corrie* at the Seattle Rep, a play with tremendous local appeal based on the life and writings of the forever twenty-four-year-old Olympia native and peace activist who was run over and killed by an Israeli bulldozer in the Palestinian city of Rafah in the Gaza Strip.

...

Bryce and Emma rolled their ten-year-old Lexus into the driveway behind Sally's Prius and got out. "Safest car on the road," Bryce often pronounced. "Like a family tank."

Renae, looking out the window, noted for perhaps the thirtieth or fortieth time the entertaining phenomena of Bryce's bulk and Emma's petite figure, Bryce emerging from a car like a giant roly poly opening its shell, and Emma like Tinker Bell fluttering about. Listed as six-five and two-hundred and forty pounds when he was a linebacker for U-Dub, Bryce had no idea how much he now weighed and didn't care at almost fifty and three children past his glory days on the gridiron. Once he was no longer playing, he never weighed himself, but he was keenly aware that his belly looked like a medicine ball ballooning over his pant waist, while Emma was the same pixie she had been when they got married. Despite their advanced ages (Bryce seventy-four and Emma sixty-seven), they both still worked, Bryce as a history professor at Washington State and Emma as a fourth-grade teacher in a private school in Pullman.

They were barely out of the car when a black SUV pulled up to the curb, and Renae's daughter and son-in-law got out. Heather and Sky and their daughter, Kaylee. After leaving home when she was eighteen and a freshman in college, Heather had gone to Seattle intent on becoming an actor. She worked various waitressing jobs (and still did) and got acting gigs in a few small theaters, some of which paid the minimum union wages and some of which paid nothing at all. I thought she and my boy Larry would love getting together for drinks and chatting. What with the acting and the odd jobs, they'd have a lot to talk about. But almost three thousand miles separation made that unlikely.

It was while acting in one of those minimum-wage gigs that Heather met Sky Mope, a handsome fellow actor of Jamaican heritage standing six-foot-three, muscular, with a deep operatic voice. He would not be continuing on to Orcas Island with them because he had the lead in a stripped-down musical comic lampoon of *Hamlet* called *Et Yet Brute* that opened that week. "It's a ridiculous play," he said, "But it's a paying gig." Opening night curtain was a few hours away.

"Hey, guys. Welcome," Diane said, standing on tiptoes to hug Sky and kissing Heather's cheek. "You're just in time for lunch."

"Gee, I wish I could stay for lunch," Sky said. "And I double wish I could go to the island with you. I've never been there."

"Oh lord, what you're missing," Diane said. "It's a beautiful, memorable, relaxing, never-get-old, leave-it-all-behind ferry ride from Anacortes to Orcas Island, a place where you feel time slow down, you take a breath, and feel a million miles from home. Welcome back is the feeling the minute I drive off the ferry."

Sky said, "Dang it, maybe I oughta give up my acting career and retire to Orcas."

"You'd give up the millions you make and all the adoring fans and retire to an island?" Heather teased.

He replied, "It would be a sacrifice but ... you know."

...

They picnicked on a table in the shade of a giant pine tree in the backyard. Cheese sticks and crackers and hummus and peanut butter and fruit cocktail—most of it made from scratch by Diane with help from the boys, who sometimes liked preparing meals better than eating them. Martin and Joe picked at their lunch; Luke played with his, and soon Joe got up from the table. Diane stopped him with "Josiah Johnson, you did not ask to be excused."

"May I be excused, please?"

"Yes you may."

"Me too, please," Martin said, and they scurried away from the table to throw pinecones back into the giant tree from which they had fallen and watch them bounce limb to limb, while the adults updated one another on happenings over the past year. "I can't believe it's been a year since we all got together on the island," somebody said as Luke smeared peanut butter on a cracker and on the table and all over his face.

Bryce excused himself to go to the bathroom, and while he was in the house he poured himself a large glass of milk and drank it in three great gulps and then hurried back out to the picnic table and ate more peanut butter and crackers, feeling slightly guilty about drinking all their milk, not knowing they had a case of it stashed in the garage (their no-dairy milk came in boxes and didn't need refrigeration until opened).

"How's the restaurant doing?" Emma asked.

"Not bad," Sally said. She and Renae had opened their little downtown restaurant called Fresh Meadows two years earlier. They specialized in vegetarian lunches and a huge variety of smoothies and juices. After a shaky first six months, Fresh Meadows was beginning to build quite an enthusiastic following. There were only three little tables, but they did a lively takeout business.

One of the pinecones the kids were tossing about tumbled over near the table. Bryce picked it up and threw it high in the giant pine tree where it ricocheted like a ball in a pinball machine and landed right back on the table. Bryce picked it up again and tossed it back at the boys. Asher said, "Boys! Find something to play that doesn't involve throwing things."

"Sorry," Bryce said. "They bring out the kid in me."

Martin the first grader shouted, "Freeze tag!" and immediately took off running with little brother Joe in pursuit around the side of the house to the front yard and back.

Sally said, "What about you guys? Emma? How's your teaching gig going?"

"Great. Loving every minute of it."

Bryce asked about Lizzy.

Renae said. "We haven't seen her in ages."

Addressing everyone, Sally said, "Maybe we should swing out and see her before heading up to the island. We're headed back to Olympia after the play and plan on visiting with Helen and Eva. They're pretty close. Maybe we can all get together. Maybe talk Lizzy into going to the island. Helen says she's dead set against it."

Asher said, "I hear she has some kind of heart problem. Had stents put in or something."

"Yeah," Renae said. "Like Billy, but not as bad. We visited her in the hospital, and we went out there to that chicken farm to see her before Thanksgiving. To tell you the truth, she didn't make us feel very comfortable. And that place of theirs, oh my god."

"Nothing like the enticing aroma of chickenshit and wet feathers," Bryce said with a hearty laugh.

Diane had gone into the house. She came back out carrying an ice chest, set it down on the table and said, "Beer and soda. Dig in."

"Oh boy!" Bryce said. He grabbed bottles for all who wanted and used his Swiss Army knife to pry the caps off and passed the cold drinks around the table. Only Diane and Kaylee opted for soda. Icy foam bubbled out and trickled down across their hands, which they licked off before it dried sticky. It was plenty warm enough in the yard for the cold liquid to feel good.

Sally said, "I don't think she's doing so well."

"Who? Lizzy?"

"Yeah."

"Is she still smoking?"

"Uh huh. Like a chimney."

"That shit will kill her."

At that point, Asher said, "All right, enough about Lizzy. Every damn time this family gets together everybody talks about

Lizzy who's so self-centered she can't bother to join us. What's with that? Why do we all …"

Before he could finish what he was trying to say, all the adults piled on with—

"Because we're family."

"The squeaky wheel."

"Because we care."

Asher said, "Sorry. Sorry. Yeah, you're right, all of you."

Getting back to health and aging, Renae, who walked three miles every day and had a figure like a thirty-year-old and the stamina to boot, who was six years older than Lizzy, yet looked like her younger sister, said, "She can barely walk from her house to the chicken coop without having to stop and hold onto something and gasp for breath. But let's face it, it's not just her. We're all getting pretty old,"

"Speak for yourself," Asher said, and everybody laughed in an all-embracing way.

In truth, only Bryce and Renae and Sally were anywhere near elderly, and of those all but Bryce exercised rigorously and watched their diets. The other adults were in their forties and fifties. Renae mentioned something from their childhood, and that set the older adults off on a wild romp through memory land, retelling tales from long ago, half of them disputing the others' recollections of what happened. When Renae said, "Billy wrecked the speedboat," Bryce said, "That wasn't Billy. That was Buddy."

Emma jumped in with, "Nah, nah, nah. Buddy was in the boat, but Billy was driving it. Came too close to a sandbar and ended up sideways against a tree." Renae shot back with, "Hey, they're my memories. Y'all get your own. You weren't even there, Emma." She wasn't, but she got a kick out of commenting on what she had heard, true or not. It was good-natured arguing all around.

Diane and Asher were not even born when most of the events they recalled happened, but they got a thrill out of hearing the old tales, many of which they had heard before.

Renae said, "Playing pirate. My god. How often did we play pirate!"

Sally said, "How could we not when we were all descended from the famous ..."

"Notorious," Bryce corrected her.

"Yeah, notorious. The notorious Pegleg Josiah Johnson."

"Billy would never let us forget that," Renae said.

Rather than playing cowboys and Indians, Harlan Johnson's kids played pirate, each playing a character based on pirates from *Treasure Island* and *Peter Pan*, the only pirate movies they had seen. Being the oldest, Billy, always got his choice of characters, and his choice was always Long John Silver, not exactly a character any kid should want to emulate, but he was Billy's favorite because he was such a colorful character and because he had a peg leg like their infamous ancestor. Renae, next to choose, usually picked Captain Hook. She thought playing the villain was more fun than playing the hero. She liked curling her fingers to simulate a hook. Lizzy, the baby sister, was assigned the role of Smee—a comedic role in the Disney film, but elegant and dashing the way she played him. She moved like a gazelle and leaped like Nureyev. Oh, how it must have killed her that she could no longer move like that.

The descendants of Josiah Johnson exhausted the cast of movie pirates with Hook, Long John Silver and Smee, so Marilou played Maid Marian from *Robin Hood*, and Bryce was always Little John.

They recalled a time when play acting a sword fight with sticks for swords got out of hand and Billy's Long John hit Renae's Captain Hook a painful slash to her shoulder. Renae went wild, throwing away her stick sword and pummeling Billy with a flurry of fists. Despite being four inches shorter and three years younger, Renae was almost as strong as her big brother and was a more furious fighter. And let's not forget that despite his bad boy reputation, Billy was hesitant to fight girls. Harlan had drilled it in Billy and Bryce: never hit a girl, never hit a girl. So Renae immediately had him backing up and fending off her flying fists and even calling for Mama to save him. Renae never let him forget it.

Bryce said, "You kids probably never knew it, but our daddy, y'all's grandaddy or great uncle of whatever—I'm talking about big Hairless Harlan—he was a world-class athlete. Remember? He claimed he set some kind of scoring record in football in high school and was recruited by some of the biggest and best, including Notre Dame and UCLA and Alabama, but he decided not to go to college."

"Yeah, we know. He told us about it 'bout a thousand times," Bryce said.

Renae said, "Yeah, I think the old man might have exaggerated a bit."

"Lied his ass off," Sally said, guffawing.

Bryce said, "Poor Billy, he wanted more than anything to be a great athlete."

"I thought we were talking about Harlan," Renae said.

Ignoring her, Bryce said, "I can remember so clearly trying to impress him when I was, you know, twelve years old. But by the time I actually earned a football scholarship to U-Dub, it didn't much matter to me. Maybe because I knew I could. Didn't have to prove anything. But Billy, he was never more than just a little bit above average, and I think that just about killed him."

Renae said, "He plays golf now, and he's dang good. I played with him once and he beat me handily. There were two other golfers playing with us, and he beat us all."

After lunch, they played t-ball with the boys, Sally and Renae both running the bases quite energetically for women their age. But soon they got winded and went inside where they took turns holding the baby. Sally said, "Don't you wish we could have another baby?"

"No, never, not on your life, Grandma," Renae shot back.

At about three o'clock the family walked to Twin Ponds Park, Diane carrying the baby in a cloth sling draped around her body. It was a good long walk through a residential neighborhood and then through a wooded trail past the two little murky ponds that gave the park its identity—a slice of wild nature smack dab in the heart of the city. They stopped at one of the ponds to watch frogs on a log and ducks swimming in lazy circles, a mama duck and three little ducklings periodically ducking their heads, and they went past the soccer field where they held up for a few minutes to let the kids watch older boys play, and finally they reached the playground where Martin and Joe climbed on the jungle gym while the adults sat on a bench and watched, some heavy breathing from Sally, who then walked a safe distance away and lit a cigarette. Her second of the day.

"Let's go on an adventure," the older boy said. His idea of an adventure was following some of the smaller paths into the woods. Not knowing where the path might lead.

Asher said, "Not without an adult," and Bryce said, "I'll go with them," and they took off, the boys running ahead and Bryce working at keeping up with them. They came to a small slice of water, a runoff from one of the ponds no more than two feet wide.

"Help us get across," Martin said.

"OK. Hop on."

Martin climbed onto Bryce and wrapped his arms and legs around him. "You too. All aboard!" And Josiah climbed on him too, and Bryce took a huge step across the little creek and then sat down on the grass with the boys hanging onto him, and they wrestled on the ground until Bryce said, "Enough. This old man is worn to a frazzle."

Renae and Sally caught up with them, and stepping across the little creek Renae slipped and cut her arm on a sharp rock. Diane, who always carried extra cloth just in case something like that happened, wrapped her arm. "Thanks, hon," Renae said. "If this is the worst thing that happens to me on this trip we'll be cool."

. . .

That night Renae and Sally, and Bryce and Emma journeyed into Seattle in separate cars to watch the special one-night-only performance of the show about Rachel Corrie. Entering the theater, they had to walk the gantlet through pro- and anti-Israeli protesters facing off against each other on the covered walkway outside the theater. The women politely refused the pamphlets proffered by each side while Bryce accepted all.

The play was a wonderfully acted and emotionally draining one-woman performance with the actress playing Rachel Corrie telling the tale taken from Corrie's real-life diaries. There were gasps and cheers from the audience, and thankfully nothing from the protestors who I guess disbanded as soon as everyone went inside.

Throughout the play, Bryce kept drifting off to sleep, and every time he did Emma elbowed him in the side.

Bryce and Emma checked into a hotel in Seattle after the play; Renae and Sally drove quickly into traffic on the freeway that was unusually hellish for that late at night.

Heading to Helen and Eva's place in Olympia, they got caught up in a two-hour delay on I-5, inching forward and frequently coming to a full stop for minutes at a time. "Jesus Christ a-ready, I'm getting one of my sick headaches," Renae muttered.

"There's Ibuprofen in my bag," Sally said. Renae rummaged through her purse for a while, an increasingly desperate look on her face, and finally she said, "Feck. It ain't here. We'll have to stop and get some. If I don't take something ..."

"I know."

I had been with her a few times when she had one of her sick headaches. I could see it coming on—see it in her eyes, in the pallor of her face, sometimes her trembling hands. So I knew that if she didn't take something when she got one of those headaches, and take it right away, she would get nauseous, and she'd break out in a sweat. It was not a pretty sight. On the road south to Helen and Eva's farm, both of them knew that the anxiety of being stuck in traffic would make it even worse.

After another half hour of crawling south on I-5, they got off in a village called Fife and found a grocery store that was open late. Sally said, "I'll go in. You wait here."

"Pick up a gallon of ice cream, too," Renae said, her voice a rasping whisper.

Sally picked up a large bottle of extra strength Ibuprofen and a container of chocolate ice cream, hoping it wouldn't melt before they got to Eva and Helen's. "Stupid, stupid, stupid," she muttered under her breath when she picked up the ice cream and headed to the checkout, afraid it would never last but getting it anyway because Renae had asked.

There were three self-check stations and only one regular checkout. Nobody was at any of the self-checks. There was only one customer at the regular checkout, a young woman wearing hot pink shorts and a T-shirt with what Sally assumed must be a band name she didn't recognize. The Agonizer Centipedes. Her basket was filled with cartons of drink and a roasted hen and bread and what looked to Sally like enough groceries to feed an army. *If she had an ounce of decency in her she'd let me go first*, Sally thought, but the woman glanced her way for no more than a second and started loading her groceries onto the conveyor. *Damn it, there's nobody in the self-check. I could zip right through there*, Sally thought. But she refused to use self-check on the assumption that it takes jobs away from union employees. She had been taught from childhood by her father, who came from a long line of union workers. *But damn it all to hell, this is no time to be so hardheaded about principle. My wife is out there suffering with a raging headache, and I'm refusing to take the easy way out and rush to help her.* She didn't really think all of that, not in words, but in a wordless fleeting second that was what went through her mind.

Not only did the woman in front of Sally have a huge stack of groceries, she slowed the process as much as the construction or collision or whatever it was that had brought traffic to a stand-still by arguing with the checkout clerk about an expired coupon, while Sally impatiently drummed on the handle of her basket and shot the woman withering looks. Out in the car, Renae couldn't take the wait any longer. Despite being sick, she got out of the car and went in to see what the holdup was. She joined Sally in line. Sally said, "You all right, honey?"

"I will be. I hope," Renae croaked.

The woman in front of them jerked to attention when she heard the word *honey*. She wheeled about to face them and quoted with an imperious voice, "If a man lies with a man as with a woman, both of them have committed an abomination; they shall be put to death; their blood was upon them. That's from the *Bible*, and it goes for women too, faggot."

Sally wanted to scream at the woman but knew that would only make matters worse and delay their getting out of the store, and Renae was not able to respond at all due to pain. A war was being fought behind her eyeballs, and the only thing she wanted to do was get the hell out of that store and back in the car and swallow a couple of pain pills.

It was not the first time Renae and Sally had been smacked with such homophobic remarks. Sometimes one or the other, usually Renae, was able to come up with a cutting comeback, but not always; sometimes they were flummoxed and speechless.

Renae could not say anything. She felt like she was about to throw up. But she muttered just barely loud enough for Sally to hear, "Fecking daughter of a dog," and Sally thought, *she's gonna be all right. By jiminy.* But she was at a loss for what to do or what to say. What came to her mind was to pretend they were deaf, which seemed completely off the wall and useless. Nevertheless, she started making sign-language-like motions with one hand. It confused the obnoxious woman enough that she said, "Sorry. I didn't realize you was deaf and dumb," and she quickly paid for her purchases and huffed out the door with her loaded cart.

The clerk, as it turned out, knew some basic sign language but had not paid close enough attention to realize Sally's signing had been meaningless. She signed her apologies, to which Sally said, "I have no idea what you're signing. We actually hear quite well and ... I just ... well, I really didn't know what else to do."

"Oh," the clerk said. "That was like a really, really cool way to handle her. Please accept our apologies and ... your stuff is on me. No charge."

SAPPHO FARM

By the light of an almost full moon, they could see past a corner of the house to the shed out back and the tall evergreens silhouetted against the early morning sky that was steel gray against a lighter gray. Barely visible in the east was the dull pink of the approaching sunrise, not yet making an appearance but waiting in the wings for its cue. It had taken them almost seven hours to get to the little farm southeast of Olympia. Sally lit a cigarette and blew the smoke out the window. Renae said, "Should we go in and wake 'em up, or should we wait for some sign of life?"

"Maybe we'd better wait. Let 'em wake up on their own."

Helen and Eva's lumbering mutt (Helen called him a Heinz fifty-seven variety) and their noisy and rambunctious little yorkie rushed out to the car begging for attention. Renae remembered that the yorkie was named Lil'Bit. Neither of them could remember the big mutt's name. He reared up on his hind legs and stuck his snout in the open window, and Sally petted him vigorously but not happily. In my mind I can hear her thinking *If you scratch my car I'll feed you to the alligators.* As if there were alligators in Western Washington.

After what the dogs apparently thought was a suitable amount of petting, they settled down in the grass next to the Subaru.

The women did not get out but reclined their seats and closed their eyes and dozed off and slept fitfully, Renae in the passenger seat, with her head on Sally's shoulder. Downing two Ibuprofen while pulling away from the store in Fife and resting the back of her neck on the car seat had eased but not cured her headache.

The dogs got up and ambled off behind the house where the goats were grazing and where chickens pecked at whatever they could find to eat in the grass and dirt. Sally woke and looked out and then nudged her wife and said, "Somebody's up."

Still no lights on in the house, but they saw two figures silhouetted against the foggy sunrise. It was Helen and Eva's grown children, Brian and Melony, heading out to milk the goats and gather eggs. They looked ghostly in the early morning fog. The women waited until the two of them were heading back to the house before getting out of the car and announcing their presence. "Good morning, kids," Sally said.

"Renae! Sally! Wow! We thought you guys were coming last night," Melony gushed.

Sally said, "We thought so too, but I-5 ... ye gods and little fishes."

The four of them walked across the slightly slippery grass and through the kitchen door into the house, where Eva and Helen were drinking coffee, both wearing pajama shorts and T-shirts. Eva was seated on a sagging couch with her feet on the coffee table. Helen was standing by the stove scrambling eggs with one hand while holding her coffee mug with the other. Bread was in the toaster.

"Oh my god," Helen said, "What took you so long?" She set her cup down and rushed to hug Renae and then Sally. "We thought you were coming in last night."

"Yeah. Well, it was quite a day at Asher's, and the trip back down here was a nightmare," Renae said.

Sally added, "We got here about four-thirty or five and decided to sleep in the car until you got up."

"Aw, you didn't need to do that. You could have come on in. You know the house is unlocked and the guest bed is always here for you."

Helen scooped out the eggs and plopped them on plates. "For the weary travelers," she said. "I'll cook more for us."

Eva said to Renae, "You look like you've been ridden hard and put up wet. Can we get you anything?"

"Yes, thank you. Some coffee, please. And some water,"
Renae unscrewed the pill bottle top.

"Another one of your sick headaches?"

"Uh-huh. It's beginning to ease off thanks to these babies and a short nap in the car, but I figure more drugs can't hurt."

Coffee and more pills finally eased Renae's pain. Helen asked them, "Have you guys seen my father? How is he?"

"Big and jolly as usual," Sally said.

"Ha! Yeah. What about my mom? How was she? And don't say little."

"I was going to say petite and sweet."

"She is all of that," Helen said.

When they told Eva and Helen about their encounter with the homophobe in Fife, Helen said. "I woulda been tempted to slap the holy hell out of that bitch,"

"Please, no, don't say that" Renae said, chuckling. "It hurts when I laugh."

Sally put the ice cream in the freezer. "It's probably melted, and I don't know if it's any good."

All Renae could eat was some toast, and she almost vomited it up. After eating they went into Helen and Eva's bedroom to take a nap, drifting off to the sounds of the Indigo Girls.

Hours passed. Eva gently woke Renae and Sally and said, "It's time to go, guys. And guess what. Change of plans. We're going to go to Lizzy's place first, and then to Anacortes."

BILLY WAKES BELLE

That same day, a cool morning in July, while Eva and Helen and Renae and Sally argued over whether or not they had time to visit Lizzy before heading to the ferry, eighty-two-year-old Billy Johnson, still spry despite a laundry list of illnesses some of which nearly killed him practically flew out bed. Enthusiastically he ripped the sheets off Belle, shouted for her to, "Get your lazy ass up," and took a few skipping steps toward the closet and suddenly gasped, "Eeeyow!" and grabbed his back.

"Ripped your back, huh," Belle said, carefully pushing herself out of bed. "Serves you right for acting like a ten-year-old."

Her actions, however, were gentler and more loving than her words. She massaged his lower back while standing. She had done it many times and knew precisely how to ease the pain.

Billy bitched about old age but fought against letting it slow him down—behavior that had become typical for him over the past decade. He still went to work at the dealership two and three days a week and could still wrestle to submission a good-sized salmon out of Puget Sound, and he still played golf and did other things with Betty Clyde at least once a month. Five years younger, Belle could keep up with him in most ways. The two of them enjoyed their semi-hermetic life in their Steamboat Island home, where they often wished nobody would ever visit.

No matter how warm the day on the shores of Puget Sound, once the sun went down, Billy and Belle shivered in the chill of summer nights. Not that a bit of shivering was a deterrent to sitting out on the deck on a cool summer night wrapped in blankets and sipping hot toddies or a hot buttered rum late into the night in silence until, with a mutual look, they signaled it was time to go in. They slept under piles of quilts and blankets by wide-open windows. Billy loved the comfort of the heavy quilts but cursed them when he had to get up during the night to pee—three times a night at the very least—kicking

116

and pushing like a netted fish, trapped by the weight of those blankets. The night before, he must have fought his way out from under the covers at least five times. He tried keeping count but couldn't. He got up at 10:33 after having only crawled in bed a mere half hour earlier, and then again at 11:03 and at a quarter to midnight, every time trudging barefoot into the bathroom and then back to bed, thinking *maybe I need a goddamn catheter.* He wasn't even sure if he went to sleep at all between trips to the bathroom. Often, he could not tell the difference between dreamtime and tossing-and-turning time. The only thing he knew for sure was that he had to pee far too often. When he had to fill out a questionnaire at the clinic, he always checked the box for excessive urination, and from time to time he asked the doctor about it, but the doctor acted unconcerned. He said, "You're old, Billy. That's life for old men."

"Thanks a heap, doc."

What concerned Belle was not so much Billy's frequent urination as it was his insisting on sleeping by an open window. Night chills could bring on pneumonia. "Besides, thieves could get in through the open windows."

"No need to worry about that," Billy said, "Not with my Smith & Weston in easy reach on the nightstand."

"Yeah. That's something else to worry about. I'm scared that if somebody did break in, you'd grab for that gun half asleep and shoot your own damn self. Or me." She had read somewhere that people who keep guns for self-protection are more likely to shoot themselves than they are to shoot a burglar. Or that the burglar—younger, bigger and stronger than them—would snatch the pistol right out of Billy's hand and blow both their brains out. She had a horror of someone climbing through the window and raping her. It was an old fear from ages ago. *Would he kill me before or after? Would he force Billy to watch? Oh what horrible thoughts we think in the dark.*

At 5:30 this foggy morning after jumping out of bed and straining his back, Billy dragged himself into the kitchen, brewed a pot of coffee and drank a cup.

"Wash your face and brush your hair, deadhead. Today's the day we go to the island. We gotta get a move on."

"Go away," Belle mumbled, turning her back to him and shuffling into the bathroom. Outside the large window by their bed lay the serene blue-gray waters of Squaxin Pass. Billy turned for a moment to look at Hope Island in the distance. They had kayaked all the way across to the island once, six, maybe seven years ago, which was one hell of a distance for an old couple like them. They agreed that kayaking was too much work, and the kayaks were put away in the boathouse and never again hauled out.

Billy and Belle so loved the view out that window and from their deck, and they loved their forested property with the gently sloping path down to the beach and the small pier and the boathouse that housed a fourteen-foot aluminum fishing boat and the no-longer-used twin kayaks. The property on Steamboat Island was their dream retirement home, and by retirement, they meant not only little to no work but isolating themselves from the rest of the world to whatever degree they could. Billy had long since decided he didn't like people. Except for Betty Clyde and a handful of others he tolerated. If he could have his way, he and Belle would live a hermit's life, but necessities like grocery shopping and checkups with the family doctor prevented that. The other exception to their isolation was the annual family retreat on Orcas Island. Every spring when he wondered aloud if maybe they should quit doing the retreats, Belle said. "It's up to you. You're the one that initiated them, and you're the one who perpetuates them. It's your baby. Do what you want."

His response every year was, "Maybe this year should be the last."

...

Twenty-something years earlier, Billy had commissioned an architect and contractor to build their rustic-modern log cabin to his specifications on the wooded shores of Puget Sound. The house looked like a country estate from the eighteen hundreds but had up-to-date insulation, heating and air, and modern appliances. There was a deck that wrapped around two sides of the house and a massive fireplace with an even more massive stone chimney on a corner of the house. The fireplace was open to both the living room and the front porch so they could sit by the fire both inside and out. One of Larry's large paintings hung in the living room. It was an abstract painting, and Billy admitted he didn't get it, but he liked the colors, and over time it had come to have the same soothing effect on him that the fireplace and the view across the water had.

The floors were slate with many throw rugs throughout. All of the furniture was oak, cabinets were glass fronted. There were sliding glass doors that opened onto their redwood deck on the back wall of the wide-open combination living room, dining room and kitchen. There was a seldom-used dining table on the deck that sat eight. They loved sitting on the deck in all kinds of weather. When the weather was balmy, in shorts and T-shirts, light jackets and blankets at night. They also liked to cast off the pier for coho, king and steelhead. They never had fishing licenses. "It's our own property," Billy argued. "They got no right to make us get a license to fish off our own property."

Belle had long since given up fighting over that one. *Let him pay the fines. See if I care.*

The only exceptions to their self-imposed isolation were the annual get-togethers at Christmas and Thanksgiving when everyone came to their house—"Why is it always our house?" Billy wanted to know. "Because ours is the only house big enough," Belle answered— and of course the annual Johnson family retreat at Peter Puget Resort on Orcas Island.

If you asked Lizzy or Renae or Marilou—the only ones of Billy's siblings who lived close enough to Billy to visit as often as Billy allowed—they would tell you the main reason they steered clear of Billy's home on Steamboat Island was that Billy was a tyrant who never got over being the big brother in a home where the parents were often missing in spirit if not in actuality. Belle let him get away with bossing everybody around. Take off shoes when entering, eat only at the table, scrape dishes into the compost bin and put them to soak in the sink, no smoking in the house and no talking during the evening news, Billy demanded all of that while commenting non-stop about everything the newscasters said. Visiting Billy and Belle was like being in the army. Granted, there could hardly be a more idyllic army base.

...

Billy complained about being old, but compared to his father, Harlan, who lived to be ninety or his grandfather, Auvergne, who hung around until he was a hundred and three, he was a young whippersnapper. He was lucky to be alive, and he knew it. Three times between 2000 and 2003 Belle had to call for an ambulance to rush Billy to the hospital, sitting by his side and holding his hand and generally getting in the way while medics worked on him. He had triple bypass surgery the first time, and over the next few years, he had a half dozen stents put in his veins. He jokingly called himself the bionic man. What with the stents, glasses, hearing aids and false teeth, he said he had more replacement parts than a classic Ford.

After the first heart attack, his doctor said, "If you don't quit smoking, you'll be dead within the year."

"I hear you, Doc, and I'm quitting. Right now." And he did quit. Or so he told the doctor and Belle, and even himself. In Billy's mind, sneaking an occasional cigarette, anything less than every day, was not smoking. He could go three or four days without a single cigarette. He was proud of himself for that. Most days he had one or two, down from a pack or two before the heart attack, and he was sure those few couldn't hurt him. The only family member who knew he was sneaking smokes was his sister-in-law Sally, because at one of the family retreats he sought out an isolated spot to sneak a smoke and Sally was there puffing on a one herself. It was their little secret, and it became an annual ritual. In their special spot a quarter mile from the hotel where a horizontal tree trunk resting at the perfect height for sitting under the shade of some broadleaved tree created a comfortable shaded bench overlooking the water where Billy and Sally, who rarely spoke to one another, became, for ten minutes, the closest of friends and allies, so much so that for a few seconds after they tossed their cigarettes into the sound Sally felt an unexpected urge to hug him. *Jesus, I shudder to think.* She no more followed through on that urge than he followed through on his promise to quit smoking.

Billy and Belle had both been runners until they were in their sixties. He managed grueling races despite being a smoker. They ran half-marathons and five-Ks, never a full marathon, always finishing

120

somewhere in the middle of the pack. Once he was awarded a ribbon for placing second in the over-fifty division in a half marathon, and she got a similar ribbon for placing third. They were running side-by-side for the last fifty yards, holding hands and vowing to each other to cross the finish line together, but Billy could not resist the urge to spurt ahead of her at the last second. "Second Place, Billy. That's been me my whole damn life," he grumbled. "I'm not going to be second place to my wife."

...

The hospital where he was treated for his heart condition had a support group for patients who had undergone heart surgery. Their spouses were encouraged to attend meetings with them. They called it the zipper club because the patients each had a scar that ran the length of their chest like a zipper.

The physician's assistant who facilitated the group did not believe in sugarcoating, "I won't lie to you. You can expect to die of a heart attack if you don't drive off a mountain or get run over by an eighteen-wheeler or get cancer first. I know that sounds harsh, but you need to accept it. Our job is to keep you as comfortable and as healthy as possible for the time you have left. But know this: what you have undergone has done a lot of damage that can't be undone. With rest, avoiding stress, taking your meds religiously, moderate exercise—and most important of all, no smoking—you can live comfortably. The no smoking includes vaping and it included marijuana if you think that's somehow safer than cigarettes. And avoid stressful situations, you can have up to twenty more good years."

Billy whispered to Belle, "He's just like my old man, trying to scare me into being good."

"Hey, he's saying you can have another twenty good years. Don't knock it. You'll be eighty-eight in twenty years. That's not bad."

Billy and Belle attended only one meeting of the zipper club. They remembered there was one woman in the group who kept asking about vacuuming. "Is it safe to vacuum?"

"Yes, of course," the physician said. "Any regular housecleaning is fine. There shouldn't be any normal activities you can't do so long as you pace yourself. Stop and rest when you feel tired, and especially if you feel chest pain or pain in your arm. You have nitro pills. Put one under your tongue if the pain doesn't ease off. Just be sensible about it."

"Even vacuuming?" the woman persisted.

"Yes, even vacuuming."

Someone else asked, "What about sex?"

There was some laughter at that. "Quit twittering like sophomores." The facilitator said, "That's the most common question we get. And yes, sex is fine. Just take it easy and stop if you feel any pain or shortness of breath."

Billy turned to Belle and said, "OK, Babe. We got this."

Once he finally and totally quit smoking, Billy did not have any more problems with his heart. They no longer ran grueling races, but they went for long walks almost every day, and he took his meds conscientiously. They still made love once in a great while, and they seldom had to stop or slow down due to pain or shortness of breath. When one or the other of them was in the mood, they would say, "You feel up to vacuuming?"

Neither of them ever said no to that.

...

"Get out from under there," Billy said, and pulled the sheet down nearly to her waist. "We got to get up and get packing and get ready to go."

"I'm not wearing underwear," she said. "What's underwear got to do with anything?"

They exchanged quizzical looks then laughed at one another realizing she must have misheard. "Oh, I said under there, not underwear," Billy said.

"Oh. I thought ..." (She was wearing a long T-shirt.)

"I know what you thought. Come on, we gotta go. We can vacuum on the island."

"I gotta go, all right," she mumbled, and she kicked herself free of the sheet and went to the bathroom. He heard the faucet running, her trickle in the toilet and said, "Don't flush ..." just as she pushed the handle.

It was Lizzy who had taught them the importance of saving water by not flushing every time. Lizzy had a sign in her bathroom, hand-lettered in her calligraphic style:

IF IT'S YELLOW, THAT'S MELLOW.

IF IT'S BROWN, FLUSH IT DOWN.

"We ought to get her to letter us one of those," Billy said. But they never did.

Belle shuffled back into the bedroom, mussing her hair and running her hand along her jaw, blinking. Sunlight beginning to burn through the fog created an aura of light around Belle's snow-white hair that tumbled across her shoulders.

Coffee downed, clothes on, Belle fed the animals—a cocker spaniel named Goldie and a calico cat named Sweetness (in honor of Walter Payton)—and shuffled into the kitchen as Billy was dishing up pancakes and pouring a second cup of coffee. "Don't reckon you're gonna mention our anniversary, are you?"

"I forgot."

"Of course you did. As always."

"Which one is it?"

"Fifty-seven."

"Dang. That's a long time."

"Yeah. I don't know how I put up with you that long. But don't you go taking me for granted. I got my eyes on that blond fellow that works at the little store." *Why do we never joke around like this when we're with other people*, she wondered.

...

For no reason he could put a name to (he told me years later), Billy picked that moment to recall a visit with his little brother Bryce a few years earlier. Bryce had driven across the mountains for a conference at South Puget Sound Community College. Billy and Belle invited him to stay with them. "No sense in forking out money for a hotel," Billy said. "And you don't want to drive all the way back across the Cascades after a full day of whatever y'all do at educational conferences."

Emma came with him and spent the day with Billy and Belle while Bryce attended the conference. The next day, after Belle cooked a big breakfast for the four of them, talking around a mouthful of cheese and bacon omelet, Billy said, "It's the weekend. You don't have to be back right away. Why not spend one more day and drive back in the morning?"

Turning to Belle, Bryce said, "Who is this effusive guy and what's happened to your husband?"

Belle replied with a shoulder shrug.

Billy packed cheese and crackers and bologna sandwiches on white bread in a lunch sack and a six-pack of some cheap beer in his ice chest, loaded fishing gear in the boat, and he and Bryce climbed in and chugged out into the waters of Squaxin Pass and spent most of the day out on the water drifting and talking more than fishing. After eating their sandwiches and while drinking their second beer each, Billy said, "You know, there's something's been buggin' me a lot lately. Last time we were together I said something nasty about President Obama. I don't remember exactly what it was."

"You called him the n-word."

"Oh. Yeah, you would remember that. But yes I did, and I'm ashamed of it."

He paused and Bryce waited, and then he said, "I tried to claim it didn't mean anything. and you called me a racist."

"Uh huh."

"Well I've been thinking about it a lot lately."

"Good. You should."

A breeze was picking up. The boat was rocking. Choppy waves. Dark clouds overhead. He looked to the sky, to the water, and said, we're gonna need to go in soon" and then, "Well, all right then. The thing is ..." he paused a few more dripping seconds, took another big swig of beer and propped his spinning rod against the gunwale. "You called me on it, and I guess you were kinda right. I reckon I am kind of racist. I don't mean to be, and I never thought I was, but ... the thing is, when I think about a colored person, I think the n-word in my mind. I don't mean to and I never say it out loud, but there it is, a part of who I am. I don't know where it comes from."

"I do," Bryce said. "It comes from Louisiana, from kids at school. From everywhere. Eenie meenie miney mo, catch a n-word by the toe. Don't n-lip that fag. Remember that one? How about there's a n-word in the woodpile. There's even a kind of nut that we called n-toes. Everybody did. I was grown before I knew that wasn't its real name. That kind of casual racism has been pervasive throughout our entire lives. Nobody ever gave it a second thought."

"Yeah. Like that. I guess it's been there forever, you know. But I'm not a racist. God, you know that. It's not like I'm a freaking Klansman. I never tossed around the n-word. I mean, I was all in favor of equal rights back in the sixties."

Bryce raised an eyebrow, pursed his lips, said, "You don't have to hate Blacks to be racist. You just have to believe deep down inside that they are inherently less than us. Less intelligent, less worthy. It takes hard work over a long time to overcome that."

Bryce set his rod down too. He said, "We're all racists inside, all white people, even the ones that have fought for civil rights. We don't like to admit it, but it's true. If you grow up white in America, man, you can't help it."

Billy took another big swig of his beer. "I don't know. That's ... that's kinda crazy."

"Uh huh. But it's true."

"Well what can I do to change?"

"What you're doing right now. Think about it, talk about it. Be awake to it. Don't let defensiveness rise when it comes up. That's just what you're doing."

...

In his second year teaching at Washington State, Bryce married his graduate assistant, Emma Hall, a tiny girl with a laugh large enough and wit sharp enough to match Bryce's. They had six children, three of whom were adopted after an illness left Emma unable to have more. Only one of their children, Helen, remained in

Washington after she grew up. She married Eva, a schoolteacher who was painfully shy back then but definitely not anymore.

Bryce was playful and loving with the Johnsons, as he was with the bulk of his students. Even into his "dotage," as Emma liked to call Bryce's aging, he would get down on his hands and knees and play horsey with his grandchildren. They said of him he never grew up.

...

Making a conscious effort to lighten the conversation, Bryce said, "You know what? I read somewhere or maybe heard on some radio talk show that changing your routines from time to time helps keep you younger."

Phew. Thank God we're not talking about racism anymore, Billy thought.

Bryce said, "I remember us talking about that routine thing when we were college age. Or I was. Come to think of it, it was our daddy who said that about routine. Lord knows where he might have heard it. Probably from Billy Graham or Paul Harvey."

"Probably. He listened to them all the time."

Harlan loved Paul Harvey. So did Billy. "They don't do talk shows like that anymore," they said. A statement everyone who heard it took as gospel. Unquestionable. Or if they didn't agree they didn't bother responding. That was all of Billy's friends anyway. "You gave me that piece of advice back when we lived on Bethel and you were driving to work five days a week," Bryce recalled. "You took it to heart too. You made a conscious effort to vary your route from time to time because Paul Harvey said to. Yes, it had to have been Paul Harvey. Yeah. So anyway, you said you enjoyed the variety. You got a kick out of seeing different things and different people along the different routes. Seeing what kind of foolish lawn decoration that guy on Central was going to put in his yard next—remember him? Or the guy with all the pink flamingos and the rock garden with running water and a little windmill. The idiot's done turned his yard into a goofy golf course. And there was the house on Central with the little ceramic black boy peeing into the pool. There's the casual racism we were talking about."

"Uh-huh. I remember. I remember seeing what political signs people put up. I cursed at most of them."

Billy remembered how he often passed the mail carrier and shouted at him, "G'morning, Randy!" and Randy the mail carrier would shout back, "Morning, Mr. Johnson." If instead of taking Central with all those dang speed bumps he took Puget to Fourth, he always passed by a cute young jogger who reminded him of Marilou when she was that age. Fun-loving Marilou, sharp as the point of a hypodermic needle and quick to laugh or to anger, always battling her weight and always struggling with weak self-esteem. I believe Billy still thinks of her as a chubby little insecure girl even though she lost the weight as well as the insecurities sometime in the mid-to-late fifties when life was an adventure, when there was joy in looking forward.

Nowadays Billy seldom varies his routes because they hardly ever go anywhere except the grocery store. Now that they're semi-retired and have the time to do it, they no longer eat in restaurants, and they don't go to movies or plays. Other than his weekly drive to the Safeway on Cooper Point and his monthly drive to Costco, about the only times Billy drives his car is to take it into the dealership when it's time for service, which he does strictly by the manufacturer-recommended schedule. And every Friday evening when they drive into town for fish and chips at the Martin Way Diner. He always has a Budweiser with his fish.

Every other day of the week at five o'clock he drinks his beer in front of the television while watching Fox News after a long and relaxing soak in the hot tub and while Belle is cooking dinner. This is the man who had believed varying his routines would keep him young. The older he and Belle grew, the more important routines became, and if something or someone interrupted those routines—even if it was something or someone they enjoyed—Billy's knotted-up guts became a raging volcano rumbling deep inside but never quite erupting. He so teeth-grindingly desperately wanted to tell whomever it was that so thoughtlessly interrupted his precious routine to get the hell out of his house. But of course he would never do that. He was nothing if not polite. He would offer his guests something to drink and seethe inwardly while trying to act the perfect host—wishing he could kick their asses because they talked during the news. He was incapable of splitting his attention between the visitor and the newscast. He would mute the TV and turn on closed captions at Belle's insistence but not turn it off.

Belle took such interruptions of routine more in stride—their almost immutable daily routine was her feeding the animals in the morning while he made the coffee. They drank two cups each while watching the morning news before breakfast, always one of the local network affiliates until they started repeating stories, and then he switched to Fox. After breakfast, they spread out mats and did yoga for half an hour. They attributed their longevity and good health to these routines and to their single glass of red wine every night at bedtime.

. . .

Before Billy and Bryce put their rods away and came in for the day, Bryce caught a six-pound steelhead. "Here's dinner," he said. "I'll gut her and clean her, and Belle will cook her up nice."

...

On the morning of the last day before going to Orcas Island where they knew their daily routines would be shot all to hell, Marilou and I showed up unexpectedly at Billy and Belle's just as they were getting ready to do their yoga. *Dammit it all to hell, Marilou, have you ever heard of calling ahead,* Billy wanted so much to say. But he welcomed us perfunctorily and even smiled. He gave Marilou a brotherly peck on the cheek and slapped my back. A surprisingly hard slap.

Belle welcomed us more jovially, saying, "Have you had breakfast? Can we get you anything? Coffee?"

"Coffee would be great," Marilou said.

Marilou was a mere five years younger than Billy, the same age as Belle, yet Billy still had a hard time thinking of her as fully grown. Eighty-two and seventy-seven, for Christ's sake. It was past time he should stop playing big brother. But habits are hard to break. Growing up with parents who were not the most attentive in the world, it had often fallen to Billy to take care of his younger siblings, a position he reverted to quite easily.

"Have you been by to see Helen and Eva lately?" Billy asked.

"Not recently. I think they're doing fine. You know, of course, that Eva's son is living with them now. He's a student at Evergreen."

"Yeah, yeah. I heard that. I'm happy for 'em."

Even though Helen and Eva lived on a farm a mere half an hour away from Billy and Belle, they hardly ever saw them. Eva and Helen were almost as much homebodies as Billy and Belle, a fact for which they periodically berated themselves. One or the other would say, "We need to get out and do stuff more often," and they both agreed but rarely did anything. Their lives could be summed up in two short sentences: Helen stayed home and worked the farm. Eva taught school. Eva did, however, occasionally stop downtown on her way home from school and walk around Capital Lake. They seldom even went into town to shop; the kids did that for them. Routine for them was much as it was for Billy and Belle, something sacred. It had not always been so. Settling into safe and, let's face it, boring routines had been their way of coping with a traumatic incident two years earlier when Eva got shot.

Marilou and I led fairly routine/boring lives too, but I didn't mind.

So we were uncomfortably making small talk with Billy on the morning before going to Orcas. Belle brought four cups of coffee on a tray with sugar and creamer, saying, "Sorry, I can't remember what you take in your coffee."

"This is fine," Marilou said. I said I'd take a little honey in mine if they had it.

"Sorry," Belle said. "We don't have any honey."

"No problem, honey," I said, thinking I was being terribly clever. "Sugar's fine."

Belle said, "Let's take this out to the deck. It's too nice a day to be cooped up inside."

Seated on plastic webbed chairs around the glass-topped table on the deck, Billy took a good look at us like he'd never before seen us. This is what he saw: a Billy-like sister much shorter than Billy with still a youthful and curvaceous figure, big hands, big eyes, muscular arms and shoulders. She was an attractive woman who did not look her age. Same age and close to the same size, I had put on weight since retirement, I had one of those heavy necks that looked like it came straight out of my jowls. Looking soft overall with long, thin white hair, every time I looked in the mirror I told myself we needed to exercise more, which we did, but not for long. Once or twice a week we got out into nature and walked. Squaxin Park, McClain Creek nature trail, the watershed off Henderson. God, that last one was a killer. I endured the walks, enjoyed the scenery, but the exercise was a killer. I'd much rather be right where I was relaxing on patio chairs at Billy's house even if it was Billy's house.

Marilou took a big gulp of her coffee and set her mug down so hard it was a wonder she didn't break the glass table top. She said, "We're worried about Lizzy."

"That's why you're here?" Billy asked.

"Uh huh. We think you should go out and check on her. See what she needs, ask what we can do for her."

"Why don't y'all check on her? You're just as capable as I am."

"Yeah, but you're the big brother. She'll listen to you."

"Ha!" Billy chortled. "Lizzy has never listened to anybody."

I stayed out of that. Marilou conceded that Billy was probably right about Lizzy not listening but insisted that he should be the one to talk to her. He resisted but finally said, "I will. But not until after the retreat."

MARILOU WOKE PARKER AND DELIA

Billy and Belle did not drive out to Lizzy's place. They did not smell the chicken shit and put up with the noisy dogs or the cacophony of the punk rock or hip-hop or whatever kind of excuse for music it was that Buddy played non-stop. They did not try talking Lizzy and Buddy into joining the family on the island. What a senseless waste of breath any of that would be.

Neither did Marilou and I embark on that Quixotic quest, although Marilou did attempt to convince me we should at least try. My reply to Marilou, which I felt was imminently logical, was, "You'll just end up feeling let down and insulted that she doesn't want to spend time with us. Face it, Lizzy doesn't give a damn about this family. She has no interest in spending time with us. She's as grumpy as those nasty chickens of hers and has no intention of ever changing."

"Wow! Talk about grumpy. Here lately you've gotten to be the grumpfather of all grumps." Marilou let me have it with both barrels. She wanted to know why I was getting to be such a curmudgeon.

"It's called old age, my dear. It's a disease we all have."

We had just left Billy's house, and I guess something of him had rubbed off on me. So that was the gist of our conversation as we drove to the farmstand on Harrison where we stocked up on fruits and vegetables—snacks for the trip to the island. We agreed that there was little if anything we could do about Billy being such a curmudgeon. Same with Lizzy. Same with me too, I guess. At least one of us agreed.

At the farmstand, Marilou said, "We could get all this stuff free of charge from Helen and Eva."

"Uh huh, and spend as much on gas as we'd save."

All the way home to Royal Court we didn't say another word to each other. I fantasized, as I often did, that I finally published my novel and it was a gigantic success, and I imagined a big book-signing event at which I could not control my trembling hands. The thought of that mortified me. I asked Marilou if she had noticed that my hands sometimes shook.

Marilou said, "Uh huh. I have, a little. Maybe we should switch to decaf, and maybe quit drinking coffee after a certain time of day, say, after lunch. Maybe you'd feel better if you got out once in a while. Did something. Spent some time with other people instead of spending all your time in our little house on this little cul-de-sac in the little town of Lacey with little neighbors we hardly even know."

"Way to sum up our miserable little, little, little lives. Did you forget about the long walks you drag me out on?" This conversation took place as we entered our little castle in Lacey, and I went immediately to the refrigerator for a bottle of beer. Hey, hey, no caffeine in beer.

Lacey, an addendum to Olympia, two towns of practically the same size and stitched together like conjoined twins. It was impossible to tell when you left one and entered the other. It was the same with Tumwater and Olympia, although Tumwater, smaller than the other two, was more unique in both good and bad ways—home to the horribly ugly abandoned brewery which was next to the most beautiful park in the area.

Almost fifty thousand people called Lacey home, yet it was a stepchild to Olympia, the state capital. Marilou and I were two of those almost fifty thousand souls.

We had put a down payment on the sweet little suburban home on Royal Court on the day we were married. It was a pink house. We vowed to paint it white right away, but we didn't get around to that for years. There we tended a perfect lawn and watched uninspiring television and had insipid discussions and arguments and frequent and hot sex which had lately become infrequent and ho-hum. *When did that happen?*

I often reminded Marilou that we were lucky to live in such a place. "It's a sweet little house."

"If you say *sweet* or *little* one more time ..."

"Nothing fancy but comfy, and the neighborhood is just perfect for raising kids." Variations on this conversation had been happening often over the years since we bought the house. But not the part about raising kids, because ours were now all grown. Larry was

132

in New York, and Maryanne lived on the West Side with Wanda, and Parker and Delia and Baby Randolph had moved back in with us after he got laid off from his last job. We sometimes said that Maryanne and Wanda needed to come around more often. "Maybe if we invited them," was Marilou's usual response to that.

Living on Royal Court was tolerable to Marilou. Only tolerable. "It's nothing but strip malls and big box stores and vast swaths of housing developments," she complained on bad days, but she loved the relative peacefulness of the neighborhood and the convenience of shopping and the comfort of the house. Every house is just like every other house was her major complaint. "And where is the character? Is there anything that makes Lacey unique? Hell no, there certainly is not. It could be Federal Way or New Jersey or the suburbs of Memphis, Tennessee. People who live here can search all day and never find anything that can be called downtown. And after fifty years or however long we've been here, we hardly even know the neighbors. They've come and gone but mostly just stayed in place like hermits. Like us. We're like mimeographed, stereotypical suburbanites fitted properly into our mimeographed little houses on Royal Court, all of them and us as well.

"Let's have another of those beers."

"Except we know the Rappaports," I said, stepping over to the fridge.

"Whoopee! Let's hear it for the Rappaports." We clinked bottles and laughed, our rancor wearing off.

The Rappaports lived next door and were co-in-laws. Parker's wife was their daughter. We and the Rappaports tolerated one another for the sake of our middle-aged stuck-in-the-mud kids.

. . .

No one who lived on Royal Court had the slightest idea why it was so named. Nothing royal about it. But there it was, a cul-de-sac built in 1951 with six houses on each side of the street and around the circle at the end, half a dozen cars and trucks spilling out into the circle, more cars than people, every house built to the same floor plan: a tiny kitchen, a reasonably large living room, three small bedrooms, one bathroom and a carport; the quintessential little house made out of ticky-tacky. Every last one of them at some point had wall-to-wall shag carpeting in every room except for the bathroom and kitchen, which had black-and-white checkerboard linoleum flooring. That was the way it was when we bought the house in the 1970s for barely more than fifty-thousand dollars. The master bedroom had flower-print wallpaper, and the bathroom had striped wallpaper, orange and ... I can't remember the other color. Maybe olive green.

The first thing Marilou said when we moved in was, "We gotta get rid of this wallpaper and paint these walls white. It's gonna make me want to puke every time I look at it."

It took us almost twenty years to get around to stripping the wallpaper and painting the walls and replacing the by-then badly stained carpet with laminate flooring.

One thing we loved about the house on Royal Court was the bathroom. It was humongous, not at all like the bathrooms in other such row houses that were popping up all over the place from the end of the war to ... well, I guess they're still popping up all over the place. Ours, and I guess all the ones in our cul-de-sac, had the biggest bathtub I had ever seen. It was one of those old fashioned tubs that sat on claw feet, big enough for me and Marilou to get in together. We used to carry drinks into the bathroom—beer or wine—and climb in together facing one another and sip our drinks and bathe one another.

Also kind of nice but mundane, were the patios. Every house on Royal Court had aluminum siding and a three-foot-by-three-foot concrete-slab front stoop, and a door on the carport side that opened onto a short walkway to a concrete-slab patio. Right away I built a brick fireplace on the patio with a metal grill that could slide out for cleaning. I was boastful of my accomplishment because I had never built anything like that. In fact, I had never before built anything other than a small bookshelf. We still use that bookshelf, and I'm still quite proud of it.

The only variation between the houses was which side the carport was on. That and the color. The houses were originally painted in a variety of pastel colors: bubblegum pink (actually baby girl pink, but Marilou gave it the other moniker), baby boy blue, desert rose, and a dull yellowish color called cantaloupe that looked like sour milk diluted with orange juice. Over the years, residents repainted according to their personal taste, and a couple of residents enclosed their carports and converted them into dens or dining rooms (the original "dining nooks" were part of the living room). Converting was what we did—a faux rustic den with knotty pine paneling. We bought a new dining set for the new den, shiny aluminum legs and a red tabletop and matching aluminum chairs with red plastic seat cushions—all the rage at the time although I can't imagine why.

I hung plastic fish on the walls, a leaping marlin, a swordfish, and a silver-scaled tarpon. They were life-size and looked like real caught-and-taxidermy fish. Hung above the plastic tarpon was a fishing rod with a monofilament line playing out to a hook stuck in the fish's open mouth. "Clever, huh?" I said to Marilou. She shrugged her shoulders in answer.

There was also a fake oil painting (meaning a photograph of a painting printed on canvas) of a fly fisherman casting in a mountain stream. Not once in my life had I gone fishing, but I vowed that someday I would. I bought a fiberglass fly rod in anticipation. It collected dust in the little storeroom off the den.

I also vowed, almost forty years later, that before I passed away I would finish my novel. I had been writing and rewriting it forever, and I knew deep down in my bones it would be a best seller. Except for the times I feared I was a no-talent bum who had no right to call himself a novelist. People would take notice of me. They would say, *Good lord above, I've known Rudy Briggs practically forever, and I never suspected he was such a genius writer.* Yes they would, oh yes they would. When the novel was finished and published to rave reviews and the movie won the Best Picture Academy Award, I would at long last no longer think I was a big fat zero. Jesus! Me and Billy. I keep discovering ways in which we are alike.

Realistically, I accepted that I was never going to go fishing. In all truth, I didn't even want to. But I had no doubt I would someday finish the novel. When I expressed my doubts about the novel, not about fishing, Marilou reminded me that dear big brother Billy had such doubts about almost everything, and thank God I didn't take it out on friends and relatives the way Billy did.

...

"Surely you can't remember that," the therapist I went to for a short time said.

"I most certainly can," I shot back, highly offended that he would question the veracity of my memory, which was probably the main reason I quit seeing him. He was a crap therapist, Freudian mostly I suppose. It was Marilou who talked me into counseling anyway; I never thought I needed it. When I was four years old, my mother gave birth to cute-as-can-be twin girls. Never ever ever were there girls so cute as my little sisters. I grew to love them to death, but not at first. At first, I was the only child, and my parents and my aunts and uncles and grandma Andrea all thought I was the most precious child in the world. But when my baby sisters came along it was suddenly like I didn't exist. I told that to the therapist, and I also told him about my feeling of being invisible. He linked the two: the sudden change from being pampered and smothered with affection by my parents for the first years of my life, then being set aside when twin sisters came along when I was four.

Until I went to school, I was seldom around other kids. Not counting the little sisters who were so wrapped up in each other that they hardly knew I was there. So I learned to play alone; to build fantasy kingdoms out of blocks and anything and everything I could find around the house, and I learned to read before I went to school.

In school, I did not know how to socialize with the other kids. Throughout first and second grades, I pretty much stayed to myself— always reading. In the third grade, I decided—maybe from something I had seen on television and maybe from something I read—that the way to be liked by the other kids was to be the class clown. I tried my dead-level best, but my clowning was ineffectual and went unnoticed by the other kids. They just thought I was weird.

I seldom paid attention in class, except when my tenth grade English class studied *Macbeth* (I liked the witches) and when everyone was assigned to choose a poem, memorize it, and recite it out loud. My choice was "The Raven," the only poem I ever memorized. Unless you count "Now I lay me down to sleep, I pray the lord my soul to keep." I loved *The Raven,* but what I loved more than any poetry was mystery and detective novels.

I was an avid reader. My absolute favorite in my youth was a writer of detective novels whose name I can't even recall now. All his books were about the same urbane detective whose name I also can't remember. All I remember is that the detective was Ratpack cool like a combination of Dean Martin, Peter Lawford and James Bond. Women fell for him. He had a Zippo cigarette lighter he loved to flick open and fire up. He smoked a lot; so did I during my high school and college years. I remember that there was a scene in one of the books at an outdoor restaurant in the shade of a ginkgo biloba tree in Hawaii and that in at least one of the books firing up the trusty Zippo was a lifesaver. (I can't recall how it was a lifesaver. Perhaps he threw the flaming lighter at the bad guy to distract him while he dashed in and snatched his gun out of his hand.)

...

When I was in high school, the fictional worlds of Holden Caulfield and the Joad family and the brothers in *East of Eden* became the only worlds in which I felt at home. It was no longer detective stories I escaped into. I soon got bored with them; they were all too much alike. I fell in love with Hemingway and Steinbeck and Philip Roth and Joseph Heller.

I went back to college when I was twenty-five. I tried to make friends, but the art of socializing was still a mystery to me. I had no real friends and still felt I was invisible.

After college, I went to work for the Department of Transportation which was where I ran into Marilou Johnson once again. She had been working part-time as a clerk for her grandfather at Bobo's Hardware but quit that to get a different job. "Too damn much family chaos at Bobo's," she grumbled when telling me about it. "It was like we were the damn mafia," was the way she put it, "And I didn't want to be a part of that."

Marilou appreciated my love of literature, and we could talk about books and plays and movies and current affairs. She went to college while holding down the job at Bobo's Hardware. She majored in English. Then she got a part-time job in a bookstore and later a job with the state in the same department I worked in. Somewhere in there, between college and the bookstore and working for the state, we got married—and I became invisible all over again, lost among all the descendants of the pirate Pegleg Josiah Johnson.

...

Just as the houses on Royal Court were essentially the same, so were the people who lived in them. Most worked in dull office jobs and their family incomes slowly climbed from slightly more than minimum wage to around $70,000 in the late years of their working lives. Like me and Marilou, most of them had lived there for decades and had seen their children grow up and move out and come back to visit at Thanksgiving and Christmas, or in some instances come back to stay indefinitely with their spouses and children when they couldn't afford a place of their own. That was our son Parker and his wife and son.

There was no social life for us on Royal Court, although Marilou was neighborly with some of the wives. I knew only a handful of the neighbors well enough to nod and say hello, and didn't know the others at all, even though some of us had been neighbors for decades. There were the Rappaports next door, Adrian and Brenda and their daughter Delia, who was about the same age as our son Parker. For the longest time, I could not remember the nextdoor neighbors' names. Rappaport. What a high-falutin' sounding name. Brenda and Adrian Rappaport. Sounds like they thought of themselves as the Asters or Rockefellers or Jay Gatsby stuck in the suburbs. Huh! I didn't even know them well enough to know what either of them did for a living until well after they became Parker's in-laws. Yeah, that's right, their daughter Delia married our son Parker, and they now live with us. The kids, not her parents. Ye gods and little fishes.

In the circle at the end of the cul-de-sac lived an elementary school teacher who always nodded and sometimes waved when she saw us. Neither of us could recall how we knew the woman was a teacher. She was gorgeous. "That woman in the blue house is a schoolteacher, right? Her name is Marilyn or Marianne or something like that. And the big guy with the riding lawnmower? Oh, it's right on the tip of my tongue. I don't think any of them know us. We should introduce ourselves. I think the schoolteacher would be fun to get to know."

"I know them, Rudy, and I'm pretty sure you've been introduced to them. You forgot. Or you weren't paying attention," Marilou said with a wink.

The schoolteacher's name was Sheila, not Marilyn or Marianne. She was petite and wore glasses.

There was also Allen George and his wife, Grace. Marilou called Grace a nervous little bunny rabbit. Allen was big and boisterous, an outdoorsman and a big football fan. U-Dub Huskies frippery all over, probably had husky tattoos on his ass. My name for him, just between me and Marilou, was Macho Man. He drove a Jeep and was a fly fisherman. I knew he was a fly fisherman only because I saw him loading his gear in the jeep. I assumed that if I told Macho Man I was writing a novel he'd think I was some kind of nerd. And he'd be right as rain and okay by me.

Allen and Grace were nasty people. They never spoke to anyone. When I waved at them—just trying to be neighborly—they gave me withering looks. Their house was right across the street from ours. While sitting on our couch watching the six o'clock news, we often glanced out the window to watch Macho Man driving home from work or wherever. He'd swing the Jeep into his driveway and out onto the grass so fast it was a miracle he didn't murder the matched Labradors his wife walked every day at about that time. I tried putting them in my novel, but it didn't work.

...

In the backyard of each Royal Court house stood two large oak trees evenly spaced in a line across the ten lawns to create a leaf-canopied pathway that ran straight west past four houses, made the circle at the end and straight back to about where to about where it started. Everyone called it the promenade. Kids used the promenade as a football field and racetrack. Out front, they biked and skateboarded and played basketball in the street. In spring and summer, the adults cordially greeted one another while tending their gardens and relaxing on their patios. Most were friendly but not friends, so Marilou and I fit right in.

...

On the rare occasions when relatives on the Johnson side of the family got together, they spoke to me perfunctorily at best. Courteous. Kind. But I was still basically an invisible man. At the annual retreats on Orcas Island, I often found myself standing alone staring out across the Strait of Juan de Fuca like the way I sometimes stood in my cubical at work watching my wife across the sea of office drones, or the way I sometimes gazed across the bay on my walks along the boardwalk at Percival Landing and dreamed up stories about the people who lived in the houses across the water.

I once told Marilou, "I feel like I could walk out of the house bare-ass naked and stroll the length of the promenade and nobody would notice."

"Still dreaming your exhibitionist dreams, huh," she teased. "Just like back in school with that nudie pamphlet." Laughing, she added, "I dare you to try it."

"You're kidding, right?"

"Yeah. But maybe you should have one of the characters in your novel do it."

"Ha! Yeah." From living with her almost my entire adult life, I knew she was only partway kidding. There was a wild streak in Marilou that surfaced unexpectedly and often, sometimes to my chagrin and sometimes to my delight.

With a more sympathetic tone, she followed up with, "People see you, honey. I know that's not what you think. You are much admired. Billy and Renae have both talked about how nice you are and how level-headed. Renae said you were the most stable character in the family. Even Bryce has said you're clearheaded."

Stable and *level-headed* and *nice* were not attributes I wanted to be known for. In my heart of hearts, I longed to be considered dashing, daring, a genius, the life of all parties. I thought maybe I should take Marilou's absurd challenge and stroll the promenade in my birthday suit. Let old Macho Man and the schoolteacher and the freakin' Rappaports get an eyeful. Poor old Brenda Rappaport would think it was the end of the world. The Rapture. *Take me home, Jesus.*

I wished I had the nerve to do something, not that, but something equally audacious. Like the character in the Henry James story, I dreaded the "Beast in the Jungle."

What I really wanted was to be admired as a world-famous novelist. I had been keeping my work on the novel secret from everybody but Marilou, wanting to surprise everyone when it was finally published to great fanfare. I didn't even tell Marilou my fantasies about crowds coming to my book signings at Elliott Bay and Powell's, about being interviewed by Oprah, about Warner Brothers or Paramount buying the movie rights and George Clooney and Julianna Margulies playing the characters who were based on Marilou and me.

...

Parker and Delia and their rambunctious four-year-old son, Randolph—everyone called him Baby Randolph—had lived with us for the past three years while Parker went through the motions of looking for a job. Poor Parker. Marilou always spoke of him that way, as if Poor were his first name. Poor Parker could not find a decent job no matter how hard he tried. It was not because he wasn't smart enough or willing to work hard enough. At least that was Marilou's take on it. I was more inclined to think Parker was a freeloader sponging off us.

I was convinced that when Parker claimed to have been out looking for a job he was at the movies or the bowling alley or a bar. During the time Parker and Delia lived with us, he had managed to land a few jobs. I'll give him credit for that. But they were all short-lived—working at Office Depot and clerking in a bookstore that went out of business, and one disastrous evening walking door-to-door disturbing families at dinnertime trying to sell encyclopedias. Then he got a job he actually liked, working as a warehouseman for a kitchen supply company. He thought that job was going to turn into a career. He thought he was going to work his way up in the company. After three months, he got a raise. Confident at last and with money in the bank for a change, Parker and Delia rented a small apartment on Fourth Avenue near downtown and moved out of our Royal Court home. Whoopee! But then the kitchen supply company went broke, and they had to move back in with us. In desperation, he begged his uncle Billy for a job, and Billy gave him a shot at selling cars, but that didn't work out either. It took little time working at the car lot for Billy and Parker to be reminded that they didn't like each other. Plus, in his three weeks at Bobo Ford, he sold zero cars. He sank into a terrible depression and gave up looking for work.

Parker and Delia were not without guilt over sponging off us. Delia tried to help out by bartending at The Homestead, a downtown bar and grill. She chipped in the bulk of what she made in tips to help with family expenses.

They slept in the little back bedroom across the hall from our bedroom. It was the same room that had been Parker's growing up. Some of his old rock posters were still on the wall. They installed a little cot for Baby Randolph at the foot of their bed.

...

Back when Parker was a teenager, he often climbed in and out of his bedroom window at night. The window opened onto the patio—the patio that was practically wedded to the Rappaport's patio next door. Only a three-foot strip of grass separated the two. On a hot August night twenty-three years before Parker parted ways with Bobo Ford, seventeen-year-old Delia Rappaport climbed out her bedroom window and tiptoed across the adjoining patios barefooted and wearing shortie pajamas, and Parker opened his window and helped her crawl through and onto his bed where they made love quietly and without the use of a condom and conceived baby Marianne Briggs, who twenty years later moved into a studio apartment on the Westside near the co-op with her girlfriend Wanda.

From Marianne and Wanda's house to our house on Royal Court is a mere fifteen-minute drive. Nevertheless, Marianne rarely visits. Marilou says she suspects that Marianne thinks family members are ashamed of her because she's living with her lesbian partner. But that has never bothered any of us that I know of. We're not like that. None of us. But then what do I know? I married into the Johnson family, and I've never fully felt like I belonged either.

Parenthetically, Billy once told me we needed to tell Marianne we loved her for who she was and assure her that being gay was perfectly all right with us. I said, "She knows that. We don't need to tell her."

He gave me what-for about that, and for once, Billy was right. He said, "She needs to hear it from you."

Marilou and I were surprised that Billy even cared. In fact, we thought that Billy, of all the Johnsons, would be the one least likely to accept a gay child in the family. (Of course, there was Helen, but she was adopted and raised by Bryce, so whaddaya expect.)

Marilou vowed she would talk to Marianne about it and said we should talk to her together—to both of them, Marianne and Wanda, but the right time to do it never seemed to come around. How could we talk to them about that when we never talked to them about anything?

. . .

It was the morning of island resort day. I rolled onto my side and cupped Marilou's shoulder in my palm and gently rocked her.

"Wake up, honey. It's seven o'clock."

Marilou slung the sheet and bedspread off her body and swung her legs off the bed. "Oh my god, oh my god. Why'd you let me sleep so late?"

After scrambling out of bed like a startled spider she rushed barefoot to the closet muttering, "What am going to wear? My new blue shorts? Should I take a dress? What about a ... of course, a bathing suit. How silly of me not to think of a bathing suit. And a nice dress in case we decide to go out for dinner."

The closet was double-wide with sliding mirror doors. She slung open one side and then the other. I was shuffling to the bathroom to shave. I said, "Calm down, Marilou. There's no huge rush. I'll make coffee."

She joined me in the kitchen. "Are these OK?" she asked, referring to the khaki shorts she had stepped into. I was also wearing khaki shorts. And a T-shirt with a picture of Ernest Hemingway. I poured coffee for both of us. She was so excited she reached for the coffee and dropped it. Cup shattered; coffee splattered.

I said, "Jesus, take it easy," and we grabbed paper towels and cleaned up the mess, me stifling laughter and she holding back tears for a moment and then laughing as uproariously as me.

Marilou always panicked before any big occasion, even if it was an occasion like going to the island which we had done every summer since our first summer as a couple.

Across the hall, Parker and Delia were naked, lying languorously on top of the sheets, his cheek on her breast, she rubbing his back. He slid his face lower down and kissed her near her navel.

"Uuum, I like what you're doing," she said.

"I'm just getting started," he said. And then Marilou rapped loudly on their bedroom door and shouted, "Up an at 'em, you guys. We gotta get a move on. We need to leave in a little more than an hour to catch the ferry."

Delia pulled the sheet up over her breasts as if modesty were called for. As if Marilou would open the door and barge in without asking, "Are you decent?" She had been respectful of their privacy that way since bursting in on them in one of the first few days they were living with us. Parker said, "There are later ferries, you know. If we miss one, we'll catch the next one. No biggie."

"Yeah, 'cept we want to get there before nightfall."

Parker turned away from Delia and swung his feet off the bed. But she was not ready to let him get away. She reached around him and grasped him amorously and whispered, "You're not getting away that easily," and he whispered right back, "Whatever you say, my dear."

As it turned out, we didn't leave until much later.

COMING OUT

"Do you remember when you came out to me?" Lizzy asked.

Buddy said, "Where did that come from? That was more than fifty years ago. And it wasn't exactly coming out. It was ..."

"Close enough"

"Well I wasn't queer then, and I'm not now, and I don't think I'd be ashamed if I was. It was something I worried about at the time but for no reason. None whatsoever." Buddy was always astounded but knew he shouldn't be when she dragged long-lost memories out of the vault of her mind. Especially one like that one. There should be triggers, something said or seen or done that logically stimulated a memory, some kind of order to things. But with Lizzy there seldom was. One minute it wasn't there and then—blam! There it was, spit right out of her mouth.

They were eating a late lunch at Homeplace, the little café they thought of as their place. They liked it because it was comfortable, unpretentious, and close to home. Lizzy chuckled when saying, around a bite of burger, "You were so scared you could barely speak. Like it was some kind of big deal."

"It was a big deal," Buddy rejoined. "At least it sure as shootin' seemed like it back then. Couples got divorced over shit like that. Still do, but especially back then. Besides ..." He took a big bite of his fish sandwich and chewed slowly and let that *besides* simmer slowly, and then said, "I didn't come out. I just said I was afraid I might be. But I'm not. Not then, not now, not ever. Why in the world are you bringing it up now anyway?"

"And why are you getting so defensive?" An uneasy quiet between them and then, "Just crossed my mind. But by-the-way, you most certainly did say you were, not that you might be."

"Did not."

"Yes you did."

145

"Well, I didn't say what I meant." His irritation was starting to show.

It had first come up way back in '63 or '64, only a week or so after they moved into the farmhouse. They had just finished stripping the wallpaper in the bedroom down to the hardwood and had moved into the front room to sit together on the new-to-them loveseat they had picked up in a yard sale, the same loveseat, twice reupholstered, that's still there some fifty-odd years later. They made 'em well back then, not so much now. Buddy poured himself a beer, and she got a soda from the fridge and poured it into a pint glass. He said, "Honey, there's something I need to talk to you about."

"OK. But you can't ask for a divorce. We're not married yet."

"No. But seriously, it's uh, some ... uh, something about me you need to know."

He took a long swallow of his beer. She said, "Well, what is it? Are you a CIA agent or married to another woman or what?"

"Or what. Naw, nothing like that. It's ... oh, never mind. It's not important."

She said, "Come on. Don't do me like that."

"No, really, it doesn't matter."

It took her a long time to get him to open up with, "The thing is, I'm ACDC."

She asked him what that meant. He said, "You know. It's like ACDC ..."

"Uh, huh. I repeat: what does that mean?"

"Oh, uh you don't know what that means? It's alternating current and direct current. You know, electricity. Meaning I can go either way. Girls or boys. I can, I have. But not anymore because I'm with you now."

"You mean bisexual?"

"Uh-huh."

"Well, if you ever do ..."

"I won't."

"But if you do, let me know."

"I won't. It was like a phase or something. Curiosity. Curiosity satisfied."

"Just once?"

"Uh huh. Just once."

They were both surprised at themselves for talking about it so casually. As if—once he pushed through his initial fear—it was no more earth-shattering than, say, admitting he didn't like ice cream, which he didn't. She asked, "How was it?"

"How was what?" He was thinking about not liking ice cream.

"Doing it, whatever it was you did, I don't want details—with another guy."

"Oh that. It was all right. I mean, yeah, I enjoyed it. But it's not something I think I'll ever want to do again. And for god's sake don't ask for details."

"You don't ever imagine it? I mean fantasize about doing it again. Surely you must."

He took another big swig of his beer. Looked like he might finish the whole pint in three or four hefty gulps. She rolled a joint and lit it. They passed it back and forth. He said, "Yeah, sometimes I fantasize, but idly. It's not like imagining it gets me all excited."

"Then why do you think about it if it doesn't turn you on?"

"I don't know. It's just something I ..."

He didn't know the answer. He handed her the joint and she took a big hit and after letting it out said, "Well if you ever feel the urge, just know that I can accept it. We can work it out."

He stood up, said, "Gimme another hit," said, "What do you mean work it out?"

She shrugged her shoulders. He took a couple of steps toward the kitchen, then turned back and took the joint again and took another hit, held it in for a long time and let it out slowly. He said, "There's nothing to work out."

She said, "There's nothing to be ashamed of either. It's perfectly natural."

He said he knew it was natural and he wasn't ashamed of having tried it that one time, but, "Like I said, there's nothing to work out."

The theatrical pause that followed was long and uncomfortable for her while he cast a wicked grin her way, followed by a non sequitur, "If it's not fixed, don't break it."

Squeezing her features into a quizzical look and then chuckling, she said, "That reminded me of backwards talk."

"Didn't it if dammed," he replied.

BILLY AND BELLE PICKED UP LARRY

Heading out the door, Billy grabbed his MAGA cap and slapped it on his head.

"You're not going to wear that," Belle said.

He said, "I gotta wear something." He never went outside without a hat. Now that he had lost nearly all of his hair but for a few brave wisps, his head blistered easily in the summer and froze in the winter, and he did not like getting his glasses wet in the rain. Or his bald pate. A hat was sufficient to protect his glasses from the sun and rain unless the wind was whipping around like a loose firehose.

"You got at least ten other hats," she said. "You don't have to wear that one."

"These days it's my favorite."

"Oh god, don't I know it."

He smiled at that. She said, "Anything but that, please. You're just trying to be provocative. You don't have to advocate for your boy Donny every time you leave the house."

"I'm sorry you feel that way," he said, "but you're not going to tell me what to wear."

She said he was being defensive and antagonistic. "What am I going to do with you?"

He ignored that and strode to the car. Belle hesitated, was tempted to say *you can just go by yourself*, then hurried out to get in the car. After six decades tolerating her often-infuriating husband, she wasn't about to let it all die because of his damn politics.

She had dressed that morning in a brand-new outfit she thought made her look younger. Billy, in fact, had said it made her look ten years younger. Modeling it for him when stepping out of the dressing room the day before had prompted him to pat her rear in a way he hadn't in ages, much to the tittering amusement of the sales ladies at Neiman Marcus. Her pants were some kind of soft fabric, black, printed with clusters of flowers, and with deep pockets. topped with a sleeveless white shirt with a scoop neck, the same outfit she was wearing when they got to the ferry terminal. I saw it, and I liked it. Belle was a good-looking woman with a flair for fashion that even Billy admired and applauded.

By way of contrast, Billy was wearing old blue jeans and the same Hawaiian print shirt he had worn to the last two island gatherings. Their shopping excursion for the trip had netted Belle's pants and the top plus another pair of pants and a pair of pink shorts, two other tops and a one-piece swimsuit printed with an image of flowing seaweed. Her wardrobe for the weekend on Orcas Island was all top-of-the-line, flattering, and suitably casual for the occasion.

She hadn't needed Billy to take her shopping, but he liked doing it. He liked watching her exit the changing booth in a new outfit and prancing about for his inspection, turning in front of the full-view mirror. His own private fashion show.

On her good days, Belle could look in a mirror and be convinced that she looked barely out of her prime. Seventy-seven years old with silver hair, she saw herself—realistically, she was convinced—as an attractive older woman. Like Billy and Renae and all of her siblings, she had skin that was a little loose and puckery on close inspection, especially the backs of her hands, and she had that old lady floppy flesh on the underside of her arms, but her face was almost as smooth as when she was forty-five or fifty, and she had maintained the figure of a much younger woman thanks to gardening and regular exercise, and a sensible diet since her millennial resolution (strictly vegetarian with smart limits on carbs).

When she tried on the new swimsuit and preened in front of the mirror, turning to look over her shoulder at the shape of her butt, she felt pretty damn good about herself. And now she felt good about going to show off her young-looking old self for her nephew Larry. She was excited to be headed out to SeaTac to pick him up. She hoped the mountain would be out for him to see on their way home.

And her goddamn Donald-J.-Trump-loving husband ruined it for her just by donning a red cap with the printed legend MAKE AMERICA GREAT AGAIN.

She tried one last time as she crawled in the car. "Please, honey. Don't wear that cap. Let's leave politics aside for this weekend and just enjoy the family."

She couldn't swear to it, but she was sure that Billy was the only one in the family who had fallen for the cult-like appeal of the new president. "How could you possibly like that disgusting man?" she had asked during the campaign, and Billy had replied, "I don't like him, if you must know. Personally, I think you're right. He is disgusting. His personality is. Bragging about grabbing women by the woo-woo for god's sake and making fun of that poor disabled reporter. And ... and what was that bullshit he said about McCain, a true American hero—I prefer people who don't get caught. Shee-it. There's lots of stuff about him I don't like. But all that stuff was just him acting tough to please the rednecks."

"Like you."

"Yeah, right. Like me. See, here's the thing. He didn't mean any of that. Locker room talk, that's all it was. He's just putting on an act. And I like that. I like it 'cause we need a tough leader. But that's not why I voted for him."

"You coulda fooled me. Seems to me like you're in love with him. So what is it then that makes you wear that hat, announce your love for the man?"

"He's gonna restore the economy and bring sanity back to the government, bring about an end to the national epidemic of coddling the lazy unemployed and foreigners. That's what. He's going to keep drug dealers and other riff-raff from taking over the country."

"But Billy, he's been credibly accused of sexual harassment."

"Yeah, and so was what's-his-name, Clarence Thomas. And look at him now. He's a Supreme Court judge. And Bill Clinton for God's sake. Sexual harassment is the weapon liberals always pull out, but they never can prove it."

She couldn't understand what had happened to Billy. This wasn't like him. But then that was what establishment liberals said about the country. They said, "This isn't who we are." But to Belle's way of thinking, it was exactly who we are.

Billy and Belle had never fully agreed about politics, but he had always been willing to listen to reason up to a point. "We can agree to disagree" had been his mantra. But not anymore. It was as if someone had hypnotized him. She had thought for sure he'd ease off after the election, after Hillary won as everyone knew she would. But Hillary didn't win, and Billy wore his support of Trump like a banner.

Belle said they should change the subject. "Let's talk about Larry," she said.

"OK, sure. Larry's a good kid, even if he is a crazy artist. I just don't get his art."

"You like the painting we have."

"Sure. It's nice decoration and all, but I still don't get it."

That was the extent of what they could find to talk about on the subject of their nephew Larry.

...

They drove in strained silence the rest of the way to the airport. Larry was waiting in the pick-up zone with his backpack by his feet. Almost unrecognizable at first because he had cut off his signature long blond hair and grown a shaggy beard.

"There he is," Belle shouted.

"Jesus, he looks like Buddy."

Cursing the traffic, Billy crept into the left of two right pick-up lanes and pulled to a stop but did not get out to greet his nephew. He left the engine idling as Belle got out. All around them people were hugging and kissing loved ones and slinging suitcases and backpacks and honking and leaning out of windows trying to get into and out of parking spots. Belle gave Larry a huge hug. "Hi, Auntie Belle," he said. He opened the back door, tossed his backpack in, and hopped in himself. He said, "Hey, Uncle Billy."

Billy said, "Hi, kid. That's some mountain man beard. It looks like the hair on your head tried to get away but got caught on your chin."

"Yeah. I guess it didn't get far. D'you like it?"

"I do. Makes you look more rugged, not so much a pretty boy," Billy said as he squeezed the BMW between two other cars and headed into the southbound traffic on I-5.

Larry did not notice Billy's hat at first, but then saw it reflected in the rearview mirror: MAKE AMERICA GREAT AGAIN. He didn't say anything about it. Instead, he talked to Belle. "You're looking beautiful, Auntie."

"Well, you're a flatterer."

"No, you really are."

Larry was a flatterer and a flirter. Always had been. Belle knew it and loved it.

All the way back to Olympia Belle and Larry chatted. She filled him in on everything that had been happening with everyone in the family and asked him all about his life in New York. He talked about the gallery and about trying to find a new look to his paintings and about his girlfriend. "I wish she could have come with me. I know you'd like her. She's sharp as a knife blade and funny and quite the beauty."

It's all about beauty with him, Belle thought, chuckling inwardly. *His girlfriends are always sexpots, and they never last long.*

And he talked about his podcast. Billy jumped in now and again with friendly comments.

"Oh my god, the mountain's out," Larry gushed like a tourist from Kansas or Missouri who had never seen a mountain. He grabbed his cell phone and snapped pictures.

"It's not like you've never seen it before," Belle said.

"Yeah, but I want to show Arnie and Jodi. They've never been outside the city. Arnie says everything east of the Hudson is New Jersey."

They talked about his friends in New York and the fickleness of the art market and about Liz and Marilou and Bryce and his brother Parker. "Are they still living with you?"

"Yep. Parker and Delia and Baby Randolph."

He wanted to ask Billy if he knew MAGA caps were made in China but didn't because he didn't trust his own source on that and didn't want to take a chance on starting an argument, at least not yet.

THE DRIVE FROM PULLMAN

Emma woke Bryce before five o'clock in the morning, gently shaking him by his shoulder and saying, "Wake up sleepyhead. We've got a long way to go and a short time to get there."

Turning toward her and pulling her down for a chaste good-morning kiss, he mumbled, "We have, not we've got. Got is an ugly, guttural word that shouldn't be uttered before first coffee."

She ran her fingers spiderlike through the hair on his chest. She said, "You don't *got* to correct my speech." She kissed his chest, ran her tongue around a nipple for a moment, and then rolled out of bed and said, "Come on, let's get a move on."

An hour later, dressed and bags loaded, coffee-filled travel mugs in hand, they were in the car headed for Shoreline where they were to visit with big sister Renae and nephew Asher and his family before driving up to Anacortes for the ferry to Orcas. They talked about family—his family, her family, Lizzy's surprise seventieth birthday party (which neither of them could tell if she liked or not)—the time when pre-teen Larry before his voice changed did an impersonation of Bette Midler, the arguments they had with Billy about the Clinton-Bush campaign and what they had heard about Billy now being a rabid Trumpster, discussions about whether or not Marilou was the boss in our family. (Emma told me that. She said, "Yeah, Marilou's the boss in that family." Bryce said it seemed that way because I simply did not give a damn, because I was too wrapped up in my private thoughts about whatever it was that occupied my mind. He kind of hit that nail squarely on the head.)

So seldom did Emma and Bryce get opportunities to chat like old friends catching up that they reveled in the talk as Bryce drove through the little towns of Lacrosse and Washtucna, home to barely more than two-hundred people, and across Moses Lake to Bryce's favorite little town, Othello. Along about there they ran out of things to talk about. Emma laid her head back and fell asleep. Thoughts of beating the crap out of a detested colleague in the Washington State History Department invaded Bryce's mind. How could he entertain such thoughts? He fancied himself a Gandhian pacifist, yet entertaining such violent thoughts didn't disturb him in the least. He could joyfully dream up violent scenarios punch by punch and kick by kick. His fantasies had nothing to do with what he was really like. Or so he insisted and believed.

"What?" Emma mumbled, coming out of sleep.

"Nothing. Was I talking out loud? I was just thinking about my dear brother Billy. It's nothing. What say we stop in Ellensburg for a bit of brunch?"

CHICKEN PLUCKING

"Where is the lithe body and lustrous hair of youth? I could have taken more care of my appearance, of my health for god's sake. Screw it. Who gives a good goddamn? I sure as hell don't." Lizzy, never one to soften her speech, said that out loud to her mirror at five o'clock on the morning all her siblings were going to the island. She stepped into and pulled up her old chinos and pulled a black T-shirt over her head and down across the braless breasts that drooped way lower than they once had. "Remember that?" she asked the mirror and stuck her tongue out at her reflection. "Remember when I had perky little tits?"

Moments after telling her reflected image she didn't give a damn about her appearance, she told herself, *I'm going to start exercising, get myself back in shape. I might even start dancing again. Ha! I could have been one of the best. I could have glided down a circular stairway with Gene Kelly. I can still do it. You better believe I can. Just have to get myself back in shape. But when can I ever find the time? Never, never, never.*

The thought of gliding down a stairway reminded her of the mother-daughter dance scene in that movie based on Bob Fosse's life, and she momentarily thought how wonderful it would be to dance with a teenage daughter.

Lizzy slipped on her shoes and pushed open the screen door and trudged across the back acre on the wet grass, rocks and twigs digging into the bottoms of her thin-soled shoes. "Shoulda put my damn boots on," she mumbled out loud to the clouds and the morning mist, to the chickens and the goats and the one fat white pig that had free range of the property. She sloshed through the slick grass and islands of mud. She walked hunched forward with drooping shoulders. Her dry and scraggly hair hung straight and was the color of weathered wood in the morning haze. Her teeth were tobacco-stained; two were visibly missing. Murmuring a cloud of complaints as she headed toward the chicken coop intent on murder. *Damnable rain-soaked ground. Damn stinking ankle pecking no good chickens. Why do I keep doing this day after day after day?*

A cigarette dangled from her lip like a long-broken tooth hanging by a thread of a root—a tightly rolled smoke of American Spirit tobacco in Zig-Zag paper like the joints she and Buddy shared in the 1970s—the hippie days she had long since outgrown and he still missed. She constantly told him he should quit smoking weed, and he constantly warned her about smoking cigarettes; the reek of both permeated their plush but deeply worn chairs and the old loveseat and the throw rugs scattered about their house.

Her back hurt from too much bending and from sleeping on a sagging mattress. She thought it would be so nice to sleep in a soft bed in an air-controlled room—a hotel room, perhaps, not some low-class motel either, but something high-falutin' like in midtown Manhattan or maybe the one in Victoria where she and Buddy once spent a romantic weekend oh so long ago, where a lady in a server's uniform brought breakfast on a tray. Or hell, if I'm going to fantasize luxury, howzabout dreaming up our own multi-million-dollar goddamn mansion where a servant draws our bath and changes the linens while we bathe in the steaming water. In her most delicious fantasies, that servant drawing her bath would look like a young Sean Connery who, simultaneously in her fantasy, would be Buddy in his youth. (Buddy in his youth had been quite the catch.) In this scenario spun enroute to the chicken coop, Buddy (or the Sean Connery looking servant) would watch appreciatively as she shucked off her robe and let it fall around her ankles, and he would test the water temperature with his elbow like he was preparing the bath for a baby, and he would help her step gingerly into the huge gleaming white tub where he'd scrub her back and across her breasts and her stomach, and after helping her out of the tub he would dry her body with a large, soft towel, and he would quietly slip away so she and Buddy could make love on their king size bed. *The tub is in the same room with our bed? Yeah, why not.*

If she couldn't have that fantasy life for at least a day and a night, she thought it would be so nice at the very least to sleep until it was no longer dark and not have any squawking, crowing, barking, grunting animals welcome her to each new day. "That would do quite nicely," she said out loud to the animals who squawked, crowed, barked, and grunted right back at her.

Their dogs, two mixed-breed mutts they had never bothered to name, and a stray cat that had made a home of their farm, gathered around her, the cat getting underfoot as usual. She slung open the rickety door to the chicken coop, spit her cigarette out, coughed fitfully as half a hundred hens all in chorus started loudly clucking and gathering around her feet like rock fans clamoring to touch their favorite singer. *Noisy, pestering, Flippin' chickens.* She reached into he bag strapped to her shoulder, scattered feed on the ground, and then gathered eggs. Then she grabbed one fat hen and headed back outside dangling the bird by its bony neck. It was a quarter till six. The air was wet, and a ghostly sun hovered behind solid fog. The thought crossed her mind that her big sister Renae and her wife were probably already in town. They probably spent the night with Helen and Eva in Olympia and just might take a notion to come out and try to convince her to go to the island with them. Renae was like that.

As a child, Lizzy had idolized Renae, whom she thought of as a second mom as much as a sister, because when you're young a six-year age gap is humongous. Renae taught Lizzy how to dance and how to draw, and soon Lizzy became much better at both than Renae ever was. Renae praised her for being such a natural talent.

She would love to see Renae and Sally, and maybe even Helen and Eva. But company would interrupt her routines and keep her from ... what? The sad truth was, she had nothing to do that visitors dropping in would keep her from. Killing and plucking and cooking the damn chicken and folding laundry and watching her silly soap operas on TV—planting and harvesting and canning in the proper seasons and cooking and washing dishes by hand every day—those were the only things she ever had to do. Nothing that couldn't be put off an hour or two to visit with her family.

Please Lord, don't let 'em come out here. I love 'em and all, but I'm just not up to seeing 'em today. And I sure as shootin' don't want to have to deal with Helen or Renae insisting on me and Buddy joining 'em at that Peter Puget Resort, which I'm damn well sure they will. She was luxuriating in her misery. She didn't want her lovely wallowing interrupted.

If Eva showed up, she would try to relate to her by mentioning something about farming as if the little farm Eva and Helen lived on was the same as hers and Buddy's. No more than a half-hour drive away, it was what Lizzy called a Saturday farm, not exactly a working farm in her estimation. They called it Sappho Farm. Had a damn Sappho Farm sign on the road out by the cattle guard. Granted, they did some real farm chores. Helen milked a couple of goats and got enough milk from them to sell a little to neighbors. They had no more than a dozen laying hens, and they sold some of the eggs and a few vegetables, and they called that a farm. *Ha! Let 'em raise a couple hundred chickens and grow as many vegetables as Buddy and I grow. Then they can call themselves farmers.*

At least one of them, Eva, had a regular job outside the farm. She was a schoolteacher. Helen also, from time to time, had non-farming jobs, but at the moment, she could not think of what it was Helen did.

Near the pig pen she stopped and, still holding the hen by her neck, swung her round and round like a rodeo cowgirl with a lariat, and the chicken's neck snapped with a splatter, and blood spouted dark red from its neck hole while the headless bird ran in a bloody circle until it expired, the dogs running around after it, barking excitedly.

"You gonna be fine fried up crisp and served with mashed potatoes and collards and cornbread," she said to the plump fowl body. She picked it up by its legs and carried it into the house still dripping, making a mental note that she'd have to wipe the blood and mud up from the floor before it dried.

...

The house was square with wood siding that had been painted and repainted, now pale yellow with dulled previous coats of paint showing through. Inside there was one large bedroom and one smaller bedroom that was used mostly for Lizzy's hobbies, which she cycled through on a roughly bi-annual schedule. Drawing and painting for a few months—she still had it, she was proud to say—and then collecting dolls, followed by quilting. Her current obsession was scrapbooking—cutting and pasting pictures and words. Nothing she did in that room satisfied her for very long.

The large open and airy front room was a combination living and dining room with a large dinner table and ladderback chairs. There were two easy chairs, one plaid and one striped, and their old brown loveseat. The dining and living areas were separated by an island counter with pots and pans hanging above. A black cast-iron skillet rested on the stovetop as usual.

Lizzy brought water to a boil in her biggest pot and lowered the dead bird in. She poured herself a cup of coffee and thought about Buddy while drinking it—not Buddy as he was in the next room half asleep, scratching his still muscular body, but Buddy when he was young and sexy—when his body was rock hard, when his belly was flat and ripped. He had a shock of black hair that constantly fell across one eye back then. She thought about Buddy when she could not keep her hands off him. Man oh man, were they ever a hot couple, he six feet tall with high cheekbones and ebony hair, eyes that were like black laser beams, she a mere two inches shorter with flowing hair almost as dark as his, a long neck that could have been painted by Modigliani, a figure to make men pant like winded dogs. Yes, even in 2017, at seventy-three, she still had a youngish figure, but her skin was loose and there were dark circles around her eyes. And the veins in her hands were big and purplish. All-in-all she looked a lot like Marilou. Oh so long ago she had been a dancer. She had moved like a stalking panther. Now she walked like an old lady, and it hurt. Hurt everywhere, all the time. Getting up out of bed or out of a chair hurt. Walking to the henhouse or out to the road to check the mail hurt. Everything hurt. Bending over? Oh god! Better to let dropped things stay where they lay until Buddy could pick them up.

She thought about Buddy's cock, and a sly smile came to her lips. She told herself she was too old to be thinking about that, and it was too damn early in the morning, but she loved it nevertheless. Picturing buddy naked and horny made her happy. Not much made her happy or horny anymore, so why not enjoy recalling Buddy's cock when it was erect? Lizzy liked to hold it two-fisted and squeeze it as she bent to it and put her lips around the tip. She loved the taste and the feel of it. Sometimes when they were making love, she used to wrap her legs around him and put her feet on his back high up near his shoulders. Sometimes they'd get so rambunctious they'd throw themselves right off the bed and keep doing it on the hardwood floor. Good lord above, they fornicated with the abandon of feral cats.

That was so, so long ago. He was a cop back then. Retired now for almost ten years—could it really be that long? She wondered if the reason he had rarely been able to get it up over the past year or more could be long-delayed post-traumatic stress. God knows being a cop was stressful enough. The things he had to put up with—the almost constant fear he had to push out of his mind. Her daily fear that he might come home mangled—or not come home at all. Surely he had feared those things too.

Domestic abuse was the worst. He said he never knew when going to a domestic call if the husband was going to turn on him. Or the wife maybe, or both. Cops get badly hurt trying to break up husband-and-wife fights. Another thing that could be scary and infuriating was dealing with smartass destructive teenagers, the kind that tear things up for the hell of it. Lord, what must their parents be like, these kids that run their cars through muddy lawns just to dig circular tracks in the ground, or who speed through town hitting mailboxes with baseball bats, or who tied firecrackers to cats' tails?

He told Lizzy they were lucky not to have children, but sometimes he said it might have been nice to have had a sweet little girl. If they had a daughter she would have gifted them with grandchildren by now. Buddy could picture a granddaughter on his lap while he read to her. But since the miscarriages and Buddy's vasectomy they tried not to think about a child.

Lizzy wondered about why they so seldom had sex. Maybe it was because of the drugs they did when they were young, a delayed reaction. Or did he simply not want her anymore? There had been a time when she couldn't get naked in the same room with him without him fondling her boobs or grabbing her butt. Now, if he looked at her when she stepped out of her clothes it was a look cast with no more passion than if he happened to glance at a coffee mug left on the bedside table. She, on the other hand, looked at herself plenty enough. Wondering if she had grown ugly in her old age. Nah. A little sag here, a little bulge there, but mostly not bad for an old lady. No reason her body shouldn't still turn him on. But dammit, sexual attraction should be about something more than body parts.

She sometimes wondered if he might be gay and just never admitted it to himself. Funny that they had recently talked about that. Strange that she could think about it after half a hundred years married to him. But she remembered the way he used to look at one of his biker buddies and the way they used to mock wrestle. But nah, that could not be it. The wild sexual passion of their youth would never have been if that were the case.

Buddy ambled into the kitchen. Like the Buddy in her revery, he was bare-ass naked. That thing that used to stand up so proudly dangled like a rag hanging from a wire. Thin gray hair covered his head and chest and belly. His pubic hair was gray too. His gray beard fell all the way to his sternum, a mountain man beard cultivated over the past two years. His once-hard body had grown soft, still not bad muscular definition, but nothing like in his youth.

"Where's your pants?" she asked.

"Dang if I know. I left 'em throwed across the chair, but they ain't there now."

"That's 'cause I tossed 'em in the laundry, hun. You been wearing the same britches for five days. Go get a clean pair."

"All right," he said. "Don't get your panties in a bunch. How come you're so mad all the time anyway?"

She didn't bother to respond.

She remembered Marilou saying she asked me the same thing. Did Belle ask Billy, did Renae ask Sally that same question? Maybe growing old and grumpy was a family trait. *I mean everybody grows old unless they get run over by a truck or something. I mean is it a Johnson family thing to obsess about it?*

Buddy turned to walk back into the bedroom, scratching his butt.

Lizzy thought: I'm mad all the time because life sucks, because I hurt all over, because it hurts to bend or stretch, because I can't get up out of my chair without pushing with both hands on the arms, Because I've lost half my teeth and can't afford to get 'em fixed, and I get headaches, and there's a burning in my chest and throat all the time.

Recalling their early years together made Lizzy wonder if that long-ago version of them ever truly existed.

She rolled another cigarette and lit it. Buddy shouted from the bedroom, "Today's the day everybody's going up to the island. We could still go if you want to change your mind."

"Uh uh. No way. I do not want to spend the weekend cooped up on an island with Billy and Belle and Marilou and Rudy."

"But you love them. Jesus, gal, what the fuck's wrong with you?"

She didn't respond because she didn't have an answer.

PROUD LIZZY

Eva and Helen got dressed while Lizzy reminisced about her early years with Buddy and while Renae and Sally took a short nap. "That trip down must have been a horror," Helen said as soon as they came out of the bedroom.

"Uh huh. Poor Renae."

"I'm fine now," Renae said. "Like a brand-new woman."

Eva asked when they should catch the ferry.

"When does it leave?"

"It leaves Anacortes at 12:30 and 3 and 7. Should we catch the 12:30?"

. . .

Their hastily conceived plan was to go in three cars: Johnny and June in one because they had to get back home a day before everyone else, Helen, Eva and Melony in Eva's Kia, and Renae and Sally in the Subaru because their plan was to drive home straight to Portland without stopping back at Sapho Farm.

"Are you sure you're up to driving? You hardly slept at all last night," Eva asked.

Sally assured her their brief nap in the car was sufficient. "I'm fully energized and ready to go," Sally said. "And Renae can sleep all the way if she needs to."

But first the women in Eva's Kia were going to head south on I-5 to Lizzy and Buddy's farm for a short visit before heading to Anacortes. Windows cracked open an inch or two, wind blowing their hair and cooling their faces, Sally and Renae hardly felt or remembered the exhaustion and nerves from last night's trip. Already, the day was turning off warm, but hey knew it would still be a bit chilly on the ferry.

...

Half an hour later they turned off the freeway onto the road to Lizzy's place.

Eva said, "It's still pretty early. I hope they're up."

"Are you kidding? They're farmers like us only on a bigger scale. They get up with the chickens. Lizzy's probably already brought in a basket of eggs and rung a hen's neck."

...

Two motorcycles stood in Lizzy and Buddy's front yard, one a partially disassembled Indian leaning against a tree trunk, the other a new-looking Honda. There were also two trucks, an old Ford pickup and a Dodge Ram with cardboard duct taped to one window; and there was the eight-year-old Volvo that Lizzy had bought from Bryce a few years back for practically nothing.

Sleeping dogs perked up when the cars pulled into the yard and parked in the shade of a gnarly oak with limbs that brushed against the slanted roof over the front stoop. Lizzy was in the kitchen kneading bread dough, Buddy was on the couch thumbing through the *Seattle Times*, a steaming mug of coffee on the coffee table. Buddy was the first to hear the cars pull up and doors slam shut. "I think they're here," he said. "Your sister and them."

"Shit," Lizzy said. "I knew it."

Buddy put down the paper and stepped out onto the porch, shirtless and in overalls, carrying his coffee. He didn't hear Lizzy say, "At least you put some pants on."

"Hey, y'all," Buddy shouted. "Get on in here. Damn, it's good to see ya."

A big smile from Renae at Buddy's jovial greeting and at his cultivated good-ol-boy country brogue. Hugs all around.

Lizzy came to the door. Still barefooted and still wearing the shapeless brown dress splattered and smeared with chicken blood. Opening the screen door, she stood hip-to-hip with her husband, the picture of a contented farm family. "Hey! Hey! It sure is good to see you. I'd give you all a hug 'cept I've been elbow deep in chicken guts and bread dough."

"You butchered a hen?" Eva asked.

"Yeah."

"I can never do that. I'm too queasy. Thank God Helen doesn't mind doing it."

Buddy said, "Well y'all come on in and take a load off."

Lizzy served coffee and last night's biscuits heated up in the microwave, and spread with butter and peach jam. And they talked family talk.

Soon they ran out of family talk. The only thing left was what everybody knew they had come to discuss. Yet they still managed to put it off for the next half hour. Buddy smiled at everybody but hardly said a word. He kept glancing at the spread-open newspaper, clearly wanting to resume reading it but too polite to do so while they had company. Rather than join in the conversation, he played host. "Y'all want any more coffee? Hey, how about them homemade biscuits, huh? Jam's homemade too."

When Sally said, "That sounds great," he eagerly hopped up and rushed to the kitchen and soon came back with more biscuits and coffee.

Sally sniffed the air, and her head shivered. "Sorry about that," Lizzy said. It's the chicken feathers. I boiled the hen before plucking her. Pretty nasty, I know."

"It's all right," Sally said. Buddy opened windows and the front door. Both Sally and Renae noticed the dust on every surface and ground-in dirt on door frames but figured all of that was to be expected. It was a farmhouse, after all. Lizzy and Buddy spent their days working in the dirt and tending to animals; you couldn't expect the place to be as pristine as, say, their restaurant in Portland. Renae finally made the plunge: "I really wish you'd change your mind and join us on the island. You haven't been there in ... what? Three or four years?"

Buddy said, "More like six. I'd kinda like to go but ... " and he trailed off. He had been on the verge of blaming Lizzy but thought better of it.

Renae and Sally both squirmed in the easy chairs where they had plopped down. Lizzy had moved back to the counter to resume kneading dough and spreading it out on the countertop, all the time smoking and coughing and only perfunctorily keeping up her end of the conversation. Her contribution to the talk was mostly a sweet smile and a head nod. Renae was afraid Lizzy was going to drop ashes in the bread dough. Not that it's any of my concern, she told herself. I'm not going to eat the bread. Probably ashes in these biscuits too. Nevertheless, she took a bite of biscuit and had to admit they were delicious. She said, "We really, really wish you would come. Everybody misses you."

Sally pulled her phone out of her pocket and looked to see the time. Lizzy asked, "What time is your ferry?"

"Three o'clock. It's eleven now."

"I guess you need to leave soon." Lizzy had been spinning tales about their nephew Larry as a teen and as an adult artist.

"You know he's coming?" Eva said.

"Uh huh. I'd love to see him, but ... maybe after y'all get back." She put the dough in the oven and washed her hands, saying, "It takes about three hours to get to Anacortes. Let me fix you a lunch you can eat in the car on the way, and you can get going right away."

Sally and Renae tried to protest that she needn't go to so much trouble, but before they could Buddy said, "I'm on it," and immediately hopped to getting ingredients out and started making them cheese sandwiches with lettuce and sliced tomatoes and sweet onions."

"Really, that's not ..."

"We're family," Lizzy said firmly. "That's what we do. But before you leave there's something I really must tell you. I ... I think I owe you an explanation. Kind of a confession, I guess you'd say."

Her tone grew heavy. Hesitant. She said, "I'll tell you why I can't go to the Peter Puget Resort. You'll think I'm crazy, I know. But here it is."

She stood up and paced as she talked, stepping around the kitchen counter and back into the front room, mostly not looking eye-to-eye with anyone. She said, "It was not as if it was the first time I'd ever been to Orcas Island or to the Peter Puget Resort. I remembered earlier trips even going back to when I was in school. Glowing memories, perhaps colored by my childish imagination, the hotel with its sumptuous restaurants and glorious overlooks of the sea, the lounge which was off limits to kids and from which delicious music wafted into the hallways. It was like a fairytale castle. It looked so majestic, like a grand hotel from the nineteenth century. Or like from picture books. I can still picture its long balconies and water-facing windows. The morning mist rising over the water."

She sat down, coughed almost violently. Buddy got her a glass of water, and she took a few big gulps.

"I remember the last time, no longer a child, I had forgotten what a long circuitous drive it was from the ferry to the hotel, all the way on the other end of the island.

Renae said, "You were six years old, almost seven that first time. It was the summer after first grade for you, and I was twelve. Years and years before the family started having the annual retreats. I remember being astonished just like you were at what a long drive it was, at how big the island was. It didn't seem like an island at all, but just another town near the coast with everything you'd find on the mainland—houses and businesses. Even a mountain. And then the last time it was, like Buddy said, only five or six years ago."

They enjoyed hearing Lizzy's description of the island and the resort. Eva the English teacher especially enjoyed the telling, thinking she painted word pictures as a poet might. At first. Until she got to the disturbing part.

Slipping in and out of past and present tense, Lizzy said, "I'm thinking about that last time. No longer a child. So we drive up to the resort and I know we have to check in at the main building. We drive up to the circular drive there like where a chauffeur would drive up to let people out, and I'm looking at the other surrounding buildings, which seem under construction, some of them, or renovation, I guess. Do you remember that? We go up the stairs to check in at the front desk. My first impression is it is an old gal of a resort past her heyday. Old old old. Anyway, it seemed a little fusty with some flowery carpeting and heavy furniture, but the views of the water and a neighboring island are amazing, and the architecture is interesting and, I sort of felt, opulent even."

Eva was almost mesmerized by Lizzy's telling of this experience because it was as if Lizzy were in a trance and telling about that weekend on the island as if it were her only time there when in fact she had been on what must have been at least three other retreats at Peter Puget Resort.

Lizzy said, "So they give us the key and tell us our room is in the next building and we should go park there and let ourselves in. Back outside at the car, a closer view of the building in question makes me feel funny. As we walk up the sidewalk to it, I see some of the rooms have drapes that are pulled roughly closed like there's something heavy on the other side of them and there's actually mold at the bottoms. I can see this partly through the dirty floor-to-ceiling windows. So we're walking to try to find the entrance and I'm trying to be as cheerful as possible because I do not want Billy and Belle to think I think they've landed us in a musty dirtbag hotel. But that's what it seems all of a sudden, my fairytale vision turned to the muck of reality."

Eva and the others are getting nervous.

"At the front door, I fumble with the key, and when I open the door I am overcome with this really troubling strong chemical smell. Like they'd really been working hard to kill stuff with chemicals. I was mortified. *Please let this just be the way this long dark, dirty-carpeted, bad-artworked chair-railed hallway smells*, I thought to myself. Surely the room will be fresh as a daisy.

By this point Renae and Sally were awed as kids listening to a story of hunting pirate treasure. Eva was beginning to feel like it was a horror movie. Buddy was making sandwiches with mustard, mayonnaise, two kinds of cheese, lettuce and tomatoes. "Does everybody want onions?"

Lizzy continued: "My first impression of the room is that it looks scoured or sort of chemical-burned with whatever they were using to cover up whatever stink they were covering up. Know what I mean? The carpet, bedspread, chair upholstery and drapes were washed to within an inch of their lives, and everything has that look people get after they've just gotten an aggressive haircut: They're aware of having been shorn, of how red their ears are, how you can see their scalp, how they used to have a lot less space between their eyebrows and their bangs."

Sally laughed at that but quickly clamped down her laughter, not sure whether Lizzy was trying purposefully to entertain them or seriously describing her experience. Lizzy did not notice, so thoroughly into the telling of her tale.

"So the room is sort of cringing back at me when Rudy and Marilou walk in, and I say something cheerful as we check out their adjoining room and the bathroom. Turns out we're in a sort of half-basement with the windows right at grass level, which isn't what I'd been expecting. Hard to feel grand when you're aware that you're half-underground—and this was my breaking point really—the ground-level windows were filthy. Like someone had blown grass and dirt all over 'em and then not bothered to clean 'em."

She went on and on and on about how dirty the place was and most especially about the stench, which she said almost made her puke. Renae tried to gently tell her that she and Sally had never experienced Peter Puget like that, and Lizzy said, "I know. Nobody else has, or so it seems. I told you you'd think me crazy. But I know what I saw and what I smelled, and I simply can't go back there ever again."

...

Sally had already started the Subaru and was about to back up to turn it around when Buddy rushed out and signaled for her to hold up. Through the rolled-down driver-side window he said, "I need to explain something before you take off. Can I get in?"

"Well yeah, OK, sure," Sally said, checking the time again and thinking we damn well better not miss the ferry, and Buddy climbed in the back seat and sat with feet spread, knees up and hands on the back of the front passenger seat.

He said, "I know that stuff she said sounds crazy. But what I need to explain is that it was right after ... or not very long after, her concussion."

"What concussion?"

"The concussion she had when ... I thought y'all knew this. It was all my fault. It was in the spring of that year. The last year we went to the island. We were messing around on my old Kawasaki dirt bike, doing wheelies in the yard. Acting stupid, I know. Lizzy was seated behind me, holding on with her arms around me, when I turned a little too sharp, and the grass, it was wet, so the bike skidded out from under us. I landed in the grass with the bike on its side on top of my legs. I didn't get anything but some bruises, but Lizzy was flung off the bike and she landed headfirst against that tree right over there. It knocked her out. Gave her a concussion."

"Oh my god," Eva said.

Buddy said, "After that ... well, she never did remember any of it. Riding the bike, falling off, me taking her to the emergency room. Nothing. She still can't remember it. It did something to her brain. Especially her sense of smell, but other stuff too. Smells she used to love, she all of a sudden couldn't stand, and she saw things wrong with stuff that I couldn't see. Like the mold and some of the dirt she saw in the resort. I never saw any of that, and I was right there with her. When I told her I never saw it she claimed I was trying to say she was crazy. Some construction or remodeling was going on at the resort, and yeah, the place wasn't kept up as well as it shoulda been. But it was nothing like what she described."

"We never saw anything like that either, did we, Sally?" Renae said.

"No, we didn't. I mean the place is ancient. It's not perfect, but nothing so bad as what she said. But then we didn't go that summer. Remember, it was the summer you were taking graduate courses at UW. I think it was the year they did some renovation, which might account for some of all that."

"I know," Buddy said. "And the smell. She said it made her sick. It wasn't just there either. Other smells. Like movie-house popcorn. We used to go to movies a lot, and she loved the smell of popcorn in movies. But after her concussion, it made her sick. And bacon—to this day she can't stand to even be in the same house where bacon has been fried, and she used to love it. Well no, not really to this day. She's actually got over a lot of it. The smells, seeing things as ugly or dirty that she used to think were pretty. She's recovered

171

from most of that, but she's still scared to go back to that resort. You see, that was the worst of it. That was the first place after the accident where things went kerflooey for her, and she's terrified of going back."

All of the women expressed deep sorrow but said they had no idea what they could do to help. Buddy said, "I don't think there's anything any of us can do but just give her time. There's another thing too, and I guess this is my fault as well. It's 'cause I ain't been able to support her properly, so we don't have insurance. Oh god, I feel so sorry about this. Lizzy's in bad health, really bad. You heard her coughing. It's the cigarettes. Since she rolls her own, I don't know how many packs, but I'll betcha it's more'n two a day. And she's got those missing and rotten teeth, and she's embarrassed to be seen like that."

They tried not to think Buddy had only himself to blame for all their ills but could not forget that it was Lizzy's youthful infatuation with Wendell "Buddy" Bundrock that had killed her dream of becoming a dancer, and their seclusion on that nasty farm was what made her sick.

...

Heading back to the interstate, Sally said, "I don't want to fall into the trap of thinking a man's duty is to take care of his woman. I mean that's an old-fashioned sexist notion. But I can't help but feel Buddy has fallen far short on that."

On the Road to Anacortes

Somehow on the freeway we fell in behind Renae and Sally and
Helen and Eva and followed them all the way from just north of
Olympia to the Smokey Point rest area forty-two miles short of the
ferry terminal at Anacortes. But we didn't know it was them we
were following until I had to pee and pulled off at the next
convenient rest area.

  We first spotted the little blue Kia following close behind a
late-model Subaru while driving through the flooded plains of the
Nisqually Valley, past the Billy Frank Junior Wildlife Refuge on our
left and the hazy Mt. Ranier peak seeming to floating in air on our
right. We stuck behind them past the military base and into the
southern edge of Tacoma where all three cars of our unintentional
caravan pulled off the freeway to gas up at Costco. There were so
many cars lined up in the multiple lanes you'd think they were
giving away gas, so we didn't see any of the people but only their
cars. Still didn't know we were a honking family huddle. Our three
cars finished filling up and pulled back out onto the freeway at about
the same time—past the gynormous casino on the right where a neon
sign flashed an ad for an Elvis impersonator and for Saturday night's
wrestling match, past the exit for Fife where Sally and Renae had
run into the obnoxious homo-hater, past an older and much smaller
and dingier casino of the same name as the other one. Soon we came
to a rest area where we pulled off to use the facilities. It was there
that Marilou ran into Renae outside the women's facility and we
discovered that the accidental three-car caravan was family.

  From there we continued onward past the airport and under
the convention center in Seattle and finally, we pulled off for another
rest stop miles ahead at Sandy Point where there was a giant red
cedar stump with a square tunnel cut through it. We could not resist
a rest area.

A plaque attached to the inside wall of the giant tree trunk explained that the tree had been destroyed by fire in 1893 and almost seventy years later the tunnel was carved through it, and finally, it was hauled to the rest area in 1939.

The other two cars kept going, but we were hungry, and Marilou had packed sandwiches and chips in a paper bag and drinks in a small cooler. We sat at a table near the big tree trunk and ate lunch.

"It's funny that we met up with Renae and them," Marilou said.

"Uh huh. That was some coincidence."

"Next thing you know, we're going to bump into Bryce somewhere along the road, or Asher and his family."

"Or Billy."

Marilou crumpled up our now empty paper bag, tossed it in a trash can and said, "Speaking of Billy, did you know Larry's with them?"

Yes, I knew. Billy paid for Larry's flight from New York, and he's staying with them rather than with us because with Parker and Delia and Baby Randolph living with us, Larry would have had to camp on the living room couch; at Billy's he can at least have his own bedroom. I said, "It was nice of Billy to pay Larry's expenses."

"Yeah, well he can afford it. He's filthy rich. I wonder exactly what he's worth."

"Millions, I think."

"Do I detect a note of envy?

"Damn right you do," I said.

Billy and Belle didn't flaunt their wealth, hardly lived like a wealthy family at all. No yachts, no private airplane, no lavish trips around the world. Their house is nice but modest, and they never go anywhere or do anything.

I said, "If we were super rich, I don't think we would live high on the hog either. That's one thing I admire about Billy and Belle. The only thing I can think of that I'd want to do if we could afford it would be to move away from Royal Court, get a nice little house by the water somewhere, maybe one of those along East Bay overlooking the sound."

"I might want to travel," Marilou said, "Maybe to England. I've always wanted to visit England. Or Germany. Heck, maybe like a summer-long tour of Europe. That could be fun."

"I guess," I said. "I would like to see Rome. And Florence, the Sistine Chapel."

"The Louvre."

"Yeah, yeah. And we could donate to causes like Shriners' Hospital and Save the Children."

After a satisfied pause from seeing the world's great art and saving children, I said, "I guess the only place we're ever going to go is Orcas Island."

REBECCA AND KAYLEE ON THE BOARDWALK

Billy's granddaughter Rebecca, Thirteen-years-old, paced back and forth at the ferry terminal leaning against the guardrail over here and then again over there, looking down at the brown water lapping against barnacle crusted pilings and farther out the shining blue and gray water, her hair in the midday sun more white than blonde, feeling discombobulated for the moment but content to be there. Rebecca was the daughter of Billy's youngest son, Randy, who lived in Spokane and rarely made it across the mountains to visit his parents. For that matter, he never visited his uncle Bryce either, and Bryce lived much closer to Spokane. The only occasion for a family get-together they never missed was the annual retreat on Orcas Island, which was, for all purposes, their only connection with the rest of the Johnson clan.

On this day they were the first Johnson descendants to make it to the ferry dock in Anacortes. Randy and Jill sat in their car in line to board. They were two hours early. They were snacking on chips and cookies washed down with Cokes.

"If I was eating that crap my folks are snacking on," Rebecca said to the seabirds, "I'd put on a million pounds." She was convinced she was fat, and she hated herself for it. She had tried all kinds of diets, none of which worked. She would starve herself until she couldn't take it anymore and then stuff food down her throat until she was ready to puke. Her daddy said, "You're not fat, honey. You're pleasantly plump."

If you asked me, I'd say even calling her pleasantly plump would be too much. I'd say she had a lovely full figure for a girl barely into puberty. On this summer day leisurely wandering the ferry property, Rebecca was dressed in denim shorts with a British flag printed on the hip pockets and one of those tops that look like a bandana tied in a big bow, her belly was bare, hardly a bulge showing above the waistband of her low-slung shorts. Her daddy was right to say she wasn't fat. Her puffy cheeks and lips were pink like cotton candy.

The morning mist had cleared up, and the day had turned out to be sunny and warm as predicted, a pure cobalt sky with a few puffy white clouds. The water of the strait melded with the blue of the sky, the water so tranquil that from where Rebecca stood, she could not tell where water ended and sky began. Near the pier, water birds of various sorts floated in tranquility on the surface of the waltzing water. Seagulls sat statue-like on the tops of pilings, and a blue heron stood ankle deep near the rocky shore. Rebecca hummed along with her current favorite song, Rihanna's "Only Girl (In the World)," playing in her ear buds. It was a bright and saucy tune.

She shaded her eyes with one hand to look out over the water where she saw a ferry so far away that she could not tell if it was coming in toward land or chugging out to one of the islands.

Rebecca's relatives said she was going to be a beauty like her aunt Lizzy. Rebecca didn't get it. She couldn't see that Lizzy was a great beauty. She couldn't see that at all. Aunt Lizzy was old. In Rebecca's eyes she didn't look like she had ever been much of a beauty. But Rebecca was willing to give her the benefit of the doubt. After all, she had seen only one photo of Aunt Lizzy in her youth, and the focus was less than sharp in that one. It was a black-and-white photo of her dancing on stage with other dancers, taken from the audience. Probably with a flash which, unless things were much different back then, would not have been allowed in the auditorium. Somebody probably got hollered at for that, maybe even asked to leave. In the photo, Lizzy was wearing a flowing white gown. Rebecca thought the word to describe it would be diaphanous, a word she had only recently learned and loved to say. She thought the way it rolled off her tongue was delicious. Deliciously diaphanous. The photo was taken in the 1960s, a mythical time in the long ago to Rebecca. She thought it was kind of a magical photo, but it didn't look anything like the Aunt Lizzy she remembered from the last time she had seen her back when she was nine years old. How could she really remember what Lizzy looked like then?

Every once in a while, she looked to the car where her parents were waiting, probably listening to CDs of music from the sixties and reminiscing about good times remembered.

Rebecca kept turning to look for Kaylee, the one relative she had enjoyed the last time they went to the island. She imagined Kaylee excitedly running up to her and hugging her. Maybe even kissing her. Would that be gay? Nah. They were cousins, second cousins or cousins once removed or something like that. She was enamored of Kaylee. She wished she could be her. The two of them had been inseparable that four-years-ago summer. It had rained almost the whole weekend that year. Better not rain this time. Rebecca remembered taking the ferry. It had not been her first time ever on a ferry, but it was the only time she could clearly recall. She loved the very idea that you could drive a car right up onto a boat and then get out and climb up very steep stairs, claustrophobic walls and ceiling close enough to touch—*Uncle Bryce would probably have to duck*—up to where you could get sandwiches and drinks and sit by windows looking out at the ocean. Or could you properly call it an ocean? Puget Sound, known to some as the Salish Sea. She remembered climbing up there with Kaylee following her, hoping she wouldn't slip and fall but thinking that if she did, and if Kaylee could catch her, that would be super cool; but she knew she wouldn't be able to catch her. They'd probably both go tumbling down and land in a tangle of arms and legs with heads busted open. The other thing she remembered was the vastness of the water, water as far as she could see, with clouds reaching down to the surface. You could even go out onto the deck and stand by a rail and look over into the sea like Rose and Jack in *Titanic*. The wind was so strong out there that she rushed back inside afraid to go out again until Kaylee, poo-pooing her fear, went with her and held her around her waist.

Ah! Here comes Kaylee now. Rebecca's first thought was *she looks all grown-up. Like a cover girl.* Kaylee was seventeen. She had blossomed since her last time on the island. She looked a lot like her father but more delicate. When Rebecca had last seen her, she had already reached her full adult height and had a willowy figure with sharp hipbones and thin shoulders. Back then, she wore glasses. No glasses now; contacts maybe. Now she had a dragon tattoo on her shoulder and a two-tone hairdo, something like a burnt red and orange, all swept to one side. The last time her hair had been black and much shorter. Rebecca remembered how gorgeous Kaylee was and especially how large her eyes were, but she had forgotten how creamy chocolaty her skin was. *That's right. She is Black, or mixed race. How could I have forgotten that? Heather and Sky's daughter. Sky is Black, Jamaican or from one of those islands down there.*

As much as she worshipped Kaylee, Rebecca was also terribly envious of her—primarily because she dated practically grownup boys who had their own cars. *She's pretty much grown up now. Probably already had sex. Probably doesn't give a flip about things I'm into like Mindcraft and Harry Potter. What can we even talk about?*

But oh boy, Kaylee greeted Rebecca just as she, Rebecca, had imagined, with a hug and a friendly kiss on her cheek. "Becca, Becca, Becca! Hi there, cuz," she said.

"Hi." Nobody had ever called her Becca before. She liked it. Maybe that could be their special name for her that only Kaylee used.

After "Hi," they didn't know what to say. They looked down at the water birds and then far out over the waves and back at each other. The last time they were together, Kaylee had confessed in a delicious sounding whisper that she had almost gone all the way with ... somebody. Rebecca had forgotten the boy's name as soon as Kaylee said it.

"Were you going to ... you know?" Rebecca had asked, and Kaylee said, "What? Let him do it? Oh my god, no. But I thought about it. Like maybe we could do it when we got a little older." Quickly doing the math in her head, Rebecca thought *she was the same age then that I am now, and now she looks back upon herself at that age as a child.*

Kaylee reached into her bag and pulled out a pack of Lucky Strikes and tapped one out and lit it and blew a smoke ring that quickly dissipated in the air.

"Lemme have a drag," Rebecca said.

"You smoke?"

"Sure."

She handed her the cigarette, lipstick on the filter, and Rebecca took a drag and blew it out without inhaling.

"Have you ever?" she asked.

"Have I ever what?"

"You know. Gone all the way like you said you almost did."

"You remembered that? Oh god no. But I just might. I mean everyone's doing it now." She squeezed Rebecca's hand and said, "Don't you dare tell anyone I said that. I mean that I might," and she flicked her cigarette end-over-end into the water. For a minute, they listened to the lapping of waves and the cries of seabirds, and then Kaylee said, "To tell you the truth, I'm not even sure anymore if I like boys."

"Do you mean you're interested in girls now?" Rebecca asked, astounded and intrigued.

Kaylee said, "No, not really. I mean maybe. Who knows? Most girls nowadays are kinda fluid, ya know." She had to explain to Rebecca what *kinda fluid* meant. Rebecca said, "Yeah, sure. I get it."

Kaylee was also wearing shorts and a T-shirt. Her shirt had a picture of Bruce Springsteen. She pulled a paperback book out of her bag and opened it to where the corner of a page was turned down and began to read. Rebecca read the title. *Object Lessons* by Anna Quindlen.

"That a good book?"

"Yeah, it's pretty good."

She set the book down.

"I'm sorry," Rebecca said. "Am I keeping you from reading?"

"Nah. The sun is. It's too bright. 'Sides, I like talking to you."

Rebecca picked up the book using a finger to keep from losing Kaylee's place and studied the cover and turned it around and skimmed the stuff on the back and put it back like it was.

She asked, "Are you still dating that boy?"

"John? Yeah, sometimes."

"Right. John. Are you in love with him?"

"I think maybe I could be. He's pretty dreamy."

Do you want to marry him?"

"Oh gosh no. I'm not ever going to get married."

"What? Why? I mean if you're in love."

Kaylee said, "Marriage is a dead end. I just read something about that in this very book. Let me find it. I'll read it to you. It's good advice, I think."

She picked up her book, checked to make sure the turned-down corner still marked where she had left off, and thumbed through the pages. Rebecca saw that sunlight on Kaylee's hair made it glow like embers in a fire.

"Who did your hair?"

"Me. All by myself."

"Cool."

"Here it is," Kaylee said. "It's two girls like us talking. They're about our age." Rebecca almost swooned when Kaylee said *about our age* as if the four-year gap between them were nothing. "These girls, they're talking about what life might be like for them twenty years in the future when they're old. Like almost forty. Listen to this. 'Somebody like my sister, she's already on her way to a decision. In two or three years she'll start dating some guy and she'll get used to him and he'll get used to her. They'll go a little further each time they park, until they don't have any further to go.'"

"Ooh, yummy," Rebecca said.

"They're talking about making out."

"Yes, oh yes. I get that. I'm not a kid anymore."

"So it goes on. '... don't have any further to go. And their families will get to know each other, and everyone will expect them to get engaged and pretty soon they will. And then they'll be married and the kids will show up and so on and so forth 'til the end of time.'"

Rebecca said, "I don't get it," and Kaylee said, "The point is, most people just stay where they are and do what people expect them to do, and whatever dreams they might have had when they were growing up are like fruit that was never picked but dies on the vine and falls to the ground and rots. They never *do* anything. They're like our aunt Lizzy. You know she was supposed to be this great dancer, I mean like on Broadway and stuff. In the movies even. But she fell in love and got married, and that was the end of that."

Why does everyone always talk about Aunt Lizzy, Rebecca thought. She said, "That's funny. I was just thinking about her."

"Who?"

"Aunt Lizzy."

"Oh yeah."

"She was the one that had all the potential. Grandpa Billy and Aunt Renae and all of them talk about how she was such a beauty and so talented, and how she went to New York to become a dancer and then she came back home and fell in love with Uncle Buddy and like the girls in the book, they went a little further each time until they wound up married and eking out a living on that nasty little farm."

"And Buddy, he was a cop for a while, but then he retired."

"Really?"

"Yeah. And look at Aunt Lizzy now. The only difference between Lizzy and the girls in the book is she never had children."

"Is it 'cause she can't?"

"I don't think so. I think they never wanted children."

"Anyway, being married is like she's in jail. That's what marriage is like, like being in jail. Look at Uncle Billy and Aunt Belle. They never go anywhere except for these summer weekends on the island. They're stuck. That's what marriage gets you. Besides, boys are disgusting."

"Even John?"

"Well no, not John. But most of 'em."

"Yeah. I guess you're right." She didn't think boys were disgusting, but at the moment she thought it was a good idea to agree with Kylee. She wanted to be sophisticated like that.

...

Helen and Eva approached the girls. "Hey girls." Eva said.

Kaylee said, "Hey. We didn't know you were coming."

"Of course. Wouldn't miss it for anything. And guess who else. Renae and Sally. They stopped by our place before daybreak this morning. And Larry too. Remember him? Marilou's boy. The artist."

Rebecca wasn't sure who she was talking about. Maybe another kid her age. That would be cool. She couldn't keep all the people in her family straight in her head. Who was related to who was a puzzle that made her head hurt. Like exactly who was Helen anyway. *Oh, I remember. I'm pretty sure she's Uncle Bryce's daughter, the adopted one. And she's a lesbian, married to Eva. Imagine that.* Rebecca knew that much at least. And she knew Eva was the one that got shot. She thought that was cool, that she survived it, not that she was shot. And Larry the artist? She didn't know who he was, but she was intrigued with the idea of an artist in the family.

Helen said, "You don't know Eva, do you? OK, so this is Eva. Eva is my wife."

"Yeah, I knew that. Cool," Rebecca said.

"Yeah. So, Eva, these squirts are Kaylee and Rebecca, more descendants of the great and horrible Pegleg Josiah Johnson."

"Yeah, nice to meet you," Rebecca said. "Do you think he really was a pirate like they say?"

Helen said, "I think he was actually a privateer. That's kind of like a pirate, but it's legal. Or kind of legal and kind of not, depending... privateers are more like mercenaries or private armies hired by the government. Blackwater for instance."

"Oh," Kaylee said. "I guess that's like for real. What's Blackwater?"

"Real as the four of us on a ferry dock."

Blackwater went unexplained.

Kaylee's wandering eyes went to Eva's shoulder, bared by a sleeveless blouse. Muscular shoulders, she thought, for a woman. There was a tattoo of a bird. Her eye slid a little farther down to a round pucker of a scar a few inches above her elbow. She asked, "Is that where you got shot?"

"Kaylee!" Rebecca's exclamation sounded shocked.

Eva said, "It's OK. Yes, that's where I got shot."

"Gosh," Kaylee said. "That must have been terrible. What was it like? Did it hurt?"

"It did. But not as much as you might think. I was kind of numb in the moment. It hurt more the next day. But it was terribly scary when it happened."

"You were probably in shock," Rebecca said.

It had been early in the school year at Beeson School. Rain had been pouring down relentlessly for three days. Students and teachers, everyone except the principal and the cafeteria workers, were gathered in the Commons. Like a ghost from years gone by, a kid named

Gregory Linden suddenly appeared in the doorway. Gregory had been expelled near the end of the previous school term for threatening to bring a gun to school and kill everyone. And there he was, carrying his father's old hunting rifle. Just like he had threatened. "I gonna kill ever one of you," he said with a shaky voice, the rifle jerking in his hands. He began firing at random. Four bullets went harmlessly into a wall, the fifth glanced off a sixth grader's heel. The kid screamed and hobbled out the door into the hall, passing within inches of the shooter, who ignored him. A sixth bullet hit a girl in her back near her shoulder, where, fortunately, it did no permanent damage. And then Gregory's gun was out of bullets. He tried to reload. Trembling hands fumbled with the bullets. Grabbing the opportunity, the football coach, standing five feet from Gregory, made a diving tackle and knocked the gun out of hi hand. The gun skittered across the tile floor and came to a stop next to Eva. Instinctively she picked it up, and the cops who were just bursting through the door saw her and shot, thinking she was the shooter.

I'm a teacher, you idiots! Eva thought but didn't shout it out. Pure bedlam in the Commons. People shouting, scurrying away, running for the doors. Many of them shouted variations of "Not her. That guy. He's the shooter."

Helen said, "Eva's a teacher. Did I tell you that? That's why she was there."

The cops handcuffed Gregory, who by then was sobbing like a baby and saying, "I'm not queer. I'm not no damn queer," and "I'm sorry. I'm so so so so sorry. Please, please, please."

"See, that was why he did it," Helen said. "The other kids bullied him, called him queer."

Eva said, "Coach Sims held a jury-rigged compress to my wound and walked me to the nurse's clinic where the nurse cleaned the wound as best she could without attempting to remove the bullet, and bandaged it, and an ambulance showed up and took me to the emergency room at St. Pete's. After they fished the bullet out and gave it to the cops—evidence, you know—and after cleaning and bandaging the wound again, the doctor released me, and Coach Sims, who had followed us to the hospital, walked me to his car."

Helen said, "Before the coach could even start the car, they were waylaid by reporters with a volley of questions. What do you know about the shooter? What did getting shot feel like? Is it true that the shooter is gay? Was it the police that shot you?' "Just all kinds of questions. And oh yeah, it was the cops that shot her. I wanted to shoot them. Right then and there. Soon's I heard about it. I still can't overlook their stupidity. But Eva, she forgave them right away. Said it was a mistake anybody could have made."

Eva told the reporters she could not answer their questions, "Not right now," and Coach hustled her back to the school, and from there she drove herself home.

"I, of course, had heard about it on the news," Helen told the girls. "I was working out in the orchard in the rain, gathering up the last of the apples that had fallen and were rotting on the soggy ground. Somebody called me and told me I had to turn on the news immediately. Funny, I didn't normally answer my cell phone unless I knew who was calling, but that time something told me to answer. So I was waiting for her to get home. Believe me, I was a wreck. I thought I'd have to calm her down, but it was Eva who had to comfort me."

Kaylee said, "If you weren't there, how do you know so much about how it happened?"

"I don't. I'm just going by what Eva told me."

"Was that the way it happened, Eva?"

"I guess. I don't know for sure. I don't remember much of anything between when Gregory started shooting and when I got home. Really not until a while after I got home. But if that's what I told Helen, then that must have been the way it was."

Her voice was weak and shaky as it always was when she tried to talk about it. When she got home the evening of the shooting, Helen met her at the door and hugged her and walked her inside. They clung to each other, both of them shaking all over. Eventually one of them fixed hot buttered rum, and they sat together on their couch with a blanket wrapped around their shoulders. It was early in September and not cold, but they wrapped the blanket around themselves because they were still shivering from the adrenaline overload. They talked little for the rest of the evening, heated up leftovers for dinner, and Eva went to bed before eight o'clock.

185

For days after that, reporters haunted her. They wanted to know if it was true that Gregory was gay and had been bullied by his classmates. Eva didn't know how to answer their questions. She wanted to be able to tell them—to tell the whole world, because she thought truth should be told—but she didn't know if Gregory was gay or not and thought it was nobody's damn business anyway. If he came out on his own, then yes, the story should be told. But Gregory claimed he wasn't gay. He might have been, and was in denial, and, yes, the other kids had been harassing him mercilessly for at least the last year or two. The only thing she would tell the reporters was that she did not know and that his sexual orientation was nobody's business.

"Gregory was a special kind of problem kid," Eva said—not to the reporters or the police or school officials back then, that horrible year ago—but to Rebecca and Kaylee on the landing at Anacortes, "I worried about him a lot."

He spent some time in jail, and Eva visited him when she could. He told her she was his only visitor and that his parents had disowned him. Eva tried, with great care and trepidation, to convince him that if he were gay there was no shame in it and that he would be much happier if he could admit it to himself, but he insisted he was straight. She told him she was gay, thinking that if he knew that he might be more willing to tell her the truth about himself.

"Was he or wasn't he?" Kaylee asked.

"I honestly don't know. I think he probably was … is, and he hated himself for it and wouldn't admit it. God! How could he have possibly admitted it to his homophobic, rock-headed parents?"

Once that summer, she decided to visit his parents and see if she could convince them to accept their son, whoever he was. As it turned out, they lived not very far from her in a rundown little house on a street of similar little rundown houses. When she pulled up to the curb and parked in front of their house, she was shocked to see in the yard of the cross-the-street neighbor a big yellow plywood arrow pointing at the Linden's house with the printed legend "Queer Lives Here." Gregory's father said, "You see that? That's what all this shit has come to. I called the cops on them, but the cops said they have a right to put up whatever kind of sign they want on their own damn property. Can you believe that? If you look closely, you'll see there's two bullet holes in the sign. I put those bullet holes there. Damn right I did. The cops told me if I did it again they'd arrest me. Arrest *me*! Can you believe it?"

The longer he talked, the louder he talked. And faster. Gregory's mother seemed to shrink into herself.

Eva was flabbergasted when Gregory's father said, "This whole mess is your fault. You're the one that encouraged him to go to that faggot club."

He told her to get the hell off their property. As she was backing off to get in her car, his wife said, "I'll pray for you, dear."

...

For some time after the shooting, Eva and the football coach who had wrestled the gun away from Gregory were treated as local celebrities. They were on TV and in newspapers all over Western Washington and talked about on blogs. And then they vanished from the spotlight and were simply teachers again, doing the important but thankless job teachers have always done. Almost a year later, Eva started having flashbacks to the shooting and she could not bring herself to go into the Commons where the shooting had taken place. She was overcome with unexpected crying jags. She took a six-month sabbatical from teaching and started seeing a therapist. She started talking to other teachers and of course to Helen and even to some of her students about the shooting and the incidents leading up to it and the aftermath. "Thank God," she often said, "For summer vacations."

When she went back to Beeson School the following school year, she talked the principal into letting her start the LGBTQ support group he had not let her start the year before. Not the one already in existence but a new club specifically for kids like Gregory who were in denial or kids who were questioning their sexuality. It had some neutral-sounding name—the idea being to allow kids who might be closeted gays or unsure of their sexuality to feel a little safer attending the meetings. They met in Eva's classroom.

...

Helen had slipped into a peaceful silence while Eva and the girls wound down the shooting story. She had leaned against Eva with her head on her shoulder and almost fell asleep standing in the sun. She opened her eyes and looked around at the water and the sky, watching the birds, the people coming and going. Activity picking up as it grew closer to ferry time. She spotted her parents waiting in line in Bryce's old Lexus. "There's Mom and Dad. I'm going to go over and say hello to them." She ran to the Lexus and leaned in the window and kissed her daddy.

"Hello, sweetheart," he said.

Distracted only for a moment, the girls turned their attention back to Eva. "You're like a character in a movie," Rebecca said.

Eva chuckled at that. Kaylee said, "Tell us more about ... well, everything."

"There's not much more to tell. Gregory spent a year in juvie and was required to go to counseling after he got out. His father refused to let him back into their home. Get this, he said, 'No goddamn queer is gonna live under my roof.' Excuse my language, but that's just what he said. Exactly."

"Hey, it's OK. I'm like the world's champion cusser," this from Rebecca.

"I'll bet you are," followed by, "I don't think the old man gave a hoot about the shooting or about his son being in jail. All he cared about was the shame of having a queer son. After Gregory got out of jail and when he packed up his things and left the house for the last time, his mother said, 'I'll pray for you, son.'

"Gregory is living on the streets now. You can see him most any day down by the artesian well and the Respect & Love Olympia mural. I think he's probably doing drugs pretty heavily now."

...

Helen rejoined the group and suddenly pointed out at the water and said, "Look at that."

Where she pointed, a large turtle was sitting on a floating log, and they saw that a seagull had swooped down and was standing on the turtle's back. It stood there for a long time, until the turtle slowly slipped into the water and the gull took off to find another place to perch. Kaylee pulled her phone out of her pocket to take a photo, but she was too late.

Marilou and I, and our son Larry had been watching the group from our car. Larry had come with Billy and Belle, but once they got to the ferry terminal, he came and crawled into our car and gave us each a big hug and said, "Jesus Christ in a tutu, how does Aunt Belle put up with him?"

After a good chuckle over that, we talked about what had been going on with him, and then he decided he wanted to go talk to Eva and Helen and the young girls.

...

"Hey, hey, hey!" he shouted loudly and jovially. And all turned to see him approaching, a megawatt smile flaring across his face.

"Larry!" Helen shouted and ran to him and practically knocked him over when she leaped on him with a strong hug. Eva, less enthusiastically, hugged him too. The two young girls stared bug-eyed.

"And who are these beautiful young ladies?" Larry teasingly asked. He knew good and well who they were.

Kaylee said, "Cool socks, Dude."

The socks were argyle in shades of blue stuffed into red Crocs. The rest of his outfit consisted of a brownish button-up shirt unbuttoned over a red T-shirt and cargo shorts.

Larry talked flatteringly to the two young girls, and they both giggled and blushed. Helen then asked Larry if he came alone.

"Yep. Just me."

"No girlfriend this time?"

"Nope. You can be my girlfriend while I'm here if you want. Both of you. All of you." He laughed jovially at that, and none of the women and girls responded with words. They all smiled, and Rebecca looked at the ground and blushed.

Kaylee said, "You didn't have a beard last time. I like it. It makes you look like a mountain man."

He didn't respond for a moment, and then Kaylee said, "I wish I could touch it."

Rebecca gasped. Larry said, "Be my guest."

Kaylee rubbed his beard with her fingers and said, "It's soft. I thought it would be ... you know, bristly."

Helen and Eva remembered the last time Larry came—how long ago? Four or five years? Some dingbat of a girlfriend came with him. Nobody liked her. As much as everybody in the Johnson clan loved Larry, they never liked his girlfriends. He went for sexy, not character or personality or intelligence, none of which any of his girlfriends seemed to possess. Helen thought he would probably grow out of that, probably already had. After all, he had been just a little over thirty then and would now be about forty; an age at which men do mature if they're ever going to, Helen thought—Helen who was born mature and serious; yet still fun-loving.

"How about the two of you? Is it just you? Are Brian and Melony coming?" Larry asked.

"Yeah, they're coming. In Brian's car, because they're going to have to leave early. He has to get back to work or something."

Larry said, "Brian has a car of his own? They're old enough to drive?"

"Yep. Plenty old enough. And he earned the money himself."

"Time do plunge ahead, don't it? I still think of Brian and Melony as eight or ten years old."

"I know. They're both in college now."

Laughing at himself, Larry said, "Hell's bells, I still think of my brother Parker as ten years old, and there's hardly more than a year's difference between us. This Johnson family. Man. Great greats and triple greats or whatever and a pot full of other relatives. The whole damn shebang of this Johnson clan is weirdly obsessed with family history. It's all gobbledegook to me. All held together by a freaking pirate."

"Maybe even psychologically worrisome." Helen said, and Larry said with a wink and a crooked smile, "Any incest or inbreeding?"

Helen said, "Blame it all on Billy. He's the one that stokes that obsession."

Eva said, "Johnny's coming too," and after a brief pause, "Do you even know about Johnny?"

"No, I don't. Who is ..."

"Johnny. He's my son by my ex. Remember? I was married before. To a man. Before you were even born."

Rebecca was drop-jawed at that but didn't say anything.

"After we got divorced—oh sweet Jesus, I can't believe you don't know about this—my asshole ex kidnapped our son. If I could have got my hands on him ... well, it's a good thing I didn't, or I'd probably still be in jail." She said this with a self-effacing chuckle. And then, wiping the smile off her face, "Johnny was only two years old, Two. Imagine. Stolen away from his mother. And for sixteen years I didn't know where he was. I reported it to the police, called everyone I could find who knew my ex, even hired a private eye. No luck. But Johnny found me. Smart kid. His father told him I was dead. But Johnny figured it out somehow. It's a long story. Anyway, he and his girlfriend played detective and found me. They're living in Olympia now and going to Evergreen, both working parttime. So anyway, yeah. They're going to be here too. He went bananas when I told him Renae and Sally were coming and that they owned Fresh Meadows in Portland. He said it was his and June's favorite eatery down there.

"Wow!" he said, "I met Sally. But I had no idea she was related to me. Somehow we never happened to be there when Renae was there, and we didn't know. I mean Jesus. All that time chatting away with Sally and I never knew she was married to my aunt."

Stunned into silence, Kaylee and Rebecca kept looking at each other as if to question, "Did you know any of this?"

Eva's eyes teared up. "It's a miracle," she said.

Larry said, "That's fantastic. More members of this huge and already confusing family. I don't know who half of you are. I'm not even sure who I am."

They all laughed at that and agreed that it was impossible to keep track of who was who. One of them mentioned that I had talked about creating a family tree, which was true, but I hadn't yet done it.

After a while, Larry asked Eva if she was still teaching school.

"Yep, still teaching."

191

Kaylee said, "Not only teaching, she's a hero. She saved the school from a mass shooter."

"Please, let's not tell that whole story again," Helen said.

And Larry said, "Not to worry. I know all about it. What I want to know is, is the school OK with you being a lesbian."

"Yeah. We've joined the twenty-first century out here. Actually, Olympia is pretty liberal. You shoulda known that. It's one of the more gay-friendly towns anywhere. And Tacoma—get this— old blue-collar Tacoma—remember the aroma of Tacoma?—it was voted the most gay-friendly small city in America."

"By whom?"

"*The Advocate*. A few years back."

"Damn! That's cool. Unbelievable but cool."

Before they could talk anymore, Bryce blew his horn and shouted out the window, "Hey guys! It's time to board. Let's go."

...

On the upper deck, Johnsons by the dozen gathered in small groups to chat and reminisce— *What's new with you? Are Heather and Sky here? Who's heard from Lizzy. Kaylee, you've grown so much. Did y'all go to the Puyallup Fair? What's the name of your restaurant again? You're looking good, Marilou. You too, uh, Rudy.* That last one was Heather; for a second she couldn't remember my name.

...

Billy and Belle ordered bowls of chowder, telling the others that eating chowder on board the ferry was a sacred tradition. "Well, we must honor tradition," Bryce said, and he ordered chowder for himself and Emma.

Helen said, "If Mom and Pop are eating the chowder, I guess I better too," and she ordered a bowl for herself. She and Eva took turns eating from the same bowl using the same spoon.

"That right there, that's true love," Larry said. "Sharing them cooties."

192

"I think it's sweet," Bryce replied. He asked Larry who he would be staying with on the island, and Larry said he was sharing a cabin with Billy and Belle. Bryce said, "My condolences," and Larry couldn't tell from his tone or from Billy's shooting him the bird, albeit with a smile on his face, if they were kidding or not. Of course, the exchange was said with a smile, but what was underneath those brotherly smiles? Larry had heard that when all of Hairless Harlan's children were growing up the oldest and the youngest, Billy and Bryce, were constantly at each other's throats, and he knew Billy could be gruff but that his gruffness was often couched in kidding. Billy was hard to read.

A slew of Johnsons and Johnson spouses and Johnson in-laws soon headed out to the open deck to stand in the wind where they had to almost shout to be heard. Someone asked, "Where's Lizzy and that dreamy husband of hers?"

"She's become something of a hermit," Billy said. "She never leaves that stinking little farm."

Sally said, "We went out there early this morning and tried to talk her into coming with us, but she didn't want to talk about it."

"She's in really bad shape," Billy said. "But she's only got herself to blame. She just doesn't take good care of herself."

Renae said, "She said Peter Puget Resort was dirty and smelled bad," and Sally told them about Lizzy's concussion and how all kinds of things smelled bad to her after that. "I don't think Lizzy would want it to get back to her that he told us about the concussion and all."

Marilou, crunching on potato chips, and Johnny, eating his chowder out of a paper bowl, were late arrivals on deck. Jumping in on the tail end of the conversation, Marilou asked, "Y'all talking about Lizzy?"

"Yes."

"Yeah, I'm afraid she's in one hell of a mess. I honestly don't think she's going to last much longer. And I don't think she even cares."

"Wow! That's radical," Larry said. "I really like her. I was looking forward to seeing her. Maybe I could go out after we get back to Olympia, if somebody would take me."

Helen said, "We could take you. Right, honey?"

"Sure," Eva said.

...

Eva's son Johnny asked them all to squeeze in close together for a family picture, and they did, and then Kaylee said, "OK, you get in there now and let me take one with you and everybody."

Her other son, Brian, was wearing an old Green Bay Packers hat he had picked up in a yard sale for a quarter. Moments before Kaylee snapped the last picture it blew off his head and sailed over the rail like a frisbee and skipped into the drink. He said, "Oh well. I never liked that hat anyway."

"So why'd you buy it?"

"I was drunk."

Later, Bryce said to me, "Too bad that wasn't Billy's MAGA hat."

"I see he's not wearing it."

"He probably left it in the car, but I'll bet you he'll be wearing it at dinner tonight."

After the picture taking, Renae asked me how my book was coming along.

Taken aback, I said, "I didn't think I told anybody about the book."

She said, "Your wife's a snitch." An exaggerated shoulder shrug from Marilou.

I told them the writing was slow going. I was pleased that at least one of the Johnsons cared enough to inquire. *Bless your heart, Renae. And yours too, Marilou.*

"You're writing a book?" Kaylee asked, undisguised astonishment in her voice. "What kind of book?" She couldn't have been more enthusiastic if I had told her I hit the walk-off homer in the last game of the World Series.

"It's hard to explain. It's about a family," I said. "Kinda sorta like our family."

...

Kaylee and Rebecca looked over into the water and saw dolphins leaping in the wake of the ferry. "Look! Look!" they shouted.

"They love to do that. Sometimes they'll stick with a boat for miles and miles," Marilou said. They jumped and they jumped, and they jumped, and then one leaped high out of the water and did two complete twists in the air before landing back in the water, and its companion followed suit.

"They're performing for us."

Someone else out on the deck shouted, "Whales!"

"Where?"

"Ahead. Off the port side. Right. Right side."

Everyone rushed to the rail to look. No more than forty yards away was a pod of orcas with their distinctive black and white markings tumbling on the surface. It seemed that, like the dolphins, they were playing with us humans. Everyone pulled out their phones and started snapping photos. Kaylee exulted, "I got 'em on video!"

Soon the dolphins and then the whales took a final dive and did not surface again.

"Show's over, folks," I said. "They took their curtain call, and now they're gone."

The wind was getting to be too much out on deck, and most of us went back inside.

Helen and Larry found seats together on the long benches. Helen asked him how his career was going, and he told her he had a new show coming up in January.

"That's great. By the way, I love the beard. Are you still with the Sullivan Gallery?"

"Yeah."

The gallery was highly regarded but, as Larry put it, not bigtime. "They're just one step down the ladder from the really bigtime galleries. But that one step is huge. I've been with 'em more than three years now, but this will be my first solo show. Greg indicated this show might be make-or-break." He paused to run his fingers through his beard, exposing a touch of gray, then said, "Indicated hell. He came right out and said it, didn't beat around the bush. He said he's going to invite some big-time collectors and critics, and it's going to either elevate me to the next level—whatever that might mean—or it's going to be sayonara for me and him. I gotta tell you, I'm pretty damn nervous about it. Hopeful but scared shitless."

"Well good luck with that. What else is new? Any new love in your life?"

He told them he had a new girlfriend. "She's a doctor. How 'bout that, huh? And I've started something new, a podcast."

"We know. We listen to it," Helen said.

"Dang. I never think about how you can get it way out here. Do you think it's any good?"

"Uh-huh, but I know I'm prejudiced."

At that point, Eva slid in next to them with dessert items enough to share all around. She said, "You're talking about the podcast, right? It's great. We laughed our asses off at the one with that actress that was in *Rent*. Did she really moon the audience? Bare butt and all?"

"Yeah, she did. It's in the script, I think. Pretty sure. There've been lots of actors played that part, and they all mooned the audience."

"And I reckon you went back every time to see all them butts," Helen quipped.

"I do figure drawing at the Art Students League once a week. Nude models. Naked butts are nothing new to me."

Eva said, "I wonder if they could get away with that in community theaters out here,"

"They can. They have. Or so I've heard," Helen said. "They did it at that theater on Fourth Avenue, the one that went out of business—not because of that, mind you—and I heard they also did it in a theater in Tacoma."

Eva said, "I think it's really clever how you find all those actors and artists and writers to interview. How do you do it? I mean it sounds like you just happen to meet up with them, but they're all brilliant and accomplished."

Larry laughed at that. "It's serendipity, it's magic." And then, "Seriously. It's two things. First, I don't *just happen* to meet up with them. And second, I'm an artist; all my friends are artists of one sort or another. Theater people, writers, musicians. Heck, it's New York City for god's sake. It's where creative people come to get rich and famous or starve and vanish into oblivion. Hopefully I'm helping them to not vanish."

...

If seen from high above by passengers in an airplane, the water through which the ferry sailed would look like a giant spill that seeped around land masses that look like gargantuan mushrooms, green ones, or some kind of strange pods floating on the surface. The Strait of Georgia, the Strait of Juan de Fuca, Desolation Sound, Orcas, San Juan and Lopez Islands, and numberless other islands, some dotted with buildings and others uninhabited—all of that comprises Puget Sound, a body of water only lately dubbed the Salish Sea after the Coast Salish indigenous people. This inland sea extends from British Columbia all the way south to Olympia. Theoretically at least, Billy Johnson could put a sailboat in the water at the pier below Peter Puget Resort and sail south until he docked at his own pier on Steamboat Island. It's an enchanted slice of earth and water, and nobody falls for the magic more so than Kaylee and Rebecca and Larry. Artists and youth believe in enchantment long after the rest of us have grown jaded and no longer give a damn. Even Billy, the most jaded of us all, silently stood hand-in-hand with Belle on the stern watching the ferry's wake as island after island and boat after boat receded in the distance. He was mellow and nostalgic, and he wondered what it would have been like to have been a pioneer exploring these waters for the first time. Just imagine launching a boat at Port Angeles or Anacortes with nothing but water and a few distant islands in sight and no idea what might be beyond the horizon—like mariners in ancient days fearful of deep-sea monsters or sailing off the edge of the earth.

FIRST NIGHT

Billy called everybody at the retreat together. He used a bullhorn fashioned out of paper for theatrical effect. He tapped his water glass with a spoon so hard Belle was afraid he would shatter the glass, and he shouted out in imitation of a circus barker or an old-time prophet, "Gather ye together all ye children. All a y'all." They were in the Trawler dining room which Billy had reserved for the evening: dining tables of various sizes with linen tablecloths and cushioned Victorian sofas and chairs, a large fireplace that was not in use because it was summer, and in front of the fireplace a couch and three lounge chairs creating a family lounge area currently occupied by Asher's family. The water-facing wall was lined with windows offering a panoramic view of Cascade Bay. Billy liked the Trawler lounge because its rustic comfort reminded him of his Steamboat Island home.

Standing next to Billy and copying his staged manner of speech, Belle sang out, "Hey, everybody. Come together, come together right now," and Bryce sang out, "Over me-eee!"

For the oldsters, the ones who had been coming every summer, it was time to put on their best performances, imitating speakers from Congress to preachers to circus barkers to vaudevillians. In most cases badly, but they loved every moment of it. Larry, having changed into jeans and a Hawaiian shirt after his brief afternoon swim, his long, now-braided beard swinging from his chin, laughingly joined in the performance. "Brothers and sisters, we're gathered here today ..." sounding like a preacher at a funeral, and Renae sang out a slurry, "Oyez, oyez, oyez! Come all ye Johnsonseses."

Rebecca whispered to Kaylee, "Are they all drunk?"

"Nah, they're just kidding around. They always do this."

The Johnson descendants had been milling about the room, many with drinks in hand, chatting in groups of two, three and four. Asher and Diane and their children had driven up from Shoreline early in the day, having arrived on the island well ahead of everyone else and set up camp in Moran State Park before lunchtime—tent camping instead of staying in the resort. They claimed the kids wanted to camp, which was true, but the difference in cost had not a little to do with their choice. They were gathered in front of the fireplace, Martin and Josiah playfully wrestling on one of the big chairs and Diane nursing baby Luke.

It was getting on toward sunset, and slantwise sunshine poured through windows that were overdue for a thorough cleaning. Renae and Sally could not help but notice the lack of pristine cleanliness after hearing Lizzy's tale and after what happened when they checked in. They were given keys to their room and were surprised to notice that the room they were assigned looked like—most definitely must have been—the exact room Lizzy had described when telling about her last trip to the island. It was called the Vancouver Room. Renae said when they stepped through the door, "Oh my god, it smells musty. Just like ... you know."

I think you're imagining it," Sally said.

"Maybe. I don't know. I'm still discombobulated from the trip from Olympia to Shoreline and back and the headache and lack of sleep and that homophobic bitch in Fife, and finally Lizzy's bizarre behavior."

Sally hugged her and assured her they were not entering a Lizzy-inspired nightmare, and Renae laughed about that, and they talked about maybe not going to the family gathering in the Trawler room but decided that, no, they should go. God knows what people would think if they simply didn't show.

"Just to play it safe," Sally said, "let's open the windows."

One of the windows was stuck shut; they got the other one opened. Renae said, "I swear on my grandmother's grave, this is the room Lizzy stayed in. Didn't she say there was a window painted shut?"

"And it's still shut? Welcome to the twilight zone."

"No way it could have remained stuck all those years. Hundreds of guests and the resort maintenance staff failed to get it unstuck year after year after year." Again, they laughed it off, and they showered and went to the lounge and had a glass of wine, and Renae leaned back in her chair by an open window overlooking the water and almost fell asleep. They ordered hummus and crackers, and after they ate a few, Sally wiped the hummus off the knife blade and slipped the knife in her purse. Back in the room, which no longer had that odor, they changed clothes and grabbed lightweight jackets, knowing it always gets cool after the sun goes down. Before going to the welcome get-together, Sally used the table knife she had pilfered from the lounge to open the stuck window.

They were late getting to the Trawler dining room. They shot one another loaded glances and put the creepiness out of mind and laughed heartily when Billy called everyone together in his circus-barker voice and when his imitators mocked him.

Renae said, "Oh boy, here we go again. A string of begats to put the Bible to shame."

They were sharing a table with Marilou and me and Parker and Delia. Sally said, "Billy does this every year."

"We know. Oh god, do we ever know," Marilou said.

Parker, who had not gone the past few years and must have forgotten what it was like, was ecstatic, laughing and clapping and practically jumping out of his seat.

The gathering was colorful to say the least. All ages and all wearing bright clothing, many in shorts and T-shirts or bright floral shirts, hair coloring mostly in the blonde-to-light brown range with a few rusty gingers and Billy's shiny dome covered with his red MAGA hat. Seated somewhat apart from the others at a table by a window were Bryce and Emma with Helen and Eva. Bryce commanded the table by size alone. His hair, once black as night, was now shockingly white, what little of it there was, and his skin was shiny mahogany, inheriting his generous dosage of melanin, everyone assumed, from great grandma Gertie. He was even darker than Kaylee, who got her melanin unadulterated from her father.

People outside the family often assumed Bryce was mixed race. There had been a time, before he grew to be huge and fearsome, when other kids thought he was Native or African American. They teased him about the color of his skin, some even calling him Tonto or Sambo. In middle school a boy named Johnny White dared to say, "Your mama must a done the deed with a colored man."

Those were fighting words in small town Louisiana in 1955, the year that 14-year-old Emmitt Till was beaten to death for whistling at a white woman in Mississippi. Few of the other kids laughed at that, and those who did were afraid not to. Bryce chose to ignore it.

At Washington State University where Bryce taught history, he was known by his students as Dr. Johnson. Fans from his football days remembered him as Bull Johnson. He had always been a soft-spoken man whose belly laugh was explosive. His siblings and his cousins admired his brilliance and his playfulness. Even big brother Billy was grudgingly proud of Bryce. But Billy was contemptuous of what he thought of as the weirdly liberal classes Bryce taught. "Gender and Race Studies," he grumbled to Belle. "For Christ's sake that's socialism pure and simple, not proper subjects for impressionable students at Washington State. Whatever happened to reading, writing and 'rithmatic?"

...

Billy was still enjoying his moment in the spotlight. He said, "It's time you younger Johnson progeny learned about your heritage and time the rest of y'all were reminded. We come from a proud family line."

"Here, here. I'll drink to that," Renae said, lifting her mug high.

"Too damn proud," Bryce mumbled. He had left the play the night before, mad at some of the sign-wavers outside the theater who were protesting against the martyred Rachel Corrie, and he had not yet completely regained his good humor. A long drive and interminable wait in the car under a blazing sun had not helped. Seeing the red flag of Billy's MAGA cap didn't help either. Only his wife heard his mumbled comment. Others lifted their glasses in good cheer. Most were smiling or laughing. All but Emma, who could see what none of the others could because none of the others knew Bryce the way she did. What she saw was a sizzling fuse inching up to a bomb that might explode at any moment. She reached for his hand and held it firmly.

Unaware of the reaction playing out by Bryce and Emma, Billy said, "We're all descendants of the notorious pirate Pegleg Josiah Johnson, a brave and adventurous man who spat in the eye of convention."

"Hear! Hear!"

"Pegleg Johnson pirated in the Caribbean and the Gulf of Mexico. He plundered ships along the coastline from Pensacola to New Orleans to Galveston and in the Caribbean from Cuba and Bermuda to Puerto Rico from about 1868 to 1873, a short time, but oh boy. Then, putting his pirating aside, he settled down in New Orleans with the notorious madame—get a load of her name—Matilda Gertrude Hildegarde Duchamp, better known as Hurricane Gertie."

"And yes," Billy went on, "If you've heard the rumors, know that they're true. She was indeed a madame. Ran the fanciest and most notorious house of pleasure in New Orleans, and it was said she could beat the daylights out of any man that dared get out of line in her establishment. If she ever was a lady of the night herself, it was before she met Pegleg Johnson. To him, she was completely loyal, even when he was out to sea for months at a time. Even when he was with his other families, which she likely at least suspected. As for our dearly departed ancestor, he was not exactly what you'd call a one-woman man. They say old Pegleg had a woman in every port. Some say he was a bigamist many times over and had a slew of children—nobody knows how many or with how many women. He was a man's man, that's all, every bit the man's man."

Bryce whispered to Emma, "If that's what makes a man a man's man, then God help the youngsters who might look up to Billy (or Pegleg) as a role model."

Billy continued his spiel with, "Pegleg's wild exploits with pirates at sea and women ashore were documented in the dime novel *The Illusive Pirate Pegleg Johnson* by Robert Creel."

He paused and looked every one of his children and grandchildren and nieces and nephews in the eye, his own eyes like searchlights scanning the crowd. And then with a hearty laugh, he said, "Don't you believe it. Creel's book was a load of crap. Not a truthful word in it. But there was another book, *The Privateer Called*

Pegleg by Brandon Call, that was taken from Josiah's own journals and other sources that we believe were mostly true."

He held up for all to see copies of both books.

Bryce said, "That part's true so far as we know."

Billy went on, "But Gertie now, grandmother to all of us, we know a lot about Gertie. She was famous and well-loved by everyone from the stevedores and fishermen in New Orleans to the captains of industry and leading politicians of the day who frequented her establishment. It was said that when some folks were bent on cleaning up the French Quarter—like that had a chance of ever happening—when they talked about shutting down her pleasure palace, Governor Huey P. Long himself purchased her house and let her continue plying her trade in it. After that, the cops never again raided her establishment. They guarded it.

"Bullshit," Bryce grumbled, addressing his comments to Emma and Helen and Eva only. "Huey P. Long would have been a toddler when Ol' Pegleg was diddling Gertie."

It was almost ten o'clock, time for Diane and Asher to excuse themselves and get their children back to their campsite. Sky and water seen through the windows were a soft shade of fuchsia, and the tree line on distant islands was almost black. "Of all the women Pegleg knew in Galveston and Biloxi and Mobile and New Orleans, Gertie was the one he came home to," Billy said as Asher's family quietly slipped out. "Gertie's the only one we know about with any certainty."

One of the younger Johnson descendants shouted out, "Galloping Gertie!" And most of the younger people laughed at that. They were nibbling on pretzels, guacamole and chips, and paying scant attention to Billy.

Billy said, "Yeah, yeah. Y'all have your fun. Anyway, Gertie ... well she's a whole story in herself."

"And now we're going to hear it," Renae called out.

Billy said, "Gertie was every bit as notorious as Pegleg. The record was clear indeed. 'Tis true, 'tis true, she was the madame of a house of ill repute. A bordello. A bawdy house. A whorehouse. Whatever you want to call it. There are pictures of her and pictures of the bordello women and their customers in the parlor of the house printed in newspapers of the day, the men in coats and ties and the women half dressed, ladies of the night right out of Toulouse Lautrec."

He picked up his glass of bourbon from the table, took a generous swig, wiped his mouth with the back of his hand, and said, "That whorehouse she owned and oversaw with an iron will was as elegant as a castle."

"Hear hear!" Renae shouted.

Billy said, "Now Gertie, she was a businesswoman through and through. No nonsense about her. And she was big and strong. They say she was six feet tall and weighed two hundred pounds. Pegleg was not so big. He was maybe five-nine or ten, slim and muscular. They loved each other fiercely, and they had five children. We know their names and when they were born and when they died, because all of that is inscribed on their graves in a mausoleum in the heart of New Orleans."

"Here comes the begetting part," I said.

And it came.

"Now we're getting to the part of the family most of us here come from. Pegleg's son Auvergne and his wife, Bluebird had a son named Wilson who died at one month old and another son named Harlan Bujeaud Johnson who many of us knew. A whole bunch a y'all are his direct progeny—his sons and daughters. Harlan was born in 1918 and lived to be two months short of a hundred. He was married for a very short time to a young girl named Josephine who died tragically." Then he told the gory tale of Josephine and the tiger. Then, "At the risk of repeating myself, lots of us here knew old Harlan. He was my daddy and some of y'all's, bless his soul. After Josephine was killed, he married our mama, Viola Parker. Four years after he passed away she died, some say, of a broken heart. Harlan and Viola were the ones that brought the family up here to the Pacific Northwest. Every one of us here this evening are Harlan and Viola's children or grandchildren or nieces and nephews."

Family members pounded on tables like roustabouts in some old movie—like lusty pirates in a tavern in old New Orleans. Getting restless and not wanting to hear more from Billy, a few of the Johnsons started shouting out. "Bring on the food."

"Hold on," Billy said, "Before we eat, does anybody have anything they want to add?"

Nobody spoke up for a few seconds, and Billy started to say, "OK, let's bring on the food," when Bryce pushed his chair back and stood up. Everybody looked expectantly at him expecting some witticism. But Bryce did not say a word. He gave Helen's shoulder a pat in passing and sidled sideways past me and Marilou and our boys, Larry and Parker, who had probably not sat together since the fourth or fifth grade. On up to Billy's table he marched, and there he halted and silently reached out and snatched the MAGA hat off Billy's head as quickly as a striking rattlesnake. Holding the hat with both hands, he brought it up to his mouth and bit into it and shook his head and growled like a dog trying to rip the hat to shreds, but he could not rip it. He dropped it to the floor and ground it underneath his foot. Finally, he spoke. "You will not wear that hat in my presence," he said, and then he returned to his table leaving the mangled hat on the floor.

No one said a word for a full minute, maybe two. And no one, not even Billy, dared pick up the hat. And then Bryce said, "We are going to our cabin now. Come, please, Emma."

Emma pushed her chair away from the table and stood up, an unspoken apology for all in her eyes. Or am I reading something into her expression that was not there?

Red-faced now, Billy shouted at their retreating backs, "That hat represents the president of the United States! Show some respect."

Silence fell over the room. Everyone looked to Emma and to Helen to see who would stand with Billy and who would walk out with Bryce. Helen, with a tremulous voice, said, "Daddy's right. I can't abide anyone supporting that man. But we're family, all of us. For the sake of family, Eva and I will stay and remain as friendly as possible. But Uncle Billy, I want you to know that you have driven a wedge into this family, and the break you caused may never be healed."

Day Two

Finally, the fog and the mists that had been hanging around mornings for the past few days had decided to hightail it away from the island. It was as if Bryce's volcanic eruption had blown it away. We breakfasted, not all together, and took off on our various excursions. Marilou and I with Parker and Delia went whale watching on a sleek and roomy catamaran with a two-man crew, both of whom were seasoned whaling guides.

"We can't guarantee we'll see any whales," Captain Mike said as he pulled the boat away from the dock. "After all, whales are living creatures. They do not answer to our wishes. But we see whales ninety-eight percent of the time."

"Damn," I said, "That's impressive."

What was also impressive was Captain Mike. We had expected a gruff old Captain Ahab from *Moby Dick*, but what we got was a snappy youngster who looked like a singer in a boy band. I didn't think he was old enough to handle a rowboat in a creek, much less captain a whale-watching catamaran. Parker later said he had wondered if we could trust him to get us out to sea and back.

Captain Mike said, "We not only see orcas, but—less frequently I'll grant you—we also spot humpbacks and grays. Humpbacks are spectacular to see. Plus, we of course see porpoises, seals, sea lions, dolphins, sea birds, and otters."

Parker expressed skepticism. "That's a big promise. And by the way, aren't porpoises and dolphins the same thing?"

"Not at all, and I'm glad you asked." And with that Captain Mike launched into what sounded like a prepared speech. "People use the terms dolphins, porpoises, and whales to describe marine mammals belonging to the order Cetacea from the Greek work *ketos,* meaning large sea creature, and often use them interchangeably. In fact—hardly anybody knows this—the orca, or killer whale, is not a whale at all. They are actually the largest member of the dolphin family."

His speech impressed the heck out of me, even if it did sound like he was reading from a textbook. Marilou and Parker were pretty darn impressed too. We all were.

The first mate chimed in, "Even if we don't see a single sea creature, which is absurd to even imagine, you can bet your bottom dollar you'll see some—but even if we don't, you'll get a great tour of the islands."

"Thanks, Captain Ahab," Parker said.

"Just try to enjoy yourself," Delia told Parker.

It was a balmy sixty-eight degrees and barely a hint of a wave on the glassy surface of the sound. We were twenty minutes out when we spotted the first orca pod, three adults and one juvenile slicing through the water not far from the cat. Parker got so excited he tossed his Mariners cap in the air and failed to catch it. We watched it float away. That was the third lost cap of the trip. "Too bad that wasn't Billy's," Marilou said.

"Yeah, what's with him and that freakin' cap anyway?" Delia asked.

Marilou said, "God only knows."

I said, "Oh, we all know. Now can we agree to not talk about that anymore?"

...

Renae and Sally slept until after nine o'clock, actually a bit early for a couple who ran a late-night restaurant; they generally slept until almost noon. After a leisurely breakfast of sweet rolls and coffee, they decide to go on a shopping excursion around the island and on San Juan Island, a short hop on another ferry. They dawdled until after lunch, wandering around the grounds, by the pool, along the beach where Renae picked up seashells, and back to their room for showers and to change clothes—Sally in shorts and a top that tied like a bandana, and Renae in a short yellow skirt and a wide-billed straw hat. No longer the cool and breezy morning that had seen the whale watchers off, the temperature had crept up close to eighty degrees. The sun was a fiery ball overhead, comfortable enough thanks to a cooling ocean breeze.

They wandered the streets of Friday Harbor and visited the San Juan Islands Museum of Art, where they saw sculpted heads that looked like fearsome ancient gods but were made of recycled materials, including modern packaging with brand names and slogans. In a little shop near the museum, they bought more T-shirts, including one each with the names Orcas Island and San Juan Island emblazoned under photos of the landscapes: a picture of the imposing stone tower on top of Constitution Mountain and one of the lighthouse on San Juan Island. Before going back to Orcas, they sampled beer at the San Juan Brewing Company and got pleasantly tipsy.

...

Bryce and Emma were up with the sunrise that morning. After coffee and showers in their room, they headed to the Dinghy Grill for breakfast with Helen and Eva, the only family members on the island that routinely got up at break of day.

The Dinghy was the only one of the resort's three restaurants that opened early enough for them. They took a table on the deck overlooking the sound. After placing their orders and chatting a bit about family members who weren't at the retreat, Eva said, "Rule number one: no more talking about me getting shot, no matter who asks, and no talk about Billy's MAGA hat. Everything else is on the table."

"Speaking of which," here comes our food."

The server set their plates on the table, a shrimp omelet with bacon and home fries for Bryce, waffles for Eva and Helen, and a breakfast burrito for Emma. "Oh boy, this all looks good," Helen said. Emma suggested to Bryce that they share. "OK," Bryce said. "And I get to finish what you can't."

They talked about their plans for the day. Helen said she and Eva planned on exploring the island with their kids and with Larry. "And then we're going to meet for lunch with Randy and Jill and Rebecca."

"That's quite an itinerary," Bryce said.

"I know. But how often do we get to see them? I want to get to know Rebecca better. She seems such a fascinating young lady."

"And Kaylee," Eva said. "Wherever Rebecca goes, so goes Kaylee."

Helen said, "I think it's the other way around. Rebecca follows Kaylee."

Gulping down a bite of her burrito, Emma, asked, "Which one is Kaylee?"

"She's the Black beauty." Two seconds of silence then, "I hope that didn't sound racist."

"No, not at all. She's really pretty. Young too, maybe fifteen or sixteen at the most. But precocious. She's Heather and Sky's daughter. Sky couldn't come because he had some theater thing, so I think they came with Asher and his family."

Shattering rules number one and two, somebody asked Eva about the shooting incident, but she refused to talk about it. And then they talked about Bryce's blowup with Billy the night before. It was Bryce who brought it up. "Maybe I shouldn't have been so harsh with him. I mean ... well, y'all know, Billy has always been more conservative than any of us, but that's never been a problem before. Family members need to be forgiving of one another's differences. Family unity should trump politics—forgive the expression—but Jesus H. Christ, today's right wing has gone too damn far."

"Oh lord, there he goes," Helen said to the table at large. "Please, Daddy, no talking about politics." She knew that once he got started, he would be impossible.

And he proved her right. He said, "It's not just that Trump's policies are despicable and scary, it's that voting for him is excusing sexism and racism and God knows what all. Just pure-de-hell vulgarity. 'Grab 'em by the pussy,' he said. It's on tape. Before Trump nobody could say that word in public. Now he says it and gets elected President. Fu-uuck. Who could vote for someone who said something like that for the whole world to hear?"

Helen said, "Come on, Daddy. We agreed not to talk politics."

He ignored her. He said, "He's an admitted abuser. He walked in on the teenage girls in the dressing room when they were naked or almost naked at that ... whatever it was, that beauty pageant he runs, and he bragged about it. On tv! And he advocated beating people up. Really. At a rally. On television for the love of God. He told his supporters to beat the crap out of a heckler. Sometimes I wish ... Oh, never mind."

Helen said, "Geez, Daddy. I remember when you were the laugh of the party."

Changing to a safer subject, Emma interjected, "Maybe the four of us can meet again for dinner. But not here. Some other place. We've heard great things about The Inn at Shrimp Bay."

...

After breakfast. Helen and Eva met with Larry and the girls, and Bryce and Emma checked out of the Peter Puget Resort and drove to Eastsound and rented a room in the Blue Heron. From their room, Bryce tried to call Asher and Diane but could not reach them. "Must not be any cell service where they're camping. We'll have to drive through the park and hope to spot them. A family with three children and one big tent shouldn't be that hard to spot." Which turned out to be true. Emma spotted Asher's van with its distinctive blue and green car-top carrier and the big U-Dub Huskies sticker on the back window.

They pulled to a stop behind the van. Martin and Josiah were riding their bikes around the campground; Diane was nursing the baby.

"Hey there," Bryce said. "We thought maybe we could spend the day with you guys if you'd like that."

"Sure. We'd love it."

"Great. Where's Asher?"

"He's scouting out the area. There are some great hiking trails and a nearby beach. We'll probably all go for a hike when he gets back. Maybe even climb the mountain."

At some point, Bryce and Emma, Helen and Eva, Larry, Brian, Melony, Kaylee and Rebecca all met while exploring the woods and the beaches. They chatted and wandered about gathering rocks and shells and climbed the twenty-four-hundred-foot Mount Constitution, Bryce and Emma driving up in Bryce's old Lexus, the younger family members on foot. The climbers stopped often to take in the views or take a break from walking. They passed by a house off a wooded lane that had a wrap-around front porch and a fireplace not inside but on the porch, and a large stone chimney. Bryce mentioned that it looked like Billy's house. "I could love living in a place like that," he said, "But not a million miles from civilization. The daily commute would be too off-putting. I've gotta be close to the action."

...

Everywhere they stopped, Larry pulled his sketchbook out of his backpack and made quick sketches of the scenery and his companions. Drawing was a form of calisthenics to him or maybe a form of yoga, and had been since college. He didn't think of the weekly figure drawing sessions at the League he and his loft mate went to as serious art. Mostly they did quick gesture drawings, a way to keep his hand-eye coordination sharp. Same for the casual drawings he knocked off in his favorite tavern in Brooklyn. Figurative art had not been viable as contemporary art to him for ages, granting exceptions like Phillip Pearlstein and Elmer Bishoff, but as he sketched Kaylee and Rebecca and the trees and shorelines something began to flitter enticingly in his mind. Could he make something modern and solid and meaningful out of paintings of bodies in natural environments? *I mean for god's sake, hasn't it all been done a gazillion times? Yet, yet...*

The girls marveled at how quickly he drew and at how he ignored details yet captured with a few strokes of his pencil what to them was the essence of his subjects. "How do you do that?" Rebecca asked.

"I just do," Larry said. "It's magic."

"I'll say."

He did a sketch of the two of them together on the beach, Kaylee perched on a fallen and weathered tree trunk and Rebecca standing behind her with her arms on her shoulders and leaning into her so that their faces were cheek-to-cheek. Kaylee said, "I want it. Can I have it? Please."

"Me, me," Rebecca chimed in.

"Hey, I know what," Larry said, "I can rip it in two right down between the two of you and give you yours and you yours," a big grin on his face, adding, "It's the King Solomon solution."

Rebecca said, "That's silly."

"Yeah, I know. I was kidding." A two-to-three second pause and then, "Actually, I'm going to keep this one for myself. I'll do other drawings for each of you, How's that?"

"Yes!"

"That's perfect."

"Oh, do. Please do."

And then the girls took off their shoes and socks and waded out into the water, and then Larry joined them and the three of them splashed each other. And the group of nine spent the rest of the day touring the island with Larry making drawings of them whenever they stopped for a few minutes to take in the views. His drawings were mostly sketches of Kaylee and Rebecca, although he did get one of Helen and Eva that he thought captured them nicely. He was surprised at how much he enjoyed nailing them and the island scenery to paper.

The beach where he did the first drawing was a rocky stretch strewn with large fallen tree trunks that appeared well on their way to becoming fossilized, and wooden picnic tables that looked to be almost as old as the trees. Kaylee posed for Larry to sketch her sitting on one of the logs, wearing the shorts from the day before. She put one foot on the log and raised a knee, tilted her head back and ran a hand through her hair, unconsciously inspired by cheesecake poses she had seen from she knew not where or how long ago. "You look like a girl in a 1950s *Redbook* or *Look*," Eva said. Neither of the young girls knew those publications.

On top of Mount Constitution stood an old castle-looking tower. When Larry and the girls reached the mountain's summit, they looked up to the top of the ancient stone structure, squinting in the sun to see Bryce and Emma waving from the ramparts. "Hey down there. What took you so long."

Rebecca and Kaylee scampered up the tower, and Larry drew them looking out over the island-dotted blue steel water of the Strait of Juan de Fuca with behind them the whipped cream of white clouds in an intense blue sky—interpreted in shades of gray, of course, since his only drawing instrument was a pencil. Later, he asked the girls to pose longer for a more detailed drawing, and he took his time creating separate portraits of each of them posing atop the tower with the sound as background. "Each of you get one of these," he said, and he signed them *With love, Larry Briggs*. Later, he did an even more detailed drawing of the young girls on a beach seen from behind with arms around each other.

"Hold still, damn your hides," Larry said.

They were play-tussling and giggling. Kaylee nestled her cheek between Rebecca's neck and shoulder. The portraits were featureless silhouettes of ambiguous gender, the only fully realized details being in the trees and logs and water and sky. Eva said it looked like a cover illustration for a romance novel. Larry demurred, "Oh please, not that. First ads in women's magazines and now romance novels. No wonder I stick to abstract art" —his protestations in jest because he was having the time of his life filling his sketchpad.

Pretending jealousy, Helen said, "Quit flirting with the girls. They're way too young for you. Why don't you draw pictures of me and Eva?"

He laughed and said, "Nobody wants to see pictures of old ladies on a mountain."

"Old ladies? I'm five years younger than you."

"Yeah, but Larry looks younger," Eva teased, and Helen shot back, "I'll get you for that when we get home," and she scooped up a handful of pebbles and soil and tossed them at her. Eva ducked and closed her eyes.

Larry then knocked out a nice sketch of the two of them and gave it to Helen.

...

After nine that night and finally beginning to cool down, Belle and Billy sipped sweet wine on their balcony. They had not left the resort all day, had wandered the grounds and lunched, and had taken an afternoon nap. Below them was a platform dance floor that extended over the water. A three-piece band had set up, and guests were dancing to the music, mostly lush ballads but a few upbeat swing-era tunes. Billy and Belle quietly watched. "Look at the couple closest to the bandstand," Belle said, the sound of her voice softened in the night air. "They are so smooth, almost like professional ballroom dancers."

"Yea, I guess so. Kinda showoffy if you ask me."

Billy had been taciturn all day, still pissed at the way Bryce had ruined his evening the night before. His hands were gripping the balcony rail. Belle put one of her hands over his. After almost sixty years of living with him, she knew how to deal with him when he got that way. No complaints. No reprimands. She allowed him his long pout and spoke no more than was needed. They sipped their wine, watched the dancers, listened to the music; and after a few minutes Billy spoke up for practically the first time all day. "That scene down there looks like something from the nineteenth century, like one of those paintings by that French guy. You know, he painted almost that very scene."

"Monet?" Belle ventured.

"No, the other one."

"Renoir?"

"Yeah, that's the one. Sometimes when I see that painting in a magazine or something I think it would have been nice to have lived back then. Paris. Partying on the Seine."

"Well you old romantic you."

"Yeah. Uh huh. I can be romantic." Then, "We got it as good as them. We got Orcas Island, San Juan de Fuca. Besides, in that painting, they weren't dancing, they were eating."

"Yes. But it was the mood, the gaiety."

Finally, he was over his snit she thought but didn't dare say so out loud for fear of bringing it all back. She knew his all-day pout had been about Bryce jerking his hat off, shooting off his big mouth, and he and Emma cutting short their visit and leaving the island—or did they leave; maybe they were cavorting on another part of the island and having a grand old time. "Probably with Larry and our granddaughter and that other young girl. Whose kid is she anyway?"

"Heather's. She's Renae's granddaughter."

"You'd think after we paid for his plane ticket and let him stay with us Larry would want to spend more time with us."

"Aw, you're just being crotchety. It's good the young man can spend some time with people closer to his own age. They were probably hiking somewhere too strenuous for us anyway."

Just then they heard the front door open and footsteps through the cabin. Larry dropped his backpack by his bed and called out, "Hey you guys. I'm back."

"Out here," Belle said. "Come on out."

Billy said, "Grab one of those chairs and a glass. We have some nice wine."

The music drifting up from below was muffled by the night air as if coming from some distance across the water. "Dance with me," Larry said, and Belle stood up and curtsied, and they danced to "Tennessee Waltz."

"I didn't know you knew how to waltz," she said.

"I'm full of surprises."

Billy tapped the edge of his wine glass in time with the music. A dreamy smile crossed his lips. Later, while drinking a second glass each, Larry told them that Helen and Eva had asked him to ride back to Olympia with them and said they wanted to take him out to Lizzy's. "Tired of our company already?" Billy asked—with no hint of an edge to his voice. His mood had softened with the lulling music and the pleasant night.

"No, not at all. It's just ..."

"It's fine, Larry," Belle said.

Billy said, "It's the MAGA hat, ain't it? I swear to god y'all can't disagree about politics without getting bent all out of shape."

"No, it's not that. I just want to spend some more time with Eva and Helen, and I really want to go out to Aunt Lizzy's."

With a chuckle, Belle said, "City boy from New York goes home way out west and wants to spend his time on farms with chickens and pigs. Sure. Yeah. All right. Go ahead."

"Yeah, I guess that would be good," Billy conceded.

...

Nightfall had finally settled on the island, and lights from below were still twinkling like fireflies. In the distance, someone had built a bonfire on a beach. Billy said, "I need to say one more thing about the MAGA hat, and then I'll drop it for good. It's this: family members need to be forgiving of one another's differences. Family unity should take precedence over politics. You know and I know that I love Bryce. After all, he's my baby brother, but does he have to go storming off every time we disagree?"

"Geez, I thought for a second there was going to be an apology somewhere in that," Belle said.

"Well damn it all to hell, people ought to be able to agree to disagree," Billy said.

Larry fought hard to resist the urge to argue the concept of agreeing to disagree.

POKER FACE

Back on the mainland in a private room in the back of a barbeque joint off I-5—hardly more than a mile south of their farm, Buddy was playing poker with three other men. His luck was not good. They didn't fall for his bluffs (nobody had ever told him his poker face was pathetic) and the one good hand he had, two pairs, aces and nines, was beat out by a full house. Pounding rain on the roof sounded like a dump truck load of gravel was being let loose. Buddy had consumed four bottles of beer and was down to eight dollars of the fifty he had started with. Next hand, he was holding three tens when one of the other players put down twenty dollars. He was desperate, and he knew, absolutely knew, he could win with three of a kind. "Hey guys," I've only got eight dollars left, but I've got well over a thousand in the bank, and I can put my bike up for collateral if you let me play on credit. You know I'm good for it."

They agreed to let him play on credit. The group had been playing together off and on for years and knew they could trust each other. Buddy said, "Thanks, guys. I'll see your twenty now."

One of the others said, "That's it for me. I'm folding."

The other two stayed in. Buddy turned his cards over. "Three tens, suckers."

One of the others said, "That beats me" and flipped his cards, a pair of kings.

A blast of thunder, rare in Western Washington, rattled the one little window in the back room. It was immediately followed by a strobe-like flash of lightning. The final player flipped his cards one at a time. Showboating. Buddy's heart sank. Deuce, seven; then jack-wham, jack-wham, jack-wham! "Sorry about that, my friend," and he scooped up his winnings.

"Fuck," Buddy said. "You're one lucky son of a bitch."

The winner wrote down what Buddy owed him.

Buddy lost the next hand and the next. He ended up losing more than two hundred dollars. The savings he would have to draw on to pay the debt was money they had set aside as a first payment for getting Lizzy's teeth fixed. He had promised. He knew he had to do something to recoup the losses, and he had to do it fast. Before Lizzy found out he'd gambled away her new teeth.

He thought maybe he could get busy and finish restoring the old Indian motorcycle and sell it. It was a true classic built for the US Army in 1941. Buddy was sure he could get a huge hunk of money for it if he ever finished it. "Oh baby, I'm so sorry," he mumbled.

"What's that?" one of the players asked.

"Nothing. I must have been thinking out loud."

He didn't stand a chance of getting the Indian roadworthy, not before Lizzy checked their bank balance.

Two of the players, Jack and Jason, had come together in Jason's pickup. One of them said they had to call it a night, and they left. The third player, a banker named Roger, younger than the rest, offered to take Buddy home. "Can't ride your bike in this weather."

"Nah. Thanks, but I'm not on my bike. I'm in the Ford."

"All right, Buddy. At least let me buy you another beer."

ORCAS FINALE

Larry continued making sketches throughout the last day on the island. Sketching here, sketching there, sketching everywhere. It was as if he had just discovered the allure of drawing. He also took part in some group activities such as miniature golf (he sucked at it) and a Scrabble tournament with me and Marilou and Eva. I barely beat Larry for the highest score. Mostly he hung out with the women and girls: Renae, Sally, Eva, Helen and the two girls whose names he kept confusing, much to their delight at first, but increasingly to their frustration until Kaylee finally said, "You're doing it on purpose. You're teasing us."

"Nah, I would never do that. It's just that my brain is messed up from sniffing paint thinner and oil paint."

Kaylee teased, "I think your brain is messed up period."

Helen said, "These girls are sharp. You can fool them for a little while, but then they know when you're messing with them."

Eva asked, "Are you going back to Olympia with us or aren't you?"

"Sure. I already told Billy. I think he feels slighted. But hey, you can't please everybody all the time."

"Screw Billy." was Helen's response.

Laughing, Larry said, "Be nice, now." He thought of Helen and Eva as the steadying influence, the glue that held the family together as opposed to Billy and Bryce whose outrageousness sometimes threatened to tear them all asunder. Despite that, he liked Billy and Bryce ... well, maybe not Billy so much.

...

After driving off the ferry at Anacortes, Eva and Helen in their little Kia with Larry riding shotgun headed to Deception Pass, and Renae and Sally in their trusty Subaru aimed for Portland, determined to make it home without having to stop overnight. Eva and Helen wanted to turn what remained of the vacation weekend into a sightseeing tour. They cruised through the campgrounds at Deception Pass, parked by a beach access trail and got out to hike the trail to a rocky beach, but before reaching it, the trail followed a small creek with overhanging trees where they had to duck under one low-hanging branch and step over a tangle of roots. Helen snapped pictures. Larry pulled out his sketchbook and made more hasty drawings.

"This is fabulous," Eva gushed as they stood on the beach. "What a marvelous, marvelous view! It's like looking across the water to some magical place where pirates wade to shore and search for hidden treasures."

"X marks the spot," Larry said with a hearty laugh.

Helen said, "Maybe it's the great and marvelous Pegleg Josiah Johnson's ship."

"The Jolly Ranchomongo or whatever his ship was called," Larry said with another big laugh.

Fallen and sunbleached trees were piled so thick as to form an almost impassable barricade where sand and rocks met forest, pushed there by wind and water over years if not centuries while being seasoned by salty air, water and sand. Helen slipped out of her shoes and rolled up her pant legs and waded ten yards out into the water. A stranger on the beach aimed her cellphone camera at her and Helen waved and smiled for the camera. Family groups wandered about, some wading in the water. Off to their left, parents and children climbed over a steep headland.

Near the cliffs was a small amphitheater with stadium-style seats carved into the hillside and a dirt path that circled the promontory to another part of the beach where Larry drew an island in the sound and the bridge they had only recently crossed, which from their vantage point looked to be impossibly high.

...

On the highway headed south, Renae and Sally passed a sign for the town of La Conner. "I've always wanted to go there," Sally said. "It's famous as an artists' retreat, and there's a big art museum."

"Then let's go," Renae said.

In La Conner they had crab cakes for lunch, then visited the museum where there was an exhibition of paintings by regional artists in homage to some of the greats of the so-called Northwest School of the 1930s and '40s. Most of the paintings were semi-abstract scenes of the area, all misty and moody. Renae said she wasn't sure if she liked the show. "I do," Sally said. "I wish Larry could see this show. I'll bet he'd love it."

What they didn't know was that at about the time they were leaving the museum, Larry was telling Eva and Helen that he'd love to see it. "Back in the … the thirties I guess it was, all the famous Northwest artists lived and worked here. It was like a little Paris. Mark Toby, Morris Graves, Kenneth Callahan, and I don't know who all, they were all somehow associated with La Conner. Oh, and Guy Anderson. He might have been the boldest of the bunch. There was a lot of great stuff done here."

Half an hour later as they drove into the little storybook town, Larry said, "This place is nothing but a doggone tourist trap." There were lots and lots of art galleries. From what they could see from driving slowly past the windows, the galleries were selling schlock paintings of local scenery. There were ice cream parlors, burger joints, souvenir shops. Larry thought of movie sets—false-front buildings. The town was overcrowded with tourists strolling the streets in their shorts and fanny packs and driving bumper-to-bumper, creeping through the town. Four times they circled past the museum looking for a parking spot before Larry said, "Forget it. It's not worth it. Besides, I just looked it up. The museum closes in half an hour. Let's just go."

"Oh, that's such a shame," Eva said. "I know you wanted to see it."

Twenty minutes down the road they stopped for lunch at a café in Mount Vernon where Larry delighted in watching a little girl at the next table eating french fries. She looked to be about two years old and was seated in a highchair at the head of their table. Her mother put a handful of fries on a placemat in front of her and squirted ketchup on the placemat, but when the little girl tried to pick up one of the fries and dip it in the ketchup and put it in her mouth, she couldn't manage it because the potatoes were limp, so she resorted to reaching her hands in the ketchup and licking it off. Ketchup smeared around her mouth and a bright red dot of it was on the tip of her nose.

Back in the car and headed south on the freeway past the Everett exit, Larry looked to the east at the majestic, snowcapped Mount Baker and talked about the sloughs they crossed, how they looked like something swampy you'd more likely see in some place like Louisiana or coastal Mississippi, at least to his understanding, not that he'd ever seen Southern swamps. He wondered out loud why *slough* was pronounced *slew*. Abruptly changing the subject, he said, "I wish I hadn't left my sketchbook in the car when we went for lunch. I could have captured that little girl. Maybe I can sketch her and her parents from memory."

He gave it a shot, but the movement of the car defeated his efforts. When a truck in the left lane suddenly darted into their lane too close in front of them, Eva swerved to avoid an accident and Larry's pencil made involuntary scribbles on the page.

"Damn idiot," Eva grumbled.

Helen said, "Whew." And after a few moments to regain composure, Larry chuckled and said, "Ruined my freaking drawing." Holding up the sketchbook page for them to see, he said, "The little girl looks like a wolf."

"A werewolf," Eva said, and Helen said, "I was a werewolf for the CIA. Great story idea for cable TV."

Larry said, "You write it and I'll see if I can find a producer."

Helen said, "You could have taken a photo."

"No, that would have been too intrusive."

Eva said, "You've been drawing everything everywhere we go. Do you always sketch so obsessively?"

"No, I don't. In fact, I haven't drawn like this in years. I mean I haven't drawn anything in probably four or five years, period— nothing, nada. At least not like this."

"But you mentioned some figure drawing group."

"Oh, that. Yeah, but that's different. I don't know how to explain it, but the drawings I do back in New York I don't even consider drawings. The stuff from the figure-drawing sessions, I don't even keep 'em. They go straight into the recycle bin. But I brought the sketchbook along on this trip with a notion that I might do some paintings based on sketches from the trip. I don't know why. It's not the kind of stuff I do, but I'm searching for a new look to my art. I don't know if I'll actually do anything with it or not."

"A different look? Like how?" Eva asked.

"Attitude, I guess. I never had such lovely subjects to draw."

"Ha! More flattery."

The truth of the matter was, he didn't know why he was drawing so much. He was an abstract painter. Since his grad school days, he had been caught up in the ethics and aesthetics of abstract expressionism and color field painting, in love with Clement Greenberg's theories—no recognizable subject matter, flat, no perspective, the integrity of the picture plane (a phrase he was never quite sure he fully understood but which he strove for). He poo-pooed figurative art and landscapes as outmoded and overly sentimental and trite. Even though he knew that formalist artists—that would be him— were quickly becoming dinosaurs. But then what else was there? He felt there was nothing new an artist could do. Lately, he had been pulled toward more figures and urban scenes. He was digging early Diebenkorn and the Bay Area figure painters and Phillip Guston. If only he could find a way to paint people that wasn't clichéd or hadn't already been done to death. They did it, Guston and Diebenkorn, but then Diebenkorn went whole-hearted abstract.

Larry said, "You know, I have a gut feeling I'm somehow on the verge of a breakthrough, something monumental. I don't know if it's going to grow out of these drawings or not, but I know I'm going to somehow do something new when I get back to New York."

"Well maybe you'd better hurry up and get back and get your ass in gear," Eva said.

Larry said, "Yeah, maybe. But no, I don't think so. I think I need to let it stew for a while. Maybe I should spend a few more days out here."

"Stay as long as you want," Eva said.

He said, "Pollock. I was just thinking about Jackson Pollock. When Peggy Guggenheim commissioned him to do the mural, he put it off and put it off like he was afraid to tackle it, and finally he attacked furiously, painting non-stop for hours, and it was the breakthrough that led to his famous drip paintings. I think that's what I'm doing now. I'm building up to a monumental moment like that. At least I hope so."

...

They passed through Seattle, past the Space Needle and under the Convention Center, and finally past the stadiums in the old Dome district. Boeing Field was ahead and the looming Mount Rainier that appeared to be floating above the trees.

Eva said, "The mountain is out."

"Yeah. It's glorious. You know there's a move afoot to restore its original name, Mount Tahoma. It's the name the Indians gave it. I don't know which tribe."

"That's cool," Larry said. "I could go for that."

Eva said, "Rainier was a British admiral. He fought against us in the Revolutionary War."

"Then let's expel his ass from our geography," Larry said.

Passing the exit to the airport, Larry asked, "What was with your dad getting so mad about Billy's MAGA hat?"

"We were all mad about it. Weren't you?"

"Damn right I was. But I didn't go and jerk it off his freakin' head."

"He shouldn't a brought his stupid politics into the family gathering."

"I get that, and God knows I'm not a Trump fan, but it was just a hat. I mean I thought that was overwrought."

"He gets that way," Helen said.

Eva said, "Granted, it was just a hat, and it was just Billy being Billy and Bryce being Bryce, but the whole damn family is sick of Billy's bossiness, his arrogance and small-mindedness."

"Whew!" Larry said. "I didn't know he was so ..."

"So Billy. Yeah," Helen said. "He hasn't always been like that. My dad says he was pretty nice when he was younger. He thinks Uncle Billy's assholery has increased with age. He says Billy has always felt inadequate. He's pretty good at whatever he tries to do but never feels quite good enough, and he takes it out on other people. We think that the older he gets, the more that bothers him. He's gotten grumpier and grumpier."

"I can relate to that," Larry said. "I'd better watch out and not let myself become another Billy."

Eva said, "I think he was particularly jealous of Bryce and was made to suffer by comparison. I mean when they were growing up. He was eight years older, but by the time Bryce reached puberty he was bigger and stronger than Billy."

"And smarter," Helen said. "The thing is, Dad worshipped Billy when they were kids, and he hated seeing him slip off the pedestal little by little, year after year."

"I guess boys need a father or a big brother role model, and Billy didn't have much of either."

"Yeah, maybe. Oh, I don't know," Larry said. "But they did," Helen said. "They had Harlan. How about Harlan?"

...

Renae and Sally listened to music on their way south, Sally behind the wheel as usual. The CD player cycled through an old album by James Taylor and the Indigo Girls' *Rites of Passages* and Simon and Garfunkel's reunion concert. As they passed by the big casino in Tacoma and past the dome and through long stretches of construction, Renae said, "Let's turn the music off for a while," and after a bit of quiet time, she said, "I could kill Billy, I swear to God. I've had it with these family retreats on Orcas too. He ruins it every time. This is my last one. Never again. And I don't think I'll ever again speak to Billy either."

"Whew, that's extreme. I know everybody's pissed at him right now, but you can't really mean that. He's your brother."

"So? I didn't choose him to be my brother. There's no law that says I have to like him or love him just because we had the same parents. Or the same father anyway. I mean, after all, Harlan and Viola—what kind of parents were they anyway?"

"Maybe, just maybe they were the kind of parents who didn't throw you out of the house or make you go to reparative therapy when you came out, the kind who accepted your same-sex partner without a pittance of shame. Have you thought about that?"

"OK, OK, OK, You're right, and I'm sorry. They were pretty good on that score."

"So was Billy. Despite all his other faults."

"You're right again. I'm justifiably chastised. But look how we turned out. What a screwed-up family. Billy's a living puke, Lizzy's killing herself through self-neglect. Marilou, she's all right, but she married Rudy who's got the personality of a snail. (I can't remember how her saying that got back to me.) And Bryce, I like him, but one minute he's the life of the party and the next he's the grim reaper."

"But you turned out A-OK."

With a big laugh, Renae said, "Damned if I didn't. Thanks for that. You have an easy way of making things all better."

"That's why you love me."

"Oh? I thought it was for your pretty little ass." With that, Sally turned to Larry and said, "You getting all of this?"

"Oh yeah. Every word. It's a story for my podcast."

"Don't you dare!" from both of them.

...

The air conditioner in the Subaru barely kept the car cool. Sally had been complaining about it since mid-spring, saying, almost every time she got in the car, "We've gotta get the AC repaired." So she turned it off, and they drove the few remaining miles with the windows down, outside air blowing their hair, both wearing sunglasses because they were heading directly into the lowering sun. Sally said, "There is a law that says you have to love your brother."

"Oh yeah? What cockamamie law is that?"

"It's the law of affection."

"Yeah, right. And is it written down anywhere?"

Sally thought of saying it was in the Bible, but she knew better than to bring up the Bible to Renae. Instead, she said, "It's written down on your heart. Your heart and my heart. And if you can't see it, it's because you're willfully shutting it out."

"Jesus, girl. First you tell me I'm A-OK and then you shame the shit out of me. I wonder sometimes why I love you."

"Didn't we just cover that?"

"Yes, we did." She leaned into her and gave her a sweet peck on the cheek, and Sally said, "Don't distract the driver." After a few moments of quiet, she said, "I'd give anything if I had a brother to love. Even one like Billy."

"You're welcome to him," Renae said, and they both laughed, and the tension eased off another degree or two. Renae knew that family was something sacred to Sally because she had none of her own. Her father left home when she was a baby, and she never knew him. Her mother was an addict, methamphetamines and no telling what all. Sally had become a ward of the state when she was barely old enough to remember either of her parents and was raised by a succession of foster families, more than a few of whom were abusive. The family she lived with when she was eleven to twelve years old expected her to be responsible for all her own meals and expected her to wash dishes and do the laundry and dust, sweep and mop the whole house once a week. In other words, Sally was that foster mom's Cinderella. Another foster mom called her fat and ugly. One foster father tried to reach inside her shirt. She slapped him, and he never tried that again. At sixteen, she left home and dropped out of school. While other girls her age were either looking forward to prom and finishing high school and starting college, and then starting their careers and families, Sally hung out on the streets of Olympia with other street kids and begged for spare change. Some of her friends on the street had had traumatic sexual experiences: molestation, abuse, rape, or simply loveless and unsatisfying sex. Some were addicts or alcoholics, a lot had mental health issues, mostly based on trauma. Half of her friends were queer; and boys and girls and gender-whatever alike, it seemed that most turned to giving blow jobs for money. It was easy and quick and, as they justified it to themselves, was never intimate. Wham bam and done. Spit it out and rinse their mouths with cool Olympia artesian water, and move on. They felt it was the only way they could survive.

Sally managed to avoid that. She got a job waitressing and a place to share with two other young women who were working similar jobs. She got her GED and went to college.

Renae often said, "It's a marvel how steady and solid you turned out with such a messed-up upbringing."

"I was lucky. There was this really cool outreach street worker, and she had faith in me, and some of the kids I hung out with helped a lot. We took care of each other."

They had already passed a couple of Olympia exits. It was after six o'clock.

"I gotta pee," Renae said. "And I'm hungry."

"There's a little café right off the Maytown exit. We can stop there."

"They probably don't have anything without meat."

"It's a sandwich joint. Surely they'll have something we can eat. Grilled cheese. A salad. They might even have veggie burgers or egg salad. If nothing else, we can get dessert and coffee or milkshakes. That'll hold us until Portland."

They took the exit and pulled into Homeplace Drive-In. The parking lot was full, and inside there was only one vacant table. One was enough. Sally said, "Isn't this the way to Lizzy's farm?"

"Uh huh. It's just a couple of miles. But if you're thinking of stopping off, forget it. No more stops until we get home."

...

They each had an egg salad sandwich on sourdough. They were delicious. Their server was attentive without making a pest of herself. "From now on, when we drive up this way, we're stopping here," Sally said, and Renae agreed.

"And we're going to add egg salad on sourdough to the Fresh Meadows menu."

"Again, I agree."

...

Had they been two hours earlier they would have run into Lizzy and Buddy. From shortly after dawn that morning until nearly three o'clock in the afternoon, with a short lunch break at Homeplace, Lizzy had moped around the house, lackadaisically doing what chores needed doing—washing and folding laundry, hanging sheets on a line that was strung from the back porch, sweeping and dusting while Buddy tinkered with his vintage Indian motorcycle with its faded and scarred military paint job. He had picked it up at a scrap yard for ten dollars and hoped to sell it for a couple hundred when he finished renovating it. No more than a few words were spoken between the two of them all day.

Over the past few days, Buddy had fiddled with his bikes and repaired a fence and done most of the cooking. He had always done a good share of the cooking. Lizzy knew how to do basic dishes: fry burgers, heat canned soup, scramble or fry eggs, sometimes starting out with the notion of frying them but then scrambling them in the pan when she unintentionally broke the yolks. Anything more complicated than that was Buddy's job. Seated across the table from him wearing a pair of his old jeans and a sleeveless undershirt, also his, she watched him move food around his plate with his fork while seemingly staring at nothing. She asked if he was depressed. "No, just sorta out 'a sorts," he said.

"Me too." She had been sorta out of sorts all weekend and could not believe it was because she was stuck on the farm while the rest of the family was enjoying one another on the island. "Well it looks to me like you're bigtime depressed, but you'd never fess up to it. Big, tough men like you don't get depressed, or at least you never talk about your feelings because that would be admitting you have them."

On the rare occasions when he did try to express something deeply felt, his eyes watered, which he blamed on allergies, and speaking was difficult. He would cough or sometimes laugh to cover up. It never fooled Lizzy.

...

It was night but not yet dark. Far from it. Renae and Sally were back on the freeway and passing by the exit to Highway 12 and Mount St. Helens. "I've never been to Mount St. Helens," Sally said.

Renae said, "We'll have to go sometime. But it's not like it used to be back in the first decade after she blew her top. Back then it was like being on some alien planet. Now it's probably pretty much all grown back. But you can still see the crater. That's still otherworldly."

Back on the farm, Buddy announced he was going to ride his bike.

"Now?"

"Yeah."

"Where to?" Lizzy asked.

"Nowhere in particular. Just riding. Wind in my face. Clear out the carb. See how she runs."

"Really?" She stretched the word out in a way that indicated more puzzlement than the situation called for. Like *reeeally*. "You never go for a ride without a destination."

"Yes, I do. Bikes need to be run once in a while to keep the engines from getting sluggish."

"What are we gonna do about keeping you from getting sluggish?"

"Well, you're not exactly zippy your own self, m'dear."

They had both been noticeably and uncomfortably at loose ends since Eva and Helen and Renae and Sally's visit days before, unable to concentrate or stick with any one thing for long. It was as if they were swimming through mud. Neither could explain why without blaming it on what they did not want to admit.

Buddy grabbed his light leather jacket and his helmet and leather chaps, and he slipped his feet into his boots and laced them up. He went out without saying anything more and kickstarted his bike and took off, heading toward the freeway. Lizzy stood inside the front room leaning against the doorframe watching him leave. She felt as if she were watching the end of something.

She went out to check the sheets on the line. They were still damp, but she brought them in anyway. If she left them out overnight, they'd get wet all over again with dew. The dogs and the cat, and even a few of the chickens, scurried about getting underfoot. She remembered seeing her daddy, big hairless Harlan, booting a pesky chicken out of his way and watching the hen fly through the air like a soccer ball, landing with a squawk; and she remembered, shamefully, how they both laughed at the poor hen. That was almost seventy years ago when she was a first grader in Terrebonne Parish. On this day for only a few seconds, she was tempted to kick them but didn't.

Back in the house, she draped the sheets over the back of the loveseat. And then she did something she had not done in ages. She took off all her clothes and crawled naked into bed under a thin sheet and bedspread and went to sleep. It was three hours before her usual bedtime.

Buddy didn't get far from the farm before making an impromptu stop. He parked his bike by the curb at Homeplace Café and went in and had a chocolate milkshake. Comfort food. He had not indulged in a milkshake since high school. He slurped it slowly, long silent pauses between sips, even blowing through the straw to make chocolate bubbles. He stared out the window at a large moon riding the horizon, at cars zipping by on the freeway, thinking nothing in particular, singing an old Chuck Berry song in his head.

A young family at a table by the window grabbed his attention, a mother and father, both in their late twenties or early thirties, dressed in casual summer outfits, both with long hair and the man with a bushy mustache. The children, a boy and a girl, looked to be about eight to ten years old. While waiting for the waitress to bring their food, they played Trivial Pursuit without the game board but with just the question-and-answer cards, and they were all laughing.

That tableau jolted Buddy back to his own childhood, eating out with his parents and his little sister Rhoda. She had been born with a heart defect and was always sickly. The burden of caring for her weighed largely on him since his parents both worked long hours. She married young and moved away and he saw her only two more times before she died at twenty-six. He felt only momentary twinges of guilt when he thought about how little he missed adult Rhoda. He hardly ever if ever mentioned her to Lizzy. *Does she even know I had a little sister? I must have told her.*

Buddy and Lizzy had wanted children of their own. She got pregnant shortly after they were married, but she had a miscarriage, and then another. There were complications—female stuff he never understood—and she was not able to get pregnant again, even though they tried and tried. They never told any of the family about the pregnancy and miscarriage. If you asked them why they didn't have children, neither of them would know what to say. Naturally, the rest of the family talked among themselves about it. Marilou said, "Some people just don't want children. I know it's hard for y'all to grasp that, but it's true. Not every female is born with a desire to birth little ones."

We all agreed that she was probably right. None of us knew just how much Lizzy wished she could have a daughter.

. . .

That happy family could be us, Buddy thought, *me and Lizzy and the children we never had.*

He finished off his milkshake with a loud slurp, and then he left, pulling onto I-5 and heading north.

. . .

The day after returning to Sappho Farm from the island, Larry and Eva and Helen piled into the little Kia and headed to Lizzy's farm. Eva behind the wheel for a change, Larry in the passenger seat, and Helen in the back. When the speed limit sign south of Olympia told her to kick it up to seventy, Eva kicked it up. She always drove the speed limit, never over and never under. She kept her distance from other cars; she stayed out of the passing lane except when actually passing. She prided herself on being the model of a law-abiding driver, for which Helen, Melony and Brian teased her mercilessly until one day she could not abide the teasing any longer and pitched a hissy fit. That put an end to their teasing and is probably the reason Helen does all the driving now.

They took the Maytown and Littlerock exit and passed Homeplace Café and slowed to rock along at country road speeds.

"That place is begging for a big neon sign that says EAT," Larry said.

"Lizzy says the food is good."

"There you go. I rest my case."

SLOW TO 35, a sign warning of a curve said, and Eva slowed down. Another quarter mile or so and a sign said *SLOW TO 20*. Again, she lifted her foot off the accelerator.

Helen said, "I don't think twenty-five would kill you."

"And how would you feel if it did?" Eva said, as she sped back up to forty-five after the curve.

Larry said, "Man oh man, it's really lush and green out there, trees and undergrowth so thick a mouse would have trouble squeezing between 'em."

They passed the Littlerock Saloon with its parking lot crowded with pickup trucks. "That looks like a honky-tonk out of some Southern gothic movie. Maybe a horror movie," Larry said.

Eva said, "I guess it is. I'll bet they even have a sluice crick in there."

"And probably the men's room has a tin trough to piss in," from Larry. "They need a big sign out front that screams SHIT KICKING MUSIC!"

"I'll bet Saturday nights in there are raucous as all get-out."

Helen said, "Maybe you can ask Buddy about that. I've got a feeling he's made an appearance or two in that joint."

Eva let her foot off the accelerator again, not because of any sign but because their conversation had grown languorous, and the day was lovely, cool and quiet. They eased along the road, up Lizzy's driveway and into their dead-grass front yard.

...

The yard was much like the saloon parking lot, littered with cars and motorcycles, some of the cars in pieces with their hoods up. "Is that an old Thunderbird out there?" Larry asked Lizzy.

"Yep. From back when they were ... you know ... hot. We've had it forever."

"It must be from the sixties?"

"Earlier. Fifty-six."

"That must be worth a pretty penny."

"It would be if Buddy would ever finish restoring it."

Eva asked, "Where is Buddy anyway?"

"God only knows. Off riding his bike somewhere. Nowadays that's about all he ever does."

There was a moment when everyone felt a little out of place, as if they picked up on a vibe that Lizzy didn't want them there. They were standing in the front yard looking at the old T-bird. Lizzy had not yet invited them in. The moment of discomfort swooped down on them like a bird in flight and just as quickly flew away.

Lizzy said, "Buddy did the strangest thing last night. He apologized for destroying my career."

"He what?" Eva asked.

"Well, you know. Before I met him, I had my heart set on becoming a dancer. I gave that up to marry him, and I never gave it a second thought." Their dogs approached and rubbed up against Eva's legs.

"Do you ever regret it?" Eva asked.

"Not really, I… yes, I did, but not really. I think about it a lot. But I never blamed him. That was all on me, and no regrets. Being a dancer in New York was a childish dream anyway. My god, I thought we'd talked it out fifty-something years ago, and he just now brings it up."

Other than apologizing for destroying Lizzy's career, Buddy was even quieter and more withdrawn than usual the rest of that night and the following morning. He pushed his breakfast around on his plate and swigged down his coffee in about three big gulps, then got up from the table and walked into the bedroom and got dressed. He put on his black leather riding jacket, pulled it off hesitantly and then slipped it back on. He opened the bottom drawer of the dresser and reached under a pile of T-shirts and pulled out a small pistol and jammed it in the inner pocket of his jacket. He walked out the front door, and, as he stepped out, he turned and said, "I have to go out," and he mounted his motorcycle and took off.

Lizzy stood still. She was listless and worried all that day until almost sundown when Larry and Eva and Helen showed up.

Buddy was still unaccounted for. He was tooling up I-5 to a little town not far from Tacoma. On a street running parallel to the freeway, he pulled into the parking lot of a marijuana dispensary. He had driven by it many times but had never been inside. He would not be recognized there. He stood quietly shuffling his feet until the only customer in the shop left. Then he stepped up to the counter and faced a clerk who looked to be about fifteen years old. "Could I get like a dime bag?" he asked.

"What's that, man? Never heard of a dime bag."

"It's, uh ... aw, never mind." He reached into his jacket and pulled out the pistol and waved it shakily at the clerk. He said, "Just open the cash drawer and give me all the money. Put it in a bag."

He looked around desperately, still waving the gun shakily, while the kid pulled money out of the drawer. "Hurry it up," he said, which was when the gun went off with a loud blast. His hands were trembling so that he pulled the trigger without realizing it. He dropped the gun immediately as the kid grabbed his neck and fell to the floor, the gun and the bag of cash lying on the floor, paper money scattered about. From his position on the floor, the kid said, "Damn, man. What'd you do that for?"

Buddy ran for the door, stopped and spun around and ran back to pick up the little pistol and the bag, hurriedly shoving the money back in, and rushed out again.

...

Am I really doing this? Am I this desperate to replace Lizzy's money before she knows it's gone? Yes, yes, I had to. Is the kid all right? Oh my god, I pray it was only a glancing shot to his neck. Sure, he's all right. He didn't even sound hurt, just confused. Shit. I didn't mean to shoot him.

...

Lizzy was still standing outside with Helen and Larry. She was shaking her head as if to clear the mental cobwebs. She said, "What the heck are we standing out here for? Come on, let's go inside. I made a big pitcher of lemonade. Ice cold. Or we got booze if you'd rather."

Lemonade was the women's consensus choice for a refreshing beverage. Not so Larry. He said, "Booze sounds good to me. Whatcha got?"

"Johnny Walker or Jack Daniels."

He decided on the a Jack and a Coke.

Stepping through the door, Lizzy slung her arm around Larry's shoulder and said, "It's so good to see you, kid," not as an aunt would but more like another man—in a bar or at a football game.

...

Buddy's plan had been to rob the marijuana shop and put the money in their bank account to replace the money he had lost in the poker game. She would never know the money had been lost. *Stupid, stupid, stupid*, he berated himself. He felt for the gun in his hip pocket to satisfy himself it was still there. The stupid gun was not supposed to be loaded. It was a prop.

He headed into a residential neighborhood and took a few random turns, tooling slowly through … *where am I? Lakewood, I think*. His mind was boiling, not knowing where to go, what to do. He kept saying to himself, I shot a man. All my years as a cop, it never happened, and today I shot a man. A kid really. Is he dead? Should I go back? No, I can't.

He made his way back to the freeway and drove past the Army base and then back south toward home.

...

Lizzy said she was sorry Buddy was not there. "I'm sure he'll be home soon."

Where the hell was Buddy? Staying out so long without any word was not like him—well, except for lately. Helen said it was getting on toward time they needed to go. Before they left, Lizzy made Larry promise he would write to her. "Keep me posted on what you're doing. Especially about the new show."

...

It had been fully dark for an hour or more. Buddy had driven his motorcycle out to the lake where he and Lizzy had first kissed. He lay down on the grass and smoked a cigarette and thought about all the good times and bad times since he and Lizzy had been together. Then he rode to a bar and stopped off for a drink. He knew he shouldn't. He'd been gone far too long already. Lizzy would start to worry if he didn't get home soon. *Hell, she's probably already worried sick.* It was like when he lost all that money in the poker game. He knew then he should not have kept betting, but he felt compelled to play one more hand and yet another and another, convincing himself he'd win big on the very next hand, just as now he felt the urge to drink even though he didn't really want to.

(Lizzy did not yet know about his poker disaster, but he knew he couldn't keep it from her forever. If he could only figure out some way to recuperate his losses. How much money was in that bag anyway?)

The bar he had drifted to almost unconsciously was Nellie's. He hadn't been there in forever. Since Buddy and Lizzy first met there, it had been sold twice. The new owners, each of them, had retained the name and retained but simplified the menu and added more beer selections and a pool table. Nellie's was now a gay bar, or so he had heard. That didn't matter to Buddy. *If people think I'm queer, let 'em think it. No skin off my ass.* He walked into the dark tavern. The place was empty. Not a single customer. One worker behind the counter. Buddy ordered a Budweiser and carried it to a table in the back near the pool table. After a while he heard the rumble of another motorcycle parking out front, and a biker came in and ordered a beer, also a Bud, and walked right up to Buddy's table like he knew him and said, "Hey, man. Mind if I join you, fellow biker and all?"

Buddy sensed in an instant why the man had approached him. *If he tries to hit on me, I can politely say thanks but no thanks. No problem.*

"Sure. Pull up a chair." Even though he was not really in the mood for company.

The man sat down. He introduced himself.

"Buddy," Buddy said. "My real name is Wendell, but everybody calls me Buddy."

The man attempted to engage Buddy in conversation. He asked him about his bike, asked him what he did for a living.

"Farming."

"Married?"

"Uh huh."

"Any kids? Grandkids?"

Buddy responded politely but desultorily.

"How 'bout you, man? You got a wife? Girlfriend?"

"Nah. I'm not into women. Queer as a three-dollar bill, that's me. Hope that don't bother you none."

"Naw, it don't. I kinda figured as much."

They sat in silence for some time after that. sipped their beers slowly, and the man bought them each another. He said, "It seems you're nursing a big hurt."

"Yeah, kinda. Been down on myself for days. I don't know exactly why."

"I know what that's like."

Buddy said, "I met my wife right here fifty-some-odd years ago. It was mostly a breakfast joint back then, not a bar. Nineteen sixty-four I think it was. Yeah. The year the civil rights law was passed. Vietnam was heating up. Jesus, what a time that was."

"What was your position on the war?"

"Confused. I kinda wanted to go at first. Felt it was my duty as a citizen. But then I turned against it."

"Did you demonstrate against it?"

"No. I thought about it, but I didn't. I did march in support of civil rights though."

"Me too. Did you go to segregated schools?"

"Yeah. You?"

"Uh huh. So stupid. So harmful. You still married to the same woman?"

He nodded in agreement. "She was bright and beautiful, a dancer with a shitload of talent. She gave up dancing because of me. I ripped her away from what she loved and stuck her on a freaking little farm for the next fifty years because of some dumb idea it would be romantic to live off the land, grow our own food, kill our own meat. It destroyed her life. Just ate her up. She'd never say that, but I know it did. Before that, I was a cop. That was even worse for her. Every damn day when I put on my uniform and took up my gun, she worried I'd not come home. The farming and the policing, it took away her, unh ... her spark, I reckon."

He felt himself about to tear up but held it back, sniffled, said, "Excuse me. I think I'm getting a touch of a cold."

The other man said, "Shit man. I bet she'd never go back to what she was before if she had the chance, because ...I mean, I bet she loves you more than she ever loved whatever it was she might a wanted back then. And you ... well you're a good man. I can tell. A kind and loving man with a conscience as big as a barn."

"Jesus, you give me far too much credit." He took a big swig of his beer.

His new drinking buddy reached under the table and patted Buddy's knee and upper leg, and let his hand remain there on his thigh. Buddy thought about removing it, but it felt comforting. And then something happened that he wasn't expecting. "Goddamn, I'm getting a boner."

That brought a smile to his companion's lips.

Buddy had not had an erection in so long he had almost forgotten what it felt like. Assuming that announcing his erection was a signal, the man slid his hand up to Buddy's crotch. "Yep. That's a boner all right," he said.

Buddy mentally quipped, what are you, the dick inspector? Somehow the man's bold grab struck him as funny, and Buddy decided that if it didn't go beyond touching—why not? It felt good, sent his mind rushing back to when sex with Lizzy was aggressive and raunchy and frequent. Emboldened because Buddy had not swatted his hand away and because there was no one else in the café to see what was going on, and because the counterman had stepped into the kitchen where he couldn't see them, the guy unzipped Buddy's fly and pulled his cock out, grabbed it in a way reminiscent of the way Lizzy used to hold it when they were young. Buddy closed his eyes and leaned back in his chair, scooched his ass a bit to give his companion a better hold on what he held in his hand.

After what seemed to Buddy like maybe five minutes, he pushed the man's hand away and said, "I'm sorry, man. It's not you. Well, it feels good, but no. I can't do that," and he put everything back in its proper place and zipped up and stood up and said sorry again and walked out, not looking back.

NOSTALGIA TOUR

I can barely remember when Larry first announced he was going to New York—didn't say whaddaya think, Dad, 'bout the idea of me going to New York. Nope. He simply announced it like it was a done deal and his mother and I didn't have a say-so. We just about came to blows over it even though we had known since his second or third year at U-Dub, before grad school that it was what he was inevitably heading toward. Crazy damn kid thinking he could just haul off and go to New York City and become the next firkin' Picasso.

"You're too young," I said.

"I'm a grown man, Dad."

"Maybe in years, but not in maturity." And then I added, "Parker won't know what to do with himself without you around to advise him. He's always depended on you."

"Yeah, too much. Parker is a grown man too. He'll survive. It'll be good for him."

Then I said, "How're you going to survive out there, huh? New York City can be a vicious, heartless city. Thinking you can go to New York and become a successful artist is unrealistic. I hate to say it so bluntly, kiddo, but it's downright stupid."

(No, I didn't say that last bit, but I thought maybe I damn well should have.) I said, "Stay here and you can be a big fish in a little pond; in New York you'll be a minnow in the ocean."

Marilou nodded at everything I said, and she said, "Uh-huh," and "That's right. Ask Lizzy why she couldn't make it there." (He had asked Lizzy, and she had said that wasn't the situation at all.)

"That big fish-little fish argument is a cliché, Pop," Larry said.

"That doesn't make it any less true."

I could hear it coming, and immediately it came: "But you know what? Almost every successful artist in the city could have been that big fish in the little pond back home, but they chose to go to the city. Some of 'em fell flat on their asses, and some of 'em made it.

241

And some made it somewhere in between. Some do and some don't. I can make it, Dad, Mom. I know I can."

"I hope so, son. I truly do."

My big problem with Larry leaving was he was too much a dreamer. If his art were a hobby, that would be cool. Admirable. But as a career? Come on. Give me a break. He might as well take up writing and decide to be the next Hemingway or Steinbeck. *Wasn't that exactly what I was doing? Me, as romantic and impractical as my dreamer son. But at least I was doing it at home and I had a steady income.*

Despite my doubts, I was proud of Larry's gumption. He inherited that from his mother—the woman who was willing, way back in high school, to go with me to a nudist camp. Talk about gumption.

Yeah, Marilou was more supportive, but she was also scared to death he would get trampled in the big city. Scared his inevitable failure to become the next Picasso would crush his spirit or that he'd fall in with a bunch of pill-popping coke-snorting would-be artists and fry his brain. As for me, once Larry's determination was made clear, I was more encouraging.

...

Now that he has beat the odds and is a not-exactly-starving New York artist, Larry spent most of his first day back from the island relaxing at home with Eva and Helen, and part of a day visiting with Lizzy. Then they let him take the Kia to visit us—me and Marilou and Parker and Delia and Baby Randolph. We all piled in the almost new eight-seater Honda van that I bought precisely for such family outings, and we tooled around Olympia to give Larry an opportunity to see town anew and recall favorite places from when he was a boy. We walked the trail at Tumwater Falls beside the powerful waterfall and over the bridge that crossed the smaller falls where Larry marveled at the rustic beauty of the abandoned brew house (the original one, not the monstrosities that spanned either side of the street above). "Are they ever going to do anything with those dilapidated horrors?"

"Probably not," I said. (The brewery had gone out of business long ago, and the buildings were falling apart.)

We drove through downtown and strolled the boardwalk at Percival Landing and visited the Farmer's Market and went out to the McClain Creek nature trail, which had been upgraded nicely since Larry had last seen it. "Was this trail even here before? I don't remember it."

"I don't think it was. I can't remember either."

Climbing into the van after an hour on the trails, Larry said, "I'm hungry."

"Me too," Parker chimed in, and someone mentioned it was three o'clock in the afternoon and we hadn't eaten lunch. "How did it get so late so early?" Marilou asked, and she suggested we head back downtown and grab some food from the Deli at Bayview Market and eat out on the deck. There were sandwiches and ready-made salads of all sorts, and a nice breeze on the deck.

After eating, Larry and I wandered out on the boardwalk and past the boats moored there, and we talked about his life in the city and his hopes for the future and what Marilou and I saw in store for our waning years.

Larry said, "You know, in all my life, I don't think we've ever talked like this." We had never been extremely close. Come to think of it, I had never been very close with any of my children. He said, "I like this, Dad. I like us connecting like this."

"Me too," I could barely get the words out. I was choking up. I had not only never been close to any of my children, I had never been able to comfortably express my feelings.

He said, "What a surprise it was hearing that you're writing a novel. I'm sure it will be great. I know you're a keen observer of life and ... and uh, you're smart, and you're really good with words. I'm proud of you already, and you haven't even finished it."

I laughed, a deprecatory laugh, and said, "Oh hell, I've finished it all right. About five times. But then I keep going back and rewriting it."

I felt like those few moments on the boardwalk were the best moments ever.

...

Back home on Royal Court after Larry went back to Eva and Helen's Sappho Farm, Marilou and I took a long nap, and after we woke up, we decided to get takeout burgers and shakes from a nearby McDonald's. Neither of us felt like fixing anything, and Baby Randolph was cranky, so everybody grabbed their burgers and drinks out of the sacks, and Parker and Delia took theirs into their room to eat in bed with Baby Randolph in front of the TV. "Mr. Bean" was on.

In the living room, Marilou turned our TV on, also to "Mr. Bean." She didn't even like "Mr. Bean," but she tuned to it for me. I loved it. When the show finished, I adjourned to the den where I had my computer set up on a small desk shoved into a corner of the room. I pulled up my novel-in-progress—tentatively titled *The Red Accordion*—and got to work on what must have been the fifth or sixth complete rewrite. I'd been writing and rewriting that damn book since before they killed bin Laden. It was a family saga spanning decades. I should have the family do a weekend on Orcas, I thought. Like us. I could put in a scene like when Bryce gave Billy what-for over his stupid hat. Damn if that wasn't fun to witness.

I could do it. I mean why not. It would fit with what I already had. The family at the heart of the story was huge. It would be easy to have them gather together for an explosive weekend with a despot of a patriarch and a couple of constantly bickering brothers. Only it couldn't be Orcas Island because it was set in the South. Locations Marilou's dad had talked about down around the Gulf Coast of Louisiana. Hairless Harlan was in it, only under a different name.

One of these days I should go down there to scout locations. Maybe the family get-together could be at a fishing camp on one of Louisiana's many rivers and bayous. Wouldn't have to be a real place, could be fictitious, maybe an island in the Gulf. Are any of those islands inhabitable? Hell, were there even any islands down there? That's what Google is for. It sure would be nice if old Harlan were still alive and could talk to me about places like that. The old cue-ball-head sure had told some entertaining stories about the Southland. But Marilou said most of 'em were tall tales.

We were both restless. I don't know why—the reality of Larry soon going back to New York, maybe. We watched a string of sitcoms and doctor shows, but neither of us could concentrate. We could not say, if asked, what was going on between Penny and Leonard on "Friends" or what insanity Sheldon was up to or … whatever. Marilou pushed herself out of the chair and went into the kitchen and opened a bottle of beer, something she seldom did but had been doing more often lately.

She knew what I was doing. Working on that dang novel as usual. She would have figured it out that I'd changed out of my day clothes. She would assume I was naked beneath my robe and probably thinking I should wind it up soon and go to bed, hoping she would come in and get naked and crawl in with me. Like that ever happened anymore. We'd like to. Both of us thought about it often enough. But seldom at the right time or at the same time. By the time we went to bed, we were usually too tired. Plus, I was a reader in bed. No matter how horny I might be. Hell, even if Marilyn Monroe was under the covers with me, I wouldn't put my book down until I got to the end of the chapter. And I don't know about Marilyn, but Marilou would be asleep by then.

Sometimes I was afraid she resented my compulsion with the never-ending novel, but I think she admired my never-give-up attitude.

...

An hour later the TV was off and we were reading by the light of our twin bedside lamps. Nothing but thin sheetrock and empty space separated our bedroom from Parker and Delia's. Through the wall, we could hear muffled talk from them. None of their words were distinguishable. Marilou whispered, "I think they're arguing."

"Maybe. Maybe they're getting it on."

"Probably. Hmmm, and arguing at the same time. That's pretty much all they ever do. Argue and screw, screw and argue." I thought of telling Marilou we had to get them out of the house once and for all and into a place of their own, even if we had to pay the rent for them.

Around midnight I got up to trip to the bathroom only to find the door was locked—another reason to wanted Parker and Delia out of the house, only a single bathroom for the five of us. Me and Parker nodded at each other when he came out of the bathroom. Three minutes later, silence from across the hall in Parker and Delia's room, and I could not get back to sleep. I picked up the book I had been plowing through over the past week, a Faulkner book I was having the Dickens of a time comprehending, my back to Marilou, who lay in silence with a sleep mask over her eyes.

After some time she whispered, "Are you awake?"

I didn't respond. She knew I was awake because I was still holding the book open.

"Rudy, can we talk? Put your book down, please." She removed her mask, a sign that she was serious.

I closed the book and set it on the side table. She said, "I've been wanting to talk to you about something for quite some time. It's Parker and Delia. I can't take them living here much longer. I mean I love them and all, but ..."

I turned onto my side to face her. "Thank the Lord. I've been thinking the same thing for ages, but I was afraid to bring it up."

Naming their litany of reasons for asking Parker and Delia and Baby Randolph to find a place of their own was like shooting targets in a sideshow booth to win a stuffed animal.

"We can hear 'em every time they get in an argument."

"Every time they have sex."

"Oh good lord, yes. Did I ever scream like Delia?"

"You did. Yep."

"I didn't."

"Oh yeah. And you could again if they weren't in the next room."

"And if we weren't a gazillion years old."

"And Baby Randolph. He's constantly making messes. And do they ever bother to clean up?"

"Hell no."

"Sometimes I'm afraid to go to the bathroom because of all his stuff scattered in the hallway. Clothes and balls and roller skates he's too young for and will never use."

"We can't dare walk from here to the bathroom barefooted."

"And the messy underwear on the bathroom floor."

"Lord god, my nose may never recover."

We started laughing cathartically at the laundry list of complaints.

"And Parker is always around."

"Underfoot almost as much as Baby Randolph."

I don't think he'll ever get a job so long as they're living here. There's no incentive for him to really try."

"Let's face it, we're getting set in our ways and don't need another family under our roof."

"It seems like we have more disagreements with them every day."

"How to parent the little monster."

"Who's turn it is to do the dishes, take out the trash."

"Why can't they wipe off the counters when they do the dishes?"

"And rinse them well before putting 'em in the dishwasher. Half the time we have to wash 'em again."

"And when was the last time one of them cleaned the stove top?"

"But really, the worst of it is hearing them having sex."

"Oh my god. You said it."

"We can't have sex ourselves for fear of them hearing."

"I'd be mortified."

"But they don't seem to care if we hear them.'

I was floored when the next day, without being asked, Delia gathered up all of Baby Randolph's toys and games and clothing that were scattered throughout the house and put the toys away and put the dirty clothes in laundry baskets and, and she swept and mopped the entire house and washed the dishes and finally said, "Whew! There. I've been meaning to do that for days. Now I'm going to take a shower and get dressed and maybe take Baby Randolph for a walk to the playground."

And to top it off, Parker mowed the lawn.

"My goodness. What brought all this on?" Marilou was flummoxed.

"I don't know. I just woke up thinking about spring cleaning," Delia said.

When she went to take her shower, Marilou whispered to me, "I guess they must have overheard us talking about them last night."

It was a Saturday. Parker and Delia decided to take Randolph to the playground at Squaxin Park and later to have lunch with friends who had a kid Randolph's age. They'd be out most of the day. What a relief!

"I couldn't sleep last night," I said. "I was up almost the whole night thinking about my book. I think I might want to change the name. *Trouble in Paradise* is starting to sound corny to my ears. Besides, I found out it is the title of a 1932 movie and a Rufus Wainwright song."

"What would you change it to?"

"I don't know. We'll think of something. But there's something else. I'm done. *Fini*. I just realized it—it is really, really done by God. Now I need you to read it and critique it. After all, you were the English major, and you read all the time. Who better to critique it?"

She said, "Guess what. I have read it. More than once." She'd been reading it little by little, over and over, when I wasn't in the house. She said she was hoping I would ask her to critique it "because frankly, it needs some serious editing. It's good. Damn good. But not there yet."

...

Parker and Delia's exemplary behavior lasted two whole months, during which the family enjoyed conviviality and good weather. Marilou on a Friday evening and Delia on a Monday and again a few days later cooked sumptuous meals, and the five of us enjoyed sharing the dinner table. Parker and I weeded the garden together and trimmed the willow tree.

Even after they slacked off on helping out around the house, harmony in our Royal Court home continued throughout the summer and into fall, and we thanked our lucky stars for the slew of good deeds and adult behavior from Parker and Delia.

And then it happened.

...

"What lord-deserted imbecile did this? Look at this mess!" That explosion of invective from the mouth of Marilou would have deserved five or six more exclamation points if it had been put on paper. She had just fished out of the refrigerator a big pot of leftover soup and four slices of cornbread she had wrapped in plastic wrap and refrigerated after the previous evening's dinner. She buttered all four slices and put them in the oven to heat up and dished up four bowls of tomato and bean soup and opened the microwave and shouted out in horror her shock at the burnt-red splattering of last night's tomato soup that coated the inside of the microwave.

Delia was on the couch with her slippered feet on the coffee table watching the five o'clock news. She jumped off the couch as if stung by a bee and rushed to see what had made Marilou explode so loudly. *Good lord above! She was always bitching about something or other, flew off the handle over the slightest thing*—what she must have been thinking was usually something about something she or Parker did that they should not have done or didn't do that they should have. What now?

Delia had mixed together a concoction of the leftover tomatoes and beans from the previous night's meal, adding tomato sauce, onions, carrots and celery, and zapped it for a mid-morning snack. What Marilou saw that sent her into a hellacious rage when she opened the microwave door was the smeared residue of that concoction. It was splattered all over the inside of the microwave and cooked hard to the inner walls. How could it have been sloshed out like that without Delia even noticing? It wasn't just spilled; it ... Oh, she remembered. She had kind of witnessed the event but hadn't paid close attention. Delia had started the microwave, probably on too high a setting, and before it was done, she had to rush to the bathroom because Baby Randolph had an accident, poor baby, and when she came back, the microwave had turned itself off. She must have fished out the soup without even looking.

"It looks like somebody killed an animal in here," Marilou said.

Delia said, "I'm sorry. I'm afraid that might have been me."

"You're afraid? Might have been? You don't know? I don't guess it dawned on you to maybe clean it up."

"I didn't even ... oh, never mind. You're right. I'm sorry."

Marilou held the door to the microwave open and glowered at Delia. She said, "Well maybe you should do it now."

"OK. Geez. Could I at least wait until after dinner?"

"Whatever. Do what you want. We'll just heat up our dinner in your soup slop."

Delia mumbled something about martyr mode. With an exaggerated sigh, she stepped over to the sink and grabbed a dishrag and wet it, and scrubbed down the inside of the microwave. There were splatters on the bottom and all three walls and the inside of the glass door. Cleaning it required seriously hard scrubbing with soap and water.

Marilou was just getting started with her hissy fit. She could feel the pressure building until it reached the explosion point. She screamed, "Get out! Right now."

"But Mama Marilou, I'm cleaning it up."

"You could lick it off the oven walls for all I care. Just leave it. I'll clean it. I want you and Parker out of here. I mean it. I want you out of my house immediately. I can't take it any longer."

Delia exploded with loud wails and tears and rushed into her bedroom crying. Baby Randolph stopped playing with his toy cars on the living room floor and lay down on the floor with his face in the carpet and boohooed. Parker got up out of the chair and laid his book facedown and followed Delia, shooting his mother a look that could turn fire into icicles as he passed through the door into the hall.

After pouring herself a glass of wine with trembling hands and almost swallowing the whole thing in a single gulp and finally getting her breath to quit coming in gasps, and after sitting down on the floor with Randolph and rubbing his back and saying, "It's OK," Marilou said, "I didn't mean immediately. I ..." but she was speaking to nobody but Baby Randolph, so she pushed herself up off the floor and walked down the hall to Delia and Parker's room and said through the closed door, "I didn't mean immediately. I meant like as soon as you can, and, and I'm sorry I shouted. But this whole thing … all of us living under one roof, it just can't go on. It … it can't."

Silence from inside the bedroom. Marilou waited a minute, then, "I understand you have to find some place to go, and we can even help you with that if we need to. I mean financially. But me and Rudy are too old to go on sharing our home with our children. We just can't take it anymore. And you and Parker are way too old to be living with your parents. I mean gee-wiz, Parker, aren't you a little bit ashamed of living with your parents?"

"A little bit?" his voice came through the closed door in gasps. "I am mortified. When people ask me where I live, I just say in Lacey. I don't want to have to explain. It's too embarrassing. But I'm trying to find a job and a way out. I've tried. I've tried and I've tried."

"I know, honey. And I'm sorry. I shouldn't have got so mad."

Parker said, "Would you come in, please? Let's not talk through the door," and Delia said, "Yes, please. I'm sorry, terribly, terribly sorry."

Once inside their room, Delia said, "We understand how hard us living with you must be. We can stay with my folks until we can get a place of our own."

"Next door? I don't think so."

"Just until Parker gets a job."

By then I had wandered in, thinking Marilou might need backup, although frankly I knew she handled things like that much better than I did. I was surprised to see they were having a relatively calm conversation. Something had broken through, and the unspoken but constant tension that had existed between Deliah and Marilou had eased off. I said, "We can pay your rent in a new place until Parker gets a job, and you can pay us back in installments. Whatever you can afford."

We suspected, had suspected for a long time, that Parker had long since given up on finding a job and faked going out on interviews to satisfy us and to fulfill the requirements to keep his unemployment checks coming in. Not that he didn't want to find a job, but just that it seemed so hopeless.

He was depressed. We could see that. I could imagine how devastating it must have been for him. We sympathized, but we could not spend another week living under the same roof with them.

LARRY'S LAST DAY

There was one final thing Larry wanted to do before flying back to New York. The Frye Art Museum in Seattle had a Phillip Pearlstein exhibition he wanted to see. He had always admired Pearlstein. Moreover, his studio mate Arnie worshipped Pearlstein and constantly talked about him.

"No problem," Eva said. "Your flight's not until late afternoon. We can go up, see the show, have some lunch, and do some touristy things like Pike Place Market or go up to the top of the Space Needle, and then get you to the airport in plenty of time. Besides, I like his work too."

Larry said, "I could kill the whole day in the museum. I really don't care about doing any of that other stuff. But if you want to."

"Not me," Eva said.

Helen said she would also like to see the Pearlstein show. "We saw a bunch of his paintings on one of those Sunday morning talk shows once. Remember? (looking to Eva for confirmation) They were amazing. I'd love to see the real things full-size and up close. They're like the most realistic paintings I've ever seen. It's like you can just reach out and touch their skin. I'd expect them to feel soft and warm."

"Actually," Larry said, "His paintings are not realistic at all. He distorts the figures for compositional purposes that most people don't notice. They're deceptive that way. Wait until you take a long look up close. You'll see."

There was another artist in the show with Pearlstein, a painter named Joseph Park. None of them had ever heard of him.

. . .

They had lunch at a place called Trübistro, a tapas restaurant, and then on to the museum. It took Eva and Helen fifteen minutes to take it all in. After twenty minutes, Larry was just beginning to absorb it.

"This is fabulous," Helen said. "I love Pearlstein's figures. Not so sure about the other guy."

Larry nodded and smiled in affirmation but didn't say anything. The women found a bench and sat down and watched Larry. "So this is how artists look at other artists," Helen said. "I can't imagine what he sees that we don't see; what has him so mesmerized."

They watched him walk up close to a Pearlstein painting and practically rub his nose on it, then step back a few inches to carefully examine every inch of it. And then back away to look at it from all the way across the gallery. One by one he examined every painting in that manner, Pearlstein's and Park's.

"What do you think?" Helen asked when, after almost an hour, Larry joined them on the bench.

"Well, Pearlstein is great, of course. I knew that."

"I'm no expert," Eva said, "But what I like about his nudes is that they're kind of erotic without being like ...I don't know, glamorous, I guess."

Helen added, "Yeah, they're just everyday people, droopy parts and all. He doesn't hide anything."

"That's what he's famous for," Larry said. "But it's not what really makes him great. It's the colors and patterns and the way muscles and arms and legs and the crowded environments flow and contrast and blend. Ironing boards and chairs and curtains all become parts of complex patterns and so do muscles and blood vessels and hair. It's like if you could somehow forget they are pictures of naked bodies and just see the colors and shapes, you'd see that they're essentially abstract paintings. Like Kandinsky maybe but figurative. And yet they are super realistic."

"I kind of get that," Helen said. "What about the other guy?"

"At first glance I didn't like his stuff. I thought it was corny, too playful. No, not playful, but more like stilted drama. But the more I look, the more I like it. I think there's a term for this kind of painting. Pop surrealism or something like that. It might be too new for me to tell, but I think he might be good."

He said, "That's the thing about art. It takes repeated viewing over time to decide what you think about it.

The Joseph Park exhibition was called *Moon Beam Caress*, a name chosen, Larry thought, because of the air of mystery created by the prominent moonlight in some of the paintings—a moodiness Larry thought was contrived but effective. Some of his pictures looked like storybook illustrations or still frames from animated films à la Walt Disney. But Disney with a creepy twist. The paintings were bizarre, cleverly humorous, and sweetly romantic; and his technique was flawless—like Perlstein, which was probably why the museum had grouped them together. There were images of cute anthropomorphic animals like "Hello Kitty" and Japanese anime. His interior and exterior scenes were full of moonlight and shadow, like a nighttime version of Hopper's sun and shadows. He also noticeably ransacked the history of film and art for inspiration. As in two paintings that were take-offs on paintings by the great Jean-Auguste-Dominique Ingres. One titled "La Grande Odalisque" was patterned after Ingres' "Odalisque," but in Park's version the reclining nude had an elephant's head and trunk and a woman's body, and his "Bather" was a takeoff on Ingres' "The Valpincon Bather," the trick being that in Park's painting the voluptuous nude with her back to the viewer was a cuddly bunny rabbit—again with a woman's body.

Eva said, "Some of these hybrid human and animal seductresses look malevolent. Sinister."

Helen concurred, saying, "They give me the creeps."

"Me too," Larry said. "I think I love them."

...

Marilou plops the big manuscript down on the table. It's well over four-hundred pages, twelve-point Times New Roman, double spaced, smudged and marred with cross outs and hand-written rewrites. She says, "Jesus, Rudy. You didn't have this later part in what I read earlier. You can't do this. It's us. It's our story. Sure, you changed the names, barely—Marilou to Maryanne and Lizzy to Lisette—but it's clearly our family, unmistakable to anyone who knows us, with all our foibles and fuckups and even graphic sex scenes that I would be mortified to know people were reading. I mean shit, honey ..." the only times she called me honey were when she was about to reprimand me ... "do you really want John what's his name at work knowing about the kinda kinky stuff we sometimes indulge in? Do you want him talking about that with his wife and other people we know? Do you want Billy and Renae knowing we do that?"

"But it's fiction, honey," (When she called me honey I called her honey.) I protested, but I knew she was right; I'd known all along what her response would be.

That was a day or two before Larry went back to New York, not long before Buddy did what he did.

LARRY'S BREAKTHROUGH

Larry had been back in his loft in Brooklyn for six days. On the fifth day, the night before, he went to a party at a friend's apartment in Chelsea, and he drank much more than he should have, woke up late with a headache. Nevertheless, he was soon hard at work on a new painting. He'd been at it for five hours after taking three extra-strength acetaminophen and downing two cups of coffee. Thirty feet away in the other half of the studio space, Arnie was equally hard at work on his painting—a nude as usual, and he was working from the same live model he always painted—his girlfriend Jodi, a thin woman with long mahogany colored hair. She was posed next to a ladderback chair upon which she propped herself with one hand. She was blasé about posing naked in front of Larry while Arnie painted her. And why shouldn't she be? She was a longtime model at the League's figure drawing sessions.

Arnie paced while painting. He made a few strokes of his brush, mixed a bit of cadmium red, yellow ocher, and white to get a color that more or less matched Jodi's skin color, scrubbed it into an area, and then begin to pace back and forth again, studying his painting and the model and chewing on the blunt end of his brush. (He had told Larry at some point that he learned from his mother, who called herself a Sunday painter, that a mixture in various amounts of those three colors was the secret to creating white person skin tones and to mix in burnt umber or burnt sienna for Black person skin; and that a wash of either of those over—believe it or not—ultramarine blue was perfect for shadows on skin.)

"So that's your secret to sexy skin, huh?" Larry quipped, and Arnie said, "Uh-huh."

While Arnie paced, Larry sloshed a three-inch-wide house painting brush in turpentine and spread a wash of translucent blue across a yellow square. And then he stopped painting and studied his work from a distance, then started back painting.

While Arnie's habit was to pace while studying his work, Larry's was to plop down in the easy chair with the plush cushion and upholstery worn thin. Each of them took more time studying their work than applying paint. Larry once told me, "Painting is more about looking than doing."

Around two in the afternoon, Arnie told Jodi to get dressed and knock off for the day, and Larry took a break and ate a peanut butter and jelly sandwich. With mayonnaise. Always with mayonnaise. By then his headache had finally begun to ease off. There was just a bit of tightness in his neck, so he rolled his head in a circle to the left and a circle to the right to loosen the cramped muscles as Jodi stepped into pink thong panties and pulled up a pair of jeans and fastened them and then slipped into a sweatshirt and dug a joint out of her bag and lit it, and the three of them shared it.

The loft was above a warehouse, reached by way of a freight elevator. The studio space was large and open with a bank of windows along the southern wall, all of which were blanketed with pull-down shades because they preferred using artificial light. They could control incandescent lights, not sunshine.

Jodi had once commented that she thought artists always insisted on northern lights. "Not anymore," Arnie had explained, "That came from a time when electric lights didn't measure up to today's standards."

Larry painted on canvas tacked directly to the east wall, and Arnie painted on a stretched canvas on a large homemade easel against the west wall. Both worked on paintings in the four-by-six-foot range; both also did smaller paintings around ten-by-twelve inches on paper or canvas.

There was a pass-through window on the north wall and a door that opened into the small living areas, two beds and three chairs and a couple of jampacked bookcases separated by room dividers much thinner than the walls back in Lacey that had separated Parker and Delia's bedroom from mine and Marilou's, a kitchen with a dining table and three chairs and a bathroom with a shower but no tub, books stacked nearly floor to ceiling in Larry's bedroom, Arnie's walls covered with pictures of women—nude and clothed—cut from magazines. There were photos by Mapplethorpe, Leibovitz, Stieglitz,

Man Ray, and paintings by Picasso, Magritte, Wesselmann and of course Pearlstein, plus many of Arnie's own sketches and—recently added, some of Larry's sketches of Kaylee and Rebecca.

While Arnie and Jodi shared a bag of chips, Larry, still in the studio, worked on his painting a bit more and then slouched back down in the old easy chair, a beer in one hand—hair of the dog—and paint brushes in the other, staring intently at the canvas he was working on. The painting was unlike anything he had painted since his undergraduate days. There was—sacrilege of sacrilege— recognizable subject matter, *forgive me, Saint Clement*, the interior of an abandoned warehouse in tones of black, white, and gray with a few subtle blue and buttery yellow washes. *Greg's going to freak*, he thought. Depicted in the warehouse interior was a stack of boxes, two Straight back chairs, one black, one white, and some empty metal shelves. It was a nighttime scene. Desolate. Filtered light from streetlamps seeped through a bank of windows. The paint application was smooth, and all edges were soft.

It was the first of what he envisioned as a new and different series, an attempt to find something more compelling than the geometric abstractions he had been painting for years.

Over the past month, he had been sneaking into abandoned buildings at night and photographing some of them occupied by squatters who ignored his intrusion. He chose one of the photographs and projected it large onto the primed canvas and traced the outlines of windows, chairs, walls and shelves, and the stacks of boxes. And then he painted it with heavy, impasto paint, carefully adjusting and changing the colors and softly brushing the edges of objects when the paint was almost dry to give it the look of a soft-focus photograph.

He was pleased with the way it looked, but there was something missing. He puzzled and puzzled. *What can I do to give it a special flare without subverting the starkness or the mystery?* After studying the painting for a long time, he noticed something he should have seen much earlier. It was an Edward Hopper knockoff. *Crap. I do not want to be accused of appropriating Hopper.* Far too many so-called artists had tried that, creating what Larry considered wall fodder, a pejorative term, he'd been told, first used by the critic Peter Plagens. Once he saw his new painting as a Hopper, he couldn't get it out of his mind. He thought about how often Hopper would insert a single, lonely figure into his scenes—often, he thought, rather stiff figures. Hopper's paintings were not about the figure; they were about light and shadow and mood. But the figures created context, mystery, and psychological intensity. That, at least, was Larry's interpretation and what he wanted in his own paintings. He needed something that would do to his interiors what Hopper's figures did to his. And maybe something else. Maybe a sly sense of humor. Yeah! That would do the trick. Something like right out of the old Chicago Imagists, the Hairy Who and those nutjobs.

He didn't hit upon what he was seeking that day or the day after or the day after that. But he finally came up with an idea that was so audacious, outlandish, ridiculous that he thought it just might work in the current crazy art market and be something he could more than just live with creating. He would insert into his dreary scenes not lonely figures but comical creatures harkening back to the graphic novel-inspired drawings he did when he was fourteen and fifteen years old and barely beginning to learn how to make art. "I got it, Arnie. Listen to this ..." He told Arnie about his idea, and Arnie said, "That's fabulous. I can picture it. Do it, man."

Jodi said, "If you want me to pose for you, it'll cost you."

"Nah. Sweet pea, I don't need a model."

"I'll give you the friends and family discount."

"What's that? Ten cents off on the dollar?" He knew she wouldn't really charge him for modeling. She had offered too many times, but he had not been interested, which she took as an insult, but only teasingly so. Once she got peeved and said, "If you're not interested in my naked body, you must be light in the loafers."

"Oh no. I love looking at your naked body. I could gladly look all day and all through the night. I just don't want to paint it. Besides, Arnie might not be cool with that. I think he's got an inner stopwatch that tells him how long I can look."

She laughingly countered with, "Painting my nakedness is the only thing you can do with it."

"Right," he said. "But Arnie, look at these."

He opened a drawer and dug out some of the many drawings he had made on Orcas Island and chose a few of Kaylee and Rebecca on the beach at Deception Pass. "How about these?" he asked, "Painted into the warehouse scenes as human-animal hybrids."

Jodie clapped and said, "I love it."

"Me too," Arnie said.

And Larry painted the girls in the dark and deserted warehouse (in tones of yellow ochre, red and white over ultramarine), and he gave them pigs' faces. And he painted scenes with women with alligator heads and scales and teenage girls with big bunny ears—all from his Orcas Island sketches. He painted Kaylee in her cheesecake pose as a sexy nude with a big-bearded wolf face. Would the girls get a kick out of these, or would they be horrified? Was the erotic undertone of the underage Kaylee and Rebecca paintings out of bounds? Nah. Because it was no longer Kaylee and Rebecca; they were anthropomorphized sex goddesses like Jessica in *Who Framed Roger Rabbit*. He hoped that if the girls ever saw them, they would enjoy the humor.

...

He was on a roll. Like an athlete in the zone.

It took him eight weeks to come up with enough paintings in the new series to approach the gallery with them. He lined them up propped against the wall, and looked at them long and hard. Just as he had been shocked at an earlier point upon noticing the similarity to Edward Hopper, now he realized the figures looked a lot like Joseph Park's bunnies and elephants from his show with Pearlstein at the Frye.

"I was unconsciously copying this painter I saw in Seattle," he told Arnie. "What the hell. Take a bit from Hopper, a bit from Park, put 'em together with my own unique flare. That's not stealing. Shit, Picasso did that kind of stuff all the time. If it's good enough for Picasso, it's good enough for me."

He photographed the new paintings and printed the photos on 8½-by-11 matt stock and carried them on the subway to Penn Station and walked to the gallery and showed the photos to Greg, who initially said, "Are you crazy? You've built a reputation as an abstract painter. People are going to come to the show expecting to see what they've come to think of as Larry Briggs. We have no idea what they might think if you clobber them with these new pieces."

"Come on, man," Larry argued, "If people were so familiar with my work as to have a Larry Briggs look in their heads, I'd already be selling them for big bucks. Besides, nobody should expect a painter to keep repeating himself forever. We have to change. Grow. Remember what happened when Phillip Guston quit doing AE and started doing those crazy cigar smokers and Klansmen? It could be like that."

"Yeah, well need I remind you that at first everybody hated his new stuff. I mean, based on what I've heard, he even lost close personal friends over the change."

"Yeah, well maybe. But now everybody loves the stuff he did after abandoning abstraction. It's all abstraction really. All modern art is."

"I don't know, Larry. It seems awfully risky to me. Let me look at them from a little different angle." He moved them around, looked some more, moved them again, and then said, I got to admit there's something to these. I think I like 'em. But what will my clients think?"

Larry pleaded his case and would not back down, and Greg said, "Leave the photos with me and bring in one or two of the paintings and let me think about it."

He left the gallery feeling as nervous as the first time he approached a gallery with a portfolio. Had he defied his dealer? Could it be the end of his career? Or perhaps—crossing fingers and tossing up a silent prayer to the art gods—an exciting new twist of an adventure for his career?

OK, Larry me boy, these apocalyptic musings are absurd. It's not that big a deal. Or is it?

...

Before boarding the subway back to Brooklyn, he stopped for a drink in a bar on Eighth Avenue. It was a quiet bar, one he had often passed by but never entered. Crossing the threshold was a step back into Depression-era New York. A heavily scratched redwood bar, checkerboard patterned tile floor and pressed tin ceiling, slantwise light coming through the front window. The big surprise that floored him was that there was art displayed on the walls. No beer signs, just art—contemporary art lighted by clip-on lights.

The only customers were two men at a table playing chess and a single woman on a barstool nursing a drink from a glass. The men were dressed as workmen, probably from the construction crew he had seen a block away. They didn't so much as glance Larry's way when he entered. The woman nodded in his direction and gave him a little smile. She looked to be in her sixties. Silver hair flowing down past her shoulders, glasses, large turquoise earrings. She was drawing patterns with a finger into the condensation on her glass. She gave his paint-splattered clothes the once-over and said, "Are you a house painter or just an artist?"

"Are you trying to be funny?"

"A little bit. I'm an artist too." Deep dimples in her cheeks when she smiled at him.

He laughed and said, "I guess house painters are a bit more respectable."

"At least their product is useful."

She pushed up off her stool and moved to one next to him. "Do you mind?"

"No, not at all. So you're a painter?"

"Yep."

"What do you paint?"

She screwed her mouth up in concentration and didn't answer right away but then said, "Are you familiar with Leon Golub?"

"Yeah, sure. I like his stuff."

"Good. My stuff is like his stuff." She tapped a Lucky Strike filter out of a pack and stuck it between her lips.

The bartender said, "No smoking, Linda. You know that."

She stuffed the cigarette back in the pack, offered her hand to Larry and said, "I'm Linda."

"I kinda figured that. Hi, Linda. I'm Larry."

He asked her if she was any good, and she said, "Well, I'm a good cook, and I'm good in bed, and I'm a good friend to the few friends I have. And yeah, I'm a good painter too. But I've never been very successful."

Larry thought, *I wouldn't dare respond to that good-in-bed comment, not for a pile of money*. But he knew exactly where she was coming from with the bit about no correlation between success and ability. "Tell me 'bout it," he said. "I'm not very successful either. But at least you're good in the kitchen." A shared grin and a pause and impromptu clinking of glasses and then "And bed," she said. "Don't forget in bed."

He glanced down at the sleek curve of her hip and thigh and said, "Oh no, I'll never forget that."

Continuing with the playful banter, she said, "You'll have to take me at my word for that."

"Well, what choice do I have? I'm not about to call you a liar or demand proof. You might beat me up."

The chess players finished their game, and one of them got up and shuffled his way through the peanut-shelled floor to the jukebox and played a Lou Reed song. Then they reset the game.

Linda told Larry she had a couple of paintings in a group show and mentioned the name of the gallery. "If you got the time, we can take a look-see."

"OK. I know that gallery. It's just a couple of blocks away."

"Uh huh."

...

He liked what he saw. Her paintings were huge and gritty with globs of paint piled up inches from the surface of the canvas. They were modern interpretations of classic subjects that were not easy to take: the rape of the Sabine women, the beheading of John the Baptist, Judith beheading Holofernes after the Artemisia Gentileschi version of that grisly scene, and a version of Goya's "The Third of May."

"These are really great," he told her. "You've mined the horror show of art from the Renaissance until today. They ought to be in the Modern."

"Of course they oughta. Too much horror, I guess."

"Are you making a statement about violence in the world?"

"Not really. I think I picked these subjects because I wanted to show raw emotion, but in an abstract or painterly way, not a narrative way."

"I can dig it. I was just talking about something like that with my dealer."

He told her about his upcoming show at the Greg Sullivan Gallery and how he wanted to show all new paintings and that Greg was a bit skeptical. He described the new work but didn't have anything to show her because he had left all his photos with Greg.

"The thing is, if he doesn't want to show my new work I'm shit out of luck because I don't have enough of the abstracts to put a show together." Which was not exactly true; he had a loft full of the abstracts, but most were old and had been shown. Greg's regulars would likely recognize them.

They left her gallery and headed back toward the bar, having not said anything about what they were going to do next. Part company? Go for another drink? Head to her place and test how good she was in the kitchen? The bedroom? *I gotta put the bedroom out of my mind. What am I thinking? She must be twenty years older than me. She probably has grandchildren. Married for sure. But she doesn't look old. Was that quip a come-on?*

The sun had sunk low in the western sky. Shadows were long and purple. He watched their shadows walking down the sidewalk. He glanced at her and liked that she was almost as tall as him. He liked the way she moved. Like his cousin Lizzy.

Linda said, "Tell you what. My place is nearby. So is Greg Sullivan's gallery. What say we go by Greg's and let me see your stuff, and then you can come home with me, and I'll whip us up something to eat?

...

After visiting the gallery and chatting with Greg and seeing the photos of Larry's new paintings and three of his older paintings that Greg pulled out of bins, and after stopping off on Seventh Avenue to pick up bagels and lox and eating them in her third-floor walkup, she said. "Those Mondrian-slash-Joseph-Albers-looking paintings are good, but the new stuff is much more exciting. Let's face it, man, geometric abstraction is dead. You don't want to be an anachronism. Go with what your heart tells you, dude. Don't let Greg Sullivan tell you what to paint. Gallerists don't know diddly."

"Yeah, but they hold the key to the money."

"That's true. So Whatcha gonna do?"

"I dunno." Something about what she said about geometric abstraction being anachronistic didn't sit right with him, even though he had thought it before and worried about it in relation to his own paintings. Nothing in art was anachronistic anymore. But if anything was, it was probably exactly the kind of paintings he had been showing.

Before leaving, he noticed she had a huge walk-in closet whose doors were standing open, and in the closet was a mixture of what looked like Salvation Army clothing and fancy dresses that looked like they would cost about what he made in six months. *Was this old dame just slumming down in Chelsea? Who in the world was she?*

PARKER AND DELIA MOVED

A little more than six miles from our abode on Royal Court was a neighborhood of small homes built in the 1950s and '60s, some even much older. Lots of elevated porches. Like, you know, with three steps up and a swing on the porch, and flowerpots or trellises on porch rails. Most of the pots and trellises were painted white or gray with daring red or green doors. Places to park cars in alleyways where the occupants entered their houses through back doors. It was a neighborhood of parks and wooded hiking trails and what I like to call funky little businesses along nearby Harrison, the major thoroughfare running through the neighborhood. It was the kind of neighborhood Marilou and I should have moved into when Larry and Parker were toddlers. It was in this neighborhood that Parker and Delia settled after we tossed them out. They rented a two-bedroom cottage in easy walking distance of the food co-op and a playground where they could let Baby Randolph swing on swings and climb on various playground equipment and in the warmer months run through water squirted high in the air.

We should have let them live in our house on Royal Court and moved into that neighborhood ourselves.

It was seven months past the day Marilou had blown her top about the microwave and told them to get out of our house.

The rift she had torn had long since mended. "It's not you. It was never you," she said. "I'm the one that lost my temper and ran them off."

"Well, maybe it was a little bit me," I interjected. We had talked the subject to death. We agreed for the umpteenth time that Parker and Delia would be much happier having a place of their own.

It had been my contention that after moving out on their own, Parker would have to get more serious about finding a job, and eventually that appeared to be the case.

"Here's a concept," I said to him, "Don't be so particular. Take whatever job is offered. Swallow your pride. And then, while working at your new job, you look for the one you really want."

"Good plan, Pops. Problem is, I don't know what I want to be when I grow up," Parker wisecracked. Forty years old and seemingly perpetually unemployed, Parker surprised everyone by landing a job right away. Everyone assured him it was a good job, a desk job with the Department of Corrections. Good pay but boring work. "You're going to love it there," said supportive friends and relatives who had no information to assess the job.

Parker liked his co-workers all right but wasn't exactly in love with the bosses.

"That's the way it always is in the working world," I told him. "You're an adult. Get used to it." Easy enough for me to say. I had been retired so long I hardly remembered what it was like to go to work every day.

We celebrated Parker and Delia's new life over drinks in their nice but crowded new home. They paid for the drinks and for takeout from a Thai restaurant, proud to be magnanimous for once. Back on Royal Court in the following days, Marilou and I delighted in not having to shut the bathroom or bedroom doors. We could run around naked inside the house if we wanted to. So we did. An old fantasy brought to life. The first time I dashed out to the kitchen in my altogether for something and right back to the bedroom, I was thrilled to be so daring. It felt like freedom. Exhilaration. Yet I was titillated by the thought that I might be caught streaking through the house. By whom? My wife? She was standing by the sink pouring hot water into the French press, naked as the day she was born.

After the first few daring forays outside our bedroom in our birthday suits, we tried watching TV from the couch in the nude, sometimes snuggling together under a quilt.

"Remember when you picked up those nudist pamphlets" Marilou asked.

"Uh huh. Yeah. Naked at home is better. I don't have to worry about anybody but you laughing at my body."

"There's nothing laughable about your body."

"Thanks, but I wasn't fishing for a compliment."

"So you wouldn't want to take a trial run at one of those places?"

"Oh god no. I'd be mortified."

We were careful to keep the blinds drawn on the Rappaport side of the house. The Rappaports, Delia's parents, were always trying to see what was going on in our house, like they thought we were having orgies or something or doing stuff with handcuffs and whips. (No whips, but we had tried handcuffs a few times, and we got a kick out of fantasizing about kinky stuff we'd never really do.)

The Rappaports were evangelical and—as I suspected was true of many evangelicals—they were clearly attracted to the very things they vociferously condemned.

One summer evening after we shut up the house and pulled the front room blinds down and made love on the couch, something we hadn't done in at least thirty years, we were snuggled in post-coital exhaustion when Parker and Delia dropped in unannounced and marched right through the front door without knocking. Old habit. We leaped to our feet and ran for the bedroom to the accompanying music of Parker and Delia's laughter. What horror, what shame, what delight at the sight of our flapping butt-flesh in fast retreat! From behind the bedroom door, Marilou shouted, "We'll be out in a sec!" Both of us hurriedly dressing and giggling as much as our children in the living room.

Embarrassment all around, but all of us feeling giddy, Delia said, "We came by to invite you to our place. We fixed it up really nice."

"We saw it already."

"Yeah, but that was when it was cluttered with unopened boxes."

Marilou said, "Sure, we'd love to come by. We'd love to see what you've done with it."

"When we told Helen we were getting our own place, she said she might have some stuff we could use to spark up the new place. She let me rummage through their storage area, and I found one of Larry's early paintings. You probably never even saw it. It's hanging in our living room now," Parker said.

"Great. We'd love to see it."

"Come as you are." And after a brief pause and a stifled laugh, "But not as you were when we barged in."

Parker promised us they'd pay us back for that first month's rent and deposit we had paid for them, "And something more as a token of appreciation for all you've done for us."

Marilou poo-pooed that. "We're family. That's what families do."

...

We never did get around to visiting Parker and Delia's apartment. The next time any of the family got together was Easter Sunday when all the Olympia-area Johnsons and Johnson in-laws, minus Lizzy and Buddy, got together at Billy's house. Marilou and I were there, and Parker and Delia with Baby Randolph (whom they had recently started calling Randy) and Helen and Eva, but none of Eva's now grown children. Helen was still mad at Billy about the MAGA hat debacle from almost a year ago, which still irritated Marilou as well. But on that Easter Sunday everyone agreed to keep all talk on comfortable subjects, which Marilou said was bound to make for a quiet family gathering.

"It's a gorgeous day," Billy said. "What say we all head down to the pier? Parker, you and Delia can bring those two chairs down. Rudy, can you bring the ice chest?"

"Aye aye, Captain," I said.

The ice chest was loaded with beer and soda. A picnic table and chairs already sat on the pier, snacks laid out on the table.

After we settled at the table, Billy said—like a coach trying to bolster his team's spirits—"Who's planning on going to the retreat this summer?"

"We are," Eva said.

"Us too," from Marilou. (We had not discussed it.)

Parker said they weren't sure.

They talked about Larry's big show, and Eva said she wondered if Kaylee and that boy she'd been dating—forever, Helen said—were going to get married. And Belle asked what everybody thought about the new disease everyone was talking about.

"It's not a new disease," Billy insisted. "There've been eighteen—count 'em, eighteen—previous versions of it. That's why they call it Covid 19. And none of 'em have been serious. This one won't be either."

Helen spoke up. "May I respectfully interject that you're full of shit? The number nineteen does not mean there were eighteen previous versions. There were no previous versions. Got that? None. This is the one and only. And it's a killer."

"Posh," Billy said, and Eva said, "Hey, we promised not to fight."

For no longer than a few minutes, the threat of an all-out war loomed over what to call an illness none of us knew anything about, while Billy sat back smug in his presumed rightness. Then calmness, and then consensus that Covid would soon be a forgotten chapter in modern history.

"Change of subject," Helen said. "Do any of you do pot? I mean medicinal. Like we tried some lotion for body aches, and it works wonders."

Marilou said, "We've tried some edibles. Not bad. They help us sleep at night."

Eva said talking about pot reminded her that she had read that a young man working in a pot shop in Lakewood got shot by a would-be burglar. The newspaper said the bullet grazed his neck but didn't do any real damage. He was quoted as saying it felt like a bee sting and scared him more than hurt him. Everyone looked to Eva as if expecting confirmation that a glancing bullet felt like a bee sting.

. . .

Marilou poured our nightcaps, bourbon and Coke, as if three or four beers each that afternoon hadn't been enough—we're not big boozers. We settled on the couch in our pajamas, the running-around-naked phase having become boring. Besides which, the night had turned out quite chilly. "I've got something to tell you," I said. "It's the craziest, most outrageous thing you can imagine."
"About the book, I presume."

271

"Yeah. Uh huh. Now don't laugh. Hear me out."

"I promise. No laughing."

"Here goes. OK, remember you said the characters were too obviously based on all of us."

"Uh huh."

"So I don't want to make the characters less like us. I want to make them more like us, super obviously more like us. Like a satire of us. And to make sure there's no doubt, I want to call them by their/our initials. B for Billy and She B for Belle…" an enormous explosion of laughter from Marilou and then "You must be out of your everloving mind."

"I am! I am! That's what's so freakin' great."

By then, tears were running down both our cheeks, and we were both laughing hysterically. "Sorry, I continued, "and my character will be named R, for me and you'll be M. Bryce will be B-2. No, better yet, he can be Little B. Get it? Like Little John, because he's so big. Remember playing Robin Hood when we were kids?"

"I'm starting to get it. Heaven help me."

"I know, I know."

I explained to her that all the characters will do the things that are already in the book, like the trips to Orcas Island and like Billy and Bryce and the MAGA hat, but expanded, made ludicrous, an outrageous fiction. "See," I said, "it will be a parody of our actual lives."

Marilou screwed her face up and wiped tears away and swigged down the rest of her drink. "You're right," she said. "It's crazy, but it just might work. Give me an example of how you'll expand on it."

"All right. So like the time Bryce jerked Billy's MAGA hat off. What if Billy challenges him to a duel, an honest-to-God duel, a name your weapon kind of thing? So the next morning they go into town and buy bb guns. *Bb guns* for Christ sake. And they meet up at a beach somewhere. Ten paces, turn and shoot. They both hit their targets."

"They actually shoot each other?"

"Yeah, but like they're bb guns, not real guns."

"But bb's can put an eye out."

"It's fiction, honey, fiction.   OK, so they pace, one, two, three… They turn and fire. Little B hits Big B right square in the middle of his forehead and raises a bb-size bump. "Damn you!" Big B shouts, dropping his pistol and grabbing his head. "That hurt."

"Well you hit me too, and it wasn't no little slap." He drops his gun too and rubs his wrist where B's bb had hit a glancing blow. And then, surprising everyone, B and Little B start laughing and end up hugging each other and laughing like fools."

Marilou said, "By god, I like that. It's ridiculous, but I like it. What else you got? Hot sex scenes? What about if I get dressed in skimpy black panties and fishnet stockings and …"

"Yeah, that's good."

"Hey, we're really cooking now. But we still have to come up with a better title."

"Yeah, I know. We will."

LARRY'S BIG SHOW

Five months earlier, a night in December. We were at home snuggled together on the couch under a heavy blanket. Not naked. The fog ladened night sky was a surface swept with vine charcoal. A hazy halo encircled the streetlight on the corner.

"Oh my god, I just remembered. Larry's new show is opening." Marilou pulled her phone out of her pocket, and looking at it said, "Let's see, what time is it in New York? Yeah, it opened about an hour ago. I can't imagine how nervous and excited he must be."

"We should have gone," I said. "I'm already regretting that we didn't."

"Let's text him congratulations."

It was six in the evening in Lacey. It had been fully dark outside for well over an hour on that night a week before Christmas. We were toasty and comfortable listening to tunes from our youth on one of our favorite streaming services. The currently playing song was "Twilight Time" by the Platters.

Marilou threw off the blanket and stood up in her flannel pajamas and reached out a hand. "Dance with me. Come on."

"Nah."

"Don't be an old fuddy duddy."

"I was not a good dancer when I was young, and I'm not even good at standing on two feet now," I demurred as she dragged me into the middle of the room.

"Oh pshaw. You move quite well. We walked two miles Saturday, and you didn't stumble once or grab me or support."

We must have been quite a sight dancing in our matching PJs. Other than the way we were dressed, we might as well have been in the high school gym with all our classmates swirling around the floor, music courtesy of The Dreamers in their white sports coats and red ties: Van Slayton on tenor sax and Johnny Devero on lead guitar. "Who played drums and bass?"

"Ed something on drums."

"Yeah, Ed Brown."

"Uh huh. And Van Martin on the standup bass."

"Goddamn they were good."

Reluctantly at first, but surprisingly smoothly, I danced with my wife. Holding my arms around her and swaying to the music felt good.

...

Lizzy and Buddy settled back on their comfortable old loveseat to watch an episode of "Outlander." Everybody was watching that series. High-tone porn, Lizzy called it, or a nighttime soap opera pretending to be historic fiction with lots of sex and nudity. Lizzy made a show of saying she had heart palpitations every time the character Jamie took off his shirt. Buddy leaned back and put his feet on the coffee table. Lizzy leaned against him, nuzzling her head against his chest. It was a rare romantic scene until Lizzy was wracked with a sudden coughing spell. Buddy paused the show and said, "I've got just the thing for that cough."

He went to the bathroom and got a throat lozenge from the cabinet and came back and handed it to her.

"Suck on this while I get you the real medicine." He made them each a mug of hot buttered rum and sat back by her and draped an arm around her shoulder with a hand cupping her breast. It had been many months since he had done anything like that. Since that strange day, the day Eva and Helen and Larry stopped by and Buddy went out early in the morning and stayed out until late at night with no explanation, since then they had rarely spoken. He kept to himself and brooded. She was convinced that he was going to leave her, although they had never talked about that either. And yet that cold December night, without any discussion, they ended up snuggling on the loveseat and comfortably watching TV together. Lizzy had paused the show when he went to get her medicine. She started it again, and they drank their rum.

And here they were again six months later, early on a sweltering June night, again together on the loveseat drinking rum and

Coke (not hot buttered), which had become an almost nightly ritual, their differences, their tension over the however many months, Buddy's unexplained anger and Lizzy's worry apparently forgotten.

"Uuuum, yum," Lizzy said. She slouched like a cat on the tattered loveseat wearing an oversized T-shirt as worn and tattered as the couch and a pair of Buddy's boxer shorts, her feet on the coffee table, cupping the cool drink in both hands and propping it on her belly between sips. the air around her hazy and smelly from her. A small fan fought to stir the air. It was well into the pandemic, which had proven to be much worse than anyone expected. Buddy had tried to put the memory of robbing the pot shop and shooting the clerk out of his mind. *It was an accident. I didn't mean to pull the trigger. I didn't pull it. It just went off.* Nowadays, since the news announced that the clerk had not been severely hurt, thoughts of that day and the night in the bar came up only rarely.

On the wall behind the television was thumbtacked a copy of the announcement card for Larry's big show, which he had signed "Love, Larry" and the original pencil study for the painting on the card. Lizzy and Buddy's isolated lives had become even more isolated. She had not left the house or talked to anyone besides Buddy in almost a year. She took to talking to the chickens and the goats, not the way people talk to animals but like talking to other humans, imagining their replies and talking back. Buddy had taken to long motorcycle rides at all hours of the day and night and spent hours restoring his old Indian bike, a job that never seemed to progress. They were watching a mundane sitcom on TV, Buddy reclining next to her against a couple of throw pillows with his feet laid across her legs, still dressed in the clothes he wore when replacing part of a fence that afternoon, threadbare jeans and a Grateful Dead T-shirt. It was eight o'clock in the evening, the day's heat just beginning to lessen. A typical deadeningly dull evening at the Bundrock farm. Other than a few comments about the show they were watching, neither of them had anything to say. Buddy sipped his drink. At eight-thirty he announced, "I'm gonna go out for a while. Ride my bike. Get some night air."

She said, "All right," and squashed her cigarette out in the cracked saucer she used for an ashtray.

...

A little after nine o'clock Buddy found himself in Nellie's Tavern for the second time in recent days, his twelve-year-old Honda motorcycle parked at an angle out front. The place was practically empty, as it had been the last time. He wondered how they managed to stay in business. Only recently had bars been allowed to reopen. Signs on the front door and inside walls said MASKS REQUIRED. Two guys were shooting pool, and one lonesome dude was seated at a table by the restrooms. Buddy liked that the place was practically empty. He noticed for the first time that both restrooms were non-gendered, a recent change. *Good on them*, he thought.

He ordered a Bud and took a seat in a darkened corner two tables away from the lone dude. He pulled his mask down around his neck and nursed his beer. He watched the pool players rack their cues and walk out. Bob Dylan was wheezing and whining on the jukebox. Buddy caught the lone dude's eye, and the guy nodded at him and smiled almost imperceptibly. *I know that guy*, he thought. *I know I do. Who the hell is he? How do I ... Oh, of course, I met him here. The queer that grabbed my dick. Didn't feel half bad I gotta admit. I shoulda known it was him.* He'd seen the guy's bike parked at the curb out front when he came in, and he recognized the hand-painted lightning flashes on the tank, but in the moment, he had not associated the bike with the man.

The biker stood up and, beer mug in hand, approached Buddy and said, "Hey there. You came back. I'm surprised to see you in here again."

Why? Buddy thought. *Oh yeah, because I slapped you down the last time.* The guy said, "You look like you could use some company. But if you'd rather be alone, I can respect that."

He's really polite and respectful, Buddy thought. *I know what he's after, but he's not pushy about it.* He said, "No. I mean yeah. I mean that's fine. Have a seat."

"Are you sure? I mean you looked like you were deep in thought."

"I was thinking about my wife. We met right here in Nellie's more than fifty years ago."

"Yeah, you told me that."

They each took hefty swigs of their beers and set them down. "That's the end of that'un. Deader'n a doorknob. How 'bout yours?"

"Yep, deader'n a doornail."

After he got them each another beer, Buddy said, "Like I said, I was thinking about my wife. Thing is, I been loving her pants off since Kennedy was president. But things are not the same with us now. We've grown apart, but we're still together."

"I know what that's like. It's the same with me and my husband."

They talked about the old days when Nellie's was a family restaurant during the day and a biker bar after dark, and both expressed surprise that they had not met before.

"Well, I don't get out much," Buddy said. "Except for here lately. It's the only way I can shake off the Covid blues."

"Yeah. I can dig that. Reckon we'll survive this mess?"

"Oh yeah. Things are pretty messed up now, but nothing lasts forever."

He looked to be maybe ten years younger than Buddy and a little bit shorter, thin, shaved head and a neatly trimmed beard. Buddy thought he looked like a businessman except for the leathers and the ostentatious turquoise rings on multiple fingers. He felt something like a crying jag begging to let loose, but he suppressed it. Buddy hardly ever cried. He couldn't remember the last time. So why now? Why in the past few weeks had he been having unexpected mood swings?

He said, "I killed my wife's dreams and destroyed her life."

"You told me that before. Don't be so down on yourself, man."

"Now she's perpetually sad and angry, and her health is for shit, and she probably ain't gonna live a helluva lot longer, and it's all my doing."

"Aw man, it can't be all that bad."

"I don't know. It's pretty bad. She smokes like a chimney, and her teeth are rotten, and we can't afford to fix 'em, and by God she used to be sexy, but not anymore."

"Aw, man."

Under the table he slipped his hand once again up Buddy's thigh. *OK, here we go again*, Buddy thought. He knew that if he didn't say something or push his hand away it would be just like the last time. The hand would crawl up inch by inch by inch.

He didn't say stop, and he didn't push his hand away, and the other man did exactly what Buddy knew he would. And then he did stop him before it went any further.

"Naw, man. I still can't do this."

"I don't get it. You came back. That told me something. You wouldn't a come back if you weren't interested." But then he removed his hand and said, "I'm sorry, man."

"No, don't apologize. I guess I sent the wrong signal. Maybe a part of me mighta wanted..."

Their conversation petered into silence. Another minute went by, and then Buddy got up and went to the restroom. He put his hand on the handle but did not open the door. He turned around, gave his friend a long and mournful look, and then walked to the front door and out and straddled his Honda and kickstarted it and headed toward the freeway. On the freeway, he drove south toward Centralia and Chehalis and Longview. South of Kalama he turned onto Highway 12 toward Mount St. Helens. The road up to the lookout over Spirit Lake and the crater was steep and winding, with walls of rock to the inside and huge drop-offs to the outside. He gunned the engine when approaching a big curve and did not turn with the curve but headed straight off the road and down and down and down and down.

INFLUENCE

Raymonde Alexander and his wife Sandi and their good friend Linda Alexis sat on the Alexanders' balcony overlooking Fifth Avenue and Central Park. The combined wealth and influence of the three of them was stratospheric. Inconceivable to people like Larry, who, until recently, had to weigh the cost of a movie ticket against the cost of a few tubes of paint because he could not afford both. Raymonde was a banker and inheritor of millions. His wife was a comfortably retired fashion model. The Alexanders were known as influencers in the art world. Their private collection included many of the biggest names in contemporary art. Increasingly, monied people said of them *if the Alexanders collect them, maybe we should too.* Their friend Linda was not so well known and nowhere near as rich; only a handful of people knew exactly who she was. Only a dozen fellow artists and gallerists and one old girlfriend from her college days at Purdue knew of Linda's family connections, and she wanted to keep it that way. She wanted to earn recognition through her work, not through family. She showed her paintings under the assumed name Linda Purdue, taken from her alma mater.

Linda's father was the world-famous photorealist Calvin Alexis.

On the street below the Alexanders' balcony, strollers passed by the scarlet canopy of the apartment building that Raymonde and Sandi owned and lived in. Horse-drawn carriages waited across the street at the park entrance for their tourist clientele. It was midafternoon on a mild winter morning. They were drinking daquiris. The Alexanders were dressed in matching orange turtlenecks and tan chinos. Raymonde was skimming through the arts section of the Sunday *Times*. "There's an article about our boy Larry Briggs," he said. "By Cramer, of course. He says—get this— 'Three of Briggs's paintings sold opening night of his recent show at Greg Sullivan

Gallery, all three purchased by influential collectors Raymonde and Sandi Alexander.'"

Only two were purchased by Sandi and Raymode. Linda bought the third.

"And then there's this," Raymonde said, "Larry Briggs is going to be America's next big art star."

"Yes he is," Sandi said. "And the value of those paintings we bought is going to shoot to the stars—not that we bought them for that reason."

It was Sandi more than Raymonde who had the discerning eye. Much of what they knew about art and the market they learned from Linda. They also owned a few of her paintings. Horrendous things, Sandi said with a wink.

The paintings they bought at Larry's show were a set taken from his sketches of Kaylee and Rebecca on the beach looking out toward the bridge at Deception Pass. They hung it on their living room wall next to a Frank Stella and facing the wall with an early Larry Poons.

"Raymonde is thinking of moving them to the lobby of his bank," Sandi said.

...

Following Linda's advice, Raymonde and Sandi visited Larry's studio and bought four more of his paintings, two for their home and two they put in storage. Following their example, other collectors bought paintings from Larry, and suddenly the market for his paintings skyrocketed, as Linda predicted. There was a waiting list of collectors vying for his work. A museum in Florida was putting together a show of young artists on the rise, and they included four of Larry's paintings, which were the hit of the show, which traveled to Minneapolis, New Orleans, Phoenix and L.A.

Larry still had no idea who the painter named Linda was that he met in that bar on Eighth Avenue. He saw her again at his opening, but they did not get a chance to say more than "Hi. How are you. Thanks for coming." It was only later that it dawned on him that he didn't know her last name.

LIZZY CHECKED THE MAIL

Billy emailed everyone in the family: *It's that time again, time for the annual Johnson family retreat on Orcas Island. It's the weekend of June 19-21. Please let us know how many are coming from your household.*

Right away, a response from Larry popped up in Billy's in-box. Billy read: *I'm sorry, Uncle Billy, but I'm so caught up in my work that I can't get away this time. Plus, there's the little matter of Covid. I'm afraid it's not safe to gather. Hopefully next summer.* He felt only moderately shamed considering the crowds he braved at his shows.

"Goddammit!" Billy shouted. He banged his hand on his desk, upsetting his coffee cup which fell and spilled coffee all over his desk. "Goddammit! Damn, damn, damn, damn," he muttered rushing to the kitchen to grab paper towels.

"What in tarnation are you shouting about?" Belle asked, standing up from her chair in the adjacent room and watching Billy scurry to the kitchen and back.

"Spilled my goddamn coffee." And then, "Marilou's hotshot son Larry. Look how he answered my email."

Looking over his shoulder as he sopped up the spilled coffee, Belle read Larry's email. She said, "You gotta admit it makes a lot of sense. This pandemic is nothing to sneeze at." She had been voicing variations on that since the pandemic began, but he never listened. She added, "I'm not even sure the resort is open to guests."

"Oh yeah, they are. They're smart people. They know that after being quarantined and avoiding contact during all this time people are desperate to get out of the house and go someplace special."

"Uh huh. Someplace special like the hospital or the grave." Belle was growing sick of Billy denying the seriousness of the pandemic. "Old folks like us are the ones dying from it."

Later that day Billy got an answer from Marilou. She wrote: *I think it would be wise to cancel this year's retreat due to the pandemic. I know that Rudy and I and Parker and Delia do not feel safe enough. Please consider canceling it for the safety of all.*

Bryce responded with a simple *You gotta be kidding.*

Billy, as Belle put it, was fit to be tied.

It was ten o'clock in the morning. Billy fixed himself a Manhattan while expanding his curses to include Bryce and Marilou. "Shit," he grumbled. "I might as well cancel. Nobody's coming anyway. I can't believe the descendants of the great pirate Pegleg Josiah Johnson are such pantywaists. If the old man was here (meaning Harlan), he'd be kicking some lily-livered Johnson ass."

Until recently he had never imbibed alcohol before five o'clock. Belle was beginning to worry.

Billy carried his drink back to his computer and sat down and sent out another missive to the entire family: *Y'all are a bunch of pansies.*

Belle said, "I can't believe I've been living with your nasty ass for almost a century. Looking back now, I wonder how long it took me to realize how stupid and mean-spirited you are, sir."

He stormed out, taking his drink down to the pier. He grumbled out loud to the air and water, "How do I put up with her? It's a wonder we didn't get divorced years ago." But he knew he couldn't live without her. Ditto for Belle. *Why do I stay with him? And how could I live without him?*

...

Lizzy could not go a day without thinking longingly about Buddy. She endured waves of grief attacks. See someone who walks like him; see a tall, skinny man with a long beard; hear a voice like his and a flood of grief would wash over her. Making it worse, there was a new thing on the land. It was Covid loneliness, it was Covid fear, it was Covid boredom. It had descended on the world slowly like a quilt floating down from the clouds. It had not hit Lizzy as hard as some because her life during Covid was not significantly different than life before Covid. Keeping up with the farm was somewhat harder than it had ever been, and yes, she was lonely, but not in the way of so many others who complained about not being able to go out for dinner or drinks with their friends, not being able to go dancing or go to the gym or the theater. She never went out and never entertained anyway. Life went on. But she missed Buddy.

Surprising even to herself, the family member Lizzy was closest to and regularly kept in touch with was her nephew Larry on the other side of the country. She wrote long letters to him by hand, writing mostly about artists she liked or didn't like. She acted like she and she alone discovered the artist Jean-Michel Basquiat. She searched the Web for pictures of his work, and she loved everything he did. She did not in the least like Andy Warhol. Never had. Thought he was a charlatan. Larry tried to explain why he thought Warhol was a great artist; and that it was Warhol more than anyone who discovered and nurtured Basquiat. She wasn't buying it.

About books she loved. Cormac McCarthy was her latest favorite writer. And Jody Picoult. She couldn't have landed on any two writers less like one another. She was wishy washy on home-grown boy Tom Robbins, who Larry loved.

She complained about the farm. "I hate it. I've always hated it. It's slowly choking me to death."

"Then sell the damn farm and move into town," she told herself, and Helen and Marilou told her; and she answered herself and them. "I can't. There's too much of Buddy here."

Buddy's remains were cremated. She scattered his ashes off the side of Mount St. Helens where the body and his mangled motorcycle had been found.

There was life insurance. The insurance company tried to claim Buddy's death was by suicide, but the police investigation determined driving off the side of the mountain was accidental. "He ain't the only biker to lose control on those curves," one of the investigators told Lizzy. She was surprised at how quickly the case was settled.

...

Larry wrote to Lizzy. He told her about his studio mate Arnie and Arnie's girlfriend and went on about some of the people he interviewed for his podcast. Lizzy was pleased to hear of his success. The kid had earned it. She was thrilled that museums were now buying his work, that he was written up in art journals and even had a guest appearance on network TV.

Larry wrote:

I have news that might come as a shock to the rest of the family. I have a new girlfriend. Sort of. I mean we'll see how it goes. This one is different. We're taking it slow and keeping our expectations low. Could it be I'm maturing? Ha ha! She's also a painter and comes from a family of artists, and she's really good. Here's the part that might be shocking to the family: she is a lot older than me. almost twenty years older. But she looks younger and has the energy and vitality—love of life— of a forty-year-old. Anyway, her name is Linda, and I'd love for you to meet her. Maybe if I ever get to come out that way again, I can bring her to meet the family.

Lizzy wrote back:

Talking about bringing your girlfriend all the way across country to meet the family sounds pretty damn serious. I am so happy for you, for Linda, and for your newfound and much-deserved success.

...

For two, three, or more days, Lizzy did not bother to check the mailbox again or call anybody or go anywhere. She felt like she was coming down with a cold. She was lethargic, ate leftovers and sandwiches, couldn't bring herself to fix a proper meal. One day she didn't even get out of bed at all but she read the entirety of Wally Lamb's *I Know This Much is True*. Compared to Thomas and Dominick in Lamb's book, her life was like sleeping on a soft mattress and having her meals spoon-fed to her by a Greek god.

There were no books by McCarthy she hadn't read. *Maybe Lamb will become my new favorite author. At least until Cormac gets off his Southern ass and writes something new.*

She was afraid she might have Covid. The day after reading Lamb's book she dragged herself into town and got tested. Thank God it was negative.

She hadn't seen Billy's email and couldn't have cared less. She was not on Facebook or Instagram or Twitter.

And then she checked the mail, hoping to see a new letter from Larry. She had a premonition there was something wonderful in the mailbox. She pulled a stack of envelopes from the box and sorted them in her hands as she tromped back to the house. There were three offers for credit cards, a happy birthday postcard sent to the wrong address for someone named Mary, a book of coupons for discounts at a grocery store in Olympia (she made a mental note to put it where she would see it the next time she needed groceries), buy-one-get-one-for-half-price offers from stores in Lacey and Olympia, and the only piece of personal mail in the pile: an envelope from New York with her name spelled out in Larry's recognizable handwriting. Oh boy!

She tossed all but the letter from Larry, even the coupon book, in the recycle bin. She put Larry's letter on the little table next to her easy chair and went to the kitchen to brew a pot of coffee, sat her coffee on the table and opened Larry's letter. Inside was a check for a thousand dollars made out to her with a note:

Hi, Auntie Lizzy. The enclosed check is overdue payment for art lessons. Use it for needed dental work. Let me know if it's not enough.

Love,
Larry

...

Larry answered her call on the third ring.

"Hi, Auntie Lizzy."

"Hi yourself. If you think I'm going to let you pay for my dental work you're crazier than I thought."

"Please, just accept the gift. Be gracious. I know you have it in you to be gracious."

She switched the phone to her good ear. She said, "Larry, this is embarrassing. I don't want you pitying me."

"It's not pity. It's family. It's love. I love you, Auntie, and I can't stand by doing nothing when your whole life is being affected by bad teeth."

She thought this newfound love of family must have been the new girlfriend's influence. He said, "I've got money now. I'm rolling in it."

It's much more than bad teeth, she thought. It's heavy smoking and a heart condition I've not told anyone about, and a husband who drove his motorcycle off the side of a mountain, and a life wasted.

"No, you're not exactly rolling in dough. You sold a few paintings. Big deal and congratulations. I'm happy for you. You've earned it. Now you're out of your head with pride and joy. But you can't count on the money keeping on coming."

He said, "Maybe, maybe not. But right now I've got more than I need, and you need it."

The line was so silent for a full minute that each of them was beginning to think the connection had been lost, and then Lizzy said, "You never said I love you. That's sweet."

"Well I do." A little more silence and then, "Just get your damn teeth fixed."

"Thank you, Larry. I love you too." And with that she hung up the phone and walked out to stand on the front porch and look at the rain, leaving her coffee to get stone cold.

LIZZY AT HOMEPLACE

Driving down Maytown Road, Lizzy passed by the barn red Homeplace Café, their eatery of choice since forever, or at least since she and Buddy first dropped in there for lunch on the day they moved into the farmhouse. They were sweaty, tired from lugging furniture and boxes of clothes and books and cookware into the house and wired with excitement at the prospect of starting their new life as farmers. Before hopping in their car to drive the half mile or so to the diner, they washed their faces and arms and hands, and Lizzy put on a fresh shirt (Buddy said his was fine, only a little bit sweat-stained).

A good-looking (in Lizzy's estimation) young waiter welcomed them and seated them by a window and took their order: fish sandwich and fries for both, iced tea for her and a cold beer for him. From that moment forward, Homeplace was their place. Not just because it was the closest café to the farm but because they loved the homey atmosphere and the large portions of simple food, and because they liked Freddy the waiter—who, it turned out, was the owner of the place.

On this day not long after Buddy's death, she thought she would love to see Freddy again precisely because of that stab of nostalgia and because—what a dumb, dumb, dumb reason for wanting to see him again—because he looked a little like Buddy minus the beard. Hell, every fifth or sixth person she laid eyes on (she acknowledged to herself now) looked a little like Buddy, beard or no beard.

Freddy treated his customers like they were cousins or neighbors or old chums. He said, "Welcome to Homeplace. Your home and mine." And he always addressed his customers by name. If they were first-time customers, he asked their names and never forgot them, and said, "You're at home here. Welcome to the family."

But also on this day, waves of grief still overwhelmed Lizzy. Triggers were unexpected and always caught her off guard. Thinking of Freddy and remembering their first time eating at Homeplace, she drove on past the restaurant and the freeway entrance and into the little community of Maytown before pulling off the road and stopping. She let the engine idle while she took long, deep breaths, buckling under the grief. "Damn you, Lizzy Johnson Bundrock," she said aloud, "get ahold of yourself."

She put the old Volvo in gear and pulled a U-turn and drove slowly back to Homeplace and into the parking lot, but she did not get out of her car and go in. She put on a mask and continued sitting behind the wheel. At that point in the pandemic, restaurants were under a government-ordered shutdown—curbside pickup orders only, no interior dining. Homeplace defied that order. They were notorious for it.

Lizzy reclined her seat as far as it would go and closed her eyes. She rolled down her window and lit a cigarette. For a long time, she sat in her car smoking, her eyes closed, opening them momentarily every time she heard someone going in or out of the café door and every time she heard a vehicle drive up and stop. She knew it was stupid, but she couldn't help it. Every time the café door opened, she expected to see Buddy amble out, and every time a car drove up, she expected to see Buddy, and she was ready to call to him by name before he could get to the door.

The fish sandwich—fresh cod with tartar sauce on a grilled bun—was her favorite meal at Homeplace. Buddy's favorite had been the cold roast beef sandwich. They had always ordered a big platter of onion rings, which set in the middle of the table so they could each reach it. Mostly, eating there had been a romantic outing for them back when they indulged in such things as romantic outings. Like love-smitten kids, they would sometimes feed each other onion rings, nibbling from one another's fingers. They would also from time to time hold out their sandwiches and let the other take a bite, and sometimes they would comfortably sit in silence smiling at one another long after they finished eating.

How long had it been since they ate there? Months and months. Maybe as much as a year or two years. She couldn't remember why they had stopped going—why they had stopped eating out anywhere.

For a moment she was shocked to see so many cars parked out front despite the lockdown. And then she remembered the great controversy over the owner refusing to go to curb service and takeout only in the face of Covid. A Channel 7 news van was parked near the door. *Yes, of course*, Lizzy thought. *They're here to report on the restaurant's defiance.* The reporter and cameraman hadn't decided on a whim to stop in for lunch. Heck no. Before the pandemic, reporters from Seattle didn't even know there was such a place as Homeplace. They didn't even know Maytown existed for that matter. Newscasters reporting on their defiance always referred to them as a restaurant south of Olympia, often not saying the name. The café's defiance of the law had made them hot news, and I suspect Freddy loved the notoriety even though it was costing him a pretty penny and might even put him out of business. He had been held in contempt of court after a restraining order was issued, demanding compliance with state Covid-19 restrictions—and he was faced with a $2,000 fine for every day they continued to offer indoor dining. Already they had been fined $86,751 according to a recent *Seattle Times* article.

She noted that there was nobody in the news van, figuring the reporter and cameraman were inside interviewing customers. Lizzy felt sorry for Freddy and wondered how long he could hold out. On the one hand, she admired his gumption; on the other hand, she thought he was being incredibly stupid and playing loosey-goosey with the health, and possibly the lives of his customers and anybody they came in contact with. *Don't they know what this goddamn illness can do*, she wondered.

To many of Homeplace's regular customers—especially the recent explosion of MAGA-hat-wearing, confederate-flag-waving regulars, the same people who had protested against smoking bans years before—Freddy was a hero for standing up against heartless big government. *Oh yeah, my stupid big brother Billy probably thinks he's deserving of a Presidential Medal of Freedom for saving people from the horror of having to eat at home.*

But judging by Freddy's public statements, it didn't appear to Lizzy that he thought of himself as a hero. In fact, he came across in public appearances as sensible and thoughtful if misguided. She had seen him on television explaining why he rebelled against the shutdown. He said, "This is not a protest. We're not taking a stand. We are a social gathering. If you've eaten here once we're friends and family, and we're not about to treat friends and family cavalierly. We're careful. You cannot have any symptoms. No coughs, no sniffles. Anything like that and you're outa here. Please come back when you're feeling better."

Diners were required to wear masks, but not while eating, of course, and only a third of capacity was allowed in.

Newspaper postings online were swamped with comments. Reading the comments out loud and talking about them was one of the last things Buddy and Lizzy laughed about together.

Someone signing off as Dee Dee wrote, *Let Washington businesses open! Let people get back to work!* And Billy J commented, *I thought this was America.*

Buddy said, "Yeah, Dude, this is America, where you have the freedom to act like an idiot."

"And expose your mother and your elderly neighbor to a deadly disease," Lizzy added.

Parker B wrote, *Let's rush to increase exposure just as the more contagious strain ramps up in the nation. California can share how they transformed schools into medical care centers when their hospitals were overwhelmed.*

Someone named Amy wrote, *Restaurants and other small business have NOT been shown (by data) to be spreading the virus. Data says it is social gatherings of mostly 20–39-year-olds that are spreading it. Until a business is shown to be a problem, they should be open.*

Buddy quipped, "Who is this Data person she is quoting?"

"The guy from 'Star Trek,'" Lizzy shot back. And Parker B, again, replied, *How do you not get that if restaurants reopen there will be several gatherings of 20 howsomever year olds gathering in spaces spreading the virus? Don't blame this on my generation ... we aren't the ones banging on the governor's doors to reopen.*

"Despite the atrocious spelling and grammar, I think those last two might have made sense," Lizzy said.

"Maybe. How can you tell? I wonder where they went to school."

She replied, "Maytown Elementary?"

Oly Mary wrote, *Listen, I want out of quarantine too. Trust me. But its not gonna happen if we all don't pull our frigging weight. I've stayed in my house for 9 straight months, only leaving for essential things. I am isolated, depressed, and sick and tired. Let Washington businesses open! Let people get back to work!*

"Here comes Amy again. I wonder if it's the same Amy."

While being locked down here more than any other state, lock downs are not working.

"Where in hell did she get that statistic?" Lizzy asked.

"Right out of her rear end," was Buddy's reply.

And then there was this cryptic comment from Big Willie T, *Patriots! I stand with Rain.*

"Rain?" from Buddy, answered by a shoulder shrug from Lizzy.

And Olympia Folx's plea, *Leave us small town families alone. All we want is to be able to have dinner out with our friends once in awhile. COVID IS A HOAX.* And <u>Carol</u> C's comment, *My husband's got guns and so does his friends and there going to guard the door and make sure we can eat in peace with our friends.*

"Another graduate of Maytown Elementary," Lizzy put in.

"A scary one."

Speaking of scary, <u>Ian</u> Pee wrote: *It's there first amendment right and we got a second amendment solution ready to go. Boogaloo!* And two comments later Ian Pee again with, *Don't tread on me.*

...

Lizzy could see from her seat in the car that the restaurant, which was breaking the law and probably going into insurmountable debt just by serving customers, was doing a banner business. She tossed her cigarette out the window, got out and walked into the café with a mask covering her mouth and nose. The window seat where she and Buddy had sat their first time there was unoccupied, so she took it. Ordered a cup of coffee.

"Long time no see," the waitress said.

"Yeah, it has been."

293

"I was sorry to hear about Buddy."

"Thank you."

As she sipped her coffee, she thought the waitress looked exhausted. She imagined saying to her, "Come, have a seat. Fold your arms on the table and put your head down and rest a bit," remembering the way kids in first and second grade took naps at their desks. She imagined the waitress doing exactly that, and she felt good about herself for inviting her to take a break. *Oh, but I didn't. I just imagined it.* Her mask had slipped down below her nose, and she pulled it back up, squeezing it to the bridge of her nose to keep it in place. Laying scorn on herself for taking such a stupid risk as to go into a restaurant where people without masks were eating and drinking and talking to each other. Nostalgia. That had been her reason for stepping through the door into Homeplace. Or maybe—could it be?—she was unconsciously exposing herself to Covid in hopes she would get the virus and join Buddy in heaven. *Nah. Don't be absurd.*

From no discernable trigger, she thought about her childless state, fantasized a boy and a girl, the girl a spitting image of her and the boy big and strong and handsome with Buddy's face, grown now as they would be and married and visiting her, maybe staying for a weekend or even an entire week, that would be lovely. But irresponsible. It was a good thing, she decided, that they had not brought children into such a world where people were coming to blows over whether or not to wear a mask, where people were wholesale spreading a deadly disease, where huge hunks of the population were putting on public displays of their utter selfishness.

Her attention was captured by a stir from the table where the Channel 7 reporter and cameraman were seated. First, the reporter and then the cameraman stood up and looked out the window. The suddenness of their move was like birds on a wire suddenly flying into the blue. Other heads at other tables turned in reaction. Looking through the front window, they saw a small army marching across the road and onto the parking lot. Some were carrying signs that were not readable from inside the café until the marchers got closer. Most were wearing coats, hats and gloves, because on that day at the end of December it was bitterly cold outside.

The army consisted of a dozen adults and two children. The largest of the signs they held said HAVE PITY. WE'RE YOUR NEIGHBORS. Another said IT'S THE LAW and yet another said BEWARE COVID.

Freddy stood just inside the front door looking out at the crowd and back in at his customers. Back and forth, back and forth. A large man wearing a down vest and plaid shirt and a Mariners baseball cap stood up and headed toward the door mumbling, "Sons of bitches. I'll show 'em a thing or two."

Freddy, all hundred and thirty pounds of him, reached out and put his hand on the burly man's shoulder and said, "Hold up, Bruce. Think before you act."

And Bruce said, "All right, Freddy. I'm just tryin' to protect you."

"Thanks. But I'll be OK."

Other customers, all of them, including Lizzy, stood to watch what was happening. A reporter outside was talking into a recorder, and a cameraman was scanning the protestors. "Looks like this is going to be on Channel 7 tonight," someone said.

A man—apparently a leader of the group—positioned himself in front of the crowd. He was wearing a vest like Bruce's and held a bullhorn in his hand. "Freddy Katz," he called out, "Step out please, so we can talk."

Freddy stepped out far enough to stand in the open doorway where everyone inside and out could hear. The man with the bullhorn said, "We implore you to think about what you're doing. You know us, and we know you. We're neighbors. We're friends. We're calling for everyone to be safe."

He said, "We have come together and come to an agreement that if you will put a stop to inside dining, we will assure you that you will not suffer financially for it."

"How are you going to do that?" Freddy shouted back at him.

"We will promise—every one of us will promise—to order takeout as often as we previously came in, and we will ask our friends to do the same."

Someone inside said, "That sounds reasonable, Freddy. Me and my family, we're willing to make that promise too."

"Me too," Lizzy said, surprising herself.

The man in the Mariners cap said, "Not me. I'm sorry, Freddy. I know we been friends since school, but I can't abide you giving in to the mob like that. I can't go along with it."

Freddy said, "That's not a mob. That's a small group of concerned neighbors."

The congregated dozen gradually broke up and walked across the street to their cars. A few of the customers inside paid their bills and left, while others returned to their seats and finished eating their meals. Lizzy paid, thanked Freddy, wished him good luck, and left.

She whispered to the walls, "You should have been here, Buddy."

NOT A GOOD ANNIVERSARY

Billy and Belle's wedding anniversary was fast approaching.

"When is it?" Billy asked.

"It's the twentieth, you old coot. I mean sixty-something. You never remember."

"Ha! You don't remember either."

Could it really have been that long since they spent their wedding night in that grand old Victorian hotel in Vancouver, made love two times before going to sleep and once more before breakfast, strolled through the beautiful Butchart Gardens where a year earlier he had proposed to her in the rain, and they had climbed the eighty-seven steps up the grand oak staircase to the tower at Craigdarroch Castle (Billy called it Crag Rot). Their plan now, for their anniversary, was to stay in the same hotel and repeat the things they had done on their honeymoon—all but dragging their ancient bones up those eighty-seven castle steps.

But it was not to be.

To be allowed into Canada, they needed proof of a recent negative Covid test. So they went to a drive-up testing site. Belle's test came back negative, but Billy's was positive. "Shit! Damn!" he bellowed. "Now what can we do?"

"Nothing, I'm afraid," Belle said.

"I can't be sick. I feel fine. Just a little bit of a tickle in my throat."

He grumbled all day, but she was clearly right that their anniversary plans had to be scuttled. She called the hotel and canceled their reservation. The next day he woke with a much worse sore throat that over the next two days developed into full-blown cold symptoms that quickly turned into what felt like the worst case of flu he had ever had. Fever, chills, racking coughs, chest pain. Wednesday morning, the fourth day of his illness, he collapsed when trying to get out of bed and pissed himself. An immovable puddle of man and piss. He couldn't pull himself back to his feet. Belle called for an ambulance.

"Oh crap, honey. You gotta clean me up. Dress me," he croaked. "I ain't letting nobody see me like this."

She pulled his pants off, washed and dried him, helped him get into a clean pair of pants and pull himself up to a chair. It took the ambulance half an hour to get to their house. Billy was breathing but barely. The strapping young emergency technicians, one male and one female, lifted him onto a gurney and rolled him out to the ambulance.

They would not let Belle ride with him. "He's too infectious," they said, and the same two ETs and the attending nurse, fully outfitted in hazmats, would not let her in the room with him at the hospital. "I'm already exposed," she complained.

Their only response was a shrug and, "Protocol."

She stayed in the waiting room checking on his condition with the nurses almost hourly. There was never any change. Marilou, Eva and Helen, and even Lizzy came to sit with her. At night, Belle slept sitting up in the waiting room, refusing to let anyone spell her so she could get some real sleep. Three days later Billy was dead.

"I tried and tried to warn him," Belle said, "But he absolutely refused to wear a mask in public places. You know what he's like. Was. Was like."

She asked one of the attending physicians if Billy had said anything before he died. "He mumbled something right after we brought him in. After that, he never said a word, and what he did say that first day was complete nonsense. Probably fever induced."

"What did he say?" she asked.

The doctor said, "He said he never really had a peg leg."

...

The memorial service was attended by the immediate family, all wearing masks. Billy was laid to rest in the Johnson family plot in a cemetery in Lacey next to his father, Harlan Johnson, and Harlan's wife, Viola. When they lowered his body into the open grave, Belle said, "Goodbye, you old satyr."

LIZZY SOLD THE FARM

Suddenly there were two widows in the family, and this was a bit of a crisis among the descendants of old Pegleg Josiah Johnson. What to do with them? Would memory and celebration of the old pirate fade now that Billy was gone? Would it be a welcome relief if that were the case, or would the family shatter like the little pigs' house of sticks?

Marilou and I became frequent visitors with both Belle and Lizzy—oddly enough considering that over the past half-decade we had hardly ever visited either of them. Other family members called one another and visited more frequently than before. Bryce, way over in Pullman, pulled out his cell phone and called Belle and Marilou so often that Belle finally said, "I don't mean to be rude, but would you please just stop goddamn calling me?" And then she immediately apologized. "Just kidding. Maybe!"

What to do with the widows? Who to take care of them? Did they even need taking care of? If the women had died, would they be asking about the surviving men? We knew that Lizzy would surely rebel against the idea of needing care. "I'm nobody's damn invalid," she complained when first Helen and then Marilou said she should "sell that godforsaken chicken farm and move into town close to relatives. There's a house up for sale on Royal Court. We could be neighbors."

"Live on Royal Court? God forbid," Lizzy said, "I don't need a whole dang house. If I ever leave this farm, I want something like a studio apartment. Maybe clean out of Washington. Maybe New York, a fifth-floor walkup in a brownstone in Chelsea where I can sit on the fire escape and smoke and drink to my heart's content. Besides," she needled, "being on the same street with you and Rudy is the last place I want to be."

"Well thanks heaps, Sis," Marilou said.

Belle, on the other hand, did not object to the notion of needing care. She said she'd be as happy as a six-year-old on her birthday if she could get a little apartment near us where we could look in on her from time to time. "Time to time, you understand, is all the looking after I can stand."—also a case of good-natured needling. Maybe she could even move in with us now that Parker and Delia had moved out. Would that be OK with us? I don't know.

My mind was broiling with images of what could happen to her way out there. She could fall, break a leg or an arm, forget the turn off the stove and awaken with the house in flames in the middle of the night. Oh, but how she would miss the house on Steamboat Island if she moved away. All of us Johnson progeny thought Lizzy and Belle were too old to live alone. "Why couldn't they live together?" Eva mused.

"Are you kidding? Helen said. "I don't think they even like each other."

It was true. Belle did not much like Lizzy. After all, Lizzy hadn't even bothered to attend the last three or four family retreats. Those retreats had been Billy's babies. They had been his idea right from the beginning. He had done all the planning, and the two of them had made the arrangements, invited everyone, and more than a few times she and Billy had paid other family members' way. That included ungrateful Lizzy. Her avoidance of the family retreats had been an insult to Belle and would now be an insult to the memory of Billy. Nevertheless, Belle knew that she and Lizzy both needed familial support. *I'll be double damned if I want to end up in some assisted living home.* She was dealing with increasing physical limitations, so much so that a few months before Billy passed away, she found herself one day unable to get out of the bathtub. She could not pull herself to a standing position. Billy had to help her out, and the very next day he had a walk-in shower with guardrails installed. It might not be long before she could no longer do the work needed to keep their house presentable. Soon, it might be much worse. She had seen those irritating television commercials where an old lady says, "I've fallen, and I can't get up." The thought of becoming that old lady horrified her. The more she assessed her and Lizzy's situations, the more she had to admit that they both needed some taking care of, and she reluctantly discovered that now that they visited each other without their husbands she was beginning to realize that they liked each other more than she previously thought. Take Billy out of the picture, and everything between them was hunky dory.

Lizzy, four years younger than Belle but in worse shape physically, was in even more dire need of caretaking and was even less willing to admit it.

Larry, all the way across the country in New York, offered to let Lizzy live with him. "You'd love it," he said. "We could go to plays and concerts and dance performances and art museums. The Martha Graham Dance Company is still performing. Wouldn't you love to see them?"

"Yes, but … well thanks but no thanks," Lizzy said. "We'd love it for a little while—doing all the museums and plays and such—but believe you me, two months of that and we'd hate each other. It's like Buddy used to say, relatives are like fish, great at first, but they start to stink after three days."

Belle thought that when the time came, if it did, she could go to live with any of their children. Even better, their son Randy with his sweet wife and even sweeter daughter, Rebecca could come live with her on Steamboat Island. Anybody in their right mind would love living in such a comfortable house in such a gorgeous setting. It was big enough, and she loved it. Who wouldn't?

She was enamored of Randy's daughter, Rebecca. She thought about what fun it would be to teach her knitting and maybe even ballroom dancing—did anyone even do that anymore? —and tell her stories of the olden days. Like the one about how Billy used to do television commercials for his car dealership wearing a pirate costume.

…

Realistically, it was a foregone conclusion that Lizzy with all her fierce independence would never consent to living with relatives. She was so ornery that she'd never leave that crummy little dirt farm.

Little did any of us know that she despised that farm, had put up with living there all those years for Buddy.

Almost before his ashes were strewn, Lizzy had started looking for a buyer for the farm. She sold it right away to a neighbor who wanted to expand his holdings. She rented a little duplex apartment a block from the Olympia Food Co-op, where she would do most of her grocery shopping, and not far from Parker and Delia's place. Also nearby were Parker's grown daughter, Marianne, and her girlfriend. That little section of Westside Olympia was becoming almost a Pegleg Johnson descendants' compound, five of them now living within a four-block radius of each other, all in small apartments. "Oh, how the family has come down," Marilou said.

…

Eva and Helen and all three of their children plus Johnny's girlfriend pitched in to help Lizzy pack what belongings she wanted to keep (more than half of what she owned she had no desire to hang onto). It was clutter, all useless clutter. She rented a truck, and Johnny drove it.

The duplex was painted sky blue. The interior walls were painted blue and white. "It's a Smurf house," Lizzy said.

There was a front porch shared by both apartments, and a swing hung from a tree limb in the front yard, unusable because the rope on one side was broken and the seat dangled to the ground. It had been that way since the teenage daughter in the B-side was eight years old.

Johnny backed the rental truck up across the curb and on up to the porch, where they could let the tailgate down to make a perfect ramp for wheeling Lizzy's stuff into the house. The rest of the family followed close behind and parked on the grass by the old swing. Lizzy and Helen were the first to carry boxes onto the porch. There was a thirteen-year-old girl on the porch slider, not exactly swinging but moving lackadaisically with her feet dragging on the floor, a book in hand. Music came from inside, lush ballads from an album Lizzy had loved years ago. *When did I quit listening to music?* She wondered.

What a stunning little girl, she thought as she set down the boxes she was carrying to pull her mask out of her pocket and put it on. The girl whipped her mask out of her pocket and pulled it on as well. Her hair was as black as a moonless night and fell halfway down her back in a braided rope. Her skin was the color of coffee and looked as if light were glowing from inside, clearly, to Lizzy's eyes, a girl of Indian or Eastern lineage, perhaps Pakistani, or Egyptian. She was dressed in overalls and a sleeveless shirt. Barefooted. "Are you moving in?" she asked.

"Not all of us, just her." Helen indicated Lizzy with a nod of her head. "And my wife and her children are also helping. That's them pulling up now."

It had not been long before this when people—some cautiously and some with relief and with risky abandon—started forsaking the wearing of masks because a vaccine had become available. But the family, and thankfully the beautiful little girl in the swing, still played it safe around other people. Typically, people would wear masks when meeting with friends and say, "I'm fully vaccinated. Are you?" And if the friend said yes, they would take their masks off and say, "Thank God" and often hug one another. For a while it seemed like every time people hugged they said something like "It's so nice to be able to hug again."

The girl asked if she could help. "I'm Sitara," she announced. "Sitara Sharma. I just learned that is called alliteration; that pleases me."

"Oh, what a beautiful name. Of course you can help. It's so nice of you to ask."

Lizzy directed the move. "Those go in the kitchen. Those in the bedroom. You can leave this stuff right here. I'll sort it out later."

While unpacking dishes with Sitara's help, Lizzy asked where her parents were.

"It's just me and Mama. She's at work."

"Oh. Where does she work?"

"For the state."

Once everything was inside, Lizzy thanked Sitara for her help, and Sitara went into her own side of the duplex.

"She sure is pretty," Eva said.

It was a warm day, and the windows were open, so everyone could hear when Sitara changed the music. Another lush ballad.

"I recognize that album," Lizzy said. "It's from the eighties, by ... oh, what's her name? The singer that did 'Blue Bayou.'"

Melony said, "Linda Ronstadt."

Lizzy said, "I'm not used to living so close to other people that I can hear their music. At least she has good taste."

Johnny said, "Just wait until she starts playing heavy metal or grunge."

"Or until they start arguing and banging things around over there. Duplex living is a whole different kind of life," Helen put in, not that she or any of them had ever lived in a duplex.

"It's just her and her mom. I think I can stand that. I sure hope so. Otherwise, I might start missing the sounds of goats and chickens."

After everyone had gone home, Lizzy ate a light supper and opened a bottle of red and poured a glass and searched her CDs for the Linda Ronstadt album, the one with "Blue Bayou." She tapped the tabletop to the rhythm of the music. After a moment she stood up and took a step, another step. She bent slightly from the waist and slowly turned around. She was dancing. For the first time in more years than she could remember.

Crazy old lady. Cut it out, she admonished herself. *Act your age*. But she continued dancing until the music stopped. She could not remember when she had felt so exhilarated. Or so tired.

...

Up early the next day, Lizzy ate a light breakfast and put away a large portion of her stuff. Mid-morning there came a light tap on her front door. At first, she thought it might be the wind banging the screen door, but then it came a little louder. When she opened the door, there stood Sitara, dressed in red denim shorts and another sleeveless blouse, and holding a peach cobbler. A woman, obviously her mother, stood behind her. Each had the same braided black hair so thick it looked like black hawsers falling down to their waists.

"Welcome to the neighborhood," the woman said with soft and carefully enunciated words. "Sitara said you're fully vaccinated and it's safe not to wear a mask."

"Yes. There's no Covid here."

The mother said, "This cobbler is our welcome gift to you. I hope it is not presumptuous of us. I am Mira Sharma." She extended her hand, and Lizzy took it and noticed that Mira's flesh was smooth and spongy to the touch. "I am Lizzy Bundrock," she said, unconsciously foregoing the more casual contraction *I'm* in reaction to Mira's more formal sounding speech. "It is so nice to meet you." She said, "Oh, Mira, what a lovely name. And you ... you are much too young to have a daughter as big as Sitara."

Mira was dressed in a kind of dress Lizzy would eventually learn was called a salwar kameez, a flowing silk gown—at least it looked like silk to Lizzy—with simple straight lines, flaming pink with large snowflake patterns and a split up one side all the way to her hip with underneath white pants with red floral patterns. Mother and daughter both had ample bellies and broad hips.

For a few days after meeting them, Lizzy didn't see either of them, but she heard them through the walls. An almost constantly playing of their eclectic music collection: early rock, be-bop, hip-hop, classical, and what Lizzy assumed was Indian music. She wanted to ask about their nationality and if they had immigrated to America or were first-generation Americans. She assumed that the daughter was born in the U.S.— Sitara didn't have an accent, but Mira's accent was heavy; she had the command of the language of someone who had been speaking English for a lifetime, but with what Lizzy assumed must have been like her English speaking neighbors in India. Lizzy had heard from somewhere that most Indians learned to speak English practically from birth. She was afraid that inquiring about their homeland and their customs and why they were now in Olympia, of all places, could be insulting. *I don't know how to talk to people of other nationalities. I'm always afraid of accidentally saying the wrong thing.*

After some time had passed and they exhausted their store of chit-chat topics, Lizzy did ask the questions she wanted to ask, and Mira and Sitara were happy to respond.

"I am so glad you want to know about my country and why we came here to this country, which I have grown to love. The giant trees, the mountains, the people, all the delicious foods that were new to me when we first arrived. But yes, I was born in India and grew up in a village near New Delhi. Sitara was born here. In Seattle. She is one hundred percent American. Sunil, my husband, was in grad school at the University of Washington when she was born. He called it U-Dub, like American boys, but I feel awkward saying that. It was not long after he graduated that he started getting sick. The poor guy. I saw it coming. His diet was terrible, and he was under constant stress, first in grad school and then in his job at Microsoft. He put on weight and started smoking and drinking, and all I could do was watch him deteriorate day by day and month by month. He died at thirty-one. It is a shame Sitara has very little memory of him."

"I'm so, so sorry to hear of your loss. And with a young daughter too. I can't imagine."

Mira thanked Lizzy, and Lizzy said, "I lost my husband too. Just in the past year." They commiserated with one another and shared their tales of sorrow, Lizzy saying Buddy's death was an accident.

...

"Sunil was a successful businessman in New Delhi before we came to America. He taught himself how to build a computer. He was a wiz at anything involving computers. Like so many young men in our country, Sunil was drawn to America's West Coast by Microsoft and Intel and the whole high-tech explosion. He had a friend who went to graduate school at University of Washington who told him he had to come to Seattle."

Mira was only six when she met her future husband. For a short time, he was her only playmate, and throughout their growing up, they remained friends. Their families visited often. She was seventeen when their parents arranged for them to become betrothed.

"Wait. It was an arranged marriage? I thought those didn't happen anymore."

"Oh, but they do. And it is not like you might think. If there were statistics, and I imagine there are, I just have not seen them, I think the statistics would show that arranged marriages can be more successful than marriages based on some romantic notion of love."

Sitara, who was seated nearby, broke into a big grin at hearing that. She loved hearing the story of her parents' betrothal.

306

"I thought Sunil was a nasty little boy," Mira said. "He made fun of me because my teeth were crooked and because I wore glasses."

But the crooked teeth were soon straightened, and Sunil no longer made fun of her. "We were friends, not lovers," she told Lizzy. "Until we were married."

Their parents' agreement that Mira and Sunil should be married was based on a myriad of factors, all sensible. For starters, the two families had friends in common and lived in similar circumstances. Large celebratory gatherings of friends and family were frequent among Hindu people, and at such gatherings Mira and Sunil would dance and chatter and laugh. Both were physically attractive. The parents were sure Mira would grow up to be a beautiful woman and Sunil a tall and handsome man. That was important because how could they build a loving relationship if they thought one another unattractive? They were both intelligent, and their families—especially Sunil's family—had the means to provide them with a good education, thus assuring at least a reasonable chance of a comfortable living.

"Also, in India it is important for the future bride to be proficient in one or more of the arts. As a child, I played multiple musical instruments, and I could dance, and I loved reading," Mira said. "At six years of age and much more so as I grew up, I was the picture-perfect future bride, a bride out of storybooks." She laughed at saying this.

Mira and Sunil came to the U.S. in 2003 on a direct flight from New Delhi to Seattle. They arrived in late September. "It was rainy and cold when we got off the airplane at SeaTac, and I immediately wanted to go back to India."

"Not used to the rain, huh?"

"No, it was not that. The rain was no big deal. It rains a lot back home in monsoon season, which follows scalding hot summers. The weather can be extreme. It was the constant gray skies that left me depressed, and the cold was a different kind of cold. And over here we never had the kind of big gatherings of friends and family that we had at home. I missed that, but I got used to the new ways of living, and there is so much about this part of the world that I love."

"Like what?" Lizzy asked.

"Oh, well like the culture. You know, the music and films and television shows. And everyone is so much more casual. I like that. But I do not like it that teenagers disrespect their elders." She flashed Sitara a warning look when she said that.

Sitara was born two years after they arrived in Seattle. After grad school he worked four years at Intel down past Tacoma, a commute that seemed to grow longer day after day as the number of cars and trucks exploded—especially the trucks, oh my dear sweet lord. And then, feeling the need for more family time and the need to get away from the relentless hustle in Seattle, he applied for and got a tech job with the state government in Olympia. Mira went to South Puget Sound Community College and then got a job with the state as a programmer. Life was sweet.

...

There was a big snowstorm in Olympia when Sitara was in elementary school. None of the Sharma family had ever seen snow before coming to America, and only a few light snows here. Sitara lay down and almost sank out of sight in a deep snow drift and refused to get up and come in the house when her father called her. He laughingly said, "All right then, just stay there and freeze. See if I care," and he went inside and watched her through the window until she finally got up and came inside to stand shivering in front of the space heater in the front room. She said she wished it would snow like that every day all year, said that with chattering teeth.

The family returned to India for short visits when Sitara was five and again when she was eight. She didn't like India, saying it was too hot and there were too many people. "I love Olympia," she said.

...

In the first week Lizzy lived in the duplex, Sitara helped her unpack and put away her music and books, which stimulated a lot of conversation. "This box of books is non-fiction, and those are fiction. Fiction goes on the bookshelf in the bedroom and non-fiction in here, and they have to be alphabetical by author."

"First name or last?"

"Last."

"What about the music? Here's Dave Brubeck, whoever he is. Does he go with the Ds or the Bs?"

"B for Brubeck. I'll have to play this one for you. Everyone should know his music."

Sitara was fascinated with the range of music in Lizzy's collection. "You're just like us. You like all kinds of music. Do you have any Bruce Springsteen?"

"No, but I like him. Which album would you recommend?"

"Oh, get the greatest hits album."

She was overjoyed when she saw Ravi Shankar's "Chants of India."

"You have Indian music!" she exclaimed.

"I do. But I'm afraid Ravi Shankar is the only Indian musician I know. Maybe you can introduce me to others."

"I can. I have CDs by O.P. Nayyar and Neha Kakka and so many others."

"You'll have to play them for me."

"I will," Sitara said. "But first I want to hear some of yours. I mean if that's OK."

Lizzy played some Brubeck and Leonard Cohen and a Thelonius Monk. Sitara said Monk was "just weird. I don't think I like him."

"He'll grow on you," Lizzy said.

Sitara almost choked trying to hold back an involuntary laugh."

"What?" Lizzy asked.

"Oh, I'm sorry. I was just picturing a big black American with a pointy goatee and a funny hat sprouting out of my belly button."

...

While alphabetizing the books, Sitara said, "It looks like you've got everything John Steinbeck ever wrote. I read *Grapes of Wrath*. It was great. The ending where she nursed the old man, that was heartbreaking."

That was when Lizzy said to herself, this girl is something special. That night Lizzy drew a picture of Thelonious Monk sprouting out of Sitara's belly button and gave it to her the next day. Sitara said, "Is that supposed to be me?"

"Uh huh. Doesn't look much like you, does it? It's been ages since I tried my hand at drawing."

Sitara was in the eighth grade at a middle school close enough to home for her to walk. Also close to home was a park with a hiking trail through a deep ravine that followed a little creek among dense trees and ferns and blackberry vines and across bridges narrow enough that people meeting on them had to hug the railings. Lizzy would soon learn that this was typical of walking trails in the area. There was a steep staircase down into the ravine.

A typical conversation when meeting someone on the trails went something like this: "Careful. Watch your step," while lending a hand to help steady them across a bridge or over a steep incline.

"Thank you. It's a beautiful day, isn't it?"

"Yes, it is."

...

When not at school or doing her chores at home, Sitara spent hours tramping through that park. The far end of the trail exited onto another kind of park. Pristine, few trees, a manicured lawn, on the shores of West Bay—lovely scenery but too formal for Sitara's taste. She preferred her woods a little wilder. When the weather was just right, she often sat in the grass and read from a book carried in her backpack. Whether exploring various urban parks or wandering the neighborhoods, she usually tarried until she had to run to get home before her mother got there.

Other days after school, she went straight home and played music and danced. She loved dancing. She did not yet know that Lizzy had been a dancer.

When feeling lazy, Sitara would lie on the couch with her legs flopped over the back and her head hanging down toward the floor and read one of the books Lizzy loaned her. Her bookshelves were a treasure trove.

One day she was dancing with broadly sweeping movements of arms and legs and body to some melodious big band tune. Lizzy was napping next door. The music woke her. She listened for a while recognizing the band. It was the Benny Goodman orchestra. *I would never in a million years imagine that a girl like Sitara would be into Benny Goodman*, she marveled.

She stepped out on the porch to better hear the music. She stood at the open window and watched Sitara dance for a while, and when the music ended, she tapped on the window and said, "That was beautiful. Have you taken dance lessons?"

Sitara mouthed words Lizzy couldn't hear, and in response to Lizzy shrugging her shoulders and cupping her ears. Sitara motioned for her to come in. Inside, Lizzy asked her question again.

"No, I never took lessons. I just move the way I feel it."

"Well, that's what dancing is all about, and it comes naturally to you. You're quite the little dancer."

"Not so little," Sitara said, patting her belly.

Lizzy said, "I used to be a dancer too when I was in high school and after. I even studied with a famous dance school in New York."

"That is so, so neat," Sitara said.

...

Over the next month, Lizzy got to know mother and daughter well enough that it became an afternoon routine for Sitara to come over, with her mother's blessing, for afternoon snacks of fruits or cheese or peanut butter on crackers, avoiding sweets, except for fruit, and avoiding meat. Sitara and her mother were vegetarian and leery of sugar, which was fine with Lizzy. She was drifting in that direction herself. Often when she was alone listening to the swish and rumble of cars passing by their not-heavily-traveled street or walking along the nearby Garfield Nature Trail, Lizzy would think *oh how I wish Buddy could have known this precious little girl. We could have adopted a girl like this. Why didn't we? Because I had the weird obsession that my child had to grow in my womb. Like that would make her any more mine—ours— than if we adopted her and loved her.*

311

...

Lizzy took up drawing again, and she and Sitara took turns sketching each other. Lizzy's drawings were heavy and expressive with dark, slashing lines. Sitara's were delicate, hesitantly drawn. She loved the poster from Larry's show Lizzy had on her wall. It was signed "Love ya, Auntie," with an autograph Sitara could not make out.

"Who is the artist?" she wanted to know.

"He's my nephew. He lives in New York, and he's getting to be quite the famous artist."

"That's cool," Sitara said. "Maybe you could be my auntie too. Could I call you Auntie Lizzy?"

"Sure. I'd love that."

...

Lizzy regaled her with harrowing stories of the pirate Pegleg Josiah Johnson and his descendants down to the present day. "He was my great great grandfather. I think just two greats. Every summer the whole family gets together for a weekend gathering at Peter Puget Resort on Orcas Island, where we hear all the stories about him over and over and over again. I never get tired of it. And then we explore the islands. There are beautiful beaches and a mountain to climb and shopping. It's great fun." She didn't tell her she had not gone to any of the retreats in years and had not particularly gotten along with her big brother Billy and was not exactly crazy about her little sister (my wife) Marilou. and could barely stand our son Parker—all of that being my possibly erroneous judgement.

"That's sad," Sitara said. "Brothers and sisters should love one another."

"Oh, we do love each other. We just don't much like each other."

Another time, after listening to Lizzy's stories about the trips to the island, she said, "Wowee! You really live a fascinating life. I never get to go anywhere. Just school and home, school and home."

"You've been to India. India is not nowhere. I think getting to visit India would be fabulous."

"Yeah, I guess it's kinda cool. I saw the Taj Majal. That was really something."

Brightening with inspiration, Lizzy said, "You know what? If your mom says it's OK, you could come with me to our next island retreat. Maybe even someday before I die you and I—and I guess your mom (she added with a snicker)—can all go to India and visit the Taj Majal "

"Wowee! I'll ask my mom."

Another day, Sitara pointed to a group of old sepia-toned photographs on Lizzy's wall, saying, "What are these?"

"They're dancers."

"Well duh. I can see that. They look prehistoric."

"Ha! I guess they do. They are from the summer of 1963."

"Like I said, prehistoric. Pre my history anyway."

Lizzy said, "The older woman in this picture is Martha Graham. She was probably the most famous American dancer ever. She ran a school of dance that was also quite famous. And see the younger woman next to her, the tall one?"

"Uh huh.?"

"That's me. When I was eighteen years old. I studied dance with her."

"In New York?"

"Uh huh."

"Wow!" Sitara said. "Are any of the others famous?"

"You bet. I mean not these, not in this picture; but see the Black woman in the next picture? She was world famous. Her name was Josephine Baker."

"I never knew there were any famous Black dancers."

"Oh yeah. Alvin Ailey, Gregory Hines, Bojangles."

"I've heard of that last one. There's a song about him."

"Uh huh. You bet."

"You say you bet a lot."

"Uh huh, I do. You bet. Josephine Baker, she was just about the most famous of all. Not so much in America until after she died, but in France, where Blacks were not discriminated against the way they are here."

Sitara said, "Some of the kids at school discriminate against me. They think I'm Black."

Lizzy said, "I'm so sorry."

"It's OK. Tell me more about Josephine Baker."

"I really don't know that much about her, but I think there was even a movie made about her. Maybe I can find it online and we can watch it together."

"Cool."

"She was something special. Not just as a dancer, but during the war—that would be World War II—she was like a spy or something for the French Resistance, a real hero.
Sitara asked, "Was she your friend, too?"

"No. I never knew her. I never saw her dance except on film. But oh my, she was so graceful. Her dancing was erotic. I hope that's all right to say."

"Hey, my mom reads the *Kama Sutra*. I've seen it on her bookshelf, and I even read some of it myself. If we can read that, I guess it's OK to say Josephine Baker's dancing was erotic."

"Well, you are a very grown-up little girl."

Again Sitara said, "Not so little" and patted her belly, adding to that a wiggle of her hips and a solid slap on her butt. Lizzy mimicked her much to Sitara's delight.

...

One day Sitara asked if Martha Graham was still teaching dance. Lizzy said, "No, she died about thirty years ago, but her school is still active, and they still teach her techniques."

Sitara said she wished she could go to that school. "Maybe someday you can. And maybe I can teach you some of what I remember."

Lizzy taught Sitara some of the moves she learned in the Martha Graham school. There were many rigorous and challenging exercises, some called the 16 bounces, and others called pleadings, brushes, high curve and triplets, a kind of walking in waltz time with a dip on every third step. She also taught her to "Become the music. Don't think about it. Just move with it. Move everything, not just your arms and legs but your belly, your neck, your toes, everything."

It was not easy, but Sitara loved it. So did Lizzy. She pushed her aging body through the moves as well. Beyond dancing, they went on long walks on nature trails, and they talked, and they watched videos together (but they were never able to find the Josephine Baker movie).

"You know what?" Lizzy said to her, "You're making me younger and stronger. You're bringing out a good part of me I thought I had lost forever."

ANOTHER RETREAT

"We can't let this family tradition die. The annual retreat on Orcas Island must resume," Belle wrote in an email to the Johnson family. "Oh my god, she has cloned her dead husband," I joked when I read it, and Marilou said, "Behave yourself."

Two summers in a row, we had cancelled the retreat because of the pandemic. Now Belle was convinced it was time to get back to normal. Never mind that the pandemic was still raging. For hardheaded people like Belle, the answer to an unsolvable problem like Covid was to accept it as an unavoidable condition of life and learn to live with it. Or die from it as her husband had.

Belle had rebuffed every attempt to convince her to move into town, possibly to live with some relative if any were willing to have her. She loved her Steamboat Island home too much to leave it, and after wavering a bit had decided that nobody could pry her away from her personal view of Puget Sound and the fireplace she could sit by both inside and outside. "Christ in a nighty, if I were to move in with one of you guys or downsize to one of those little senior living apartments down by Percival Landing, I'd have to get rid of three-fourths of my stuff, and my stuff is precious," she said to whomever she thought would listen. Marilou sympathized. To lesser degrees, some of the rest of us did too.

In a move that thank God Billy's wealth made possible, Belle hired a full-time live-in caretaker, a sixty-year-old woman named Beth who was porcine and deceptively strong; she could easily lift Belle off the ground if need be, who was kind and loving with a quirky sense of humor, and who couldn't string together six words without a cussword. Without Beth, Belle could not have sent that email to the family. Her arthritis made typing unbearable, so she dictated the email to Beth, who typed it for her.

The family worried about her—Belle, not her piggish caretaker. Lizzy, to everyone's astonishment, including her own, was the first to suggest, "We all need to make a point of visiting her as often as we can."

Marilou replied, "Me and Rudy will for sure, and we'll visit you often too." That was in a group get-together on Zoom, something instigated by Marilou.

Everyone was surprised to hear Lizzy say, "And by the way, if any of y'all are interested in knowing, I plan on going to the next retreat."

...

Kaylee and Rebecca were excited to go back to the island. After much pleading and many calls and text messages back and forth between them and their parents and grandparents, it was decided that the two girls could go without their parents if they solemnly promised to wear masks whenever they were with other people. Indoors anyway.

In one of their frequent late-night phone calls, Rebecca said to Kaylee, "I asked my mom if we had to wear masks even if it's just the two of us in our room, and she said yes, even then."

Kaylee laughed at her. She said, "Haven't you learned yet that when it's just me and you alone we can do any damn thing we want to?"

"Oh, you're so bad," Rebecca said.

The plan was for them to stay with Sally and Renae. Rebecca took the Amtrak from Spokane. Kaylee drove up from Seattle. A grown woman now at twenty-two, grown in her own evaluation anyway, it was the first time she had taken such a trip alone. It was a surreal time for her, for reasons she could not stick a pin in, a time when she felt glued to a revolving conveyor belt to nowhere—going to college at U-Dub but not knowing what to major in, indeed, not knowing why she was going to college, a member of a sorority she had no interest in, still dating the same boy she had dated in high school, and having no idea what she wanted to do after she graduated. She had spent most of the last two years smoking pot and hanging out in loud and raucous bars in the U-District.

. . .

As before, Sally and Renae drove up from Portland, stopping in Olympia to visit with Eva and Helen but not in Shoreline to visit Asher and his family this time. They'd see them on the island.

Unbelievable to most people, the third summer of the pandemic was upon them. *Three years. Jesus H. Christ.* People worldwide were terrified of the virus, but so sick and tired of it that a large and growing segment of the population defied safety precautions. Kaylee's father admonished, "Don't you dare go anywhere in public without a mask. People will say they're vaccinated when they aren't."

"Why would they do that?"

"Because they're idiots. You can't trust anybody."

...

Sally unlocked the door to their room at the Peter Puget Resort, and Renae and Kaylee and Rebecca stepped in and dropped their bags any old place on the scuffed hardwood floor where they remained like random cow pies in a field. Sally slid open the closet door and placed her bags inside and then pounced on one of the side-by-side queen-size beds with a big sigh. The girls rushed to the window and opened the blinds to look out over the deck at the water. "Claim your drawers and hang clothes in the closet," Renae said.

"I'm wearing my drawers," Rebecca wisecracked, then pulled her stuff out of her backpack and put it all away. Kaylee pushed her backpack into the closet and said, "That's good enough."

"Let's get settled in and then head for the bar," Renae said. "We need a drink after that trip."

Sally said. "You girls can come with. But no booze for youze." She quickly apologized to Kaylee, saying, "I forget that you're over twenty-one now."

"Thanks," Kaylee said. "I don't think I want to hang out in a bar with old people anyway. I want to shower and change clothes and maybe even take a nap."

"What about you, Rebecca?"

"Nah, I guess not. I think I'll wait for Kaylee. Maybe we can meet you there later."

The door shut tight behind them. Kaylee watched them walk away and then reached for her mask and jerked it down and tossed it on her bed. She said, "Screw this."

Rebecca said, "Oh my god, we can't ..."

"Don't be such a little Chicken Little. We're cool. We're family. We can't wear 'em twenty-four-seven."

"But Grandpa Billy died of Covid. It's not safe."

"*Uncle* Billy—make that great uncle Billy. He was like eighty thousand years old. Practically dead already. We're young and healthy. Young people don't get it. 'Sides, we're vaccinated and boosted."

"But my parents said ..."

"Posh on that."

Tentatively, Rebecca slipped the elastic off her ears and pulled her mask off, saying, "This is so daring. You're so ... so fearless."

With a mischievous grin, Kaylee pulled an already rolled joint from her bag and said, "If you think taking masks off is daring, what do you think about this?"

"Oh, I like that," Rebecca said.

"Have you done it before?"

"Sure. Lots." *Lots* meant four times total.

They took a few tokes off the joint and waited for it to hit. Rebecca said, "I gained about a billion pounds since the last time. I must look gross to you." She posed in front of the dresser mirror, turning side to side, checking herself out.

Kaylee said, "You don't look gross. You're beautiful. Sexy. I think a sexy chick looks better with a little bit of a belly. Look at me. I'm a freakin' scarecrow, nothing but knees and elbows and ribs. I'm the one that oughta be ashamed of my body."

"Are you kidding me? You're gorgeous. Gee wiz, I'd give anything for your bod."

"Really? You think so?"

For reasons that could be explained by anything other than the marijuana, they fell into a laughing jag. They gobbled down the sandwiches they had brought with them and brushed the crumbs under their bed. Rebecca said, "All righty, here's the multi-million-dollar question, "Are you still going with that same boy, and have you done the deed yet?"

"Yes and yes. Sorta. I mean we're kinda on again-off again."

"Oh, I better have another hit with that. Was it delicious? Doing it."

Kaylee passed her the joint, and she took a good long hit on it. Kaylee said, "It was good, yeah. While it lasted. It took him 'bout half a second." Another huge giggling jag ensued, and then she said, "The second time was better. Gimme another hit."

Rebecca asked, "Did you use protection?"

"I'm on the pill. Mama took me to the clinic to get on it."

"Wow! I can't imagine my mom doing that."

They let that sit awhile, mulling it, grinning expectantly and knowingly at each other. And then, and then ... "Now here's the million-and-one dollar question. Have you ever kissed a girl?"

"No, never," Rebecca said, not with a shocked expression but with a happy face. "Have you?"

"You betcha. Many times."

"Oh my god, does that mean you're a lesbian? Maybe you inherited it."

"I don't think so, silly. I don't think you get it that way. Being queer. Or maybe you do. Who knows? Who cares? Besides, everybody is fluid now."

"Whatever. But you're doing it with your boyfriend. So I don't get it." She didn't know what she meant by *fluid*, but she liked the sound of it.

"So yeah, the first time didn't count 'cause it wasn't even a wham-bam. It was just a wham." Rebecca pretended she knew what that meant. "Then we really did it, and that was ... oh boy! Since then, it's just been oral, I don't think that counts either. And we've only done it two other times. I'm not so sure I like it. I think I liked kissing girls better."

"Oh my. Then you are ..."

"You're such an innocent. What are you, ten?"

"Eighteen."

"You don't have to be a lesbian to kiss a girl, silly, and it doesn't have to mean you can't still do it with your boyfriend."

They were sitting on the bed, barefoot. Kaylee bounced up and down and then off the bed.

"Hey, I'm gonna take that shower now." With that, she pulled her shirt over her head and stepped out of her shorts and walked into the bathroom and into the shower, leaving the bathroom door open and her bra and panties on the floor.

Rebecca listened to the shower run for a minute or two and then said, "Aw heck, why not?" and stripped off her clothes and folded them and placed them neatly on a dresser with her mask on top and said, "Here I come." A brief pause and then, "Don't look."

Kaylee shot back, "Of course I'm going to look, Sillikins."

The cascading shower was deliciously warm, and Rebecca and Kaylee soaped each other and rinsed off, then got out and dried themselves.

Wrapped in towels, they smoked another joint. Kaylee challenged Rebecca to kiss her. "Come on, let's do it. I want to see if you've got the guts."

"Oh, I've got the guts all right. Just you watch and see if I don't." And with that, she threw her arms around Kaylee and kissed her lips, and Kaylee opened her mouth, and Rebecca moved her tongue in Kaylee's mouth for a few seconds that felt like eternity, and then pulled back and expelled a deep sigh and then laughed and said, "I think I need another toke."

...

The joint had gone out. Kaylee lit it again, and they smoked it down to a tiny roach, looking into each other's eyes and smiling broadly. She asked Rebecca if she wanted to kiss again.

"Not now," Rebecca said, "Maybe another time. I liked it, but I'm not sure I'm ready to follow through with that. I mean with the next level, you know?"

"Yes, I know. Whenever you're ready."

They got dressed quickly and fanned the air in the direction of an open window, praying they could get the marijuana smell out before Sally and Renae came back.

...

Spawns of the notorious pirate Pegleg Josiah Johnson were scarcer than usual that summer. Larry was not there. Neither were Bryce and his family or Billy or Buddy of course. But Lizzy was there for a change. And Sky, Kaylee's father, who had missed the last few summers, was there. He came separately from the rest of the family because he had to get back home a day earlier. "Rehearsals, you know."

Someone said, "I guess Larry's too busy for us now that he's a big shot artist."

"That's kind of true," Lizzy said. "It's not like he doesn't want to be with us, but he had commitments before any of this was planned."

...

The first night gathering became an impromptu eulogy for Billy. Belle did the talk Billy had traditionally done. She made it more entertaining than any of them thought she could.

"Oez, oyez, oyez. Here we are again. Yadda, yadda, yadda and stuff Billy would have said. That's all."

"No, you don't. Give it your best shot," somebody shouted.

"All right. You asked for it. So each and every one of us by blood or by marriage is the spawn of the notorious pirate Pegleg Josiah Johnson, who fought and screwed his way from the Bahamas to Haiti to Puerto Rico to Cuba to Miami to New Orleans to Corpus Christi— Body of Christ."

After a long pause, she said, "Now we're all here at the Peter Puget Resort Hotel, so eat, drink and try not to throw up." Quiet ensued like at a stage play when the audience doesn't know if they've come to the end or not and finally a few people start clapping, and then more and more. By the same process, the descendants of Pegleg

Josiah Johnson began, table by table, to carry on conversations. And then, shouting it out for the whole room, Belle said, "I know for an indisputable fact that everyone here hated Billy."

"What? What? Did she say what I thought she said?" and similar words from each of the tables followed by a chorus of "No, no, no, we didn't hate him. Don't be silly," answered by Belle with, "Yes you did, all of you. And I know you loved him, too. I know. Me too. I loved him, and I hated him too, probably more than you suspect. Oh my god, he could be so infuriating. But he gave me a lifetime of love and support and three wonderful children who, sadly, couldn't make it this year, and one beautiful granddaughter who is right over there looking all grown up and stunning."

Rebecca blushed.

Belle and Marilou and Lizzy and me, we each spoke about Billy. Lizzy said, "I owe a lot to Billy. He always challenged me." With a big laugh, she added, "Everything worthwhile I ever did, I did it to spite him 'cause he said I couldn't or wouldn't. I took up dancing and art to spite him, and I think I married Buddy at least in part because Billy thought he was not good enough for this high and mighty Johnson clan. And Buddy. Oh my god. We lost Buddy last year, too. Good ol' Buddy. Wendell by God Bundrock. Betcha half of y'all didn't even know his real name."

A moment of silence was followed by Lizzy's "Goodbye, Buddy. I'll always love you."

I usually kept my thoughts to myself at family get-togethers, but this time I shouted out, "I love you, Buddy, and you too, Billy. God speed you both."

"You tell 'em," came a woman's voice, either Lizzy or Belle.

...

Everyone at the retreat was overjoyed but not particularly surprised to see that Lizzy was there. New teeth, no longer smoking, seemingly a new and more hopeful outlook on life. "Could it be Buddy's death had lifted a burden?" Sky asked Marilou in a whisper. "I can imagine Buddy could have been hard to live with."

"No, it wasn't that. Not at all. Buddy was a good husband. Maybe a little eccentric, but then so is Lizzy," Marilou said. "It's the money. The insurance settlement, and Larry sent her money, and she got her teeth fixed and sold the farm and moved into town. She looks ten years younger now, and more vital than she has looked in ages."

I said, "Yeah, it's all of that. And it's also, maybe more than anything, that little girl she brought with her."

"The chubby little Indian girl? Who is she, anyway?" somebody asked.

And I said, "She's the daughter Lizzy always wanted but could not have. Her name is Sitara. She's Lizzy's neighbor in the other half of the duplex she moved into. Getting to know her has revitalized Lizzy."

We felt comfortable talking about Lizzy as if she weren't in the room because she wasn't. She and Sitara had quietly snuck out. I also left for a few minutes. I don't think anybody noticed. It was part of a plan cooked up by Lizzy and Sitara. From the next room I could hear silence descend, everybody thinking, not yet saying out loud, *What's going on? Where's everybody going?* Which was my cue to return with a CD player and set it on a table near the windows and plug it in.

Sky and Marilou wound up their conversation, and Sky excused himself to refresh his drink. and I surprised everyone—I know I did—by stepping into the leadership role that had previously been Billy's and then Belle's. I cleared my throat and rapped on an empty glass to get everyone's attention and said, "Listen up, everyone. We have a very special treat for you tonight." I waited for the murmuring to quieten and said, "Hey, hey! I said Listen up. Now... Ladies and gentlemen, descendants of the all-powerful and wonderful Pegleg Josiah Johnson, may we present for your entertainment the dancing duo of Lizzy Bundrock and Sitara Sharma."

In they came, barefoot and wearing matching shorts and blouses. Sky turned off the lights and aimed three lamps at Lizzy and Sitara. I put a CD in the player, and Lizzy and Sitara performed a simple but delightful dance routine to Benny Goodman and Peggy Lee's "On the Sunny Side of the Street."

LINGERING EFFECTS

Back at home, no school and nothing in particular to do for the rest of the summer, Rebecca read a lot and spent a lot of time reminiscing about the retreat. She especially thought a lot about Kaylee, and a lot about Lizzy. What a surprise Lizzy was! And what an elegant and charming older woman! Rebecca had heard a lot about her but wasn't sure if she could remember ever meeting her. Living on the other side of the mountains, what her Western Washington relatives call the dry side, Rebecca got to see her wet side cousins and aunts and uncles only at the Orcas Island retreats, and Lizzy never came to those. But then she did. And what an awesome surprise she was. She was glowing, robust, charming, full of life. Yes, she was old. Her hair was silver and somewhat wispy, and there were lines etched around her eyes and across her high cheekbones, and her body as revealed by the tight shorts and flowery top she wore was thin but in no way skin and bones. Her appearance was regal and exuded joy. Rebecca had heard other family members talk about her being constantly sick and hardheaded and grumpy. She had pictured a shriveled old crone with bony hands and bad teeth and icky breath constantly saying "eh? eh? what?" because she couldn't hear for shit. But the Lizzy that showed up at the retreat—showed up with that beautiful Indian child with dark chocolate skin—looked to be no more than fifty, maybe fifty-five years old, and quite the looker for an old gal.

But why am I feeling so lousy? It must be exhaustion, Rebecca thought. She had worn herself out climbing Mount Constitution and walking on the beach, and maybe she was suffering some kind of mental confusion after kissing Kaylee. Could she possibly be gay? Her brain wandered from Kaylee and Lizzy and mountain climbing, and jumped to Lizzy and the Indian girl and their dance routine, and *Am I gay? No, I don't think so. Can't be*. She could not hold onto a simple chain of thought for more than a few seconds. *That little Indian girl sure was cute.*

She felt dragged down, unable to work up energy for anything. Also, she was having headaches—not bad, but worrisome because she seldom had headaches. *Oh my, I can't remember the last time I had a headache. Shit. This is no fun at all. Kaylee said she liked fat. Did she mean it? She said they did oral. Oh lordee, that's icky.*

She told herself her sick feeling was just the to-be-expected letdown after an exciting weekend on the island with Kaylee and other family members, a kind of hangover.

"I'm coming down with the sniffles," she said to her mother.

"Do you think it could be Covid?" her mother asked.

"Don't be silly, Mama. I don't even feel very bad. Just a little bit of a runny nose."

"Did you wear a mask the whole time?"

"Of course I did."

Despite her protests, her parents took her to get tested, and she tested positive for Covid.

She was quarantined for a week.

"I got it," Rebecca said to Kaylee on the phone. "You must have it too."

"Uh uh. No way. I don't know how you got it, but I'm fine."

Talking to her mother two days later, Rebecca said, "Kaylee doesn't have it. I called her. She said she's all right. Her mom was smoking a cigarette, holding an empty Pepsi can to use as an ashtray. She smoked only when she was nervous. She kept a pack of Camel filtered handy just in case.

"Why did you call her?"

"Because we were together the whole weekend and ... I kinda fibbed a little bit. We didn't wear masks when we were in the room alone together. I mean, you can't expect a girl to wear a damn mask twenty-four-seven."

"I know. It's OK. I'm not mad at you."

Two days later Kaylee called to say she got tested, and she had it too, but she didn't have any symptoms. "I feel hunky dory," she said.

Rebecca grumbled that it was not fair that she was sick as a dog and Kaylee had no symptoms at all. She recovered within a couple of weeks, but she was left with lingering effects, fatigue and difficulty breathing. Brain fog. Hot rages coming on from out of nowhere. Weirdly, there was the smell of ashes all the time, especially when she was stressed or tired. And most troubling of all, heart palpitations.

The doctor said those were typical aftereffects that, so far as medical science knew, could last a lifetime or simply go away in a few days or weeks or months. After all, the disease was too new to know about long-term effects. Rebecca called every one of her friends and told them she had it and had horrible aftereffects. Sarcastically, she said, "The doc said it could last all my life. How's that for a cheery prognosis?"

Kaylee sailed through her imposed quarantine without feeling sick for even a moment, and two weeks later she was making love with her boyfriend, both secure in the notion that having once had Covid they were immune.

ELLIS COVE

Weathering the isolation imposed by the pandemic had wrapped us all in a blanket of monotony, debilitating boredom, loneliness. In the first year of Covid, everyone had gotten used to wearing masks in waiting rooms, in grocery stores, and in theaters once they reopened. And then almost everyone stopped wearing masks altogether. They had simply had it with the damn masks. Typically, in a supermarket a few weeks or months back you might have seen fifty or sixty shoppers all wearing masks, albeit some of them with masks not pulled up over their noses. And a month later it might have been twenty, and now only three.

We got used to seeing delivery vans in the cul-de-sac three and four times a day because people had been forced to shop online, and they liked it. They kept it up even after in-person shopping was considered safe. Less than a year ago Helen had taken a job with the state but stuck with it for only eighteen months. Tending their little farm hardly took any time. School was out, so she and Eva had nothing to do. So they started walking almost every day. "It's funny how many other walkers we see," Helen said. "I think it must be Covid that draws them out."

"That and unseasonably beautiful weather," I said. "Count your blessings."

In the first years of the pandemic, walkers would wear masks pulled down below their chins and pull them up to cover their mouths and noses when meeting others on the trails and sidewalks. "Here comes another couple." Up with the masks, a polite nod or wave and smiling with their eyes or maybe saying "Hi" or where it was convenient simply stepping out of the path or into the road to create a safe space, and then pull the masks back down. After vaccines became available, friends started gathering on patios for drinks and snacks, hesitantly comfortable with their togetherness but still leery of gathering inside. "Are you vaccinated?"

"Yeah."

"Me too." And the masks would come off and people would hug and say, "Thank goodness. It's so nice to hug again." Every time it was like greeting a new spring day after weeks of gloom and drizzle.

Trader Joe's and Costco did away with the long lines to get in. Safeway customers ignored the one-way-aisle signs—well, many had ignored them all along. Schools restored in-person learning, but only with strict precautions. Even theaters started doing live shows again while requiring masks and at first proof of vaccination. And then no proof of vaccination required. Then came an uptick in cases and at least some of the people started being more diligent about wearing masks again. Do, don't, do, don't, maybe. Nobody knew what to do. They should have, but even the authorities gave into mounting pressure to go back to normal long before it was safe.

Helen and Eva and Marilou and I became walking partners. Walking around Capital Lake one day, Eva remarked that more people than usual were out walking. I said, "I think it must be because of the pandemic. People are sick and tired of being isolated, and they're ... hell, we know from personal experience, everybody's put on weight and they're told by their mirrors and by pants that pinch their waists that it's time to start thinking about getting back in shape."

"Yeah. Maybe. Most folks around here have always been health conscious. Always been nature lovers. It's the great Northwest, where people conquer mountains and keep an eye out for mountain lions and Sasquatch. It's me and you who are the wimps. Do our shopping online, tinker around the house, watch TV."

"Yeah. Except at least we're walking."

Neighbors on Royal Court who never spoke to one another started saying, "Hey, how's it going?" when meeting on the street. The schoolteacher that I had a kind of a crush on always greeted us with "Have a good walk." I still didn't know her name.

On a Wednesday afternoon Helen and Eva decided to drop in on us unannounced. Marilou broke out the Scrabble set and the four of us set up a card table on the patio and played and drank tea. Eva easily won. After an hour or more, she said, "We were planning on going for a walk in Squaxin Park. They have some great hiking trails. We'd love it if you could come with us." The park, called Priest Point

Park for eons, had recently been renamed Squaxin Park in recognition of the Native Americans whose land it had originally been.

Marilou said, "OK. I guess that would be all right if the trail is not too rugged. We're too old for climbing big hills."

"You always say that, and we always tell you we can stop and rest as often as you like."

I tried to beg off but gave in when the three women insisted.

I must have wanted them to talk me into it. Helen, well she must have known what was going on with me—better, I think, than I understood myself. I wanted to go, but I was afraid I wasn't physically up to it and didn't want to admit it. Frankly, it would be embarrassing to let three old women outdo me. Helen said, "There are some pretty steep hills to climb, but there are steps and places you can sit and rest. We'll stop and rest with you. God knows I'll need to take breaks too. And it's not like it's a race or anything. Come on. It'll be good for us."

. . .

We went in Eva's Kia and parked by the playground. A little more than a dozen kids were climbing over the nautical-style jungle gym. It looked like only two of them were wearing masks. I eyed the nearby restrooms and wondered if I should try to pee before hitting the trail. I didn't think I could pee, but if I didn't try, I'd probably have to halfway there. Goddamn old man bladder.

From the parking lot, two different paths were marked BEACH ACCESS TRAIL. "There's a better path down this way." Helen indicated a direction and took off, and the rest of us followed. A short walk out of the parking lot carried us to the Ellis Cove trail, the most exciting and challenging trail in the park as Helen remembered it. Eva said, "Yeah, I think I vaguely remember. We attempted it before but were unable to make it all the way to the water."

"This time we're going to make it all the way and back if it kills us," she said. "And it just might."

Laughing at her, Helen said, "Don't tempt fate." She picked up a broken limb that was the perfect size for a walking stick.

I grumbled, "Damn your lying faces. Telling us it wasn't too challenging."

It was the third time Helen and Eva attempted to conquer the Ellis Cove trail, but twice before they had failed to make it all the way to the water.

"Come on, guys. It'll be fine," Helen said.

I shrugged my shoulders, thinking I'm not gonna let a pair of old lesbians outdo me. Five minutes down a trail that skirted an intimidating gully, I said, "Hey, you said it was easy. We're almost eighty years old. Have mercy."

Eva said, "Don't look at me. I didn't say it was easy."

Helen said, "I said we could take it easy and stop and rest when we need to. It'll be fine."

With a big heaping pile of reluctance in her voice, Marilou said, "Well, we're here now. Might as well."

That was typical Marilou, taking on whatever came her way. Heading into the woods and down a steep hill, I picked up a fallen limb to use as a walking stick and mock-challenged Helen with, "My stick's bigger than your stick," and, "If we survive this, I'm going to murder a couple of beloved relatives."

Helen said, "I was just remembering when Billy and Belle were runners. My god, that was such a long time ago. This trail would have been nothing to them back then. A piece of cake. A mere bagatelle."

"I was remembering playing pirate, Billy and Bryce pretending to fight with staffs," Marilou said.

It was gray and cold, a summer day that felt like early fall, with a slight mist in the air. Under a light windbreaker, Marilou wore a T-shirt with a picture of a dragon and the legend "Assuming I'm just an old lady was your first mistake." Eva and Helen both wore hiking boots and baseball caps.

The dirt path we traipsed was barely wide enough for a couple to walk side-by-side. We hiked in and out of a tunnel of trees with Helen and Eva leading the way, and through a dense forest of gigantic firs and pines and many other trees with moss clinging to trunks and hanging from limbs. On our left was an incredibly deep ravine, and on our right a clifflike hillside green with vegetation. Tall firs and spruce

331

grew upright on the steep slopes, some standing perpendicular to the hillside. Fallen trees like scattered pickup sticks, maples, madrones with their gnarly, peeling brick red bark, yellow-green moss on everything, elderberry, mock orange, bright orange wallflowers, flowers of red, blue and purple that none of us could identify, berries that might or might not be edible. And a gigantic fallen spruce that over time had turned into a nurse log with many young trees growing out of it. Eva snapped pictures of everything, which I was glad of for two reasons: first, I wanted to be able to see and share her photos, and second, every time she stopped to snap pictures it gave me an excuse to rest.

I knew I should have used the bathroom when I had a chance. Now my bladder was threatening to release a torrential waterfall. "Hold up," I said. "I gotta pee. Can't wait."

I looked both ways to satisfy myself that no one was coming, and I stepped to the edge of the trail and, turning my back to them, I cut loose into the bushes. Marilou said, "You men, whizzing in nature."

I said, "You're just jealous you can't do it."

"Don't fool yourself. If I had to go badly enough. . ."

Then we continued walking. Slowly. Taking it all in, talking little, Eva and Marilou now both snapping pictures.

We had not gone far before my leg began to burn and throb. I leaned more heavily on my walking stick.

"Are you all right?" Marilou asked.

"Yeah, I'm fine. Just a little tightness in my thigh."

We came to a bench and sat for a minute or two. I rubbed my thigh and stood up. "I'm fine now," I said.

"There you go. You're a trooper," Eva said. A few moments after we resumed our trek she said, "Hold on. I think I've got something in my shoe."

She held onto Helen's shoulder for balance and lifted one foot to remove the shoe but could not unlace it while holding onto her wife. She laughed at the absurdity and hobbled ahead until they came to a fallen tree where she could sit to take her shoe off. She shook out a tiny pebble.

"How in the world did that get in there?" I asked.

"Beats me."

We soon came to a place where we could see the cove through the trees. It looked to be about a half mile away, sparkling water with blue-black shadows on the surface. We stopped to rest for another minute or two and then plowed ahead.

"Shit. Now I'm getting a cramp in my other leg," I said.

"Do you want to give up?"

"No way, I'm not going to let this damn trail defeat me."

"That's the spirit," Marilou said, not sounding very sure.

After stopping again to rest no longer than a minute, we came to a place where wooden steps were built into the ground with guardrails made of tree limbs. The twisty steps went down, down, down, switched back, crossed a wooden bridge, and climbed back up the other side. "This was it, our giving up place," Helen said. "It was as far as we got on previous attempts.

The ground, still wet from a recent rainfall, was packed hard, and it was slippery underfoot. Thankfully, there were those guardrails to hold onto. Slowly, we went down, past the first switchback and then the second. Stopping to take a few deep breaths and looking far ahead to see what awaited us, we saw that the steps went up again, perhaps thirty to forty feet, and then around a slight bend and back down again. *The beach must be close.*

"From here on it's a brand-new adventure," Eva said.

The creek at the bottom of the ravine was swollen with rainwater that flowed in spots over the little bridge. I stuck a finger in the water. "It's only half an inch deep," I said, "maybe an inch at the deepest point. We can make it."

Helen said, "Take it slow and hold on. The planks will be rubbed slick and covered with moss."

We inched ever so slowly across the bridge. It was no more than four feet to the other side. A young couple came from behind and passed us on the bridge, saying, "Excuse us." We hugged the rail to let them by. Halfway across, Eva's feet went out from under her. She held onto the rail but fell nevertheless, and I grabbed her, and we both went down kerplunk in the water. The young couple that had passed us stopped and came back to help me lift Eva to her feet. "Are you all right," they asked.

Eva said, "Yeah, I think so. My butt is sore."

We thanked the young couple who took off again at a quick clip.

Sunlight glancing off the water at the beach was a welcome sight when we finally reached our destination. Brilliant but soft-not-blinding sun after a day of fog and mist. Eva's face aglow, Marilou and Helen in shadow yet also aglow. I saw them as they were thirty years ago: attractive, not movie star beautiful, rather plain elderly women yet somehow gorgeous. Eva alight with pride and happiness at the ferry landing telling the young girls about the shooting at her school, Helen solid as the oaks and firs and nurse logs in the woods, Marilou as she was at every age from when we met as teenagers to how joyful she appeared while putting our bacon and eggs on the table this morning. I remembered her telling me we should visit a nudist camp and laughing at me when I said I could never do such a thing. Thoughts of sitting with Billy and Belle on their pier and not believing him when he said he once rowed a kayak all the way to the distant island, and thoughts of Lizzy with her new white teeth dancing with Sitara.

"Family," I muttered.

Helen asked, "What?"

And I said it again. "Family."

No one asked what about family. They sensed what I meant.

Driftwood and whitened tree trunks lay where the beach met the forest. It was like the beaches on Orcas Island and Deception Pass. We found a smooth trunk to sit on and rested there. I massaged my aching thigh, no longer worried about appearing weak, and Eva rubbed her sore behind. "We're the ass rubbing brigade," Helen said.

Eva said, "Pretty little asses."

To our right, a tree grew parallel to the beach out of the steep cliffside as if the earth had been twisted forty-five degrees to its left. Near the tree were young families, two couples and three children. The men were running remote control cars in the sand, and the children were chasing after the cars, righting them when they tipped over. Farther down the sandy and rocky beach, the young couple who had helped us on the bridge walked hand-in-hand. "Look at them,"

Marilou said, "That could have been any of us in our youth. We're lucky, you know, to have each other."

"Crazy as it sounds," Eva said, "I miss Billy. And Buddy."

Like soldiers sounding off one, two, three, each of us in turn said, "Me too, me too, me too."

In the distance, we could see the town's skyline and the capitol dome, and in the opposite direction and farther in the distance, snow-covered mountain peaks. I pointed at the mountains with my walking stick and asked which range it was, the Olympics or the Cascades? Helen said, "The Olympics, I think."

From out of the woods emerged another family: mother, father, and a boy who looked to be about twelve. The boy was lugging a box kite. He played out his kite string and ran back and forth in the sand trying to get the kite into the air. He could not get it to rise more than six or seven feet. I read the father's lips more than heard him say, "Lemme show you how it's done." And the father took the string away from the son and ran back and forth trying to get the kite to fly with no more success than the boy.

"Smartass father," I said to Marilou.

"He reminds me of you at that age," she replied with a grin.

We sat and enjoyed the view and the quiet. Marilou snapped a bunch of pictures.

Half an hour later, Marilou and I looked at each other and Marilou said, "You ready?"

"Ready as I'll ever be. You guys?"

"Sure." And we started the slow trek into the woods and up and down and up again back in the direction of the parking lot. We stopped four times to catch our breath and wait while the burning and throbbing of our legs subsided. The third time we stopped, an old man came running past going downhill, and a few minutes later he came running back up. "How the hell does he do that?" I marveled.

Helen said, "He's doing repetitions. That's freaking amazing."

"What are repetitions?"

"It's something runners do for training. Find a steep hill and run up and down, up and down, up and down."

"Well, more power to him. He must be at least our age. Maybe even older. We'll probably hear about him in the news someday, running a marathon at a hundred and one."

"Well good on him. But you know what? We made it. We freaking made it. All the way down to the beach and back up. So good on us."

...

The next time the four of us got together, we reminisced about our trek to Ellis Cove. Eva said, "Marilou sure was excited about conquering that trail." She said she was excited too. "I was determined to make it. Thank goodness you guys had to stop and rest a few times because it gave us an excuse to rest too, without having to admit we needed it."

"Yeah. So how are you feeling now?"

Eva said, "Tired and gratified and wonderful. Despite this horrible disease playing hell with our lives, and despite the deaths of Billy and Buddy, I think we're all doing better. I know Lizzy is, and you, Rudy, seem to have blossomed."

"Me? Shucks. Life has never been better."

I think Helen was right about me. After our long walk to Ellis Cove and back, I felt better than I could remember feeling in a long time, despite being exhausted and aching all over. As soon as they dropped us off, we went in, locked the front door behind us and shucked off our clothing. Marilou fetched us a couple of beers, and I filled the tub with hot water and soaked with beer bottle in hand.

"Here, hold mine," Marilou said, and she handed me her beer and stepped into the tub. So there we were, squeezed in the tub together, and before we could finish our drinks I began to feel so sleepy I could Barely hold my eyes open. Out of the tub and into pajamas and under the sheets, she said, "How do you feel?"

"Great," I said.

"Me too."

"Do you think you might want to do that hike again?"

"Yes, I do. But not for a few days at least."

PROMENADE

A year had somehow slipped past since the walk in the park with Eva and Helen. I had devoted that year to trying to get my novel published. We spent two months, me and Marilou, practically locked in our little Royal Court house going over the manuscript together, reading it out loud, sentence by sentence by sentence, and discussing (arguing) everything—the arrangement of chapters, strict chronological order or jumping back and forth for back story, word choices, whether or not to use dialect. Everything. And then there was the researching of agents and publishers, the laborious writing of a synopsis, query letters; writing and mailing them to agents and directly to publishers—this one wants the first 50 pages, that one a synopsis only, many ask to see the first chapter—and then we waited and waited and waited for responses. So nerve-wracking, so frustrating. Half of them sent back form thanks-but-no-thanks letters; the other half never responded at all.

We continued our walking routine as well, usually around the neighborhood, usually the two of us together alone, and sometimes with Eva and Helen, and sometimes even with Lizzy. We met her at the Homeplace Café near her old farm and went with her to the strange and mysterious Mima Mounds, a not-too-good place for walking on a sunny day because there's no shade. And yes, we did do the Ellis Cove trail down to the water again.

With nothing else to do but wait for more rejection notices, it was easy enough to get out for an hour or two whenever we wanted. We explored all the parks and woodland trails and waterways in the area: Watershed Park off Henderson Boulevard, Squaxin Park many times, Garfield Nature Trail (Sitara's favorite), Burfoot, McClain (my favorite), Nisqually. We were healthier and happier than we could remember. And still I checked my email and the post every day with no replies from agents or publishers, or with bland and impersonal rejection letters. "I swear to the almighty," I said to Marilou, "My efforts to find a publisher have been so disheartening that a lesser man would have hung himself from one of those oak trees that line the promenade."

"Don't give up, honey," she said. "Be like that ancient runner that passed us going and coming in Squaxin Park."

By my count, I had sent queries, sample chapters, outlines and synopses to seventy-three agents, each having different requirements. From those, I had gotten back two encouraging rejection letters and forty-three form rejection slips; the remaining twenty-eight, so far, had not bothered to reply in any fashion.

And then, in the middle of May, I got the letter I had long since given up on receiving. It was from an agent at the Courier 12 Literary Agency saying she would love to represent me and could guarantee she would make a good deal with a reputable publisher.

She wrote:

Dear Rudy Briggs:

I beg you to be patient. These things can seem like they're taking forever.

…

Refusing to get excited yet, I researched the agency and found that they were indeed legitimate—not big, not showy, but an honest to God literary agency. The agent's name was Heloise. She called me twice over the next two months to update me on what she said was progress. And then, much sooner than I expected, I got confirmation that a publishing company had agreed to publish my book. They offered a three-thousand-dollar advance. I had no idea how that compared to what other companies advanced first-time writers, and I didn't care. To me, that three thousand was a shower of gold from heaven.

…

I immediately made up my mind not to say anything to Marilou about it until I got a contract. Didn't want to jinx it. I can picture in my mind what I must have looked like when I finally made my announcement. A crazed and delirious joker, eyes like I had splashed water in them, wet and shimmering, a huge grin on my lips.

338

My hands were shaking as I walked into the kitchen clutching the letter. Marilou sensed something momentous. She was seated at the table in her fuzzy pajama bottoms and an old T-shirt reading the morning paper.

"I got it," I announced, trying my damnedest to sound all nonchalant about it.

Marilou folded her newspaper shut and set it on the table and looked up at me questioningly.

"They want to publish my novel. For real. *The Descendants of the Pirate Pegleg Josiah Johnson* by Rudy Briggs, published by Timberline Press. I've got the contract right here in my hand." I handed it to her. "One of their editors suggested tagging on the subtitle, *A Novel of Family Love and Strife.*"

Marilou said, "I never heard of Timberline Press."

"It's an independent press. I never heard of them either, but I looked 'em up. They're the real deal."

"Hot damn! That's fabulous." Finally, she showed some enthusiasm.

I stepped up to the island counter to pour myself a cup of coffee and join her at the table. She read the letter, glanced over the contract, set both on the table and said, "It looks like the real thing all right."

"It's not exactly like I dreamed, not like some big-league publisher like Random House or Doubleday or ... or Harper or whatever. Maybe they're not going to send me on a multi-state book tour like we fantasized about, no appearances on Oprah. But by God it's a real publishing house, and they'll get it out to bookstores all over the place and hopefully advertise it in all the trade publications."

Marilou stood up, a mischievous grin twisting her mouth. She said, "All right, baby. Now you've got to do it. I dare you."

"Do what?"

"You know what. Come on. I'll do it with you."

I didn't know what, but then I did. She pulled her shirt over her head and tossed it on a chair, grinning wickedly. She pushed her pajama pants over her hips and down her legs and then stepped out of the pants and pulled her panties off and stood by me completely naked but for the fuzzy slippers on her feet. *Well all right. I knew we sometimes enjoyed hanging around the house without any clothes, but this little striptease came out of nowhere.* She said, "All right, baby. Let's do it."

I broke into a smile as big as my laptop keyboard and said, "You're crazy as a barn owl, but what the hell," and I stripped my pajamas off much more hesitantly than she had, marveling at my newfound courage, and we walked to the door on the Rappaport side of the house and stood for a moment encouraging one another with our eyes. Two proud elderly citizens standing buck naked with all our wrinkles and bulges and sagging parts exposed to the air and, if we stepped out that door, to the world. Our intent, which went unspoken, was to walk naked the length of the promenade just as my avatar did in the book.

Having grown up in Harlan Johnson's household with ballsy little sister Lizzy as a role model and having to stand up to Billy all her life, it was not so intimidating for Marilou as it was for me. It had taken me ages to get used to nakedness, even when it was just the two of us at home alone. On our wedding night, we had gone into our bedroom after having a drink, and Marilou immediately stripped off her clothes while I slowly took off my pants and shirt and shoes but left my boxer shorts on and stood by the bed looking at her nakedness and—I'll be double damned if I know why I did this—put my hands protectively over my crotch, and Marilou knocked my hands away and tugged my boxers down to my feet, and I slipped under the covers. I didn't even remember to take off my socks until after we made love and after Marilou had fallen asleep. In fifty-seven years of marriage and after raising three children conceived in nakedness (under the covers), I had let Marilou see me completely naked no more than a dozen or so times—until the past year after Parker and Delia moved out.

Now we were standing naked in a door open to the uptight Rappaports and potentially all of the residents of Royal Court. Marilou took my hand in hers and pushed open the door, and hand-in-hand we stepped out between our house and the Rappaport house. There was still morning dew on the grass. The sun hovered just above rooftops in the east. The air was pleasantly warm, not yet as hot as predicted for later in the day. I hoped no one was awake yet. Marilou, proudly naked, and me, nervously naked but giddy, paraded our somewhat paunchy bodies across the grass to the oak-canopied strip of lawn known as the promenade where only our Royal Court neighbors could see us. If they happened to be awake and looking out.

I clutched Marilou's right hand in my left, and we each reached a hand high in a power salute as my character had done in *Pegleg*.

Next door, Mrs. Rappaport—always an early riser, I should have known—looked out her kitchen window and called to her husband, "Get in here, Johnny, and get a gander at what these fools are doing."

"They've finally gone stark raving mad."

"I'm going to call the police. They should be arrested," Mrs. Rappaport grumbled. But she made no move toward her phone.

Three houses down, Allen George and his wife, Grace—the hulking outdoorsman and his rabbity little wife—were painting patio furniture. Allen shouted, "Goddamn, Rudy! You go, man!" and also threw up his own power salute.

I said, "I didn't think he even knew my name."

"You think nobody knows you, but you're wrong."

In one of the houses at the end of the cul-de-sac where the street circled lived the schoolteacher I had long wondered about, had wished I could befriend. We did not properly know her, but if we were all out in our yards at the same time, we always waved at each other. She never seemed to have company, and from what we could tell never went anywhere but to work and, I guess, the grocery store. She was a small woman, standing about five-foot-two and probably weighed no more than a hundred and twenty pounds. She had short brown hair sprinkled with gray, and she wore glasses. She watched our naked parade from her patio and before we reached her end of the promenade she said, "Hot damn" and stripped off her clothes and ran out to join us. "I don't know what you're doing," she announced, "But I'm with you all the way." *Talk about being flabbergasted*. I felt like my tongue was dragging near the ground.

The three of us, Marilou and I and the cute little teacher, marched in all our naked glory saluting our neighbor's houses and wondering how many of them were watching out their windows. The schoolteacher said, "I'm Sheila Cranston. I should have introduced myself long ago. What are we doing?"

"I don't know what you're doing, but I'm having the time of my life," I said, guffawing, tears of joy on my cheeks.

Both women laughed at that, and Marilou said, "We're celebrating."

"Celebrating what?"

"Rudy—that's this guy here, my husband—he just sold his novel. By-the-way, I'm Marilou."

"Well hot damn," Sheila said. I want an autographed copy as soon as it comes out."

Allen and Grace laid their paint brushes down, and hurridly consulting one another, took off their clothes and ran to catch up with us. George said hello to all of us, calling each by name, and Sheila said, "This guy here's a writer, and they're celebrating his ...what is it? Your first published book?

"Yeah."

"Cool," Allen said, and to Sheila, "You're looking good."

Simultaneously, Sheila and Grace said, "Don't get any ideas." Somehow, that brought home to me the absurdity and the illegality of what we were doing. I said, "Probably one of our friendly neighbors has called the cops by now. Maybe we oughta grab up our clothes and get inside."

"And be ready to deny we were ever naked," Sheila said.

As quickly as we could, the five of us went home, each to our own home, dressed and met again gathered around our dining table. Marilou said, "Y'all get closer. I want to get a group shot."

Photos were taken, and Marilou texted them to Lizzy and Eva and Helen and Belle, telling them, "Minutes ago the five of us neighbors were buck naked and walking around outside in a victory march because Rudy sold his book."

Soon Lizzy showed up with sweet rolls and a fruit tray, and before much longer Belle appeared, and twenty minutes after her, Eva and Helen. For the first time in my life, I was the center of attention. Everyone peppered me with questions about the book. And after sufficient time had passed, I said, "I guess none of our neighbors called the cops after all."

THE JOHNSON FAMILY TREE COMPILED BY RUDY BRIGGS

Note: There is a lot of guesswork and speculation in this family tree.

The notorious pirate Pegleg Josiah Johnson was reported to have had a woman in every port and children by each of them. It is not known if he married any of them. The only one we know about definitively was Matilda Gertrude Hildegarde Duchamp, commonly called Gertie. She was the madame of a house of ill repute in New Orleans. Pegleg and Gertie had a child named Auvergne, born in 1875. **Auvergne Johnson** married his cousin Wanda, known as **Bluebird**. **Harlan Bujeaud Johnson,** known as Hairless Harlan, was Auvergne and Bluebird's son. His teenage bride was **Josephine Warnock.** They had one child, **Billy Byron Johnson**. Billy married **Belle Crenshaw.**

Josephine was killed by a Sumatran tiger in 1935. After her untimely death, Harlan married **Viola Parker.** Harlan and Viola gave birth to:

Marilou Johnson married **Rudy Briggs.**
Bryce Johnson married **Emma Hall.**
Lizzy Johnson married **Wendell Bundrock,** called **Buddy**
Renae Johnson's lover was **Sally Crawford.**

Concurrently with the above, **Beauregard** called **Bobo** moved in with **Nellie (last name)**, and they had a daughter named Viola, who later married Harlan (see above).

Billy Johnson married **Belle Crenshaw.**
Marilou Johnson, married **Rudy Briggs.** Marilou and Rudy gave birth to: **Larry Briggs** and **Parker Briggs.**
Parker married **Delia Rappaport.** Their children were **Maryanne** and **Randolph.**
Bryce Johnson married **Emma Hall Johnson,** They had an adopted daughter named **Helen** who married a high school English teacher in Olympia named **Eva McRoy.**

ALEC CLAYTON

Alec Clayton was born in Tupelo, Mississippi, and grew up there and in Hattiesburg, Mississippi.

Along with his wife, Gabi, he founded the literary arts quarterly *Mississippi Arts and Letters*.

In 1988, the Claytons moved cross-country with their children to Olympia, Washington.

Alec has worked as a reporter and columnist for various publications and is currently editor of *Oly Arts* magazine. He and Gabi are co-owners of Mud Flat Press. *The Descendants of the Pirate Pegleg Josiah Johnson* is his thirteenth novel, and he has published two books about art.

More about Alec Clayton at:
https://mudflatpress.com/alec-clayton/
https://www.alecclayton.com/